MW00629234

Rosefire

Carolyn Clarve Sing

ROSEFIRE

Carolyn Clare Givens

Bandersnatch Books
North Carolina

This book is a work of fiction. References to real people, events, establishments, organizations, or locales are intended only to provide a sense of authenticity and are used to advance the fictional narrative. All other characters, and all incidents and dialogue, are drawn from the author's frabjous imagination and are not to be construed as real.

Rosefire
Copyright © 2021 by Carolyn Clare Givens

All rights reserved. No part of this book may be used or reproduced in any manner whatsoever without written permission except in the case of brief quotations embodied in critical articles and reviews. Anyone found in violation of these copyrights may be fed, in part or in whole, to the frumious Bandersnatch we keep in the spare greenhouse. Printed in the United States of America. For information, address Bandersnatch Books.

P.O. Box 2473
Indian Trail, NC 28079
bandersnatchbooks.com
info@bandersnatchbooks.com
803-610-1223

Library of Congress Control Number: 2021932089
Hardcover ISBN: 978-0-9988454-2-5
Paperback ISBN: 978-0-9988454-3-2

The text of this book is set in 11-pt P22 Stickley Pro.
Book layout by Carolyn Clare Givens
Cover art by Kelly Collins
Cover design by Jason McFarland

For Christine and Saritha

*Without you, Karan would
never have finished telling her story.*

PROLOGUE

From the writings of Brother Ezra, Helper

Seventh day, sixth month, in the ninth year of King Saran's reign

THEY tell me that roses burn sweet—that there is something of their scent that endures through the flames and rises in the wisps of dusky smoke. This is what they tell me, but I do not know myself. Rosefire has only ever been the province of the great Masters of the Ancient Writings, and it has been so long since a Master has practiced Rosefire that it has become a myth, except among the most faithful.

There are rules that prohibit novices from practicing Rosefire. Still, they are nearly unnecessary, for the Legends wield great power among those who practice magic, and the Legends tell of great disasters that have befallen any who attempted the practice of Rosefire before they were ready. According to the Legends, not a single novice has ever survived the act. To my knowledge, none has tried in over a thousand years. And most think no one ever will.

PART ONE

A faithful account of the genesis and activities of the Followers,
here written by Karan Adamaris

haps, some of the anger in my father's eyes came from that loss so many years ago.

Richard started up from the sofa where he was reading and came over to me. "Karan, what are you doing here?" he said. "You know Father wanted you to study this evening."

I nodded up at his concerned expression. "I know," I said. "But I can't study in my rooms—the sea is too loud. I wondered if you'd help me."

Richard chuckled. He moved back to the sofa. "You're lucky you made it past the page. What did you do, bat your eyelashes at him?"

I put my chin in the air. "No, I didn't have to."

Richard waved me over to the sofa. "But you were fully prepared to, weren't you?"

I sat at the other end of the sofa, opening my text flat in the space between us. "A little flirting with the servants has saved me from far more trouble with Father than you've ever been in, O Beloved Son."

"And broken the hearts of two stable boys and a footman, if I'm not mistaken." Richard turned to face me. "What are you studying tonight?"

"The Written Histories. I have an exam tomorrow on the age of the Kings. Will you quiz me?"

"Who was the first King?"

"Toran Aurelias."

"And how did he come to power?" Richard asked.

"The power of the Priests weakened over the years of their age as their followers lost faith in the Ancient Writings. The land grew poor under their rule, and Toran

Aurelias led an uprising against the Priests, promising prosperity to the people. He and his followers overthrew the Priestly line, and Aurelias took the throne."

"Did King Toran deliver on his promise of prosperity?"

"He found gold in the north and opened the ports for trade, turning Asael into a prosperous nation of miners and merchants," I answered.

Richard continued to quiz me, taking me through a thousand years of history in about an hour, helping me to remember names and events. We went over the rise of the noble class, as well as the continued tensions between the nobles and the Keepers of the Ancient Writings. Finally, we came to the modern day.

"And the current king is?"

"King Saran Aurelias."

"The greatest concern of his reign?"

"Lack of an heir. For almost a thousand years the bloodline of Kings had been unbroken, but for the majority of King Saran's reign, he was without blood heir. After nearly forty years on the throne, he produced an heir, Prince Loran."

Richard smiled at me. "And who's had a crush on Prince Loran ever since she was five years old?"

I picked up a pillow from the floor and threw it at him. "I do not!"

"He's too old for you, you know," Richard continued, ignoring my indignation. "He'll be twenty-five this year... then again, if it's meant to be...."

I closed my text and stood. "I don't have to stay for this."

Richard went on. "I know Father sent an invitation for your eighteenth celebration to the palace. Maybe Prince Loran will be able to make it."

I walked toward the door. "Goodbye, Richard," I said.

"If he can't come to your eighteenth, maybe you can get an invitation to court sometime soon. I could see if the Makrams could take you along next summer when they go."

He continued talking as I opened the door to look out and see if the hall was clear. I was about to step out when the bell at our front gate began clanging. I know this sounds absurd—for how can a bell sound different than it ever has?—but there was an urgency to the tone that I'd never heard before. I think Richard felt it, too. He stopped mid-sentence and joined me at the door.

We stood there for a moment, unsure what to do. The bell continued to ring. Richard's room was within easy distance of the entryway, and we listened for the footsteps of the servants in the front hall. I heard a maid's shoes clicking across the marble floor and the noise of the heavy wooden door being pulled open. With that, the sound of the storm drowned out any clarity. I heard voices, but words were indistinguishable. The hum of the voices went on for some time. The quiet droning grew in volume, still undecipherable, but the tones sounded agitated. From our vantage point at Richard's door, we could see the main corridor that led from the central stair to the back of the house. The page, who'd so conveniently been dozing earlier, went running past the end of Richard's hall toward the entryway. Another page followed, and it sounded like other servants were joining them on the lower floor.

Out of the growing din, a voice, clear and sweet, rose up. "Please don't make me go! I have nowhere else."

The words seemed to jolt Richard and me out of our stupor. I dropped my text, and we ran together down the hallway to the wide main corridor. We came out nearly at the top of the central stairs above the front hall, looking down into a small crowd of servants, some of whom were trying to shut the door while others held it open.

On the steps, drenched from the pouring rain, was a girl. She might have reached her twentieth celebration, but it was difficult to tell her age. Her hair was dark, almost black; it lay in dripping strands across her face. Her skin was pale. She wore a dress that was little more than rags; even in its drenched and bedraggled state, one could see it had been simply cut from cheap material. She was looking up into the face of the maid in the front of the crowd, her expression pleading.

She spoke again. "Please, give me shelter."

Her voice was beautiful, delightful even. In the midst of the hubbub and confusion in the hall, even with the din of the storm surrounding her, it resonated like music. At the sound of it, those who were trying to push the door closed hesitated, and the servants keeping it open pushed harder. Richard and I stood silently at the top of the stairs, once again unmoving.

From below us, at that moment, my father entered the scene. I felt his presence before I could see him as every servant in the entryway tensed. He stepped out into the middle of the vestibule.

"What's going on?" My father's voice rumbled.

The servants scurried out of his way, leaving the maid who'd opened the door standing alone with the girl on the steps before her. The maid looked away from the girl to my father.

"This peasant asks for shelter from the storm," she said, bowing and stepping aside.

My father stepped forward and looked down at the forlorn creature crouched before him. Her appearance should have softened the heart of the cruelest man, but my father put his hand on the wooden door and began to swing it shut.

I do not know what made me speak. Until that moment, I had never outwardly defied my father in anything. I was expert in avoiding his notice, fearing his rage more than anything in the world. Even my quiet rebellions were never about anything of great importance. But as my father started to move the door, I spoke.

"Stop." My voice was quiet, steady.

The silent servants all looked up at me, and my father froze. He dropped his hand to his side and turned to face me, his eyes glinting, his jaw tight. "What did you say?" he asked.

"Stop," I said. "Let her in." I moved a few steps down the stairs.

I have reviewed the events of that night over and over again in my memory, and I have only ever found one explanation for what happened next. I did not know it at the time, but it was that moment that put me on the path to becoming a Follower.

I don't know what I expected to occur. It was likely my father would slam the door shut on the girl. I was certain I would feel the results of my disobedience for weeks of hard stares and stony silences. But I continued down the stairs, strangely calm, and stepped forward to face my father.

"Let her in," I said, looking directly into his glinting eyes.

His jaw not softening, his eyes unchanging, my father stepped aside.

I reached out my hand to the girl. "What's your name?" I asked.

She looked up at me, the dark hair hanging in her face, framing bright green eyes. She reached up and put her hand in mine. "Sephanya," she answered.

CHAPTER 2

I pulled the girl to her feet and helped her across the threshold. She stood beside me as I closed the door and turned to face my father once again.

He breathed quickly, heavily through his nostrils. "What are you doing?" he asked.

"I'm giving her shelter," I answered. "Tonight, and for as long as she wants to stay."

"I do not give free housing," my father said.

My miraculous bravery held. "Then she can serve me as a personal maid."

My father's face flushed. The girl beside me shivered. I stood still, awaiting judgment. I hadn't heard Richard come down the stairs, but he appeared at my other side. "Oh, let Karan keep the girl tonight at least," he said, not even looking at her, his tone casual. "And if she wants to stay, let her stay. She'd certainly serve better than that old biddy Karan's got right now. Anyone would."

Richard's voice calmed the roaring seas. The vein that had been pulsing out in my father's forehead receded as he took a deep breath. He scoffed. "What does it matter?" he said. "You want the dregs of a stormy night? Take it." He flicked his hand at us, then turned on the servants who still stood around the edges of the entryway. "Haven't you all work to do?" he said, ice in his tone.

The servants scurried away like mice, one or two looking back at Sephanya as they went. Richard gave me a sidelong glance and nodded his head toward the central stair. I put my arm around Sephanya's shoulders and guided her up the steps. Glancing back from the top, I saw Richard turning our father toward his study and guiding him away.

I led Sephanya down the broad short corridor to its intersection with the second cross corridor. There we turned right toward my quarters. The once-dozing page had returned to his station and stood at attention in the main corridor. I stopped in front of him and asked him to have a bath drawn in my quarters and a maid sent with clean clothing. He nodded and departed. A few more steps and we reached my door. I turned the knob, opening to the plush carpet and vivid picture tapestries I'd left only an hour earlier. The girl beside me had not spoken since giving me her name on the doorstep, but she gasped as we entered my rooms.

"It's beautiful," she said.

I looked around, trying to take it in from her eyes. I found it impossible to imagine what it was like for a peasant to see a noblewoman's quarters for the first time, so I turned quickly to watch Sephanya take in the room. She paused just inside the door and let her bare feet sink into the carpet, closing her eyes and wriggling her toes. Then she opened her eyes again and stepped to the wall, putting her hand up to finger the delicate stitching on the tapestry, as if marveling at the minute intricacy that created the greater whole. She glanced at the bed and sofa but made no move to sit down.

I cleared my throat, unsure what to say. My mind flitted aimlessly through the topics I typically covered with other noble girls when we visited the Capital, but none were appropriate for the moment. Finally, it alighted on a simple formality. "My name is Karan," I said.

"Sephanya." She repeated her name. "You can call me Anya."

"Anya. Why don't you sit down?"

She glanced down at her wet and ragged dress. "Perhaps I should wait," she said.

A knock at the door interrupted my moment of embarrassment. It was two footmen carrying a bath, followed by a maid with a fresh set of clothing. The footmen set the bath in the tiled room off of my dressing room and quickly filled it, bringing buckets of hot water from a tank room at the end of the hall. They bowed at the door before going out and closing it behind them.

The maid guided Anya to the small tiled room and showed her the towels and clothes laid out for her before taking leave as well. While Anya bathed and dressed, I ran out to the page in the corridor again and asked for a cot to be brought to my quarters. By the time Anya emerged from my dressing room, a bed was set up for her by mine, complete with silken comforter and soft pillows.

I'd set two chairs near the fireplace, so Anya's hair could dry in its warmth, and we could talk for a little while. She sank into one, sighing, and I sat in the other. Her hair, now clean and brushed, hung straight down her back without a ripple of curl. No longer covered by strands of dark hair, her green eyes jumped out of her pale face. The dress the maid had brought for her was a black gown of simple material, but the bodice hugged her figure and the skirt fell smoothly around her legs as she sat.

I shifted in my chair, then spoke. "Where do you come from?"

Anya looked into the fire for a moment before answering. "I—I'm not really sure," she said.

"Not sure? Are you lost?"

"I don't know," she said. "I can't remember."

I blinked. "Well, how did you end up on our doorstep?"

"The first thing I remember is walking on the bluffs this afternoon. Then it began to rain. I kept going as it grew dark, thinking I would find a town or shelter somewhere, but the first place I came upon was this. Where am I?"

"My father's estate," I said. "Marinel. My father is Lord Adamaris, one of the nobles of Asael. Do you know Asael?"

Anya nodded. "Yes. I do."

"But you don't know where you're from?"

"I have no memory of my life."

I looked at her closely, not sure whether to believe her. There was earnestness in her face and truthfulness in her eyes. "Judging from your clothing, you are a peasant," I said.

"I suppose so," said Anya.

"You have nothing with you?"

Anya reached up and pulled at a chain I hadn't noticed around her neck. Tucked in the bodice of her dress was a pendant on the chain. She tugged it out and held it toward me. "Only this."

I leaned forward and took the pendant from her hand, tilting it toward the fire to catch the light. It was exquisitely worked in plain silver, a knot of vines, covered with leaves, I assumed, with tiny flowers all along it. "It's lovely," I said.

"I have no idea where it came from, but I was wearing it."

She seemed unworried that her memory of her own life went back no more than six hours, and her ease spread to me. I was about to say as much when a thought jumped into my mind. "My text!"

"What?"

"I forgot my text in Richard's room. And I'll have to have it for my studies tomorrow."

"Richard?"

"My brother."

"Can't he simply give it to you in the morning?" Anya asked.

"There's nothing simple about it. I wasn't supposed to be in his quarters this evening. If my father discovers I was, I'll pay for weeks. I have to go get it." I stood.

Anya rose. "Can I help?"

I smiled at her, as if we already shared the bond that, at that point, I didn't know would grow between us. "How quiet can you be?"

We stole down the hallway to the main corridor and peeked around the corner to see the page. He was dozing again. On tiptoe, we traversed the empty corridors to Richard's rooms. At the door, I knocked. It was late, but I knew he would still be reading.

"Come." Richard's voice was clearly audible through the door.

I opened the door, and we both slipped inside. I shut the door behind us and turned back to see Richard gazing at Anya. I looked again at the girl and saw how the excitement of the trip through the hallways had brought a rose to her cheeks. She was smiling over at me, a merry, bright expression on her face. She was beautiful, literally breathtaking. Anya shrugged her shoulders at me, a gesture that would soon become familiar, and turned to face Richard.

She paused, her eyes caught in the gaze of his dark ones. The smile gradually faded from her face, and she took a long, slow, deep breath. For a moment I felt as though I shouldn't be there, like I was intruding on an intimate conversation, though not a word was spoken. They weren't smiling, or talking, or moving at all, but somehow I felt that they were communicating the deepest parts of themselves through their shared gaze.

Richard broke away first, shaking his head a little as if to wake up from a trance. He looked over at me. "Twice in one night?" he asked. "You really just want to make him angry, don't you?"

"My text," I said. "I dropped it earlier." I felt Anya break from her abstraction next to me.

Richard gestured to the sofa and chairs. "Come in, sit." We crossed the room and seated ourselves on the sofa. He picked up my text from an end table and handed it to me. "Be more careful with that," he said. Then he sat across from us in a chair and looked at me. "Where did tonight's display at the door come from?" he asked.

The reality of what I'd done washed over me. My father was a hard man—a description that applied as much to his physical appearance as it did to his personality. He was not tall, but I never thought him little. I had seen him stand face-to-face with a burly farmer approaching with a request, and my father, though he had to tilt his chin up to look the man in the eye, stared him into a shrinking, cowering child. Mounted on a horse, he was even more imposing—his dark hair swept by the wind, his square jaw set, his head erect. He carried himself well in the saddle, back straight, every muscle chiseled, his thick arms in complete control of the reins. He would ride into the village, pull up at the door of Thayer the tailor, and demand his order—while demanding the lowest price.

He was a man with strict rules and fierce hatred. I never knew why he hated the old ways and the followers of the Ancient Writings so much; I only remembered his anger when he discovered that our old cook was a practitioner of magic. I was only a small child when it happened, the day he found her murmuring a spell as she wrapped my brother Richard's finger with a bandage dipped in the oils and herbs she'd collected and combined.

Father didn't abuse her with blows or rage against her with loud yelling, but his whole person grew rigid, his body tensed. He grew cold, drew himself up stiffly. His black eyes glinted—coal turned to crystal. The muscles in his face tightened, drawing the straight planes of it into even sharper angles. Quiet wrath emanated from every pore. He spoke, and his voice was flinty, the words chipping out, sharp, clipped. "I will not have such things."

"My Lord," said the poor woman, quaking already at the harsh expression he directed her way. "It's just simple spells!"

"Vile lies!" Father spat the words at her. "There is nothing simple about them. Take your disgusting practice and depart." He turned to stride out.

She began to protest once more. He wheeled around at her and, for the first time in the conversation, raised his voice. "Now!" His deep, resonant voice echoed off the stone counters of the kitchens.

The woman broke, and as he stared her down, she melted into blubbering incoherence. He watched her, an eyebrow raised slightly, his nostrils contracted as if he smelled something foul. His eyes didn't soften at the mess of weeping humanity before him. Rather, he scoffed, called to Richard to follow, turned back around, and continued out of the room with his long, purposeful strides.

I was ignored.

And now, I'd directly defied my father and drawn myself to his attention. I sucked in my breath and felt the blood drain from my face. My hand was unsteady as I reached out to pick up a pillow and play with the fringe. "I don't know what made me do it," I said, rolling the tiny silk ropes between my fingers. "I didn't even think; I just spoke."

Richard chuckled. "Remarkable speaking it was. With one word, you saved a girl's life, defied a nobleman of Asael, and impressed an entire household of servants. You should try speaking more often."

I looked up at him. "It's not a joke!" I said. "Is he very angry?"

"Yes," said Richard. "But he won't do anything. If he didn't punish you in the moment, he won't punish you at all." He paused, leaned back, and looked us both over. "And, for some reason, he didn't punish you in the moment."

I glanced over at Anya. She had been sitting quietly, looking back and forth between Richard and me as we spoke. "Perhaps it was meant to be," she said, her musical voice breaking between us.

I scoffed a little at her. "What, He Who Knows Men's Thinking ordained your arrival on our doorstep in the rain, destitute and without memory?"

Anya nodded. "Perhaps."

Richard turned a quizzical eye to me. "Without memory?"

"She doesn't know anything about herself earlier than this afternoon."

Richard raised an eyebrow, turning to Anya. "Nothing?"

"Nothing at all except my name."

"Sephanya," Richard said.

"But I'm called Anya."

"In your non-existent past," said Richard.

"Richard!" I admonished.

"I'm sorry," said Richard. "I've never met anyone without a memory. Are you injured? The court medics once published a text on how injury to the head can cause memory loss." Richard stood and moved over to Anya. He reached out his hand to her head. "May I check?"

Anya looked up at him, nodded. He put his hand on her head, like a Priest giving a blessing, and she closed her eyes under its weight.

"Tell me if it hurts anywhere," said Richard. Once again I felt as though I was intruding on a private moment. Richard ran his hand back over Anya's head, almost a caress. He reached up with his other hand and started at her temples with his fingertips, slowly moving around until his fingers interlocked at the nape of her neck, under her hair. She opened her eyes and looked up at him, still for a moment. "No pain?" Richard asked.

"None," Anya said.

Their eyes caught again, and Richard slowly drew his hands away, his fingertips tracing the line of her jaw from ear to chin. He tore his gaze from Anya's eyes, asking, "What is the necklace?"

Anya reached up to the chain and pulled out the pendant again. "I was wearing it." She held it out to him, and he examined it in the lamplight, his head bent close to hers.

"Are those flames? No—is it leaves and flowers?" he asked.

"I can't tell," I said. "Perhaps."

"The metal is plain silver, inexpensive, but the work is that of an artisan," Richard said. "Work like that would cost dear." He handed the pendant back to Anya, and she tucked it away under her gown. Richard moved back to his seat. "So, we have on our hands a destitute peasant without a past, who wears expensive jewelry and speaks with a more gently trained voice than half the ladies at court."

I looked over at Anya. "Perhaps not a peasant after all," I said.

She gave her shoulders their habitual shrug. "I don't know," she said. "I feel no compulsion to discover my past. I am here now. That is what matters."

"Will you stay?" asked Richard. Anya looked over at him. "I mean, you're welcome to," Richard went on. "And if you did, I—we could keep searching to find out where you came from. You would have to work; Father would put you out on the highroad if you didn't."

"But I promise that life as my personal maid will not be drudgery," I said. "I think we might be friends."

Anya smiled at me, the merriment back in her features. "I'm sure we would be," she said. "I think—"

She broke off at the sound of the bell on the front gate. It clanged for the second time that night with the same kind of urgency as the first. Quickly following the bell was the sound of fists pounding on the heavy wooden front door. Richard crossed the room in three steps and opened the door to the hall. Muffled by distance and the sound of the storm, we could only just make out the words a voice was shouting outside the door. "Open! Open! Message from the court! Message from the king's court!"

CHAPTER 3

I joined Richard at the door of his rooms. He poked me in the ribs. "Perhaps it's Prince Loran's response to Father's invitation." He looked back over his shoulder. "Anya, if you stay, you'll get to see my sister flirt with the Prince at her eighteenth celebration next month."

I heard the clicking of a maid's shoes in the marble entryway. "Hush!" I said to Richard. "He wouldn't send a response by special messenger. Something's wrong."

We heard the front door swing open, and the voice of the messenger echoed up the stairs. "I bring a message for Lord Adamaris. Take me to him."

Richard glanced over at me. "You'd best not be seen about the house again tonight. Stay here." He slipped out the door and walked down the hall toward the central stair.

There was nothing to do but wait. I shut the door and rejoined Anya on the sofa. We were quiet for a few moments before Anya took a deep breath and turned to me.

"I'm sure it seems strange," she said. "That I am unconcerned about my past, I mean."

I looked at her. It was strange to me.

"But—" She paused. "Have you ever simply felt as though you belong? Not so much in a certain place, but with certain people?"

I have very few memories of my mother. I was so young when she died. But the few images I have are what I fled to in my mind whenever I felt the fire of my father's rages or his icy anger coming on. The memory of my mother's arms around me comforted me. I knew I had belonged in them. "Yes," I said.

Anya looked deeply into my eyes. I could see she knew I understood. In that moment, I became inextricably linked to the girl who'd appeared at my door without a past. I knew that this girl beside me would never be my servant. I had found a friend, an equal.

The door opened behind us, and together we stood and turned. Richard entered and shut the door after him. He paused and looked up at us, taking in our united front. He smiled at the sight, but it faded quickly. A curtain was drawn over the warmth that usually flowed from his eyes. They were still.

"What is it?" I asked.

Richard crossed the room and returned to the chair he'd vacated earlier. Anya and I sat again upon the sofa.

Richard looked up, his face grave. "Prince Loran is dead."

I gasped. Richard had always joked that I had a crush on the Prince. It was a foolish bit of teasing neither one of us took seriously. But I did respect the Prince. Tangled as the Written Histories were, my study of them made one thing clear: Loran was the hope of Asael. We lived in a land in need of renewal and restoration. Without it, the kingdom would sour and corrupt. For twenty-five years those who saw the land as I did had trusted that Loran would one day set all things right. Though blood-heir to the throne, Loran stood head and shoulders above most of the kings of the last age. His sharp wit, keen understanding, and calm diplomacy had already strengthened his father's following. Without his son, King Saran was merely an elderly old man who held onto his throne with the tips of his fingers.

I couldn't speak. I wanted to doubt my brother's word, but I couldn't conjure disbelief. Richard's tone, his eyes, his demeanor—all asserted his truthfulness. The reality of the loss was crashing about me, and my mind was drowning in the ramifications.

"How?" asked Anya.

Her voice drew me back toward the present. Richard seemed to find strength in it. "An accident," he said. "Near here, actually. Not ten miles off. Thrown from his horse while descending into the gorge. He must have fallen a hundred feet."

I shut my eyes, trying to block out the image. I knew the gorge well; the River Maris had worn a deep cleft in the land on its way to the sea. To cross it, one followed a rocky switchback trail down to the ford and then up again on the other side. The craggy cliffs rose two hundred feet from the rushing river to the moors above. A fall from anywhere on either side would be fatal. If you weren't killed by hitting the rocks on the way down, there would be little to keep you from plunging into the frigid rapids far below.

I opened my eyes again and saw Richard's face. His eyes were blank, his complexion grey.

"This changes everything," I said.

Richard's eyes tried to focus on me, but they failed. His eyelids slid down, hiding the dark, expressionless irises. "Everything," he whispered.

Anya sat quietly beside me. She reached out and grasped my hand. We all sat silent for a time. After a while, Anya squeezed my hand, giving it a little shake before letting go. "There is no more to be done tonight," she said. "We should all get some rest."

Richard took a deep breath and shook his head a little, as if trying to clear his foggy brain. "Yes." He stood. "If Father finds you about now, you'll pay."

I picked up my text. "Yes," I said. I had nothing else to say.

Anya gripped my elbow and pulled me to my feet as she stood. She glanced up into Richard's still-blank face. "I remember the way we came," she said. "We'll get back to her quarters quietly."

For the first time since he'd reentered the room, Richard's expression cleared, and the curtain over his eyes was pulled back for a moment as he looked at Anya. "My thanks," he said.

Anya guided me to the door, opened it, and checked the hall before we stepped out. With a glance over her shoulder back to Richard, she shut the door behind us.

I barely recall the journey back to my rooms that night. The storm outside had abated little, and when Anya opened the door to my quarters, the muted sound of the surf crashing at the base of the cliff filled my ears. Anya took my text from me and set it upon my desk. She corked the inkwell I'd forgotten earlier and blotted the pen.

Coming back to the center of the room, she grasped me by the arm and guided me to my bed. She helped me remove my dressing gown and lifted the silken comforters for me to slide under. I settled on my pillow while she slid her feet out of the shoes the servants had found for her and loosened the bodice of the dress enough to slip out of it. She hung the dress on a hook in the wardrobe. Barefoot in her shift, a strand of hair falling across her face, she reminded me again of the girl who had arrived at our doorstep in rags. I wondered that it had been only a few hours since that first bell clanged. I had not realized then that the courses of kingdoms can be changed in a matter of moments.

Anya turned down the lamp and slid between the sheets of her cot, next to my bed. "You do need a maidservant," she said.

I blinked in the darkness. "Oh," I said. "I suppose so."

The pounding of the surf filled the next few moments with its steadying rhythm. Then Anya spoke again. "You said Prince Loran's death changes everything."

I turned onto my side. I could barely see her in the gloom of the night. "He was the hope of Asael," I said. "King Saran can scarcely hold the nobles to one purpose by himself."

"You think Loran's death spells doom for the kingdom?"

"I fear it might."

She was quiet again. The surf had nearly lulled me into sleep before I heard her voice. "There is the Rose."

It took a moment for her words to reach into my mind. When they did, my sleepiness vanished in an instant. I sat up in the darkness. "Are you one of the faithful?"

I heard the cot creak as Anya shifted. "I don't know," she said. "But I know the tales."

I lay back again among my pillows and tried to keep the scoffing note out of my voice. "Everyone has heard the tales," I said. "No one believes them but peasants and Priests."

"And if the peasants and Priests are right?" Anya asked.

"Well—they—" I stopped, flustered. "There have been plenty of hard times in Asael, and no Rose has ever come. Why would he now?"

Anya didn't reply. The covers rustled; the cot squeaked. Finally, I heard her voice again. "You really do need a maidservant," she said. "I think I'll stay."

She fell silent, leaving me in the darkness, my mind whirling through possibilities of corruption and ruin. The road ahead was a dark corridor. The faithful put their trust in myths and legends, but I was a realist. As I looked at the future, though, I was hard-pressed to hold onto my realism. Without Loran, I thought as I listened to the throbbing surf, we would need a miracle to redeem Asael.

Chapter 4

I awoke the next morning in the light shining around the curtains at the window. The surf had quieted in the night, back to the low, constant thrum of clear weather. The window light mingled with a yellow glow from another direction: the burning fire, I realized. I sat up, alarmed, and blinked. Anya's arrival the night before washed back over me. She had built up the fire, warmed water in the kettle, and found the tea things in the sideboard. Through the tiny hole in the lid of the pot I could see a curl of steam rising.

Anya turned quietly to look at me, seeming unsurprised by my abrupt wakening. "Tea?" she asked.

I blinked again. I tried to bring my mind back to the present. I scooted out from under my covers and let my feet find my slippers. Absently, I grasped my dressing gown and shrugged my arms into the sleeves, tying it around me as I made my way to the chair opposite Anya by the fire.

"It was real," I said, sitting down.

She picked up the teapot and began to pour. She answered me without seeming to need an explanation. "Yes." She set down the teapot and looked at me. "All of it."

The second part of the previous night suddenly crashed back into my consciousness. I gasped. Tears pricked at my eyes. "Loran is dead," I choked out.

Anya stood and came to my side. She knelt and put an arm around my shoulders, gripping them and pulling me toward her. "Yes," she whispered. She held me close as I wept. Sorrow I did not understand wracked my body.

Anya stroked my hair as sobs shuddered through me. "You are right to grieve," she said. "You have lost what might have been." Anya held me until I quieted, and then, giving me one more squeeze, stood and returned to her seat. "Tea," she said, gesturing to the cup on the table, now cooled to a drinkable temperature.

I grasped the cup in both hands and sipped, letting the liquid course down my throat, feeling its warmth flow from my center to my extremities, soothing tense muscles and ragged nerves as it went. I felt my whole self calming, emotionally and physically. I closed my eyes and took a deep breath. "Thank you," I said.

"No one comes to make up your fire?" Anya asked, after a few more moments of quiet.

I gazed into the crackling blaze. "Not until I ring the bell."

She shook her head, her eyes also on the flames. "You do need a maidservant."

"You sound like Richard. I have made up a fire on my own before. I take it you have, too?"

Anya looked out of the corner of her eye at me. One side of her mouth curled up. "I don't know."

"Still nothing?" I asked.

"Nothing."

We'd already established a short-hand method of conversation. I should have been surprised to find rapport so quickly, but I wasn't. Everything seemed to come easily with Anya.

I gulped the last of my tea. "Richard will be down in the breakfast room soon," I said, standing. "We should ready ourselves for the day."

Anya slipped into the dress she'd been given the night before, and I pulled the bodice tight for her. She helped me with the layers of petticoats and skirts I was bound to wear as a noblewoman. As she pulled the silk fabric of the overdress down and made sure it hung evenly, I found myself envying her simple attire. I'd never before thought about my clothing; it was simply what I wore. But comparing my gown's opulence with the minimalism of hers, I began to wonder if noble ladies might learn a thing or two from the peasant women.

My clothing and hair were finally arranged, and we left my quarters. We turned down my hall toward the central corridor, then forward to the central stair. I glanced sideways at Anya as we passed through the foyer, wondering if she would react to the memory of what took place there the night before. Her face was impassive. We reached the breakfast room, and I reached out for the handle. I stopped, my hand resting there, and turned to Anya.

"My father rarely eats his meals in company," I said. "I don't expect to see him this morning."

Anya looked back at me silently.

I took a breath and continued. "But if he comes, it will be—" I searched for the appropriate word, "—unpleasant." The word did not carry the force of the reality of my father's wrath, but Anya seemed to understand. She nodded. I opened the door and entered.

Richard was sitting by the head of the table, in the place of honor. He looked up as we entered and paused, his fork still in the air before him. I watched his eyes seek past me to Anya. They seemed to go slightly out of focus for a moment, and then he pulled them back to me. I could see lines of red in the white sections around his irises. He hadn't slept.

We took another step into the room and Richard stood, his fork clattering against his plate as he put it down. He gestured to the sideboard. "The eggs are delicious this morning," he said. The words were casual, not so very different than what he'd said to me the morning before. It was hard to believe the world had changed eight hours earlier.

Anya gestured that I should sit, then went to the sideboard and filled a plate for me. When she brought it over and set it in front of me, I glanced at Richard. He'd sat down again but seemed to have lost interest in his meal.

"Will you join us?" he said to Anya.

She looked up at him.

"But Father—" I began.

Richard interrupted me. "He left early this morning."

I looked to Anya. "Then join us," I said.

She walked to the sideboard and filled another plate. Bringing it back, she sat beside me. Richard half stood and leaned to the center of the table where the teapot stood on its service tray. He poured a cup for me and one for Anya, and we reached out to take them from him.

I took a sip. "Ugh. It's not hot." I set my teacup down in front of me.

Anya set hers beside it. She spread her hand out, palm facing downward, about six inches above the cups. "*Aestus*," she whispered.

Steam began to rise from the liquid in the cups, whirling and twirling off the surface, nearly alive in its dance upward.

I gasped.

Anya looked up, and her green eyes widened. She seemed surprised to see Richard and me staring at her, our mouths agape. "What is wrong?" she asked.

"You—you're a Practitioner!" Richard stuttered.

Anya shrugged. "Yes," she said. "Just simple spells."

I blinked. Our old cook was the only Practitioner I'd ever met.

Richard cleared his throat. "*Aestus* isn't a simple spell," he said.

Anya looked at him, a puckered line between her eyebrows. "I'm sorry?"

"Producing heat is one of the more difficult acts," Richard said.

"How do you know that, Richard?" I asked.

"Our old cook. Do you remember her?" He turned to Anya and explained, "We had a cook who was a Practitioner before our mother died. I used to sit with her for hours and listen to her stories about magic. She said producing heat was complicated because it was the creation of energy. That *aestus* was a spell rarely used."

I looked over at Anya. "Do you know where you learned your magic?"

She stared at the steam rising off our tea. "I didn't consciously know I had it until right now, when I needed it."

We all watched the steam for another moment. None of us knew quite what to say. Richard and I didn't realize we'd seen something that would change our lives forever. We were simply dumbfounded that, to add to every other mark against her, this peasant who had arrived upon the doorstep of the house of Lord Adamaris—of all people— was a Practitioner of magic.

CHAPTER 5

ONE sip at a time, we consumed our hot tea. I secretly thrilled at the thought that I was partaking of something my father would abhor. I had hesitated slightly, before my first sip, wondering if tea heated by magic would taste different. It didn't.

We finished our meals without much further conversation. I was certain we would go to the Capital for the funerary services, but I knew that until the decisions were made, I would still need to attend to my studies. In my father's home, even the death of a Prince did not change my tutor's schedule.

We rose from our breakfast, and I looked to Richard. "When will Father return, do you think?"

"Soon, I imagine," he answered. "He only went to find out what he could about the accident and the plans for the funeral."

I turned to Anya. "I must go to my lessons. You could stay in my rooms this morning."

"That is probably wise," Richard said. "I think we want to stay out of Father's way today."

Anya nodded. "I shall do so."

She and I glanced at each other and, by unspoken pact, turned to go out together. As I opened the door of the breakfast room and stepped into the front hall, I heard my father's boots on the front steps. There was no time to move through the hall before the door opened and my father came through. In an instant, I remembered Anya's plate on the table and the three empty cups of tea. I determined that meeting my father in the hall was less dangerous than in the breakfast room. I reached back and grasped Anya's hand, pulled her out of the room behind me, and whispered to her, "Stay a step behind me."

We began to walk down the hall toward the staircase at the center of the house. We'd not gone three steps into the front hall before the door opened, and my father stepped in. I paused and turned to face him, keeping my head upright but my eyes lowered, hoping to avoid direct confrontation.

"Karan!"

I caught my breath, my chest tightening. I listened to my pulse hammer, each beat of my heart reminding me what it was like to face Father's fury. I felt Anya square herself behind me, a little to the right. I clenched my teeth, bracing myself for an onslaught of anger. I raised my eyes to meet his.

My father's eyes burned in his dark face as he bore down upon me from the doorway. I'd seen the look before.

It was always followed by words of bile and vehemence. The harshest language I'd overheard from the stable hands couldn't compare to the vicious words which could spew forth from my father's mouth when he was angry.

His steps across the hall seemed to take forever. I watched the muscles of his mouth move, working up the spittle to moisten his mouth for words. Then his eyes passed beyond my face and moved on to the one behind me.

And in an instant, their expression changed, faltered. He had opened his mouth to speak, but at the sight of Anya, he hesitated. His words seemed to become stuck in his throat.

His eyes widened. He seemed taken aback. Then his gaze returned to mine, and the flint was gone, replaced with a bewildered expression. He seemed to be trying to comprehend something.

It was the first time I saw such a reaction, and at the time, I had no idea what to make of it. I still cannot explain it, but over time it has become familiar. It is my guess that I had a similar look on my face nine hours earlier when I helped a rain-drenched young peasant woman to her feet at our front door.

It took my father a moment to focus his gaze upon me. He closed his mouth, paused, then spoke, "Going to your studies?"

"Aye, sir."

"Good." He continued past us to the breakfast room, opened the door, went within, and closed it behind him.

I had no time or energy to hope that Richard had been quick-minded enough to clear away the extra dishes from the table. Anya returned to my rooms, and I went to my lessons. My mind was far away from the history exams I was taking. Time after time, my tutor had to recall me to the present. The events of the past twelve hours had upset my understanding of the world around me.

Prince Loran was dead. I never thought of death when I could avoid it. I had lost my mother when I was very young, but I didn't like to think about what might have happened to her immortal soul. Was she experiencing pain? Was she happy? What was existence after death? Perpetual nothingness? I hoped not. I might complain about my brother's teasing about my crush on Loran, but I did like him. I liked everything I had ever known or heard about him. And I didn't want to imagine him in nothingness. I didn't want to imagine him in pain. But nothing in my experience had really convinced me that the soul's existence after death was anything good. My father feared death, I knew. My father, who feared nothing in this world, feared death.

I thought of his hesitation in the hall. Anya's appearance had thrown everything out of balance. My father had hesitated before her this morning. A nobleman who need only bow before the kingwas not assured in Anya's presence.

I tried to ignore her skill with magic. It was so unfamiliar to me that I found it frightening. I told myself it was of no importance.

I have little recollection of that exam. I must have passed, for my tutor did not berate me the next day. Had I failed, he would have had no shame in telling me so. When I finished, I returned to my rooms, looking for Anya.

I entered to find her standing at the tapestry on one wall, tracing the woven images with one finger. I stood quietly by the door, watching her. Her hand moved across the textured surface. For the first time in years, I noticed the image portrayed: a great map—twisting rivers, turning roads, green meadows, craggy mountains—scattered across it, small, wreathed images of what I can only imagine were pilgrims on a journey across the map. Anya's finger would trace along a road then catch a wreath and follow the vine around the image before returning to the road and the next pilgrim.

"Where do you think they are going?" she asked.

I answered her absently, my eye still caught by the wreathed images. "They're gathering somewhere—do you see the wreaths?"

Anya's finger paused on one. "My necklace?"

"Aye," I said. "It's the same pattern."

Distracted from her initial question, Anya pulled her necklace out from the bodice of her dress and held it up to the stitched wreath of vines, leaves, and flowers. "It is." She looked away from the tapestry back to me. "How was your examination?"

I shrugged, feeling myself take on her distinctive movement. "No idea. I'll find out tomorrow."

She smiled. "Have you eaten? I can fetch a lunch from the kitchen."

I had once again forgotten that she was to be my maid-servant. "Oh! Make it large, so you can eat, too."

"Yes, milady." Anya stepped quietly toward the door and went out. She did not ask for directions, and I assumed she'd found her way through the back corridors to the kitchen in the course of the morning.

I sat in a chair by the crackling fire, glad of its warmth, though the night's storm had given way to glorious sunshine that streamed in the windows. The air beside the glass was still chill to the skin. My gaze idly lingered over the tapestry, tracing paths across the landscape from inset pilgrim to inset pilgrim. For the first time, I looked at the people. I had to marvel at the handiwork of the artist who had done the weaving; the people were vibrant, alive, and... I paused, looking for a word to describe the expressions on their faces. Expectant.

I have seen the look, now, on many faces. The pilgrims who arrive, after long journeys, having finally come to the place of the One they are seeking, have such a look. But at the time, I had no experience with such expectation. I found it mysterious. What could these travelers be seeking with such hope?

After about ten minutes, the door opened again, and Anya reentered, bearing a tray laden with more food than the two of us could eat.

"Did you clean out the kitchen?" I asked. "Or was Garima feeling particularly generous?"

"She gave me all this. She said Master Richard would be joining us."

I started giggling. Anya set down the tray and looked at me, waiting for the giggles to stop.

I gasped, trying to regain my composure. "Don't... don't ever try to call him that to his face!"

"What?" she asked.

"*Master* Richard!"

"It's what the cook said," she protested.

I again tried to calm myself enough to speak. "I'm sure it is, but it sounds so funny when you say it!"

"Why?"

"I don't know. It simply doesn't fit."

"What should I call him then?" Anya seemed truly disturbed.

I had hold of myself by that time, and her distress raised my compassion. "When we're alone, call him Richard."

"I can't do that in public," she said.

"No. Try to avoid 'Master,' though. It sounds wrong."

The door had opened, and Richard entered as I said the last sentence.

"What does?"

"Anya calling you *Master* Richard!" I couldn't help another giggle.

Richard smiled. "Aye. That does seem wrong."

Anya looked from one to the other of us. "So?" she asked. "What am I to call you in public?"

Richard and I looked at each other. He picked up a chair and pulled it toward the table with Anya's tray upon it. He sat down. I could tell he was thinking through all the titles we'd been given. "The young Lord Adamaris?" he suggested.

I nodded. "It works most of the time. And you can call me Lady Karan. But not here! It—" I broke off, unable to explain what seemed so wrong about hearing Anya use our titles.

Richard finished for me: "I don't think either one of us thinks of you as a servant." He smiled at Anya. "We've started off too unconventionally for that."

She seemed to relax under his smile, the distress leaving her expression.

"Sit," Richard invited her. "Even destitute peasants with no memory have to eat."

Anya smiled and sank into the chair across from me, pulling her legs up comfortably. Richard reached for a long roll and broke it in two, handing half to each of us. We began to pick over the options on the tray and create sandwiches for ourselves. And from that moment forward, we were a trio, friends bound together as equal companions.

We sat together for a long time, first eating, then talking. Richard had spoken to Father in the course of the morning. The funeral was to be held in the Capital three days later. We would leave the morning before to travel down. My father owned a house in the city, and we would spend a night there before presenting ourselves at court for the funeral. All my life, I had wanted to be presented at court, but in the situation, I found it was no longer something to look forward to.

Anya seemed excited about it, though. She was appropriately subdued, but underneath there was an energy running through her. Her eyes shone with it as we spoke, and she would interject questions about life in the Capital. Richard answered her. He had been to court before. I watched them as we talked. Somehow, in a few hours, Anya had forged a connection with Richard as strong as our own. There were moments when they communicated with only a glance, as she and I could already do. I remembered her words from the night before about feeling at home. Not a day earlier, Richard and I had not known she existed. Already, I was certain neither of us wanted to experience another day without her.

As we finally rose from our meal and Anya began to clear away the dishes and leftover food, I suddenly realized that my worries about the future of the kingdom without Loran were gone. I still grieved the loss, but I had no fear. The day felt completely ordinary, with no looming danger in the background. Then Anya dropped a cup.

It happened quickly. The cup slipped from the edge of her tray as she picked it up. Richard and I both reached for it automatically, but with no hope of catching it. We were too far away.

Faster than either of us, Anya balanced the tray with her left hand and reached toward the falling cup with her right. "*Capere*," she said.

The cup stopped in midair as if caught by an invisible net. She leaned over, still balancing the tray, grasped the cup, and set it back on the tray.

Richard and I were frozen. I felt my mouth hanging open as I stared at her.

Anya turned as if nothing had happened and walked toward the door. "I'll return this tray to the kitchens and be back, Karan," she said. Nimbly, she balanced the tray again and opened the door with her other hand, walked out, and pulled it shut behind her.

We remained standing still for a moment after the door closed. Finally Richard spoke. "I don't think she quite realizes she's doing it."

"If it happens in front of Father, he'll kill her," I said.

"We'll hide it from him," said Richard.

I shook my head. "Our old cook could hide the dash of magic she used in her healing ointments to make them work so well. This—this isn't simple magic."

Richard looked at the door again. "Well, we'll try. That's all we can do."

Fear of the future swept back over me. We had stepped into the unknown and couldn't turn back. Something loomed ahead, but I could not even tell if it was dangerous. I stared at the door, too. "All we can do," I repeated.

Richard looked over at me. "This changes everything," he said.

CHAPTER 6

WE made our way to the Capital of Asael two days later. In the course of the two days, I'd seen Anya practice magic three more times. It seemed natural to her, as if she'd been doing so her whole life, as if she came from a world where the practice of magic was a normal part of life—not an antique custom, so out of use it was thought by some to be mythological.

Thus far, we'd kept it from my father. Anya had noticed our discomfort with her gift and tried to be careful about using it, but like that day at lunch, there were times she did so without thinking. I worried, a little, about living in my father's town house for a week. We were much less spread out there than on the estate. The quarters did not have their own sitting rooms, so we spent most of our time in the parlor or salon, and my father would enter those at any time. I feared, too, that he would note Anya's ease with Richard and me.

I said all this to Anya as we traveled, she and I enclosed in a carriage as my father and Richard rode on horseback with their men. I wanted to ride—I did so almost every day on the estate—but my father was a stickler for propriety. No daughter of his would be seen by the nobles at court riding into the Capital on horseback. The only benefit was the privacy it gave to Anya and me. I was able to share with her the details of life in the Capital. I had not been formally presented at court as a young woman, but I had visited when we were in the city. And for my whole life, I'd been trained in the etiquette and rules of life among the nobles. I cautioned her carefully about the distinct classes and the expectations of ladies in waiting in the city. I knew my father would not be the only one watching.

In the end, I probably did not need to worry quite so much. I discovered when we arrived that the death of the prince had thrown the city into chaos. Throughout the time we were there, the nobles paid little note to anything but their own grief and their own schemes for power.

Still, I found myself concerned. I worried that any misstep on our part would find Anya banished from my life—and though she'd only been a part of it for four days, I knew I couldn't go back. Richard and I both seemed to be discovering a new life, one we'd never imagined before that rainy night. In the moments when I saw Anya practice her gift, I felt as though I were in the presence of something bigger, deeper than anything I'd ever experienced before that. I didn't have words to explain it at the time—I've since read about the concept of eternity in the Ancient

Writings, but at the time, I only knew that I was experiencing something more. More than I knew.

We arrived in the Capital late in the afternoon of the day before the funeral. We found our house opened and waiting for us; a bevy of servants had gone down a day early to prepare for our arrival. Richard handed me down from the carriage, and I saw him glance over my shoulder and give Anya a quick smile, but he stuck to the proper forms and offered me his arm to go in, ignoring my lady-in-waiting under the gaze of my father and the household staff.

I led the way up the front stairs and to my room on the second floor. This room looked over the front street. As a child, I used to watch the activity below me with fascination. In my mind, I likened the waves of people to the crashing surf—the same, but more colorful.

Anya closed the door after herself as she entered behind me. "Welcome to the Capital," I said.

"It is smaller than I expected," she replied, moving to the window and looking out.

"They deliberately built it to be small. There is only a short section of the river that is calm enough and narrow enough to build along. The river widens immediately above the stone bridge and goes through the monks' fields, and then upstream from that are rapids, and just downriver the delta begins."

"The kings of old chose their placement carefully," said Anya.

"Aye. All north-south travel must come through the Capital," I said. "They charge tariffs."

I joined her at the window, surveying the scene. The bright colors of the people were all muted—black armbands and hats were signs of what tomorrow held. The golden banners typically hanging from each building had been replaced with long swathes of black fabric that rippled in the wind.

We stood silently for a few moments, watching the movement below. Then Anya spoke again. "The prince was beloved," she observed.

"Aye." I nodded. "The city is quieter than usual."

"I wonder if he knew," Anya mused.

Still looking out the window, I raised one eyebrow and cocked my head before responding. "Do we ever know what people really think of us?"

"Only if we are very fortunate, I think." She smiled a half-smile. "Or unfortunate, in some cases."

I thought of Richard and my father. I saw what she meant.

"You should dress for the meal," Anya said. She turned to the wardrobe and opened the door, running her fingers over the row of gowns that filled the space. "Crimson," she said, pulling a deep wine-colored gown off the rack. "It will complement the crepe well."

I pulled shut the curtain and began to unfasten the hooks on the back of my traveling attire. As Anya helped me shed the stiff traveling clothes and put on the stay-filled undergarments required by such a gown as she'd chosen, I once again envied her simple dress.

"There are so many buttons!" I said.

Anya fastened them one by one, from the small of my back up to the high collar. Then she turned me around. She was slightly taller than me, and she tilted my chin up so that I was looking her in the eye. "You are a noblewoman. Buttons are a sign of wealth."

"Because someone has to button them all up," I said. "So, in reality, they are a sign of the oppression of the peasant classes."

Anya chuckled. "Does coming to the Capital always bring out your political side?" She turned me again and began to wrap a piece of black crepe around my upper arm, expertly tucking it into itself.

"It comes from the hours of Richard's tutoring." Her question had distracted me. I hadn't fully considered Loran's death from a political standpoint; I'd been too caught up in the grief of it. I remembered the first night. The first words I'd said: *This changes everything.* And it did. Every nobleman and woman traversing the streets of the Capital had a stake in Asael. Loran's death placed the future of the monarchy in question, and with it, the future of the noble class.

"Half the men at the funeral tomorrow will be scheming for power while they stand there and pretend to grieve with the king," I said. "My father among them."

Anya had moved to fix my hair. "How many noble families are there in Asael?"

"Too few, if they were ever challenged," I said. "The nobles are significantly outnumbered by the peasants."

"So, if the peasants arose..."

"If the peasants followed a single leader, Asael would be a different place." I remembered Richard expounding on the topic for me a few months earlier. "But there has never been a uniting figure."

"I can see why the stories of the Rose are not popular among the nobles," Anya said.

I nodded. She stilled my head with one hand, the other holding a braid she was twining together.

"The Ancient Writings are a dangerous text. Richard once had a tutor that said the only people the nobles in Asael fear more than one another are the monks, the Keepers of the Writings."

Anya sat me down before a mirror and pinned the braids up on the back of my head, weighting it down enough that my chin rose. "The faithful would never step into the place of He Who Knows Men's Thinking," she said.

"Perhaps not," I said, looking at her in the mirror. "But what if they were convinced they'd found the Rose?"

I watched her eyes widen slightly. In our conversations over the past few days, I'd discovered that she knew at least as much of the Ancient Writings as I did—though, frankly, my knowledge was fairly limited. There were varied interpretations of much that the Ancient Writings said, but everyone who believed them agreed on one thing: the Rose was the hope of Asael.

The bell below rang, calling me to the evening meal. I stood from my seat before the mirror.

"Turn," Anya commanded. I rotated slowly. "Perfect," she said. "You look like a noblewoman should look in the Capital."

I grinned at her. "You've never been to the Capital," I said. "How do you know?"

"Oh, hush," she said, smiling back.

"You can find your way to your own meal?" I asked.

"I'll figure it out."

"Thank you," I said, looking down at my dress and smoothing the skirt. "You are masterful at handling the signs of the oppression of your class."

Her smile widened. "You're welcome," she said. "You manage to wear them without looking offensive."

I laughed aloud as I walked out of my door. Richard had come out of his rooms across the hall. He smiled at the sight of me laughing then offered me his arm to go down to dinner.

"What's so funny?" he asked as we walked.

"Politics," I said.

He shot me a quizzical look.

"Oh, never mind," I said. "Tell me about something serious. I shouldn't look too cheerful when we go in to dinner."

Richard shook his head. "Politics is funny, and you're having trouble thinking about something serious the night before a funeral," he said. "She's a good friend for you."

His observation sobered me quickly. "I know," I said. "We can't let Father see. Anything."

He gave my arm a squeeze with his elbow. "He won't. He Who Knows Men's Thinking wouldn't allow it."

My head snapped so I could stare at him, but we had reached the dining room door, and the servants opened it before I could respond. Richard was looking directly ahead, seemingly unaware that he had just said something shocking. I quickly composed my features as we entered the room where our father stood at the head of the table ready to sit. Still dazed, I allowed Richard to lead me to my seat and then performed the charade of my role in the evening meal for the next hour, passing the salt when my father asked and carefully cutting my meat into appropriately bite-sized pieces as I'd been taught. But my mind was spinning, coming back round and round to the quiet confidence in Richard's tone. He had sounded like a *believer*.

CHAPTER 7

DINNER flowed into an evening in the salon, our normal routine for the Capital. My father and Richard flanked the fire, each reading. I sat on a settee across the room, book in hand, but paying it little attention. My mind continued to reel, coming up with question after question and discarding half of them. I had to ask Richard what he'd meant, but I didn't quite know how to do so. I'd nearly forgotten my short conversation with Anya a few nights earlier about whether she was one of the faithful. Apart from her, if one could classify her as one of the faithful, I'd never even met a believer. As far as I knew, Richard hadn't either. But the words had rolled off of his tongue unthinkingly.

I could only hope that Richard would outlast our father and I would have a chance to speak with him. I watched them out of the corner of my eye, counting the chimes on the clock at each quarter-hour. Richard began to slow in his pace, the pages turning less and less frequently.

Then his eyelids seemed to grow heavier and heavier, each blink longer. I glanced at my father, and my heart sank. I watched his eyes scan rapidly over the page before he quickly flipped to the next.

Finally, Richard stood. I closed my book, hoping I might have a moment to speak with him in the hall while our father remained behind. But as Richard rose, Father looked up.

"Going to your rooms?" he asked.

Richard yawned. "Too many late nights recently," he said.

My father put a finger in the book to save his place and stood as well. "I'll finish my book by my own fireplace."

I clenched my teeth. Richard looked at the closed book beside me. "You going up, too, Karan?"

I stood, caught. My questions would have to wait. "Aye."

Together the three of us left the salon and made our way up the stairs. Anya opened the door to my rooms as we approached, giving me no excuse to linger in the hallway. As I passed through the doorway, I saw Richard yawn again and turn to his door, bidding my father goodnight. Father continued down the hall and turned in at his own quarters.

My face must have betrayed my frustration, for as soon as the door closed behind me, Anya asked, "What's wrong?"

I didn't know how to explain it. I didn't want to until I'd determined what I thought about it. So I deliberately smoothed my features out.

"Nothing."

Anya helped me with my buttons and the layers of petticoats underneath. She told me about her evening with the servants, sensing that I didn't want to speak. I listened with half an ear, still trying to wrap my mind around my brother's tone. As I slipped my nightgown over my head and pulled it down around myself, my mind came back around to the question of whether she was a believer.

"You're familiar with the Ancient Writings, aren't you, Anya?" I asked, interrupting whatever she'd been saying.

She paused. "I think *familiar* might be the only way to describe it," she said. "I couldn't say I know them. I have no memory of ever reading them. But they are familiar—as if I once knew them well but haven't thought of them in years. Why do you ask?"

I sat down on my bed. "I read them as a child. My mother had instructed our tutor to expose us to them. They were a regular part of my lessons until I was ten. Then my father discovered it and fired the tutor. He said we should focus on the Written Histories rather than fairy tales."

She sat beside me. "But you know them well? The Ancient Writings?"

I grimaced. "Not well. Not deeply, anyway. I have a broad knowledge of them—I've read most of the texts. But I never understood them. My tutor never discussed the texts with us. He simply assigned them as readings. And it was so long ago. Lines and phrases from them are familiar and come to mind from time to time, and I remember the stories. But beyond that..." I trailed off.

Anya looked closely at me. I could tell she wanted to ask where the train of conversation had come from, but I wasn't ready to talk about it. Richard's confident tone had disturbed me. I shrugged my shoulders in Anya's way. "Never mind," I said. "We should sleep. Breakfast will be early."

Anya's bed was in the dressing room at this house. There wasn't enough room in my sleeping room for a cot.

She stood. "Good night, then." She carried my dress and petticoat with her into the dressing room and shut the door behind her.

I turned down the wick and blew out the lamp. Lying down, I watched the strip of light under the dressing room door until it went out. I tried closing my eyes, but my mind wouldn't stop whirring.

Richard's voice came back to me over and over again. *"He Who Knows Men's Thinking wouldn't allow it."*

Then, suddenly, a bit of my conversation with Anya from that afternoon ran through my mind.

"The faithful would never step into the place of He Who Knows Men's Thinking."

"Perhaps not, but what if they were convinced they'd found the Rose?"

I sat up. What were the signs of the Rose? My familiarity with the Writings failed me. I remembered the passages existed, but not what they said. How would the faithful know the Rose?

Richard's comment was no longer the most pressing question in my mind. I needed to remember more about the Rose. My thoughts went to the library downstairs. I knew Father wouldn't have discarded the text, despite his reluctance to allow us to read it. He had never talked to us about magic and the beliefs of the faithful, but I could tell he equally hated and feared them. So, if my mother had ever had a copy in this house, it would be in the library.

I listened carefully for any sound in my dressing room. Anya seemed to be asleep. I slid quietly out of my bed, not bothering to rummage for my dressing gown in the dark. It would make too much noise. I crossed to the hall door and eased it open. The hallway was dark, and no light came up from below. The entire household appeared to be asleep. I looked down to the far end of the hall, checking for light under my father's door. Even that was dark.

As silently as I could, I slipped out the door, closing it behind me, and moved down the hallway toward the stairs. Gripping the railing in the darkness, I made my way down, step by step. Once down, I circled to the left. The library door opened off the back of the foyer. I found the handle and gently turned it, glad my father's servants were too afraid of him to allow anything to fall out of repair. The hinges worked smoothly and silently.

I felt my way along the shelves that covered the walls until I found the desk. My eyes were fairly well adjusted to the dark by that time, and I was able to make out a candlestick holder and a box of matches. I picked up the box, struck a match, and touched it to the wick of the candle. It flamed to life, and I blinked, momentarily blinded by the brightness.

I turned once my eyes had adjusted and surveyed the library in the light cast by my candle. It didn't reach far, but I'd spent enough time here to have a fair idea in which corner the text I was looking for would be. I made my way across the room. On the wall across from the door were windows. The shelves on that wall were low, and artwork decorated the walls between the windows.

The wall opposite from the desk had stacks jutting out from it, forming three cubbies about the size of the stalls for horses in a stable. I was making for the corner of the third stall, along the windowed wall. Once there, I sank to my knees. The oldest books were at the bottom in this corner. I held up the candle to the bindings, scanning the titles.

It didn't take me long to find what I was looking for: a leather-bound copy of the Ancient Writings. The volume was thick; the binding was about the width of my palm. I pulled it out then redistributed the other books on the shelf so that no one would notice the empty space. Somehow, I knew that I would not be returning the text to the shelf. I set down the candle on the floor in the corner and laid the book down before it. I opened it to the middle, looking for the passages I remembered. I scanned the text, then flipped forward a few pages, and scanned again. It was a few moments before I found the passage that had been niggling at the edges of my memory.

And you shall know the Rose by this sign. This One will practice Rosefire, though never trained. All the signs which come before will be confirmed in this one act. And the act will save the line of kings.

I rocked back on my heels, my eyes wide. *The act will save the line of kings.* For all intents and purposes, Loran's death had brought an end to the line of kings. I couldn't imagine King Saran fathering another son at his age. He had been close to sixty when Loran was born. Prince Loran's mother had been Saran's third wife, less than half his age. And since her death fifteen years earlier, Saran had not taken another.

I remembered the thought that had crossed my mind a few days earlier, that it would take a miracle to save Asael. I knew little of Rosefire, except that it was very difficult magic, at the level of only the most advanced masters of the craft. I remembered reading a story in the Writings where a Practitioner used it to bring someone back to life. But I couldn't recall where the story was in the text.

The only way to find it would be to start at the beginning. I flipped to the very first page of the text. I was too excited to sleep, so I began to read, starting with the first passage in the first chapter.

The Creator formed beings like Himself, and called them men. The Creator made the men like Himself, with minds to think and wills to act. And the Creator knows the man's thoughts and the man's will—better than the man himself...

Hours later, I was only about a third of the way through the text. The sky was beginning to lighten, making the windows stand out from the dark walls. I'd burned through three candles; the final one was guttering in the holder. I stood, holding the text, and blew out the candle. I eased open the door and moved quickly back to my bedroom before anyone saw me about. I hid the book under my pillows and lay down. Closing my eyes, I tried to catch an hour of sleep before breakfast.

I smile at myself now, looking back on that night. For in my distraction over a single line of the text, I'd forgotten

Richard's words and my consuming need to know what he meant. Even the question that pulled me down to the library that night had been forgotten in my pursuit of a new question. And I'd given no consideration to, perhaps, the most revealing line of the text I read that night: *All the signs which come before will be confirmed in this one act.*

I see now the hand of He Who Knows Men's Thinking in that night. My distraction was only another step in the exploration that led me to where I am today. But at the time, I completely missed what was right before me, and I went to the funeral looking for entirely the wrong thing.

CHAPTER 8

ANYA woke me an hour later. I came to consciousness slowly. The sleep had done little to refresh me; I'd simply lost the excitement which kept me alert through the night. My head still on my pillow, I stretched. My hand found its way under the pillows and touched the text I'd stolen from the library. The contact was like a shock. It brought me fully awake, and I sat up. Immediately, my mind was spinning again, eager to see what would happen at the funeral. Would He Who Knows Men's Thinking reveal the Rose?

I didn't see what was happening. I was so caught up in my own thoughts that I could not take a step back and see the larger picture. A day earlier, I would have scoffed at anyone expecting He Who Knows Men's Thinking to act. Somehow, without conscious recognition of it, I had begun to think of He Who Knows Men's Thinking as a reality instead of a myth.

Anya seemed to note my strange behavior, but she made no comment. She turned to my wardrobe and pulled a black gown for the funeral. I scooted to the edge of the bed, glanced over to see that Anya was occupied, and reached back to slide the text into the drawer of the bedside table. I closed the drawer and stood, picking up my dressing gown and throwing it over my arm. When I turned back, I found Anya watching me with one eyebrow raised.

I walked over to the wardrobe and examined the dress. "I wish I could wear a dress like yours," I said lightly.

Anya followed my lead. "It certainly is a simpler gown."

"It looks much more comfortable than mine."

"Aye. I daresay it is."

She helped me dress quickly. As I sat at the dressing table and she arranged my hair, I found my attention drawn toward the drawer in the bedside table. Anya had to straighten my head more than once as I tried to look in that direction. On the third or fourth time, I glanced up in the mirror and caught her questioning eye. I flushed and tried harder to concentrate on preparations for the funeral.

When she had finished my hair, we switched places, and I braided her long tresses. Once, I caught her eyes sliding toward the bedside table. I considered confiding in her, but something—fear of her reaction, perhaps—held me back. I should have realized, thinking back on all the strange events of the days before, that Anya was the best person on earth to confide in; her strange arrival in our lives, with no past and no knowledge of her unique gifts, had equipped her to accept the unknown and the incomprehensible. I was not yet ready to be open about this erratic excitement, this unknown presence I seemed to be aware of, to be expecting.

As I considered sharing with her, there was a knock on the door. I finished pinning the braids in my hands and went to open it. Richard stood there.

"Are you ready to go down?" he asked. "I believe Father is waiting."

I nodded.

Richard's eyes slid past me. I turned and included Anya in the conversation. "You'll be ready to go with us to the funeral?" I asked. "We'll depart after the meal."

"I'll be ready," she said.

I joined Richard in the hall and again felt the urge to share, to say all that I had discovered and thought in the hours since I'd seen him last. But he seemed preoccupied and strode forward without a word. We went down the stairs, and he paused at the door of the breakfast room to offer me his arm. The footman opened the door, and we entered in formal array, properly subdued for the occasion.

My father was sitting at the head of the table, always an intimidating figure. I moved to sit on his left, and Richard, after holding my chair for me, sat at our father's right hand. Without a word, our father motioned the footmen to serve our plates, and we ate in silence. He was Lord Adamaris this morning—a nobleman of Asael. Richard has told me stories he heard from our mother of a time when our father was a softer man, but we have no recollection. The man at the head of the table that morning was little more than a fearsome stranger to me. Across from me, Richard barely glanced up from his meal.

Meals pass quickly when there is no conversation. It was less than twenty minutes later that I rose to find Anya.

"I have ordered the carriage to depart in five minutes," my father said.

I nodded and glanced at Richard before walking from the room. I caught again the preoccupation on his features and wondered if there might be something else in his expression—but I wasn't sure if my own eagerness was tainting my vision. I felt like a wire in a piano, pulled tight and ready to vibrate if struck by the hammer. I forced myself to walk slowly, not run, up the stairs. Once out of sight, I quickly moved down the hallway and opened the door to my room.

Anya stood on the far side of the bed, by the window. She turned on my entrance, her cheeks flushed. I glanced past her and wondered if I'd left the drawer to the bedside table open a crack. I couldn't remember.

"Is it time?" Anya asked, distracting me from the table. "The carriage is outdoors."

"Aye. We'll need cloaks; we'll have to stand outdoors while the procession leaves the cathedral."

Anya gestured to the bed, where my cloak was already laid out. I picked it up and threw it over my shoulders, fastening it under my chin. Anya handed me a muff, and I hung it around my neck, one hand in, the other free. She picked up her own cloak from the chair and put it on.

There was a pair of old leather gloves that she wriggled her hands into—muffs were only for noblewomen.

We looked each other over.

"Decent?" I asked.

Anya smiled quickly. "You look proper."

I didn't feel proper. Even the shock I'd felt at Loran's death would have been more appropriate for a funeral than the state of buzzing tension I'd been in all morning. Expectation rushed through every part of me—an eagerness to get to the funeral that almost seemed like some sick thrill at the macabre. It wasn't—but at the time I thought no one understood, and so I kept it locked within.

Anya stayed a step behind me while I walked down to the central entryway. Richard was there with his valet and my father with his. All forms were to be kept—we would enter like the nobility we were, servants in tow.

We climbed into the carriage, the valets riding behind for us to have room within. The silence from breakfast followed us into the carriage. I sat across from Richard and studied his face, trying to read behind the curtain in his eyes. Was there a change in him? Had the words he'd spoken the night before—the words which had, somehow, changed everything for me, meant anything to him?

Richard looked out the window, and I couldn't see if he was eager, as I was, for what might happen at the funeral. He diligently kept his eyes from Anya, which I took to be care for our secret before my father. Anya, next to me, had not lost the color from her cheeks. While that morning she had seemed confused by my mood, she now seemed to be feeding off of it, sharing some of my nervous energy. My father glowered out the other window of the carriage; he appeared to have chosen to quell the discomfort that Anya's presence had given him that first morning.

We arrived at the cathedral and were led up the steps and into the nave by a Helper, hair cropped short as a symbol of his rank. Richard was whisked away as soon as we arrived: he was to be a pallbearer. My father's position was such that our seats were very near the front. Anya kept demurely behind me, and I followed quietly behind Father and his valet: all the forms observed. We were seated, and the Helper moved to join the ranks of monks across from us. Our box faced the center of the nave; when the Priest spoke, I would have to crane my head to the left to see him. My father was closest to the altar, with an empty seat for Richard beside him, and I beside that. In seats behind us sat the valets and Anya, their seats raised slightly higher so they could see over our heads.

On either side of us was a world familiar to me. In the boxes closer to the altar were the two noblemen whose rank was higher than my father's. I knew one of the families personally; the Gennadys, near neighbors, were directly adjacent to us. On our other side were those lower in rank, some quite close, who I'd met at various functions as I grew up. The further down the line, the less I knew about the families I saw. I was not allowed to interact with many of lower rank. My father had only one set of close friends among the lower nobles. Lord Makram was his friend from school days.

Directly before us were the ranks of Monks. Like the nobles, they were seated by rank, Priests in front, closest to the altar, then long-haired Masters, Helpers behind, with the novices, heads shaven, furthest from the altar. I rarely saw the Priests and Monks. My father never set foot in the cathedral when we were in the Capital, except for occasions like that day. I think the last time I had seen the Monks would have been Loran's mother's funeral. They sat then as they did at her son's, by rank. I knew so little about the Priests. Though I'd read the Written Histories and understood their system of rank, beyond the basics, I was lost. I never had paid attention to the intricacies of a system so completely outside my experience to that point.

For the first time that day, I studied them. If the Rose were going to appear at the funeral, I reasoned, he would come from the ranks before me. Not a Master, for the Ancient Writings said the Rose was a novice with command of Rosefire. It would be one of the Helpers, and a young one, too. I scanned across the row and found the youngest faces—they were grief-stricken, confused, and out of their depth. I wondered at the choice of He Who Knows Men's Thinking to use one of these boys, younger than me. How would a child lead Asael?

The procession began, with the Head Priest of the cathedral, one of the greatest Practitioners of the era, at the front, holding the arm of King Saran, who was crippled and bent with age. Behind them came six young noblemen, each holding a handle of the casket. Richard was on the near side, first in line. I looked at him with pride. He was second in rank among the noblemen of his generation. He seemed to concentrate on carrying the heavy casket. Once, he raised his head and scanned the crowd, very deliberately looking at me rather than over my head at Anya.

Once they'd reached the front and the king had taken his seat at the head of the nobles, the Priest stood to begin the service. He dismissed the pallbearers with a wave of his hand, and Richard came to sit beside me.

The Priest began to speak. "It is the hope of Asael that one would arise to lead us into the future. We thought it would be Prince Loran. But He Who Knows Men's Thinking also knows the paths of kings and princes. We are shocked to be here today. He Who Knows Men's Thinking is not. But He may join us in our grief..."

As he continued on, my eyes wandered once again. I looked at the King. He seemed much older than I remembered, though I'd seen him only a year before. Aged by grief, I supposed. Richard, beside me, suddenly stiffened slightly. The movement was so minimal that I doubt my father even noticed it, but I, with my head craned their direction to see the King, noticed the tightening of his back and shoulders. I looked to his face. It was turned, very slightly, away from me—toward the altar where the Priest spoke, but his eyes were locked across the nave, on the monks before us.

I scanned over the ranks of monks before me once again and saw what had caught Richard's eye. Among the Helpers sat an old man. Most of the Helpers were fairly young.

It was rare for a man older than thirty not to have moved to the rank of Master, even if he never moved up in those levels. But among the young men and boys in the upper row, one old man sat, staring directly at us.

Like Richard, the monk's head was turned slightly toward the altar, and anyone glancing at him casually would have thought he was paying attention. But, caught as we were in the line of his gaze, there was no question in my mind that he was ignoring the Priest. Almost simultaneously as I realized that, I heard Anya's chair creak behind me. Without even seeing her, I could tell she'd noticed the old man's stare. The Priest's voice faded to a distant drone for a moment as the four of us stared, caught together in something I could not understand.

"Rise!" the Priest at the altar commanded in a loud voice.

His voice broke the moment. We rose, eyes averted from one another.

"Raise your hands!" commanded the Priest.

We raised our hands like everyone else in the cathedral. "We know that death is not an end," the Priest said, "that our souls are everlasting and do not fade." I felt the familiar thrill of fear that always accompanied this proclamation at funerals. The soul's existence beyond death was never questioned in this ceremony, but it always made me wonder what came next. This was it. The old monk was driven from my mind as I scanned the row of Helpers once more. If the Rose were to show himself, it would be now. The Priest continued, "We release his soul."

And it was done. The end of the funeral ceremony. Hands fell around the nave, and I stood, deflated. No act had saved the line of kings. All the tension of the morning had come to nothing. Suddenly I felt like a fool. What had I been thinking? The Rose to arise at the funeral? He Who Knows Men's Thinking to act?

We filed out into the cold, pale sunshine. In its light, my night in the library seemed silly to me. As Richard and the others passed by, carrying the casket to the hearse, I shook my head. *Back to reality*, I thought. *The Prince of Asael is dead. The King has no heir. And everything is changed.*

A tear formed in my eye and welled over as I watched them lift the casket onto the flatbed wagon that would carry it through the streets on the way to burial. He had been so full of life, Prince Loran. And I had liked him.

After they settled the casket, the pallbearers stepped away. It was the part of the Monks to follow through the streets. Richard scanned the crowd and spotted us on the steps. He joined me, a step behind my father, and reached down to hold my hand. The Priests and Monks found their places, once again by rank.

The crowd around us pressed forward, not wanting to miss a moment of the spectacle. I felt Anya as she was pressed against our shoulders. The hearse driver clucked at his horses, and the slow procession began, first the casket, then the Priests, then the Monks, in rank from the highest Master Practitioner down to novice.

I heard Anya's intake of breath, and in the secrecy of the crowd, her gloved hand covered ours. "Who is that monk?" she whispered.

I looked down at the procession and once again saw the old man, staring directly at us.

CHAPTER 9

THE days following the funeral went quickly. We spent three more days in the city, then made our way back to Marinel. I had ignored the book in my bedside table while we remained in the city in the days after the funeral, but I packed it in my carrying bag and took it back to the estate.

We arrived home midday. My father immediately entered his study, and I didn't expect to see much of him for the next week. He detested leaving the estate and always spent significant time catching up on every detail of what he'd missed. Richard, Anya, and I made our way upstairs and broke at the hall to his quarters. Our enforced silence hung about us, and Richard simply said, "See you," before turning down his hall.

Anya and I reached my rooms as the footmen were delivering my trunk, and we set about unpacking right away. Once the trunk was empty, Anya left for the kitchens to gather some food for a midday meal. I turned to unpacking my carrying bag and opened it to find the Ancient Writings sitting on top. I pulled it out and found the marker I'd left in the text. There was another marker further on than mine, one I didn't remember seeing, but I paid it no mind. Without thinking, I sat on the edge of my bed and began to read.

Those who practice magic will range in power. Some will be great, others simple, but skill does not correspond with service. The faithful are those who follow the Creator and seek His ways. Skill in practice is only a sign, a sign of who I am—

I broke off as the door opened and Anya entered, followed by Richard. Anya stopped short on seeing me, book open in my lap. Richard nearly fell over her but caught and righted himself and looked up to see me, too.

"I'm sorry—" Anya said, "I—"

At the same time, Richard began, "You're reading—?"

And simultaneous with their words, I slammed shut the book and stood, pulling it behind me. Both of them stopped speaking. Anya turned to set the tray on the table.

A moment later my brain caught up with what had just passed. "Why are you sorry?" I asked.

Anya turned from the table. "I borrowed your text to read it when you weren't there," she said. My mind flashed to the morning of the funeral, her bright cheeks, the opened drawer.

"Your text?" Richard looked at me. "You are reading the Ancient Writings?"

"No," I said quickly.

"Karan, it's in your hands." Richard shook his head at me like he always had when he caught me in a lie.

I shrugged, bringing the book in front of me. "I began. But I stopped."

"I wondered if you had," said Anya. "Your marker didn't move."

"But how did you—?" Richard broke off again, then seemed to remember something. "The library in the town house!"

I blinked at him. "What?"

"I couldn't figure out how you'd gotten your hands on a text. I forgot that there was a copy in town."

"Well, yes," I said, still a little confused. "But there's one here, too. It's in the schoolroom."

"No, it isn't," said Richard. "It's been in my bedside table for days now."

Anya and I both stared at him, uncomprehending. He looked at us both. Gesturing to the food, he smiled. "It sounds like we have something to talk about," he said. "Shall we eat?"

I dazedly crossed the room to the table and chairs by the fireplace. Richard turned a chair toward the table for me and then did the same for Anya. He pulled up the third chair and began to serve plates from the tray Anya had brought up. I set the text down and sat quietly, waiting for someone else to speak. I didn't know how to begin, so I determined not to.

Richard placed a plate in front of me. He set one in front of Anya. Then he served one for himself and picked up a fork to begin eating. I watched him. I glanced at Anya. She also picked up her fork to begin. Still waiting for one or the other of them to start the conversation, I picked up my own fork and knife. I cut a small slice of meat and stabbed it with the fork. Richard was already chewing. Anya's first bite was at her lips. I raised my fork slowly, thinking Richard would swallow then say something. But he was already lifting another bite before he finished chewing.

I dropped my fork; it clattered onto the plate. I banged my hands against the table. "What did you mean that night before the funeral?"

Richard's fork stopped, and he looked at me with eyes wide. He swallowed. "What did I mean?"

"You said He Who Knows Men's Thinking wouldn't allow Father to see our friendship with Anya. You sounded—you sounded like—" I broke off. My tongue had given way to my impatience, but my brain still tried to stop it from speaking such strange ideas.

Richard set down his fork quietly on his own plate. He picked up his napkin and dabbed his mouth. Ever the man of breeding, he picked up a glass and took a quick drink before he spoke. I had more than once in my lifetime bucked against my breeding, but I don't believe I'd ever been so impatient with it as at that moment.

Finally, he spoke. "Like a believer?"

I looked over at Anya. She too had set her fork down and was listening quietly.

"Yes!" As if a ban were lifted, the words now shot out of my mouth, "Like a believer!"

Richard and I locked eyes. The curtain that had hidden their depths on the day of the funeral was gone, but I didn't know how to read what I saw there now. Richard's expression had always been bright and intelligent, but there was a stillness in it that I did not understand.

"Well?" I asked; my impatience made me break the silence again. "Are you?"

Richard continued to stare at me, the stillness settling into his core. He took a deep breath.

Before he could speak, Anya broke in. "I am."

My eyes snapped to her face. Out of the corner of my eye, I saw Richard turn his head to look at her as well.

He spoke first. "You believe He Who Knows Men's Thinking is actively involved in what goes on in Asael today?"

"I do," Anya said.

"You believe that the faithful were right all along?"

"I do."

"You believe that the Rose is the hope of Asael?"

"I do."

I looked back and forth between them during this exchange. As Anya answered the final question, I saw Richard's expression change slightly. It was as if he wanted to ask one thing more but considered and dismissed the question.

He smiled and turned back to me. "I am, too," he said, finally answering my question.

I opened my mouth. I closed it. I looked down at my plate, then up at my brother again. Finally, the question I wanted to ask came out. "How?"

Richard seemed to consider his answer carefully before speaking. He glanced at Anya, and it once again seemed as if he would ask her a question. But he didn't. Instead, he answered me. "I began to read the Ancient Writings the day—" he paused and seemed to choose his words carefully, "the day after Prince Loran died. I read them years ago, you remember, of course. But now—well, I found them very convincing, given recent events." He turned to Anya. "How for you?"

"When Karan brought the book up to her room from the library, the morning of the funeral," she said. "I wanted to know why, and so I began to read." She gave her shoulder shrug. "It all simply felt right. Like it felt right to be here when you pulled me in the door, Karan. Like it all fits somehow."

Richard cocked his head at her and nodded, like her answer made perfect sense to him. He turned back to me. "Why were you reading the book?"

I looked back and forth between them. Their expressions were serene. The paradigm-altering statements they had made didn't seem to faze them. I couldn't understand. Peacefulness radiated from Anya. Richard's eyes still held the calm stillness. I fumbled for my words. "You—well—what you said. That night. And the way you said it. You were so...so sure." The story began to flow. "And I got thinking about He Who Knows Men's Thinking that night, and then what you had said, Anya. That afternoon, when we were talking about the faithful and the Rose. And I couldn't remember what the signs of the Rose were, so I went down and found the text and began to read. And I found the part about the Rose and the sign of Rosefire—

that the act will save the line of kings, and then I wanted to find the story about the Practitioner who used Rosefire to raise someone from the dead, but I had to start at the beginning to find it."

Richard looked over at Anya when I paused. "I'd read those first lines two or three times in the course of my studies, but this time—" He shook his head. " *'He made the men like Himself, with minds to think and wills to act'*...I don't know. Like you said, it fit this time."

"The part that caught me was the next line," Anya said. " *'The Creator knows the man's thoughts and the man's will—better than the man himself.'* I feel like I know nothing—even about my own thoughts at times, but to know that Someone does! I thrilled at that thought!"

I broke in, impatient with them both. "But it didn't work!"

They turned and looked at me, surprised.

"What didn't?" Anya asked.

"The Rose didn't save the line of Kings! Nothing happened at the funeral. And Loran is dead. The line died with him."

"The direct line died with him," Richard corrected me.

My brow furrowed. I tried to remember the Written Histories.

Anya looked at Richard. "What do you mean?"

"The crown has passed from father to son for generations," Richard explained. "But there have been other siblings who married into the noble families of Asael. Our own grandmother was Saran's younger sister."

The passing thought I'd had at the funeral came back to me. "You're the third in line for the crown!"

Anya blinked at him. "You are?"

Richard nodded. "Aye. At this moment, I am."

"How?"

I jumped in. "The Briyannes are the highest noble family. Lord Briyanne's father was Saran's brother. So Lord Briyanne is now the crown prince, I suppose."

"But Lord Briyanne doesn't have any children, so the next in line is young Lord Gennady. Old Lord Gennady died last year, but his father was the next brother in the king's family."

"But the Gennady's have only unwed daughters after that—they're younger than me!" I cried. "So next is you!"

Richard shook his head at my excitement and smiled at me. He turned back to Anya. "Our mother's mother was Saran's sister. Mother's brother died before he married. The crown passes through the male line, but, lacking a direct male heir, it may pass through the female line to the closest male descendant."

"You," Anya said.

"Until Lord Gennady or his sisters have children," Richard said.

"So the line of Kings is not broken."

"Not yet," said Richard. "But I don't know how long it is. I never paid much attention to the line beyond myself."

I laughed. "You sound selfish when you say it like that."

Richard grinned at me. "It is, rather. Don't you think?"

I turned to Anya. "It may be selfishness," I said, "but more likely he doesn't know more about the line because very few people do. Three stages into the indirect line of kings is very far—it is unlikely that the crown would ever travel even to Richard. If any before him produce a male heir, the line will redirect."

"Only the Priests and Monks keep the full records," Richard admitted. "She is right."

I bit my lip, once again observing my brother and Anya. I felt keyed up, jittery with the excitements and disappointments of recent days. Looking at them, I saw that the stillness and peacefulness had not departed. When they'd spoken of their experiences reading the first words of the Ancient Writings, they had shown an excitement that was somehow deeper than my own, but more still. I was a gurgling, bubbling creek, running quickly over rocks and ledges. They were the strong current of a deep, wide river—almost still to the eye but running swiftly beneath.

Richard picked up his fork and began to eat again. Anya followed suit. Without thinking, I did as well. The conversation about the line of Kings had distracted me from my original concern: that the Rose had not appeared at the funeral.

I looked up from my plate to see Anya gazing at Richard. He, focused on his meal, was unaware of her gaze. I'd caught a strange mix of expressions on her face. Over her shoulder, I saw the tapestry on my wall. I quickly glanced at her face and realized that she looked like the people on the tapestry—expectant. Noticing me, she averted her eyes to her plate, and the moment was lost. I wondered what the expectation meant. Then I thought of the rest of her expression. There had been a tenderness in her eyes when she looked at Richard as if she was watching someone she cared deeply about.

We finished our meal quietly. Richard did not press me further about what I'd read. We carried on intermittent conversation about a variety of topics. Finally, Richard stood and began to clear the dishes from the table to the tray. As he set down a glass, he missed the edge of the tray, and it toppled to the floor. It hit the hearthstones and broke into pieces.

"Bother," he exclaimed and bent down to pick the pieces up.

Before I could move, Anya knelt by him, helping. They both reached for the base of the goblet at once, and she pulled it away from him. He must have already had a grip on it, for as she did so, blood bloomed from a long gash down his finger.

"Oh!" Anya cried. She dropped the glass again and wrapped her fingers around Richard's to staunch the blood. "I'm so sorry!"

"No, it's—" Richard tried to protest, and they stood.

"*Sana*," Anya said quietly, cutting him off. She opened her fingers from around his, and we all watched the flesh on either side of the gash knit itself together.

Anya picked up a napkin from the table and dipped it in a glass of water. I stood, dumbfounded, as she wiped away the blood from Richard's hand with the damp cloth. Gently, tenderly, she cleaned the area. Richard stood quietly, letting her work. Again, I began to feel as though I'd intruded on an intimate moment.

Anya looked up into Richard's face, still cradling his hand in both of hers. "Are you all right?" she asked. "I'm so sorry!"

He smiled down at her. He seemed to take her ability to heal in stride. "I'm fine. It was my fault." Anya shook her head slightly as if to disagree. Before she could speak, Richard moved his hands so they clasped hers. "Thank you."

Anya broke away first and moved to finish clearing the dishes. Her hands were stained with Richard's blood. She gathered everything quickly together and picked up the tray. "I shall take those downstairs and get cleaned up."

"We'll get this." Richard indicated the broken glass on the hearth. He knelt again to pick up the pieces.

Anya picked up the tray. I gathered my wits about me enough to move to the door and open it for her. It had all taken no more than two minutes.

Anya went out, and I shut the door behind her. I turned back to Richard, who was sweeping the last bits of glass into the coal shovel with the hearth broom as if nothing had happened.

"She healed you," I said.

He dumped the shards of glass into the fireplace and set the broom and shovel back in their places. He turned to face me. "I needed to see if she could," he said.

I blinked at him. It took me a moment to comprehend. "You did it deliberately?" I asked.

"Yes," he said.

I shook my head a little, trying to clear it. "Why?"

Richard cocked his head and examined me for a moment as if estimating what my reaction might be to his words. "I know you don't believe yet, Karan," he said.

"Yet?" I asked.

"I think you will," he answered. "He Who Knows Men's Thinking isn't finished with you. I know you don't believe yet, but listen to me, please: It wasn't Loran's death that made me pick up the book." He gestured to the copy of the Ancient Writings that still sat on the floor by my chair. "It was you."

"Me?" I continued to stand on the far side of the room from him. I was still annoyed at his presumption that I would become a believer. I ignored the fact that I had gone to the funeral ready for He Who Knows Men's Thinking to act.

Richard took a step toward me from the hearth. "There's a story in there, one I read when I was very young, about a girl who welcomes a waif into her home on a cold night. She does it against the wishes of her family. But the waif brings great blessings upon the household and all they come in contact with. Do you remember the story?"

It sounded familiar, in a vague, distant way. I nodded, "A little."

"There's one line at the end that always stuck with me, even though I think I only read it once or twice. It's right at the very end. I remember that my tutor said some scholars debated its verity—since it is one of the rare occasions

92   CAROLYN CLARE GIVENS

in the Writings that the first person pronoun is used. It says, *'Thus I will come, like the unknown waif, and ye who welcome me will be blessed.'*"

I could feel a crease form between my eyebrows as I tried to remember my lessons on the Writings. "Who is it that the scholars think is speaking when the text is in first person?" I asked.

Richard took another step in my direction. "There has been great debate about it throughout history. Some think it is the interjections of the Priests who recorded the texts. Others think it is He Who Knows Men's Thinking Himself."

I began to remember a tutor's lecture on the subject. Without my bidding, the excitement I'd felt that night in the library in the Capital began to rise within me again. I took a step toward Richard. We were near each other now. "And some think it is the voice of the Rose!" I said.

Richard reached his hand out so that it was right in front of me. I looked down at the thin white line where it had been bleeding only moments before. "A novice with great skill in magic," he said.

I shook my head. "But there are hundreds of Helpers among the ranks of the Monks. Surely—"

"*This One will practice Rosefire, though never trained,*" Richard quoted, interrupting me.

"No one is trained in Rosefire anymore," I protested.

"But what if it doesn't mean trained in Rosefire," Richard said. "What if it means exactly what it says: 'never trained'?"

I peered up at him, trying to wrap my mind around what he was saying to me.

"She's come from nowhere. She has no past. She has no recollection of ever being trained in magic, yet she has skill equal to the greatest Masters among the Priests." He shook his hand in front of my face.

I moved my head from side to side, unable to protest verbally.

Richard caught my face in his hands and held it so he could look into my eyes. "Karan," he whispered. "I think Sephanya is the Rose."

I opened my mouth to respond, but before I spoke, the door opened and Anya entered.

CHAPTER 10

RICHARD dropped his hands and fluidly took a step away from me. He smiled genially at Anya. "We're all cleared up here," he said. "You didn't hurt yourself at all, did you?"

Anya smiled back comfortably. "Not at all," she said. She opened her hands to us. "All cleaned up here, too."

I tried to recover an easy demeanor. I forced a smile.

"Well, I should get back to my rooms," Richard said. "I have studying to do." He looked over at me. "Karan, why don't you come and get that journal I mentioned. I think you will be interested in one of the articles."

"Oh!" I said. "Of course." I turned to Anya. "I shall be right back."

Richard gave Anya a friendly smile. "See you later," he said, and he walked toward the door.

I followed him out, puzzled. As soon as the door closed behind us and we were a few steps down the hall, I opened my mouth. "What was that?"

Richard didn't answer until we'd passed the page at the corner of the main hallway. "I will not force her to think as I do."

"But if you think she's—" I dropped my voice to a whisper "—the Rose, then shouldn't she know?"

"She will come to the same conclusion eventually. I am certain of it. But it will be better if she realizes it herself."

"Richard!"

He stopped, seeming to hear the panic in my voice. "Everything will be all right, Karan," he said. "You'll see that soon."

"Soon?" I asked. "When I'm suddenly a believer?"

We were near the front stairs. Richard hushed me, and we turned into his hallway. We were silent until we reached his rooms. He closed the door behind us. "For you, it won't be sudden," he said. "I know you, Karan, and where Anya will suddenly feel something is right and adjust to abide by it, you will never do so. You need to seek out all the details and examine them for yourself. Do so. Read the Ancient Writings. Watch Anya." He picked up a paper-bound work from his bedside. "Take this. It's a commentary on the Writings. Study them in conjunction with it. You *will* be convinced, Karan. And you'll understand then. You'll understand why I'm doing what I'm doing."

He put the book into my hand. "Go back to her now. And don't tell her, please."

"No," I said. "I won't. What if you're wrong? I would hate to do that to her."

"I'm not wrong," Richard said. "Anya is the Rose, and that I will stand by, no matter the cost."

I glanced up at his face as he finished speaking and saw a spasm of pain cross his features. It passed in a moment, and his expressions were once again calm and genial. I almost wondered if I'd imagined it.

"Go," Richard said. "Read. And discover for yourself."

I went out into the hallway and slowly made my way back to my quarters. My mind reeled through what Richard had said, over and over again. My stubborn streak reared its head. I wanted to ignore it all entirely, simply because he was so sure I'd become a believer. But then I remembered that thrill of excitement from the night I'd read the Writings, how it had resurfaced a few moments before. I knew Richard was right: I wouldn't be able to ignore anything until I'd gotten to the bottom of it all. Then, I tried to convince myself, I would set it all aside and go on with life as normal. Richard and Anya would come to their senses eventually.

I came to my door and opened it. Anya was standing by the tapestry on the wall, again looking over the figures on their journeys. She turned when I closed the door behind me.

"He's truly all right?" she asked. "I did not mean to hurt him!"

I looked up at her and was surprised to see the deep concern, almost pain, in her eyes. It reminded me of Richard's expression before I'd left his room. "He's fine," I said. I paused. "Your skill with healing is very impressive."

Anya looked down at her hands. "It frightens me, a little," she said. "I have no memory of being trained in magic, yet the words and power flow through me when they are needed."

OVER the next week, we began to settle back into the routine we'd developed in the days before we'd gone to the Capital. Anya performed her role as my personal servant admirably. I continued my studies with the tutor, but in my time off, I read through the Ancient Writings, consulting the commentary Richard had given me as I did so. Our father was busy each day with the affairs of the estate, but on top of that, a steady stream of messengers came from the Capital with news that seemed to disturb him. Asael was in turmoil following the Prince's death, and though my father refused to stay in the city longer than absolutely necessary, he was still one of the leading nobles in the kingdom. Richard threw himself into both his studies and his responsibilities with our father with a renewed vigor that bewildered me.

Breakfasts were often quiet affairs, my father typically out of the house early, handling various tasks on the estate. If he was not there, Anya would join Richard and me, but we dared not speak of the Ancient Writings in so public a place. I would go to my studies in the morning, and Richard to work with our father. Anya sometimes spent her mornings in the kitchens or the back areas of the house with the other servants; other times, she went exploring in the country, visiting the peasants who worked my father's estate or wandering in the woods. Richard typically joined Anya and me in my quarters for the noon meal. He and Anya carried on lively discussions about this or that in the Ancient Writings. I mostly listened, asking questions when they occurred to me, but more often simply observing this strange interaction. After the noon meal, Richard would go to his work, and I would settle in at my desk with the assignments my tutor had given me. I never had spent much time on my assignments out of class, and in those days, I spent even less—pushing them aside to pull out the Ancient Writings and the commentary for examination.

Sometimes Anya and I would talk; I would ask her questions about the portion of the text I was reading, or she would tell me about her visits from the morning. I learned more about the peasant class in those days than I had in my entire existence to that point. Between the stories in the Writings and Anya's tales of Melan the farmer or Wearan the baker, I discovered that there were peasants who were quick-minded, generous, and caring. Their grief, in these days following the death of Loran, was equal to that of the nobles—for their class had known of his kindness and counted upon his rule to be one under which they found prosperity and happiness.

"He was beloved," Anya said one afternoon about Prince Loran. "He walked among the peasants when he got out of the castle. And he sat under the monks and priests when he visited the cathedral."

"I wonder how many of the nobles so keen upon spending time with him knew of that," I asked.

Anya smiled. "It's why he was in the gorge that night," she said.

"What is?"

"He had become friends with an elderly woodcutter who lived on the far side of the gorge. The man had fallen ill, and Prince Loran was in the area and heard of it. He determined to go visit the man and took the road down the switchback in the storm."

I felt my pulse quicken. "Who told you this?" I asked.

"It's common knowledge in the village," she said. "He'd been there only that morning."

I thought about how my father would react if he heard this tale. "Don't ever tell anyone!" I urged Anya. "And tell them to keep it quiet. If my father found out—" I broke off. There was no telling what my father might do if he found out such a thing. The nobles were looking for someone to blame for the way things were following the Prince's death. If the story became known abroad, they would find their scapegoat—and the peasants would feel the force of their rage.

Anya promised her silence, and I went back to my reading while she sewed patches onto one of my old nightgowns to give to charity.

I'd finished reading through the Writings once and was going back through with the commentary. I had come across another prophetic passage about the Rose: *The one who has no voice, the Rose shall hear. He who has no strength, the*

Rose shall uphold. She of sadness, the Rose shall cheer. That One will be the voice of them who cannot speak, the arm of him who cannot lift, and the joy of all. And so also will that One bring upon them their greatest agony. For torment comes through Love, and they will burn, knowing the pain of the Rose—facing the choice of pyre or pyre; redemption from fire by fire.

I sighed. It was like a knot that had to be unraveled one piece of string at a time, but there was no end free to begin at. I consulted the commentary, but it gave me no help. It merely said that most scholars agreed the Rose would be a figure of hope for the downtrodden. The commentary didn't even tackle the second portion of the passage, the confusing part about pyres and fires and torment and love. I wondered at all the imagery of fire in the text, thinking that He Who Knows Men's Thinking must have liked flames.

I raised my eyes to see that Anya had fallen into a reverie, gazing into the fire, fingering her necklace. I looked at the pattern in the pendant again, asking myself if it were flames or leaves that wrapped around the branches and encircled the flowers. Before I made a decision, Anya roused herself from her daydream and tucked away the pendant, focusing once again on the gown she hoped to finish before our late afternoon horseback ride.

Dinners were the most formal part of our day on the estate. My father required us to dress for the evening meal and to sit in our appointed seats, he at the head, Richard on his right, I on his left. When there were no visitors, we had only one servant in the dining room, who brought our plates to us, already prepared, and refilled our glasses when they were low. The job was passed between our personal servants, one day my father's man, the next Richard's, the third Anya. The system kept them each in practice for the rare days we had guests when every member of the party had a servant behind them to place each item of food onto their plates from the large silver platters. Our personal servants attended us on those occasions and oversaw the underlings who attended the guests.

After we'd been home for about a week, the Makrams, a family of nobles below us in rank whose estate lay nearly double the distance from the Capital as our own, came through on their way home. They were truly our only friends. My father had attended school with Lord Makram, and the family often broke their journey to or from the Capital at our home. Lord and Lady Makram had three children, the eldest of whom was a boy about my age, named Edmund, and the others were twin girls, Elena and Erin, perhaps four years younger than I. We'd been friends since we were small children. Lady Makram was a delightful lady, and I often wondered if my mother had been like her. Lord Makram reminded me of my father, though not quite as stern. They were often of a mind about the events of the day in Asael, so I expected that conversation at dinner would be about politics.

The afternoon of their arrival, I briefed Anya on what would be expected of her during her first dinner party at our home. "Richard cannot even acknowledge you," I said. "And all my interaction with you must be about my needs. I'm sorry—Father is a stickler for the forms of nobility."

Anya gave her shrug. "I knew when I agreed to stay that I was to be your maidservant," she said. "I do not mind service or the forms. It's rather fun, actually. I get to listen in on so much that would otherwise be out of my range of experience."

I grimaced. "Yes, listening in is all I shall be allowed to do, too. Father doesn't like me to enter the conversation when we have company. Richard once asked him why he bothered to educate me if he wouldn't allow me to speak, but Father stormed out of the room." I giggled at the memory. "Richard says he thinks Father wants me to marry up—to Young Lord Gennady—and so does everything in his power to be sure I'm prepared for such a role."

Anya sat me down before the mirror to arrange my hair. "Young Lord Gennady? Do you like him?"

"I barely know him," I said, keeping my tone deliberately lighthearted. "I like his sisters. I don't know. It will be a year before Father begins to formally bring me out as a marriageable prospect, so I haven't thought much about it yet."

Anya smiled at me in the mirror. "Richard said once that you were quite the flirt."

I almost jerked my hair out of her hands as I tried to turn and look at her. "He said what!" I exclaimed. "I can't believe him!"

She straightened my head, forcing me to look forward. "He said that half the stable boys were in love with you, and I should be on my guard as they would ask me to bring you notes and candies."

I tried not to laugh, my lips tightening. "He's a no-good liar!" I said. "I only—well, yes, I did rather flirt with some of them...it makes life so much easier when they like me and want to wait on me hand and foot."

Anya laughed, high and clear.

"It's only—" I broke off, fumbling for the words. "Father expects me to be a perfect lady, and I'm not. I never shall be. I never liked my studies much, and I'm no good at weaving or sewing. I'd so much rather be outdoors, riding, or talking with you and Richard than anything else. There's nothing I'm particularly skilled at. But I'm bound by the forms and strictures of my place, and I have to rebel, just a little bit, or I would go crazy."

"Would Young Lord Gennady stand for a little quiet rebellion?" Anya asked.

I watched my face pale in the mirror and felt the sinking feeling that always came if I thought too much about my father's plans for my life. "I don't think so," I said quietly.

Anya noticed my change in tone and looked down at me in the mirror. She leaned forward and gave me a hug from behind, placing her face next to mine, so we were on the same level in the glass. "Oh, sweetheart," she said. "He Who Knows Men's Thinking sees you. He cares. He knows your fears even when you do not say them."

I tried to relax into her embrace. I closed my eyes, fighting back the tears that were pricking at the lids. She'd dug beyond my easy façade and found the fear under-neath—the fear of living under a husband's thumb even more fully than I was under my father's. My moment of vocal rebellion the night that Anya had arrived was un-precedented. I still, at that time, did not know why or how I had spoken that night. Richard's story from the Ancient Writings tried to poke itself into my consciousness, but I pushed it away. I knew my place in my father's house, and I knew I owed Richard daily for the blind he created be-tween me and my father's eye. When I was married, there would be no such blind. And if Young Lord Gennady was anything like his father—and from the stories his sisters had told me, I thought he was—his viciousness could make my father look gentle.

"I am sorry," Anya said, squeezing me. "I did not mean to worry you." She stood and draped a tendril of curl for-ward over my shoulder. "Tell me about the Makrams."

I began to talk about the Makrams, and as I did so, the ten-sion melted from my shoulders a little. I helped Anya dress in her simple gown and brushed and plaited her hair as I told her about running on the moors with Edmund and Richard when we were children and about the tea parties I tried to have with the twins when I was eight and they were four. I'd been so frustrated that they wouldn't sit still like my dolls.

When it was time to go down to dinner, my fear was tucked quietly away into a corner, and I was able to greet the Makrams with a smile on my face. I shared a grin with Edmund and hugged the twins. Lady Makram kissed me on the cheek, and Lord Makram acknowledged me with a nod.

We sat down to the evening meal, and Anya performed her duties perfectly. I could see Lady Makram's keen eye for quality help surveying her quiet and demure activity. After a few moments of observation, Lady Makram turned her attention to her daughters; Anya had passed the examination.

The conversation quickly turned to politics, and I sat quietly listening as my father and Lord Makram began to discuss the state of King Saran's health.

"This has broken him," Lord Makram said. "I don't know how long he'll hold out."

"It's as if he will leave nothing—worse than nothing," my father said. "He leaves no heir; he is the end of the line of Kings. No one wants to be guilty of ending a direct line that's been in power for nearly one thousand years."

"But Father," Richard said, bringing up his point from our conversation a week earlier. "The line is not fully broken; there is still the indirect line."

"Aye," said my father, "but that won't count in the mind of the King. He has failed all his ancestors."

Edmund let out his breath with a whoosh. "I wouldn't want that on my shoulders," he said. "What will happen? How will the crown pass?"

Lord Makram glanced at my father. "There's talk of a Council in the Capital."

"I've heard," said Father. "I've been invited to join when the time comes."

"A Council?" asked Edmund. "What for?"

Lord Makram looked at him. "To rule when the king has died, rather than passing the crown through the indirect line. It would strengthen the role of the nobles in the governance of Asael, and many of them are in favor of it."

"Why?" Richard asked, though I could see by his face he knew the reason.

"With more power comes more freedom," my father said. "I myself would love to have greater rein over even the affairs of my own estate. Now I am forced by my position to report to the king upon all my activity. As a member of the council I could do as I pleased, without fear of interference from those above me."

Lord Makram nodded. "Aye, even I see the benefits in it, though I've not been asked to be on the Council. With more than one man at the helm, I would always have a greater chance that someone would see my point of view and stand for me among the others. As it is now if the king disagrees with what I do, I'm told to stop, and there's no redress."

"But what sort of things?" Edmund asked. "What would you do differently?"

"I'd start by ridding the kingdom of the monasteries. It's an antiquated ritual system that serves no purpose. And I would break up the villages on the estate," my father said. "When the peasants live close together like that, they begin to think that life is simpler when they rely on each other. It's only a matter of steps until they try banding together against me. No, much better for each family to be dependent directly upon me, without support from any other source."

I heard a movement behind me and raised my head to see Richard looking straight at Anya with warning in his eyes, giving a vigorous shake of his head. In an instant, he lowered his eyes to mine. Their expression changed to alarm, and then they smoothed to disinterested politeness as he turned to our father and said, "Would there be added responsibility and work for you as the estate owner?"

It had all happened in the space of an instant, and I didn't think anyone had noticed. Richard was an admirable actor. I looked up into the mirror on the far wall and saw Anya, pale-faced. Her eyes were wide. I casually glanced over my shoulder and took in her demeanor from the corner of my eye. Her hands were tight fists, her elbows and knees locked. I did not know quite what had happened, but I could tell that she was barely in control of her emotions. And Anya out of control was a dangerous thing. I wracked my brain, trying to think of a way to get her out of the room before she acted without thinking, betraying herself.

I glanced down the table and saw that Lady Makram's plate was nearly empty. She brushed away the attentions of her waiting servant, declining a second portion. I raised my hand, deliberately languid, and gestured Anya forward over my shoulder. She stepped up, stiff as a soldier, and leaned in.

"Sephanya, I have nearly completed my meal," I said. "See to it that the maids have prepared the sitting room appropriately. Lady Makram, the young ladies, and I will retire there soon."

Anya nodded and walked from the room; I could see her still clenching her fists, entirely focused upon maintaining control until she was out of the room. As the door closed behind her, I brought my eyes back to the table where they were caught by Edmund, who was sitting next to Richard. He cocked his head a little and looked at me keenly. There was a question in his eyes as he looked from me to Richard, and then at the door Anya had departed through. He looked back at me.

He had seen the whole thing.

CHAPTER 11

I felt my face flush under Edmund's gaze and glanced again down the table to see if the twins had finished their meals. Elena's plate was clean, and Erin's nearly so. I gulped down my last few bites, deliberately avoiding Edmund's eye. When all the ladies' plates were clear, we stood, curtseyed, and moved out the door of the dining room.

We crossed the main hall into the evening sitting room, where Anya was standing in the corner by a tea service. I had hoped that the few minutes would have given her time to regain her composure, but I could see that she was still angry. I wasn't certain what it was that had angered her so. Lady Makram and the twins settled themselves on the settees, and I went to Anya at the tea service to get their cups.

The system was simple: Anya would pour and prepare the cups on my request, and I would take them first to Lady Makram, then to the twins, then get one for myself. She held out Lady Makram's teacup, and I reached to take it from her. As my fingers touched the porcelain saucer, I flinched. It felt as though it had just come out of an oven. Anya's eyes grew wide as she realized what had happened. She set down the teacup on the tray quickly, as quietly as possible.

She still wasn't in control of herself. Without thinking, she'd heated the teacup hot enough to burn skin. She looked at me, green eyes round, and I scrambled for a way to get her out of the room. Suddenly a memory arose of Lady Makram once chastising me for speaking out of place: "Oh, Karan, you mustn't speak like that before servants. You never know how long they will be with you."

I smiled a little ruefully at the memory. But I had a path of action. I glanced over my shoulder to Lady Makram and the twins. "I so want to hear the latest gossip about *everything* at court," I said, gushing. Then I looked back at Anya, feigning concern. "Of course—with the serv—" I broke off and hesitated for a moment. "Sephanya." I made my tone commanding. "You may leave us; I can handle the tea things."

Anya curtseyed and walked out of the room, no longer so stiff but certainly quickly.

I poured the other teacups and delivered them to Lady Makram and the twins before picking up the first cup for myself, giving it as much time to cool as possible before I had to touch it again. I picked it up gingerly; it had cooled enough to touch it, but I found myself forced to giggle and laugh with the twins so as to avoid taking a sip of the scalding liquid.

It was about half an hour before the men joined us. A scullery maid had cleared away the tea things by that time, and I had nearly reached the end of my endurance for gossip. I was happy for the change of company until Edmund cornered me by the window seat for conversation.

"So," he said and paused, waiting for me to say something.

I had determined to give nothing away. "Your sisters seem to have had a good time in the Capital," I said.

"Don't change the subject, Karan," he said.

I tried to flash innocent eyes at him. "What subject?"

He smirked good-naturedly. "Ah, yes, the wide eyes of Karan Adamaris, stumbling block of many a stable boy. You can't get me with them, Lady Karan. I know you too well."

I knew he was right. Richard often reminded me that I couldn't lie to those who knew me, and I would be hard-pressed to pull it off with Edmund, who was one of my oldest friends. But I also knew that telling him the whole truth was not only dangerous—it was impossible for me at that moment. I wasn't sure what had happened, for one thing, and in general, I wasn't sure what I thought about anything. I was still so in the middle of it all—Anya's and Richard's new faith, my own curiosity and confusion, Richard's crazy idea that Anya was the Rose. All of it was floating about like motes of dust in sunlight, never forming but impossible to be rid of.

Edmund saw my hesitation and continued quietly. "You and Richard seem to have gotten to know your new servant girl quite well."

"Anya." Her name forced itself out from my lips. I didn't like hearing her referred to as a servant.

Edmund raised an eyebrow. "Anya, then," he said. "You didn't answer my question."

I smiled a little. "You haven't asked one."

I watched his jaw flex. I'd scored a point.

"Fine," he said after a moment. "Who is Anya?"

"She's—" I began, but broke off, realizing I had no answer. I fished for something. "She's unique," I said.

"That's not an answer," Edmund said. "That's an evasion."

I sighed. "I don't have an answer," I said. "You have to believe me. If I did, I might be able to say more to you, but I don't."

Edmund looked down at me, cocking his head slightly. "Is everything all right?" he asked.

"Yes!" I said. "Everything's...wonderful and awful and amazing! But—confusing and frightening, too."

A crease formed between Edmund's eyebrows. He seemed genuinely concerned, but I knew I could say no more. "Ask Richard," I said, and I stood from the window seat and moved to engage Lady Makram in conversation.

I excused myself from our guests as soon as it was proper and made my way up to my quarters, knowing that Anya would be there. I opened the door quietly, hoping that she'd fallen asleep.

She had not. She was sitting on the hearth, with a pile of kindling sticks beside her. I looked at the grate—there were ashes in it. Without seeming to notice me, she picked up a kindling stick and held it in her fist over the grate. A moment later, it burst into flames, and she dropped it on the grate to burn up.

I gasped.

She turned to me, her chest moving up and down as she took deep breaths. "I didn't want to touch anything else. I was afraid what I would damage."

I rushed forward and fell to my knees beside her. I reached for her hand. "Are you all right?"

She let me pull her hand out and hold it face up in between us. "I'm fine," she said. "It doesn't hurt me."

I gingerly touched the palm of her hand; it was cool.

"I feel it—the magic—it's in my mind, like a tangled vine or a ball of flames," Anya said. "It is there—I think perhaps it has always been there, but now I feel it. And all I need to do is to reach in and pull out a single branch or a single flame and put it to the purpose I choose."

I looked in her eyes as she spoke and saw power. There was a deep, burning fire in her, and it flashed out through the green irises. "What happened in the dining room?" I asked.

She took a deep breath. "I nearly lost control," she said. "I was so angry at how your father and Lord Makram were talking about the peasants. I wanted to shout out that he had no right to remove them from their homes and their villages to serve his own purposes, but I knew I could not speak. I forced the words back, but I couldn't control it. For a moment, I was completely consumed by the fire— the branches completely entangled me! I almost fainted, I think, but I saw Richard. And looking at him, I found my way out of the fire, out from the branches, and I felt it recede. It writhed and pulsed, but it was within my mind, not surrounding it."

"And the teacup?"

"I must have let my guard down for a moment," she said. "I'm so sorry! I had it in my mind, but only just, and I let a little get out."

I looked down at the pile of ashes in the grate. "And this?"

"I had to practice. If I could find out how much control I had over it—I started to deliberately let it out, like venting the steam from a pot, a little at a time. Heat was simplest—hence the kindling. And as I did so, I felt it recede more, and now I can feel it there, swirling and throbbing, in my mind."

"Is this different than what you've done before?" I asked. "The heat?"

"No, but I feel where it is in my mind now. I never did before; it simply was there when I needed it. Now it is constantly present—vibrant, alive."

I sat back on my feet and looked at her for a moment, my mind flipping through everything I'd seen and read and heard in the recent weeks. In the same way, as Anya suddenly felt her power as a vibrant, pulsing whole from which she plucked the portion she needed at a given moment, I suddenly saw the entire situation laid out before me, like a map. I only needed time to examine the roads I'd taken thus far to see the path that I should take going forward.

"You need sleep," I said. "I can see you're exhausted."

Anya took a deep breath. She closed her eyes for a moment. "Yes," she said. "I need rest."

"Are you able to?" I asked.

Her eyes still closed, she spoke. "Yes. I need only find the flame that will calm me..." Her voice trailed off, and I watched as she seemed to concentrate. A moment later, she yawned and opened her eyes slowly. "I am ready."

In the back of my mind, I watched as another stage of the path filled in. I was nowhere near sleep. "Do you mind the fire?" I asked. "I'd like to read a little."

She yawned again, and her eyelids closed and opened slowly. "No, I don't mind." She stood, shrugged out of her gown, and lay down upon her cot. Within moments she was breathing slowly and deeply.

I stood and struggled with the buttons of my gown by myself for a few moments, relegating the map to a corner of my mind until I could give it my full attention. I wrenched the final button off of the dress in my struggle; it fell to the hearth and rattled along the stones. I stepped out of the overdress and bent down to pick up the button. Tucking it into the pocket of the skirt, I tossed the dress over a chair. I found a nightgown in the wardrobe and changed into it, pulling my dressing gown on over it and, finally ready, brought the map forward in my mind.

I stared at the tapestry on my wall—a terrain with paths woven into it, and, at intervals, along the paths, wreathed images inset. I closed my eyes and scanned over the map forming in my mind, imagining it laid out like the tapestry, tracking the journey from Anya's arrival on our doorstep forward to that very moment in its inset images. I opened my eyes and sat down at my desk. The Ancient Writings were there, and I paged through them. In the week since we'd returned from the Capital, I'd finished reading through the text. I now found myself going back to particular passages one by one as I thought through the events that had happened.

I turned to the beginning and once again read the account of the Creator, who knows men's thinking better than man himself. Anya's words from that afternoon came into my mind: "He knows your fears even when you do not say them."

I paged forward and read passage after passage that spoke of the Creator, the one we called He Who Knows Men's Thinking. I brought the map to my mind's eye again and again—the path I saw on it was one related to the Rose, but before I could even consider the stages of its journey, I had to understand the terrain it was laid out upon. Were the Writings sound? Could I even rely upon them?

I flipped to the very back of the text and read a passage from the last chapter. *When the Creator made man, with will to act and mind to think, He made him to be like Himself in every way. This is man's greatest blessing—an eternal existence, from forever past to forever future. The man who remembers his Creator need not fear death. Even death is not an end.*

I stared into the fire and considered the history of Asael, the rise of the Monks, their fall, the age of Kings, the rise of the noble class—every story I'd ever studied or read. Each life history in the Written Histories ended with the relation of the funeral ceremonies. And at every funeral, the people raised their hands, and the Priest said that death is not an end; that the soul is everlasting and does not fade. We had accepted this ceremony without question for thousands of years—in that moment never questioning the soul's everlasting existence. In the age of Kings, the nobles had rejected and grown to fear the Ancient Writings and He Who Knows Men's Thinking, but that one piece had never been forgotten or rejected. My father feared death. I suddenly knew clearly that it was not death itself he feared, but the existence beyond death. In spite of everything we'd rejected, we held onto that one truth—the soul is everlasting.

And in that moment, I realized I believed it. I believed in the soul's existence beyond death—and the Writings explained why. I felt like I'd found an anchor—a reason to trust their verity. The terrain on my map was sound.

I looked away from the fire and back at the text. I closed my eyes for a moment and pictured the path I had laid out upon the map—every interaction, question, idea, and thought I'd had since Anya had arrived.

I read Richard's story about the waif and the girl and meditated for a moment on that final line: *Thus I will come, like the unknown waif, and ye who welcome me will be blessed.*

As Richard had said, there were very few occasions when the personal pronoun was used in the text. I paged through, reading each one of the "I" passages in the text:

Skill in practice is only a sign, a sign of who I am. By it ye may know me.

I shall be a voice like none heard before.

Those who would not share bread will break it together before me.

And the final line of the text, following the passage about man's eternal existence:

Not an end, but an enemy. And in the war I shall overcome.

I sighed. There were so few of these passages. They only raised more questions than they answered. While the first certainly seemed to reflect the way I'd met Anya, the others were enigmatic.

I went back to the path on the map in my mind, thinking through Anya's strange skill with magic, and the death of Loran, his funeral, the old monk, Richard's turn to faith, and Anya's fury at my father that evening. She had never struck me as a particularly excitable person, but she'd been angry enough to lose control over the plight of some peasants. I gasped and remembered the passage I'd read only that afternoon, about the Rose being the voice of the voiceless and the helper of the weak.

My heart was beating quickly. I went through in my mind all the strange things and acts of magic that Anya had performed in my presence. I sat up straight and skimmed through pages until I found that passage I'd found the very first night: *And you shall know the Rose by this sign. This One will practice Rosefire, though never trained. All the signs which come before will be confirmed in this one act. And the act will save the line of kings.*

I read it again with new eyes, no longer distracted by the final line. I noticed, then, the sentence before: *All the signs which come before will be confirmed in this one act.* I could have kicked myself. That day at the funeral, I'd been looking for the Rose to practice Rosefire. But other signs were to come first...perhaps healing, or catching a cup before it broke on the floor, or heating a cup of tea.

I flipped forward in the text and found another passage that had haunted me since the night I'd first read it. It came at the end of the story of the Practitioner who used Rosefire to bring a woman back from the dead—a complete success, it seemed. But then the scribe had written these words. *The Creator saw his thoughts, that he understood her soul was whole beyond the veil. And the Creator saw that she had once smiled upon him, and he cherished a hope for a bright future. So the Creator demanded of him his life in return for hers—for he had practiced Rosefire for gain, and without pure motive.*

I took a deep breath. I had examined the path on the map and was finding myself convinced—Anya *was* the Rose; everything that had happened thus far pointed to that as truth. But the passage I'd just read presented a whole new step. Up to this point, I had been able to examine the facts and come to sound conclusions based upon them, like Richard had said I would. The stages of the journey laid out in the map in my mind were evidence leading me to the very decision I was faced with now.

For the Ancient Writings had only one way to confirm the identity of the Rose: a novice who practiced Rosefire. But the practice of Rosefire required absolute purity of motive. It was no wonder no one had practiced Rosefire in a thousand years. There was no way of knowing when Anya would ever be in a situation that called upon her to practice Rosefire, and no guarantee she would do so successfully even if she tried.

So I stood at the edge of my map. I had no idea where the next stage would take me, and the only confirmation left to me might as easily be confirmation of my greatest doubts. I had to choose: either leap forward, trusting in He Who Knows Men's Thinking for guidance and wisdom for future steps or stop the journey altogether.

I stared at the fire until it burned itself down to ash. Dim light began to show out my window. I stood and grabbed a cloak from the rack by the door. Tossing it round my shoulders, I eased open the door and went out into the hallway, closing it quietly behind me.

I tiptoed down the hall, past the sleeping page at the junction, and forward to the steps into the foyer. I went down them slowly, attempting to avoid the ones that creaked. I quietly loosed the bolt on the front door and opened it enough to slip through to the outdoors. I wanted to walk, so I turned to the garden that went along the side of the house. There was a maze of sorts made up of rose bushes, and I moved toward it, the scent of the late roses coming toward me on the morning air. I had been wandering there among the bushes for an hour when Edmund joined me, making almost no noise on the grass beside me.

I didn't say a word. I thought of his concern from the night before. I didn't know how to begin.

Finally, he broke the silence. "Richard is a believer?"

I nodded. "Yes."

"He thinks Anya is the Rose."

"Yes."

"Does he realize how crazy he sounds?"

I smiled a little. "I think so."

Edmund shook his head. "Does he realize how dangerous it is?"

I nodded again. "Yes."

We were at the far end of the garden, hidden from the house by high bushes. It was so early that no one was about. Edmund stopped and grasped my hand, stopping me with him. We turned so we were facing each other.

Edmund looked down at me. I raised my chin and met his eyes.

"What about you?" he asked.

I took a breath. "I believe the Ancient Writings are true. I believe He Who Knows Men's Thinking is real."

He looked hard at me. "And the Rose?"

It was the moment of decision: to step out in faith or stop altogether. "I believe Anya is the Rose, the hope of Asael."

CHAPTER 12

"Do you realize what you're saying?" Edmund asked me.

"Aye."

"It's treason, Karan."

"I know."

"Your father would kill you if he found out."

I shook my head. "Worse, I think."

A crease formed between Edmund's eyebrows. "Worse?"

I looked down. "He'd marry me off to a stranger, I think. Someone far away so that he would be rid of me and my rebellious ideas."

Edmund grasped both of my hands tightly. I looked up to see the muscles around his mouth tighten.

"It would save him the political embarrassment, then. If it ever came out," I explained. "He could blame it on the stranger."

"Karan, the nobles won't take talk of the Rose lying down. They'll stomp it out wherever it's found. Your noble blood won't protect you and Richard. And Anya—well, she'd be destroyed in public view."

Tears came to my eyes. I nodded. "I know. And I'm terrified for her."

"For her!" Edmund cried. "Karan, she's practically a strang—"

I put my finger to his lips. "She's the Rose."

He spoke, muffled a little by my finger. "You can't *know* that."

"I know enough. And every day I'm so worried that she'll be caught." I began to draw my hand away, but he reached up and caught my fingers. He bent my wrist and put his lips to the back of my hand. His other hand released mine and pulled me into an embrace. He leaned his head down so that his cheek rested against mine.

He whispered in my ear. "I'm worried that *you'll* get caught." He hugged me tightly then released me, stepping back.

"Be careful," he said, and he pivoted on his heel and walked toward the house.

I took a few deep breaths, trying to slow my racing pulse before I followed him indoors.

In my rooms, Anya was awake and dressed, setting the tea things on the fireside table. I closed the door behind me, and she watched as I hung my cloak on the rack. She looked over at the bed I hadn't slept in, then back at me.

"Long night?" she asked.

"Aye," I said. I walked to the fireside and picked up a teacup. "Edmund knows."

Anya sat down in one of the chairs. I saw a look of concern cross her features. "You trust him?"

"Absolutely," I said. "He's—" I paused. "He's worried about me."

Anya smiled. "He likes you."

"What?" I asked.

"He couldn't keep his eyes off you at dinner last night," she said.

"But—" I wanted to argue with her, but Edmund's behavior in the garden that morning had put significant holes in the conviction I'd always had that he thought of me as nothing more than a friend. I changed tack. "But he shouldn't be worried about *me*," I said. "It's you that I'm concerned about. *You're* the Rose!"

Anya's green eyes flashed up at me from her teacup, and I suddenly realized what I'd said.

"You think I'm the Rose?" she asked.

"I—I." I stuttered.

"And Richard does, too." She said it as if it explained something she'd been wondering about. She closed her eyes for a moment then they popped back open wide. "Wait! You believe!"

She jumped up, setting her teacup on the table, splashing tea out onto the saucer, and threw her arms around me, nearly knocking my teacup out of my hand.

I chuckled a little at her reaction. "Aye, I believe."

"Then everything will be fine," she said. "No matter what happens, we're in it together."

There was a knock at the door, and Richard entered upon my beckon. Anya had stepped back to the table and picked up her teacup.

Richard smiled to see us both standing by the fire, again a united front. He looked at me. "You spoke with Edmund?"

I nodded. "This morning."

"I had to tell him. He saw—" he glanced to Anya. "At dinner."

"It's all right," I said. "He won't say anything."

Anya was about to burst. "Richard, she believes!"

He looked at her, bewildered for a moment, then recognition dawning, looked back at me. He grinned. "I told you you'd be convinced," he said. He strode across the room and hugged me tightly. "Do you feel it now?"

I paused, trying to determine what he meant, what I felt. I remembered the peacefulness that had radiated from Anya and the calm stillness in Richard's eyes. I closed my eyes, looking for that in myself. I was always the most excitable of us all; I would never be as still as Richard or as peaceful as Anya, but I found something within myself: a deep-seated, unfaltering conviction that all was *right*. Somehow, no matter what buffeting wind came my way—even my conversation with Edmund or letting slip to Anya that we thought she was the Rose—nothing could shake it.

I opened my eyes, nodding, remembering that Richard didn't know I'd slipped up with Anya. "Richard, I told—" I broke off, catching a warning glance from Anya out of the corner of my eye. She shook her head. I found something else to say. "I told Edmund that we realized how dangerous this is. We do, don't we?"

"I do," he said. "I know we're going to be standing against all the nobles of Asael, and judging from last night's dinner conversation, that's going to be sooner than later."

"Aye," Anya said. "When the king dies, if not before."

I suddenly remembered Anya's new knowledge of her power. I turned to her. "Do you still feel it—in your mind?"

"Yes. It hasn't diminished."

"She feels her power now—all the time, not only when she uses it," I said to Richard.

He cocked his head at her. "Since last night?"

"Yes," she said. "I nearly lost control, but once I brought it back, I was able to feel it, and it hasn't gone away."

"Show him the kindling," I said.

Anya knelt down by the fireplace and picked up a piece of kindling. She gripped it in her fist over the grate and concentrated. A moment later, it burst into flame and burned to ash in her hand. "Now that I can feel it, I can be more careful," she said.

Richard blinked. "Aye." He took a deep breath as if steeling himself to jump into icy water. "I must go get ready for breakfast. The Makrams will leave afterward." He strode out the door.

I turned to Anya. "Why didn't you want me to tell him?"

"He will tell me himself when he is ready to. I want to give him that chance."

We dressed for the day and went down to breakfast. Even with guests, it was a much less formal affair than dinner. Anya stood by the sideboard and served dishes based on direction. From time to time, I caught Edmund watching her as if trying to make up his mind what he thought. But most of the time, when I glanced at him, his eyes were on me.

There was little conversation at the meal. We ate quickly because the Makrams still had a long journey ahead of them. When my father and Lord Makram were finished, they rose from the table, and the rest of us followed suit. They went out the door to the front hall, and everyone filed after them. I was on the far side of the room, furthest from the door. Edmund hung back so that we were the last two left in the room.

He stepped between me and the door as I neared it, barring my way out. He looked down at me. "I will read the text," he said in a low voice.

I smiled up at him. The deep conviction held strong. "I'm glad."

"Only if you promise me something in return."

"This didn't start as an exchange," I said.

"It is now." He reached down and took my hand in both of his. "Promise me, if you ever need help, you'll come to me."

I looked up into his face and saw a burning look there that I had never expected to see. I knew we had to hurry and catch up before they noticed we were lagging behind. I freed my hand from his and threw my arms around his neck in a quick hug. I kissed him lightly on the cheek and whispered, "I can promise that."

His arms wrapped around my torso and he squeezed. "Good."

We broke apart, and he went out the door before me to join his family in the hall. I followed out to the hall after a moment and joined the general farewells going on. Lady Makram made promises to return for my eighteenth celebration, and the twins, who were too young to come, cried. I hugged the twins and curtseyed to Lord and Lady Makram. To Edmund, I merely bowed my head, and in return he gave a stiff nod.

My father opened the front door, and we went out. Richard handed Lady Makram and the twins into the carriage, and Father took the reins of Edmund's horse from the groom and held it as he mounted.

Richard stepped back and joined me where I stood on the steps with Anya behind me. Father stood on his other side. We called out goodbye. The girls waved out the window. The carriage moved off, and Lord Makram clucked at his horse, following after it. Before he did the same, Edmund's eyes found mine for a moment. Then they moved beyond me, and he nodded gravely to Anya.

We stood on the steps and watched until they were out of sight. Then my father turned back toward the house.

"Richard," he said. "You will join me in my study today. We have things to discuss."

"Yes, sir," Richard answered.

My father swept past me, nodding, ignoring Anya altogether, and Richard followed him.

I went to my studies that morning with new eyes. They had been opened in the night when I realized that the Written Histories showed we had held onto some of the ancient beliefs. I had a new-found curiosity about the Written Histories—what else had we held onto without recognizing the source?

I tried to ask questions that would point the tutor in my direction of interest, but he was steadfast to his purpose, and we continued in our study of the Age of Kings. I gave up trying to influence him and instead focused on the material he put before me—watching for elements of what I now knew to be truth.

Richard didn't join us for lunch. He was closed up in our father's study without a break. I spent time studying the Ancient Writings again that afternoon. The deep conviction of the truth of what I believed never wavered. Only a day earlier, I had been reading the text, struggling through every line. That day, it was as if I were drinking cool water on a hot summer's day. I was refreshed by each story, intrigued by each prophecy.

The Writings were no more easy to understand than they had been, but I approached them from a different perspective—the opaque passages were not frustrating and indecipherable; they were mysterious and promising. I might not know what they meant that day, but someday, I thought, I would.

About mid-afternoon, Anya and I were both sitting in my rooms. Richard knocked, barely, before opening the door and hurtling through it into the room. "Oh good!" he said, stopping short at the sight of us before the fire. "You haven't gone riding yet!"

I closed the text. "No, but I was thinking about it," I said.

"Can I join you? If I have to spend another minute locked up indoors, I'll go mad."

"Of course," I said. I looked at Anya. "Do you want to go today?"

She had been sewing the button back onto my dress from the evening before. She set it down, smiling. "Certainly."

"I'll meet you out at the stables," Richard said, walking out the door.

Anya and I dressed to ride and went out to meet Richard. He had our horses ready for us, and after we mounted, set a rapid pace for us to keep up with. After we'd ridden for about ten minutes, I urged my horse forward alongside Richard's.

"Are we running away from something?" I asked.

Richard glanced over at me. He reined his horse in slightly. I followed suit. We had reached a wide part of the road, and Anya brought her horse up to my other side.

"I'm sorry," Richard said.

I looked at Anya. She shrugged. I turned back to Richard. "What's wrong?"

"I don't want any part of it," he said.

"Of what?"

"The politics and scheming. I spent the whole day studying Council documents. They're preparing for the king's death, planning for the day they will be in power."

"This Council idea is that far progressed?" I asked.

"It's fully developed," Richard said. "They've drafted Lord Briyanne's abdication—and he knows nothing about it. He will have a place on the Council in return, but it is a formality. Father and Gennady will be in charge."

"How will they get him to sign it then?"

"Gennady is tasked with—" he paused, searching for the right word, "convincing him."

I shuddered. I didn't like to think about what that meant.

"Does your father expect you to be involved?" Anya asked.

Richard looked over at her. "Aye. He's told me to put away my other studies altogether. It's now time to focus upon my responsibilities as the future Lord Adamaris."

Anya looked down at her hands, holding the horse's reins. She spoke in a low voice. "If ever there was a time for the Rose to arise, it seems it is now."

I saw Richard's eyes widen slightly at her words. He opened his mouth as if to speak, then closed it again. He had determined he would not tell her he thought her the Rose, and when Richard decided something, there was little that could sway him.

We rode on in silence for a while. I had no clear picture of the way forward. It was time for the Rose to arise and take action, but Anya didn't believe she was the Rose. So what steps were left to us?

We came round a bend in the road. Anya swerved to avoid trampling a man walking on her side of the road, carrying a small boy in his arms. I reined in so that our horses didn't collide, and Richard checked his horse beside me.

"Thayer!" Anya exclaimed, pulling her horse to a stop. "What are you doing here?"

The man looked up. He must have been about thirty but walked like an old, weary man. His eyes were full of grief and pain. "Miss Anya," he said, staggering to a stop. "I've taken Tay to the Healer."

I looked at the boy in his arms. My breath caught in my throat. I'd never seen a child so thin and pale. On his cheeks were bright spots of color, standing out in stark contrast to his skin, which was almost grey. The boy was gravely ill.

Richard urged his horse forward and reached out to take Anya's reins from her. She looked at him in confusion. His hand covered hers for a moment, and he looked deeply into her eyes. "Help him."

I watched her face grow pale under his intense stare. For a moment, she simply stared back, defiant—a battle of wills.

Anya broke away her gaze first and dismounted from the horse. She looked from side to side, checking to see that the road was clear. Then, she approached the man. "Thayer, may I see if I can help Tay?"

Thayer had watched the exchange between Richard and Anya with confusion on his face. He looked from Anya to Richard. "My Lord?"

Richard nodded at him. "Follow her instructions," he said.

Thayer looked to Anya.

She stepped toward him, reaching a hand out toward the boy. "May I touch him?"

Thayer shifted the boy in his arms so that Anya could easily reach him. She stopped before them and placed her hand on the boy's forehead. She closed her eyes and took a deep breath.

I looked to Richard; he wasn't breathing, watching Anya intently. His eyes were bright, his expression hopeful. I looked back to Anya and the man. She was concentrating; I could almost imagine her reaching into the whirling ball of power in her mind, finding the right strand. Thayer looked back and forth between her face and the boy's, uncertain what to expect.

"*Salutem*," Anya said.

CHAPTER 13

THE boy's breathing eased. The color subsided from his cheeks and suffused the rest of his skin. He took a deep breath and opened his eyes. "Father?"

Thayer dragged his eyes from Anya and focused on his child's face. His expression cleared. His eyes whipped back to Anya as she stepped away, their grief replaced with surprise. He looked back to his son.

"Tay? How do you feel?"

The boy tried to sit up in his father's arms. "Hungry," he said.

Thayer shifted him into an embrace. He looked over the boy's shoulder to Anya. Gasping sobs wracked his shoulders, and he hugged his son. "Miss Anya?" His questioning eyes looked at me, then went to Richard's face. "My Lord?"

Richard smiled and gestured at Anya. "She has great skill," he said.

Anya reached up to take the reins from Richard and stood at her horse's head. Thayer, still holding his son, moved to her.

"The Healer said there was nothing he could do. He told me to go home and make funeral preparations." His voice broke. "You gave me back my son, Miss Anya."

She shook her head. I could tell she disliked the attention. "I didn't— " She looked up to Richard, her expression defiant. "I only did what the young Lord Adamaris asked."

I saw Richard's eyes flash and his chin tilt down. He opened his mouth as if to speak but shut it again quickly. Thayer looked from Anya to Richard and then over to me. He had caught the tension between Anya and Richard— the air was thick with it.

Tay put his head on his father's shoulder. "Father, I'm hungry," he said.

Thayer, brought back to the immediate moment, hugged his son again. "My Lord, Lady Karan, Miss Anya, will you come back with us? My wife will wish to thank you."

Richard looked at me to see if I wanted to accept. Suddenly, I had a great desire to see a peasant's home. I never had stepped near one before. I nodded. He looked at Anya, tension still crackling between them. She gave a quick nod of her head.

"We would love to," Richard said to Thayer. "May Tay ride with me?"

Thayer smiled and handed Tay up to Richard on his horse. The boy grinned up at him and peered down to the ground far below. Thayer held Anya's horse while she mounted again and then took the reins and led us to the village.

The main road through the village was little more than a cart track. On either side, tiny houses and shops were lined up with barely enough room to walk between them. As we passed, eyes peered out from behind window sashes and the shadows between the buildings. I felt like a wild animal on display.

We came to a stop before one of the larger buildings on the street. A sign over the door said, "Hand-sewn and woven goods." We dismounted and tied the horses to the post outside the door. Thayer led the way in, and Richard followed with Tay in his arms.

Walking inside, Richard had to duck so as not to hit his head on the lintel of the door. I followed him, and Anya brought up the rear. Inside the door was an open room, about the size of my bedchamber. On one wall were stacks of fabrics and a counter in front of them with measurements written along the edge. On the other side of the room was a large loom and shelves full of large spools of threads. A woman sat at the loom, and the heavy cloth she was producing must have been a tapestry, though I'd never seen one so plain before.

I glanced at the walls without shelves and saw they were covered with plain tapestries, with a very simple pattern upon them. I'd never before considered the functionality of a tapestry; I'd simply accepted them. If they had no pictures upon them, I wondered, what could their purpose be? Before I could consider the question further, the woman looked up from her work.

"Thayer!" she cried, rising from the loom.

"Tay is well," Thayer said, and the little boy jumped out of Richard's arms and ran to his mother.

"Mama!" He ran into her open arms. "I'm hungry!"

The woman looked up at Thayer over Tay's head. "What is this miracle?" she said, her eyes wide. She looked at Richard and Anya and me, and her face paled. She stood, detaching Tay's arms from her neck, but holding him close beside her leg. "My Lord! My Lady!" She tried to curtsey but struggled to move with the boy hanging on her skirts. "Miss Anya!"

Thayer spoke first. "Miss Anya is gifted in magic," he said. "She healed Tay when the Healer said there was no hope."

His wife looked at him in amazement, then looked at Anya. She reached down and picked up her son, and in a single movement, stepped forward, grasped Anya's hand, and lifted it to her forehead as she bowed before her.

"Lanica!" Anya exclaimed. "Do not bow to me!"

"Miss Anya," Lanica said, her eyes cast down to the floor. "You never said you were a Practitioner."

"Just simpl—" Anya began to protest, then caught Richard's eye and seemed to think better of it. "A Practitioner," she said. "But still your friend."

Lanica raised her eyes. She looked to Thayer, then to Richard and me. "You brought us guests."

"Ah, yes!" Thayer seemed to suddenly recollect us. "Master Richard, Lady Karan, my wife, Lanica, the weaver."

She bowed her head to us. "Welcome to our home," she said. "I fear it is very simple."

"Not at all," I said. "But...you live here? This seems like a shop."

"Our home is through the door," Thayer said, gesturing toward a door in the back wall. "I am the tailor, Lanica is the weaver, so we live near our work."

Lanica nodded and, turning, led the way through the door into a room about half the size of the front room. Beside us were a bed and a small cot. At the far end was a kitchen, with a large open fireplace and an oven built into one side. Before it was a rough-hewn wooden table with stools around it. "Please," Lanica said. "Sit."

We seated ourselves on the stools and waited while Lanica and Thayer brought out bread and cheese. Thayer poured ale from a barrel in the kitchen, and then they sat and ate with us. I had never had a meal like it. From time to time, Lanica rose to check the stew bubbling on the hearth, or Thayer would hear the front door and go out to help a customer. Sometimes I would catch one or the other of them gazing at their son, Tay, who ate with gusto. I saw Lanica look from him to Anya and back to him as if she couldn't quite believe it was real.

Richard and Thayer kept up conversation, mostly with Richard asking him question after question about his life. I interjected when I had questions. Anya asked Lanica about her weaving. Conversation flowed comfortably, and we had been there nearly an hour before I realized Anya and Richard never addressed each other directly.

We said our goodbyes in time to ride back and dress for the formal dinner at Marinel. As we mounted our horses, I wondered if I might wake up and find it was all a dream—I had entered another world for an hour or so and wasn't quite sure what it would be like going back to the one I lived in.

We made our way out of the village and were on the road toward my father's estate when Richard pulled on his reins and steered his horse to cut Anya's off. She reined to a stop, and they faced each other.

"'I only did what the young Lord Adamaris asked'?" Richard spat her words back at her like a question.

Anya straightened her shoulders. "You did tell me to help him," she said.

"It wasn't—" he broke off, searching for the right word. "It wasn't a *command*! You made it sound like I was your ruler!"

"I am a servant in your home," she said.

"Stop that!" Richard's voice rose in volume. "You know I don't think of you like that."

I glanced up and down the road, hoping no one was close. "Richard," I warned.

He glanced at me, then looked back at Anya, his breathing ragged. "I am not your master," he said to her, his voice lower again. "I could never be—" He broke off, getting too close to his personal rule not to tell her he thought her the Rose.

Anya wasn't ready to let it go; she leaned in. "Why did you want me to help the boy?" she asked. She was fishing, trying to get him to say what he meant.

"You would have let the boy die, knowing you had the ability to heal him?"

Anya sat back. Richard had scored a point. "No," she said, chastened. "I couldn't."

Richard reached out and gripped her hand holding the rein in front of her. "I know," he said. "And I think it is time that you use your skills for those in need."

"But carefully!" I added. "If Father finds out, there's no telling what he would do."

Richard nodded. "Be careful," he said to Anya. "But you have great skill. I would hate to see it wasted." He turned his horse back toward the estate and urged it forward, leaving us to follow.

We joined our father in time for the evening meal. Anya was up in the rotation for service, and she quietly gave each of us our plates, deliberately avoiding eye contact with Richard. There was little conversation. I was concentrating on my food, trying to determine how much I had to eat to hide the fact that I'd had bread and cheese at a peasant's home that afternoon. Richard, I could tell, was trying to avoid striking up conversation with our father in the hope of evading talk of the Council.

We'd been quiet for about ten minutes when suddenly my father acknowledged me. "Karan, are you ready for your debut the week after next?"

I blinked at him, uncomprehending for a moment.

"Your eighteenth celebration," he said.

"Oh!" I said. "I had nearly forgotten."

"I have received many acceptances to our invitations," Father said. "You will be glad to know the Gennadys are coming."

My pulse quickened, and a familiar terror gripped my heart. I swallowed hard. "That's wonderful news," I said. I took a deep breath, trying to calm myself.

Richard saw my distress and jumped into the conversation. "Sir, what do you mean by her debut?"

Father surveyed me for a moment, his expression appraising. So often he ignored me that I was having trouble overcoming my surprise at the attention. I was far more used to being at the receiving end of his wrath. "I've decided that it is time to present Karan as a marriageable prospect."

I saw Anya's head whip toward us, her eyes wide.

I stuttered. "B-but Father, I thought that you wanted to wait until I am nineteen." I paused. I could feel the vein in my neck throbbing. "As is traditional," I added.

"There is so much uncertain about the future," Father said. "I'd like to get this settled before too long."

Tears pricked at my eyes. I looked across to Richard, hoping he could read my desperation.

"But sir," he said, coming to my assistance. "Surely, there is no reason to rush. Karan's so very young and—"

Father cut him off abruptly, his tone harsh. "You spent the day looking over the Council's plans. You know there is every reason to rush." His tone was hard, flinty. He turned back to me. "Karan, you will be pleasant at the ball."

I folded under his gaze. "Aye, sir."

"I will speak with those who I think would be the best alliances for you."

I could feel the fear forming into a knot in the middle of my chest. "Aye, sir."

He looked back to Richard. "She is plenty old enough. You will support me in this."

Richard looked to me. I could see the pity in his expression. He nodded to our father. "Aye, sir."

I could stand it no longer. The tears were close to spilling over. I pushed my chair back and stood. "Excuse me, sir. I'm feeling a little tired. I would like to go to my rooms for the evening."

Father waved me away. "Go," he said. I was back to being ignored.

I walked out of the door and hurried up to my rooms. I was angry. I was numb. I wasn't sure if I would burst into tears or lash out in fury. I wished, for a moment, that I had Anya's power and I could burn up kindling in the fireplace.

I was kneeling on the hearth, staring at the flames, when Anya came in about twenty minutes later. She came over and sat beside me.

"Are you all right?" she asked, putting her hand on my shoulder.

I shrugged. Tears had not come. I was still numb. "I knew it was coming," I said.

"But you thought—"

"I thought I had more time, but it makes no difference. Next year, this year—either way, Father is going to marry me off for his own political gain, and I have no say in the matter."

We sat silently for a moment. I sat back on my heels and took a deep breath, closing my eyes. "I wish I was you," I said, my eyes still closed. "You are completely free to do what you want—you could leave here tonight and never return. You could stay forever. No one would force you to do what you didn't want."

I opened my eyes in time to catch a half-smile on her face. She shook her head but didn't say anything in response right away. A few moments later, she stood. "Let's get you out of those uncomfortable clothes."

She helped me with the buttons of my gown and out of the layers of the underdress—the chains that bound me to the role of noblewoman. I sat by the fireplace and read for a few hours, then we both got ready for bed, and Anya saw I was settled before banking the fire and blowing out the lamps and candles. I heard her get into her cot in the darkness and then heard her breathing slow to a steady rhythm, matching the dull pounding of the surf out the window.

I lay there in bed, trying to imagine what life would be like as the wife of Lord Gennady or some other noble. The fear began to knot my chest again, so I tried to focus on something else. I tried thinking of my father, but the anger that had risen in me at dinner rose again, and I tried another train of thought. I thought of Edmund that morning in the garden—the moment that hope had welled up within me, and finally, the tears came to my eyes. And I began to sob, grieving the loss of what might have been, but what I knew could never be.

I cried myself out and lay, spent, sleep still eluding me. I listened to the steady rhythm of the surf. Anya's words, from only the day before, came to mind: *He Who Knows Men's Thinking sees you. He cares. He knows your fears even when you do not say them.*

I looked inside for that conviction I'd found that morning and grasped onto it as if it were a rope thrown to a drowning man. I held it and breathed deeply, trying to match the rhythm of the surf.

And I suddenly wondered, *If He Who Knows Men's Thinking is actively involved in what was happening—in Anya's arrival, and her gift, and Tay's healing today, can I speak to Him?* And I knew, without a doubt, that I could. That I didn't even have to because He knew my very thoughts, but I still could. And I began to consider my fears, not in such a way as to let them overwhelm me, but bringing them up, one by one, and handing them over to Him, as if silently, in my mind, I were telling Him all about them, and He was listening to me. And I brought up the anger I'd felt toward my father after the meal, and I handed it over to Him.

I won't say that I heard a voice in return. But I felt a presence there in the room with us, a presence that wasn't Anya's breathing or the throbbing sea. And in the midst of all my fears and my anger, I was certain, with that deep-seated conviction that I had discovered, that all would, somehow, be *right*.

CHAPTER 14

THE following weeks were full of activity. Between preparations for the ball and my ongoing lessons, I had very little free time. However, each afternoon Anya and I went out for our afternoon ride. A few days after our visit to Thayer and Lanica's home, we encountered Lanica on the road near the village. She had been to another village an hour's journey away to buy and trade threads and fabrics. She was driving a small cart, and in the back, on top of a pile of bolts of cloth, sat Tay.

"How are you, Tay?" I asked when we stopped our horses to greet them.

"I'm well, Lady Karan," the boy said politely.

"Thanks to you, Miss Anya," Lanica said.

I saw Anya shift uncomfortably in her saddle. "I have been gifted skill with magic," she said. "I should use it to help."

"He Who Knows Men's Thinking will bless you for your deeds," said Lanica. "Are you enjoying your ride?" she asked me.

"Aye," I said. The sun had warmed the day, and the leaves glowed golden in the late afternoon sunlight. "It is a beautiful day."

"That it is," said Lanica. "I am a little concerned with the unseasonable warmth."

Anya spoke. "How does that impact business?" she asked.

"Sales have been slow," Lanica said. She gestured back to the items in the cart. "I could only buy about half of our normal allotment for winter. I don't know whether to hope for a warm winter so that we don't run out of stock or to pray that the cold comes soon enough for us to purchase more before it really sets in."

I'd never thought about the mechanics of trade before that day. Of course, autumn would be a busy time for a tailor; he would be making new winter clothes for the whole village. Another thought struck, and I began to laugh.

Lanica looked over at me and raised an eyebrow. "Lady Karan?"

I put my hand over my mouth, trying to stifle my giggles. It felt good to laugh—I hadn't really done so in a few days. "I'm sorry, Lanica!" I gasped. "I'm laughing at my own foolishness!"

Anya smiled at me and waited patiently for me to calm enough to speak.

"The other day in your shop, I was trying to determine what the purpose of tapestries was beyond decoration." I finally caught my breath enough to speak. "You may think me ignorant, but I'd never seen plain ones before. And I only now realized that they keep rooms warm!"

Anya laughed aloud. I saw Lanica look from one to the other of us. I could see she wasn't quite sure how comfortable she was allowed to be with me and was trying to gather cues from Anya. Finally, she broke into a broad smile.

"Aye, that they do," she said. "I find that I'm more often called upon to make warm and functional tapestries over those that tell stories with their pictures."

I smiled at that idea. "I like that—tell stories with their pictures. They do, don't they? The big ones we have at home seem to be slices of tales and events."

"That is often the way," Lanica said. "Tapestry weaving is a centuries' old art form in Asael. It takes years of training to be able to create the images you see on the walls of your father's estate. My father wove some of them. I watched him working on them—I was a small child—but I remember him telling me they were for Marinel."

"Your father's work is beautiful," I said.

"It's what made me want to learn to weave," said Lanica. "Watching him work on those tapestries. He taught me the art of the picture tapestries, too, you know. And I so rarely get the chance to create beautiful ones."

"Someday, I'll have to commission one from you," I said. "As soon as I can think of a way to convince my father I need a new tapestry." As I said it, I remembered that I wouldn't be under my father's roof much longer. My ease left me, and I looked down at my hands holding the reins.

"I look forward to it, Lady Karan," Lanica said. I glanced up and caught her smile.

Anya noted my discomfort. She nudged her horse's flank. "We should get going," she said. "We don't want to keep your father waiting for dinner."

Lanica gathered the reins of the horse pulling the cart. "If you can come by our home again, we would love to have you visit," she said.

The simple kindness of her invitation warmed me. I looked up and smiled at her. "We'll try," I said. "I so enjoyed my time there."

We turned our horses and rode off, hearing the cart creak away behind us.

The next day my father canceled my lessons. He had brought a seamstress in from the Capital, and I spent the entire morning in her care, being measured and poked and prodded. The timing was short, but my father had decided that I needed an entirely new gown for the ball, rather than making over one of my old ones. He was absolutely determined that I would be engaged by the end of the event.

Every day new responses to his invitations were arriving. The Gennadys, the Briyannes, the Makrams, and many other families I didn't know at all would be joining us for the ball. I could imagine my father pulling out his lists of genealogies, trying to figure out the social status of each eligible young man who accepted the invitation. Lord Gennady was his first choice, and he was putting the bulk of his effort and hope on the gamble that my beauty and my dowry would win him over. But my father was never one to forego hedging his bets. There were a few other young men whose lineage was nearly as august as our own that he intended to impress. Perhaps he thought a little competition would motivate Lord Gennady to a quicker decision.

I watched the preparations with growing dread and, with each day, growing calm. I woke every morning and handed over my worries and my fears to He Who Knows Men's Thinking. It was a strange new way of functioning—as if I was not standing alone but was held up by a hand I couldn't see.

The day the Makrams' response arrived, I saw it on the hall table before my father picked up the mail. My heart leaped, and then my mind quieted it—I'd given over that hope the night I'd handed everything over to He Who Knows Men's Thinking. I knew Edmund was not on my father's list of competitors. I would say goodbye to him on the night of the ball, and I would thank him for his kindness, and I would hope every day that he would someday find the same conviction I had—because it was the only thing that was giving me the strength to make it through each day.

I saw little of Richard that week. Between the growing responsibilities our father was putting on him and the tension between him and Anya, he wasn't seeking out our company as much. The easy friendship of our first weeks together had disappeared.

Anya and I rode out again a few days before the celebration ball and found ourselves near the village. I suggested we make our way to Thayer and Lanica's home, and we turned onto the main street. As we rode between the buildings, I saw people stopping to stare. At first, I again felt as though I were on display, but I quickly realized they weren't looking at me. Anya kept her eyes forward, focused on our destination.

We dismounted in front of the shop, and Thayer came out to greet us. He tied our horses to the hitching post and invited us in and through the door into their living quarters. Lanica was pulling bread and cheese from the shelves and had a kettle of water warming over the fire for tea. It was as if this was normal—a quiet afternoon visit with the village tailor and weaver, the lady of the manor, and the Rose of Asael. And I loved it.

We'd been sitting and talking for about half an hour when there was a knock on the back door. Lanica rose to answer it. She opened the door a crack and spoke in a hushed voice with whoever was there. She seemed a little agitated and was trying to make the person leave.

Tay was playing by the fireplace, but he rose and joined his mother at the door. Thayer and Anya were still deep in conversation, but I found myself distracted by whatever was happening at the door. I couldn't see who was outside, but Lanica was obviously upset they had come.

She stood there a few moments longer, speaking inaudibly with the person outside the door. Finally, Thayer and Anya noticed the small commotion as well. I glanced at Anya as she looked up and saw a resigned expression cross her features.

"Lanica," she said. "Let them come."

Lanica drew her head back into the room. "Oh, Miss Anya!" she cried. "I'm so sorry! I didn't say a word, but people saw how much better Tay was and saw you here that day."

Thayer stood and started across the room to join Lanica at the door. "We'll get rid of them," he said.

"No," said Anya. "Let them come."

I didn't understand what was going on until Lanica swung the door open. A crowd of people stood in their small backyard, most of them crippled or sick. Their faces held all the expectancy of the figures on the tapestry in my room.

I gasped. Anya rose and moved toward the fireplace where there was more light. Thayer moved a chair over for her to sit in.

Our eyes met across the room. I didn't say a word, but she understood my question. She shrugged. "He's right," she said. "I can't let them go on like this, knowing I have the ability to help."

I nodded. Lanica allowed the first person, an old woman carrying a coughing toddler, in the door. As the woman put the child in Anya's arms, Anya looked up at me. "Go when you must," she said. "I'll be a while." Then she gently placed her hand on the child's chest and closed her eyes for a moment, reaching for the right branch of the vine, and spoke quietly, "*Allevo.*"

I watched for nearly half an hour as one after another came to her. Always with a patient smile, she would listen to them, and then focus on the person in need and bring out her power to heal or comfort them. Finally, when I had no more time, I nodded quietly to Thayer and slipped out through the shop, untied my horse, and mounted to ride home.

I reached the stables, and a boy named Marshall came out to take my horse from me. He glanced down the lane behind me as if wondering where my companion was. "Oh, *thank you*, Marshall!" I gushed, trying to divert his attention. He looked back at me and smiled a little foolishly. "Would you do me the biggest favor and wait here at the stables this evening? Miss Anya was held up on an errand in the village, and I *don't know* when she's going to be back! I'd hate to have her come back with no one expecting her. And you're so good with the horses, you'll be able to groom hers quickly before bed, even if she's late, yes?"

Marshall blushed at the compliment. "Aye, Lady Karan," he said. "I'll wait for Miss Anya and take care of her horse when she gets here."

I smiled at him, practicing my expression that said he was my hero. He blushed again and took my horse's reins. I turned toward the house and nearly collided with Richard as he came up behind me.

He shook his head, smiling a little as he watched Marshall lead the horse away, slightly dazed. "What did *that* one ever do to you to deserve this?" he said. "Here you are making another conquest when all you'll do is leave him behind."

I frowned.

Richard put his arm around my shoulders and squeezed, turning me toward the house. "I'm sorry," he said. "That was unkind."

I nodded, not trusting my voice not to break.

"Where's Anya?" Richard asked as we began to walk.

I took a breath. "You should have seen it, Richard!"

"What?"

"We were at Thayer and Lanica's, and half the village came—and they all wanted her to heal them or ease their pain."

"And she did?"

"She said you were right. She couldn't let them suffer when she knew she could help."

One side of his mouth went up in a half-hearted smile. "No, she wouldn't do that."

"You should tell her, Richard. Tell her we think she's the Rose."

"We? You're convinced, too?"

I nodded.

He shook his head. "I won't—I can't."

"So you'll—what? Argue and fight with her until she recognizes it on her own? And when you're not fighting, not even speak? It's as if you're not even friends anymore."

"I was mistaken to get so close to her. She has a purpose and a role, and I can't get in the way of it."

I sighed.

Richard steered me off the main path and into the shrubbery where we were hidden from sight of the house and the stables. "How are you?" he asked.

I chuckled, a little rueful. "Terrified. And resigned. And all right."

"We'll figure something out. It will be all right. I—I don't know what or how, but we'll get Father to delay this."

"No, we won't," I said. "He won't delay anything. But you're right." I reached down inside of myself and grasped my conviction. "It *will* be all right."

Richard looked down at me, bewildered. "How do you mean?"

"I have no idea what is going to happen," I said. "But He Who Knows Men's Thinking knows my fear. And I've given it over to Him. It's as though it's there, but I'm not the one carrying it."

Richard squeezed my hand. "We'll fix this."

"*We* can't fix anything, Richard," I said. "But when the time comes, He will show us what to do."

The light was fading from the sky, but Richard took a step back and examined my face in the dusk. "Do you know the tapestry in your quarters?" he asked. "With all the people?"

"Yes," I said. "The ones who look so—"

"Expectant." He took the word out of my mouth. "I just saw that same expression on your face."

"I saw it on the faces of the peasants gathered outside Thayer and Lanica's today."

Richard put his arm back around my shoulders and steered back to the path toward the house. "Something amazing is about to happen," he said. "The whole world is falling apart, but something is about to happen."

I glanced up at his face and saw the very same expression there.

CHAPTER 15

I woke early on the morning of my eighteenth celebration.
I slipped out from under the covers and put on shoes and a
cloak without waking Anya. I tiptoed down the servants'
stairs and let myself out through the kitchen door. At the
edge of the cliff overlooking the sea was a path that wound
down to a small, rocky beach. The tide was out, and the
breakers small.

I sat at the edge of the water on a small boulder, watching
the waves lap the pebbles around me. The steady rhythm
washed over me, and I slowed my breathing to match it. I
was eighteen years old. I had lost my mother, been raised
by a harsh, cold father, seen the death of a Prince, and
was about to be married off against my will. And I'd never
been so content. The knowledge that had swept over me
that night, only two weeks earlier, that all would be *right*
had never wavered in that whole time of preparation. I
thought of my new gown upstairs. The seamstress had finished it the night before. It was beautiful. I would shine

like my father's prized jewels which he intended me to wear. I knew I could dazzle Lord Gennady.

I heard footsteps on the beach behind me but didn't turn to look. A moment later, Anya sat down next to me on the boulder, her shoulder leaning against mine.

"Are you ready for tonight?" she asked.

"As I'll ever be."

We sat in silence and listened to the lapping waves for a few moments.

"Richard is convinced he can make Father delay this," I said.

"Can he?"

"I don't think so. I can't see any way out of it."

The waves took over the conversation for a few more moments. "You know the other day," I said, "when we were at Thayer and Lanica's?"

"Yes," Anya answered.

"You chose to help all those people."

"Yes."

"But it wasn't what you *wanted*. Not—" I tried to clarify. "Not that you didn't want to help them, but you didn't want the scene, the position or role of 'Practitioner.'"

"True."

"But you did it anyway because you have the gift, and you can't *not* help people."

She nodded.

"This is something I can do. I'm not good at many things. I don't have gifts like you. But I can influence the people I know." I paused, trying to state clearly the conclusion

I'd been moving toward over the previous days. "If Lord Gennady falls in love with me, I'll have the ear of one of the most powerful men in Asael. Maybe that's the role I'm supposed to play in all this."

Anya turned away from the sea and looked at me. There were tears in her eyes. "You would sacrifice your own happiness?"

"The Rose is the hope of Asael," I said. "Of what importance is my happiness if I can do something to contribute to her success?"

Anya closed her eyes; a tear rolled down her left cheek. She opened her eyes and looked straight at me. "You don't *know* I'm the Rose. I don't even know! I'm only a girl who is gifted in magic."

"He Who Knows Men's Thinking has a plan in all this," I said. "I don't know what it is, but this is the only path I see before me. So I will take it and trust Him to show me the next step when it comes."

"And Edmund?"

I squeezed my eyes shut as my heart contracted in my chest. I had avoided thinking about Edmund as I came to this decision. It hurt too much. I opened my eyes and looked into Anya's clear green ones. "Edmund will fight for the Rose, too. In his own way, in his own time."

She didn't answer. She looked back out to the sea, and together we watched the waves break.

Darkness was closing in as the first guests arrived that evening. I stood by my father's side by the door, a smile ready on my lips. Richard stood at my other side and greeted each guest after I did. I hadn't seen Anya since she'd finished braiding and coiling my long hair up upon my head and fastened the long line of buttons down my back, but I knew she was there, somewhere in the shadows, with me as I faced this night.

After we greeted our guests in the foyer, footmen in livery led them to the ballroom. My father had spared no expense. Everything at Marinel shone. The night was warm for the time of year, and torches lit the gardens, inviting people to walk in them.

The first to arrive were friends of Richard's, a low-ranking nobleman and his sister. Bellamy Mumina had attended school with Richard, and Richard had often gone to their home for visits on holidays. Lord Mumina's rank did not carry enough weight for him to be one of my father's prospects for me. His sister Cecily I'd met once before. She was cheery and curly-haired, someone who radiated good sense and fun. Richard greeted Bellamy warmly and grinned at Cecily as he requested a dance later in the evening.

There were already five or six families arrived before the Gennadys came. I gave quick hugs to the girls and held out my hand politely to Lady Gennady. Lord Gennady brought up the rear, and my father greeted him heartily.

"My Lord, I don't know that you've met my daughter, Karan."

Lord Gennady turned to me and looked me up and down, with the kind of expression my father had on his face as he evaluated a horse. "Enchanted," he said.

I forced myself to lower my eyelids and smile. I felt Richard beside me, taut with energy. I put out my hand, and Lord Gennady bowed over it.

"I hope I may have a dance," he said.

"Of course, good sir," I said. My skin crawled at his touch.

"Perhaps you would honor us by beginning the dancing with Lady Karan," my father suggested.

Lord Gennady stood straight and let go of my hand. "Certainly. Until then."

"Aye."

He turned to Richard and shook his hand. The difference between Richard's welcome of Lord Mumina and Lord Gennady was obvious. My father cleared his throat. I watched the muscles in Richard's shoulders tighten as he forced a smile and a few pleasantries.

Other families came, and the opening music started in the ballroom. It was almost time for me to go in to the dance when the Makrams finally arrived. Lord Makram and my father shook hands, Lady Makram kissed me on the cheek, and then I stood before Edmund.

I had seen him only two weeks earlier, but I had lived a lifetime in those two weeks. I put out of my mind his behavior in the garden the morning he left and instead focused on what he'd said in the breakfast room. I wondered if he'd been reading the Ancient Writings and what he thought of them.

I looked up into his face as I gave him my hand. He smiled. "You look lovely, Lady Karan," he said. He turned to my father. "I hope I may request the honor of Lady Karan's hand sometime this evening."

"Of course you can, my boy," my father answered. "But we must get her into the ballroom to begin the dancing." He turned to me. "Lord Gennady awaits you."

I watched pain cross Edmund's eyes at the words. In a single turn of phrase, my father had told him he was considered nothing more than a boy and who the real catch of the evening was.

Tears threatened to well up in my eyes as I was turned away from Edmund and led into the ballroom. I took a deep breath as we entered to compose myself. If I was to win over Lord Gennady, I had to put Edmund out of my mind. I smiled graciously as my father and I entered to applause. The musicians struck the chords of the first piece to ready the dancers to the floor. Lord Gennady came forward, and my father handed me over to him. I suppressed a shiver when he took my hand. He led me out to the dance floor, and we began to waltz with the first strains of the music.

As we moved round and round, I put a smile on my face and looked up at him, trying to think of something to say. I suddenly realized I had no idea what to talk to him about. I'd never be able to pretend to be silent and demure for a lifetime. I had to be sure he knew I was talkative. I raked through my thoughts, scattering them left and right, searching for something to grasp hold of—I caught something.

"Have you been busy with the Council's work lately?" I asked.

He glanced down at me, a little surprised. I suppose most girls did not start off political topics while dancing. "Aye," he said. "Do you have an interest in politics?"

I smiled. "A little. I've been raised by my father and brother, so dinner conversation has often veered toward the affairs of the kingdom."

"And what do you think of the Council?" he asked.

Well, I'd gotten myself into it. There was no skirting the topic now. "I hope they have in mind what is best for *all* of Asael." I tried to make sure I emphasized "all" enough to stress it, but not so much as to encourage too much discussion on the topic.

"We try to do so." He paused. It seemed to have worked. "Do you ride?"

"Aye, every day when we're here at Marinel."

"I love horses," he said. "Hunt?"

"Not really," I said. "Father drew the line at teaching me to shoot, but I have been out with them a few times."

"Do you read?"

I laughed quietly. "My lady in waiting says I read too much."

"What have you been reading lately?"

I considered, in a flash, what the reaction would be if I told him the truth—the Ancient Writings and commentary on them—I glanced down, grinning at the idea, but then I remembered his sisters' stories about his temper. No, it probably wouldn't be funny. "My studies have been in the Written Histories lately," I said, trying to hide my pause. I thought back to the novel I'd been reading the first night in the Capital. I told him I'd been reading that for pleasure.

"Your father has you read the Written Histories in your studies?"

"Aye."

"You ride, you've been hunting, you have an interest in politics, you read the Written Histories—is there anything you don't do?"

I thought about it for a moment. "I don't sew well," I said.

He threw his head back and laughed. I grinned. Over his shoulder, I caught a glimpse of Edmund, standing along the wall, watching us. Richard stood beside him, urgently speaking to him. My smile faded when I saw Edmund's face. All the pain that I felt when I thought of him was echoed in his expression as he watched me dance with Lord Gennady. Before I was turned away in the steps of the dance, I saw Richard put his hand on Edmund's shoulder and squeeze.

Lord Gennady returned me to my father's side at the end of the dance, and I discovered that my dance card had been filled for me. Father's list of eligibles topped the card; midway through the evening was a second dance with Gennady and one or two of the eligibles, then Richard, and finally, Edmund. There were only two empty slots at the very end of the night—my only freedom of choice. I told my father I was thirsty and turned to get a drink from the buffet. A pencil sat on the table, and I quickly scribbled gibberish names into the empty slots on my card—I would need time to talk to Edmund after we danced.

I gulped down a glass of punch and returned to my father's side to be introduced to the first of his other eligibles. I was led out onto the dance floor and began all over again. I danced all evening, passing pleasantries with nobleman after nobleman. I watched my father pull Lord Gennady aside and chat with him after our first dance, getting a read of our time together. After our second dance, he cornered him again, and they spoke for some time.

In between, my father worked the room, talking with all the great men of Asael, the members of the Council and the high-ranking nobles. He introduced Richard around and made sure that he took certain young ladies out to the dance floor. This was my night for conquest, but Father would not be remiss in finding the right alliance for Richard, too.

Partway through the evening, the musicians took a fifteen-minute break. I excused myself from my father and made my way out of the ballroom. I went quickly up the stairs to find a corner for a quiet moment alone. As I approached the first hallway, I heard Anya's voice. "What if there's another way?"

Richard answered her, "What way?"

I came around the corner. Anya saw me over Richard's shoulder. "Karan!"

Richard swung about. "Are you absolutely exhausted, Karan?" he asked, using the smooth voice he always used when he was hiding something.

"Almost," I said. "What were you talking about?"

Anya moved around Richard and came to me. "Nothing of importance," she said. She put her hands on either side of my face. "You've been amazing tonight. Dazzling when you should be and demure when it's right."

"Where have you been watching from?" I asked.

"Windows, mostly."

I laughed. Just then, the musicians began warming up again.

Richard reached out and took my arm. "You have another dance on your card, milady," he said.

He swung me away from Anya and led me rapidly back down the steps to the ballroom. When we reached the foot, I saw him look up. I glanced up to the landing in time to see Anya nod.

"I'll see you later," Richard said as we entered the room and he handed me off to my next partner and disappeared into the crowd.

It was over an hour before my dance with Richard came up on the card. Throughout the evening, I'd watched Edmund from afar, trying to think through what I would say to him when we had the chance to speak. I'd seen Richard with him more than once. I wanted to see if Richard could tell me what Edmund was thinking.

We moved out to the dance floor together and began the waltz. I'd learned to waltz with Richard, so I didn't even have to think of the steps or the movement; we'd done this a thousand times.

"How is Edmund?" I asked.

"He wants to talk with you," Richard said.

"I want to talk with him!" I cried. "But there's nothing I can do. Father filled my dance card for me and put Edmund at the very bottom."

"He knows," Richard said. "And I think as much as he wants to talk with you, he also doesn't want to have the conversation at all."

I choked back a sob.

Richard tightened his arm around my back.

I took a deep breath. "What were you and Anya talking about?"

"She told me about your conversation on the beach this morning."

"Oh," I said.

"You have been amazing tonight." Richard grinned down at me. "Who would have thought all those years of charming stable boys would come in helpful when securing yourself a husband?"

I laughed a little. "I don't see another way forward."

Richard was silent. We danced on for a few moments. As the song was drawing to a close, Richard finally spoke again. "You're remarkable, little sister. I don't know if I could do it."

The music came to a close, and we walked to the edge of the room. Edmund was waiting, and Richard placed my hand in his. "Take care of her," he said to Edmund.

"I always will," Edmund said.

He led me out to the floor and put his arms around me as the music began. I followed his steps, my mind in a million places at once. I couldn't think how to begin, and it seemed

Edmund had the same difficulty. Precious measures of the music slipped by as we struggled to find words.

Edmund found his tongue before me. "So, Gennady?"

"Since he hasn't yet discovered I'm a traitor, Father has decided I should marry up."

"And soon?"

"Aye. If tonight went well, as soon as he can make it happen."

"Tonight went well," Edmund said.

His tone was bland, but I looked up into his face and saw the pain there. My heart constricted to see it. We danced in silence a few moments. I saw Richard standing by the edge of the room talking with Lord Mumina and his sister Cecily. His attention was caught by something out the door, and he excused himself and slipped out.

Finally Edmund spoke again. "You know this doesn't change it, right?"

"Change what?"

"Your promise."

"My promise?"

"If you ever need help, you'll come to me."

A tear spilled over my eyelid and ran down my cheek. "It doesn't change anything," I said.

We gazed into each other's eyes as the music ended. There was so much more I wanted to say; I'd barely begun. "Go out to the garden," I said in a low voice. "I'll join you in a few moments."

Edmund led me back to my Father. "Thank you for the honor of the dance," he said to both of us. He made his way out the door, and I knew exactly where I would find him as soon as I was free.

My father led me over to the Gennadys, and we exchanged brief farewells as they prepared to leave.

"If you'll excuse me, sir," I said when we had left them. "I think I need some fresh air."

"Of course," Father said.

I made my way outdoors and directly to the place where Edmund and I had spoken the morning I told him I was a believer. He was waiting for me. He reached out his hands, and I grasped them.

"I saw the Gennadys leaving just now," he said.

I nodded. "Did you read the Ancient Writings?"

He smiled. "Aye. I said I would."

"And?"

He took a step closer to me so that we could see each other more clearly in the flickering light of the torches. "Well, my father hasn't figured out I'm a traitor yet, either."

CHAPTER 16

I started to laugh. And with the laughter came tears. The exhaustion and tensions of the entire evening came out in near-hysterics. I was gasping and sobbing and laughing all at once.

Edmund led me to a bench and sat me down, never letting go of my hands. "Are you all right?"

I smiled up at him. "I'm fine," I said, between hiccoughing sobs. "That's the best news I've heard all night."

He chuckled. "Glad I rank."

I tried to take deep breaths and steady myself. I freed one hand and brushed the tears off my cheeks. "You believe it? You really believe it all?"

"I've never been more sure of anything in my entire life," he said. "As I was reading, it was as if I was finally finding words for something I've known forever—that Someone created us to follow in a dance, but we've lost track of the steps."

"And the Rose?"

"I don't know your Anya, but if what you and Richard have told me about her is true, I'm well on my way to being convinced there, too."

"You should have seen her the other day," I said. I told him about meeting Thayer and Lanica, and how she healed Tay, and then our second visit and all the peasants who came.

"They know to keep it quiet before the nobles, right?" he asked.

"Of course. But how often do the nobles talk with the peasants? It's been weeks now, and none of the nobles know Prince Loran was on his way to visit a peasant man when he died."

Edmund raised his eyebrows. "No, that one hasn't gotten out. And it's a good thing, too. But if she's going about healing people right and left, word is going to spread," he said.

"We'll be careful."

He was silent for a moment. "She can really heal?"

I nodded. "Illness or injury."

"And she doesn't think she's the Rose?"

"She—" I paused. "She doesn't know."

"You've asked her?"

"It slipped out. Don't say anything, though. Richard is still convinced that he can't tell her what he thinks. And Anya is waiting for him to say something."

"Sounds like he may have met his match for stubbornness."

"He's convinced that if he tells her that he thinks she's the Rose, it will influence her somehow. He's certain that she must come to the conclusion on her own."

"And you can't sway him." It was a statement, not a question.

"Richard can be single-minded," I said.

"To a fault," said Edmund. "Once he gets his mind on something, he worries it like a dog with a bone until he's used it all up."

I nodded.

Edmund was thoughtful for a moment. "Will she go with you—Anya, to the Gennadys' when—" He broke off.

"I suppose so. I haven't thought about it." I looked over at him. The pain was back in his expression. I squeezed his hand.

He gripped my hand in both of his, lifted it to his lips, and kissed it fiercely. "How are you so calm?" he asked.

"It's my part," I said. "Richard could lead nations if he put his mind to it, and Anya can heal the sick and who knows what else, and I'm basically useless. I'm nothing more than a silly schoolgirl."

"You have never been a silly schoolgirl."

"You know what I mean," I said. "But this I can do. If I can make him care about me, I might have some little influence over one of the most powerful men in Asael."

"It's a huge sacrifice," Edmund said.

I thought about that for a moment. When I spoke again, my voice sounded small. "I can't see another way out," I said. "Father is set on my marriage, and I can only make the best of it. I can't see another way."

He sat beside me, his head hanging down. My hand was still in both of his, and I never wanted him to let go of it.

He shook his head from side to side slowly, as if silently protesting the truth of my words.

The part of the garden we were in was a long path between two hedges. We sat on a bench at about the middle of the length. Suddenly, Anya and Richard came round the end of the hedge and running toward us.

"Karan!" Richard called out.

Edmund looked up and watched their rapid approach. He stood, pulling me to my feet with him. "What is it?"

Anya hesitated a moment, glancing from me to Edmund.

"He believes, too," I said.

Richard grinned at Edmund. "I knew you would see."

"I still think we're all crazy, but I'm on board," Edmund said, smiling.

"Anya's had a brilliant idea," Richard said. "And we've figured out how to make it work."

"What?" I asked.

"I found another way," Anya said.

I remembered her words to Richard in the hall earlier. "Another way for what?"

"Another way out. You don't have to marry Lord Gennady."

Edmund's hand gripped mine so tightly he began to cut off the circulation to my fingers.

My heart began pounding. "What?" I asked. "How?"

"We run," said Richard. His eyes were sparkling with excitement in the light of the torches.

"Run?" asked Edmund. It was as if a light came on behind his eyes.

"We leave this all behind—Marinel, Father, the Council—all of it. And we find a new life somewhere. Just the four of us."

For a moment, I saw it—life with Edmund, and with Richard and with Anya, in quiet cottages in the mountains, free from the trappings of nobility with which I'd been raised. It was beautiful. I wanted it.

And then, a line from the Writings came to my mind, as if someone were pulling it forward and spreading it out over my dream: *That One will be the voice of them who cannot speak, the arm of him who cannot lift, and the joy of all.*

Just the four of us meant pulling Anya from her path. Just the four of us meant taking Richard out of a sphere of influence with which he could change the world. I couldn't do it. He Who Knows Men's Thinking would never approve of such selfishness.

"No," I said. "We can't be just the four of us."

They all looked at me. "No one else knows. No one else believes that He Who Knows Men's Thinking is real and active. No one else knows that the Rose is the hope of Asael. We have to tell them."

I saw Richard frown, and Anya bow her head.

"We can't let Father force you to marry Lord Gennady, though, Karan," Richard said. "We have to find another way."

I nodded. Now that the hope of not marrying Gennady had been dangled before me, I didn't want to give it up without serious thought. And as I thought, a new vision rose before my eyes. I thought of the people in Thayer and Lanica's yard. I thought of the conversation Anya and I had once had about the number of nobles in Asael. I remembered my father saying once that a group of people with a single purpose was the most powerful force on earth.

"We run," I said.

"But—" Richard began.

I interrupted him. "We run, and we leave this all behind—but not just the four of us. We gather followers, and together we find a way to save Asael."

I saw Richard look over at Anya. He still fought the idea of telling her he thought she was the Rose, but I could see that my idea intrigued him. He was convinced she'd come to the same conclusion we had; it was a matter of time. And if the peasants chose to follow the Rose...

I could see Anya and Edmund considering my alternative as well. Anya seemed to be weighing it out. I didn't know it at the time, but she was already well on the path of claiming her role as the Rose. She shrugged and nodded. "We run."

Richard smiled. "And we gather the followers of the Rose."

"And we save Asael," I said. I looked at Edmund. "Are you with us?"

He looked back at me. I watched as the light dimmed in his eyes and pain encroached at the edges again. "I can't run," he said.

I felt as though I'd been struck. I dropped his hand and took a step backward. "But I thought—"

He interrupted me, gripping my shoulder with his hand. "I want to go with you!" he cried. "I want nothing more than to go with you, but if you're going to do this, you need someone on the inside." He turned to Anya and Richard. "Karan was right in thinking it would be good to influence Lord Gennady. We need someone who is close to the Council, who can help. It has to be me."

"Why you?" I asked.

"Because no one knows I know Anya," he said. He came no closer to saying Anya was the Rose, but I knew we all understood him. If we raised a band of followers, she would be their leader. And Richard or I would be suspect because of our relationship with her.

"Your father's not on the Council, though," Richard said. "How will you stay connected to it?"

"I'll ask your father for a position on his staff. When he loses the heir to the estate, he'll need a secretary."

Richard nodded. Given our fathers' longtime friendship, no one would be surprised if Lord Makram's son requested a position on the staff of a Council member.

"When do we go, then?" Anya asked.

"Within the week," said Richard. "If Lord Gennady was as impressed with Karan as he seemed tonight, Father will be pressing for a wedding within the month. We have to get away sooner than later."

"Where do we go?" I asked.

"There are caves along the shoreline between here and my father's estate," Edmund said. "No one ever goes there, and they're large—they go deep back into the cliffs, and they're well-protected from the weather. The entrances are narrow; most people never even know they're there."

"Sounds as good as anything," said Richard. "We'll be roughing it."

Anya glanced over at me. "We'll limit the buttons," she said.

I laughed.

Edmund and Richard threw us confused looks.

"Never mind," I said.

"We should look at the caves on a map before you go," Richard said to Edmund. "So that I know where they are."

"Of course. Meet you in the library in a few moments?"

Richard nodded. "Aye." I watched as he and Anya turned and walked back down the lane. They seemed to have forgotten their frustrations with each other in the task of finding another option for me.

I turned to Edmund. "Work for my father?"

"I can face it bravely, knowing you're safely away."

I sighed. "Away," I said. "I wish you would go with us."

Edmund reached out and pulled me into an embrace. My head rested on his shoulder, and he stroked the back of my hair. "I wish I could, too," he whispered. "But this is a thousand, a million times better than seeing you sacrifice yourself in marriage to Gennady. This is *my* part."

"And I'm still useless," I said.

Edmund grasped my shoulders and pushed me back so that he could look into my eyes. "Karan, love, you're the least useless person I know," he said. "You're strong, and brave, and intelligent, and sacrificial, and absolutely inspiring."

I'd barely heard the rest of what he said after the endearment. For a long moment, I stood there, staring back into his eyes, trying to etch every fleck of color in my memory. And I smiled.

I didn't know what we were going in to. I'd never even considered living in a cave in my life. Anya had still not embraced her identity as the Rose. We had no way of gathering followers, no one to gather them behind, and no plan once we did gather them. But none of that mattered. I would be with Richard and Anya. I knew that Edmund would be supporting us, wherever he was.

And all was *right*.

PART TWO

From the writings of Brother Ezra, Helper

Fourteenth day, twelfth month, in the sixteenth year of King Saran's reign

I remembered today a lesson from my studies as I was going through the novitiate right after I joined the monastery nearly fourteen years ago. The memory seemed to strike from nowhere, vivid and clear. Aldan and I had been in our lessons with the Priest, and I jotted a note down in the margin of my text because I had no other paper.

I was whipped for it later by a young monk named Cormac. I am not sure what happened to him. He must have been transferred to one of the other monasteries in Asael, for I've not seen him since those early days.

He whipped me for writing in the text—not for what I wrote. I can still remember him pouring over my unstable, childish hand and reading it aloud. He said the idea was sound, and he was surprised the Priest had said it: that the Written Histories, while we do not hold them sacred, are a record of our past and a guide for our future.

I was only a child, but Brother Cormac's interest in the statement (and the whipping) is still clear in my memory. He went on for a bit about the Written Histories and said there was much we could learn from them. He told me about the men who had been leaders in the time of the Priests, men of strength and quality. And he told me about the weak men who were Priests at the end of that era, who allowed the country to grow poor and corrupt and paved the way for the Age of the Kings and the rise of the nobles.

"It was weak-minded Keepers who lost Asael," he said. For a moment, I wasn't sure he was talking to me. "Weak Keepers who would not use the tools before them to hold the land for He Who Knows Men's Thinking."

The memory came to me as I studied my texts today. Lately, I have been asking He Who Knows Men's Thinking to give me particular insights. I know I have skill with magic, but I wish I had Brother Aldan's skill with the texts. He will rise higher in the ranks than I, simply because he remembers the proper passages at the proper times.

If I wish to rise, I must know the texts. I will need guidance, and I shall look for it in the Ancient Writings and the Written Histories.

Creator, give me diligence to study the words You have given us to show us Your path.

Eleventh day, fifth month, in the twentieth year of King Saran's reign

I have been made a Master Practitioner! It is in recognition of my skill with magic that I was made a Master so young. Praise to He Who Knows Men's Thinking who has heard my prayers for such a thing and granted them.

I will begin advanced study of magic tomorrow. My responsibilities will be mainly in the infirmary, as my primary gifting is the healing of injury. But as a Master I will have the opportunity to continue my training and move up in the ranks of leadership among the monks. My gifting with magic has always made me stand out among my peers, but I have wondered before now if I've been held back from advancing for some reason or other. Now I have the opportunity to move forward. I am pleased.

I will seek to serve He Who Knows Men's Thinking with all my heart and pursue Him only in all my days.

Creator, use my gifts for your will. I seek your promised Rose, and I will practice magic as you enable me henceforth. I know Your ways are unknown to us. I thank you for raising me up this far. I wish to serve You and to follow Your ways alone.

Second day, third month, in the twenty-fourth year of King Saran's reign

A new opportunity has arisen. King Saran has asked for a contingent of monks to be present at the palace on a regular basis, and I have been asked to be among them. Rumor has it that the king is trying to appease He Who Knows Men's Thinking with the move. He has been on the throne for twenty-four years now without an heir. Since the first queen died and he married again with no issue, there have been whispers that perhaps the lack of an heir is not the fault of the queens.

I wonder at the royals sometimes. They have the greatest education in the kingdom at their disposal, and I think they've not understood a word of the Ancient Writings. He Who Knows Men's Thinking—we know this by the very name we call Him—cannot be appeased with actions.

Yet they try. And the Creator allows me to benefit from it. I shall be able to meet men of influence in the kingdom and get a glimpse of how the nobles really live and how their systems of governance work. Aldan was made a priest last month, and I had begun to despair of ever rising above my current rank. They see my skill with magic, but I think they fear it, for I am rarely called upon to use it outside the infirmary.

Twenty-ninth day, third month, in the twenty-fourth year of King Saran's reign.

I have been at the castle now for three weeks. This opportunity is greater than I had imagined it could be. If we choose to use them, we have tables in the king's dining room. I have gone from time to time, when my prayers do not interfere.

King Saran has gathered about him the highest-ranking nobles in the land. His brother-in-law, Lord Hakan, sits beside him regularly. They are close friends, and Hakan married Saran's younger sister and serves as the king's steward. King Saran's brothers have responsibilities at their own estates; Lord Briyanne holds all the land surrounding the Capital that does not belong to the king or the monks. Lord Gennady's estate is further out—about half a day's journey—but no less impressive. Other nobles fill in about the extended royal family. Over the course of the weeks I have been here, many nobles have filled the rest of the seats for a night or two. From my vantage point at the wall, I can see them all, each vying for space closer to the royal table. Everyone wants some measure of influence or association.

Last night at dinner, two young knights, brothers, were brought into the room. They had distinguished themselves in some battle, and their reward was an evening at the king's table. I watched them take in the display. They had the eyes of hawks. The younger one—he must barely have been out of school—watched Lord Hakan keenly. I could see him noting every time the king turned to speak to his brother-in-law. The young man coveted that seat; I am certain of it.

The nobility of this kingdom is a system of futility. Each one maneuvers for position, but only birth or battle can guarantee it. Those young knights—the Adamaris brothers—they are, in the grand scheme of the nobility, nothing. Their father's lands are almost as far from the Capital as you can get and still be in Asael. I am certain they received a good education—I saw the younger one talking with young Lord Makram, son of a mid-level noble, and they seemed to be friends. But it is only because the young man and his brother were brave soldiers that they have even been given the opportunity to enter the king's presence. Without war, they would be relegated forever to the edges of the kingdom and the fringes of noble society.

We monks are no different, I suppose. Though our ranking is related to giftedness as Practitioners—which comes from the hand of He Who Knows Men's Thinking. But we still jostle each other for position. Aldan is made a priest, and I am left a monk because he is better than I at remembering his lessons.

Do we monks have a better way than the nobles? Aye, we seek the Rose, but we have done so for thousands of years without finding him. Perhaps the Creator has another plan He did not give us in the Ancient Writings.

Eighth day, first month, in the twenty-fifth year of King Saran's reign.

BROTHER Cormac has been transferred back to the Capital and has joined those of us assigned to the castle. It is good to see him again. I had forgotten much of our interaction during those days when I first joined the order, but he was one of the young monks assigned to my training in the novitiate. He was very young then, though he was older than his fellows at the same rank, for he had spent a few years as a sailor before joining the order. Since he has returned, I have been remembering his lessons more and more.

He told me the other day that he had been watching my career with interest.

"Why, Brother?" I asked him. He had been part of our training for a relatively short time. "Aldan has had far more success than I."

"Your skill is natural; Aldan's is practiced," Cormac said. "Nine times out of ten, he will surpass you in an act of magic, yes. But you have the innate ability to succeed in some of the most challenging situations."

I felt my brow furrow. I was trying to remember when Brother Cormac might have seen me succeed over Aldan. "Brother," I said, finally, "I do not know what you mean."

"You would not," he said. "You have not yet been faced with a task of that sort."

"Then how—"

He interrupted me. "I know," he said. "When the challenge arises, you will shine."

He says that he thinks I have only a few more steps before I reach the second level of mastery as a Practitioner. I am pleased. If I cannot train for the Priesthood, I do wish to be of service as a Practitioner. I am gifted, I know, and I have used those gifts in the infirmaries and everywhere else I have been assigned. But what is the result? Is He Who Knows Men's Thinking better known because I am a gifted Practitioner? How does my work serve the purpose of finding the Rose? These are the questions that have been on my mind in recent days. Are we monks as futile as the nobles?

Brother Cormac is a second-level Master. He has not risen through the ranks as high as he had hoped, I think. He seems to be happy that he has been transferred back to the Capital, and he has asked me at every meal to point out the various nobles and tell him their connections to the king.

When we were speaking the other day, he brought up that memorable conversation we had when I was a young novice, before he was transferred away.

"Do you remember a conversation we had about the end of the Age of Priests?"

I told him I did. "You said it was weak-minded Keepers who lost Asael."

He nodded. "I wonder if I used the wrong description," he said. "I have begun, in recent days, to think that it was instead weak-willed Keepers who lost power over the land."

I kept silent, waiting for him to clarify.

"Your knowledge is sound, Brother Ezra," he said. "But the same can be said of Aldan. What sets you apart from him is your passion. You have natural talent, but you also have vision. That will be useful."

I cannot think what he has in mind that I would be useful for, but it is nice to be recognized for my gifts.

Twenty-fourth day, eleventh month, in the twenty-eighth year of King Saran's reign

THE queen has died, and King Saran still has no heir. We sat at the funeral today and listened to the cathedral priest speak the old words once again:

"Rise! Raise your hands!"

We stood with our hands raised, and I glanced about the cathedral. In those final moments of the funeral ceremony, there is no difference between monk and noble. All stand. No matter if you read the Ancient Writings daily or have never opened them once. All raise their hands. No matter if you have kept the offices of prayer or never bowed a knee.

"We know that death is not an end," the Priest says, "that our souls are everlasting and do not fade."

For one more moment we stand, Asael united in the king's grief. Then the Priest continues, "We release her soul."

And it is over. Noble is once again noble, monk again monk.

After the funeral, we sat in the king's dining hall, full to the brim with royals and nobles. Lord Hakan's wife and children were there. I have not seen them before. His son is perhaps thirteen years old, and his young daughter only eight or nine. I look at the boy; he seems strong and serious. I have heard stories that Lady Hakan is a true believer. There are not many these days among the nobles. Beyond the monks, it is typically only peasants who hold to the Ancient Writings. But Lady Hakan is said to be raising her children to study the Ancient Writings alongside the Written Histories.

I wonder if the boy would ever get the chance to rule Asael. It is unlikely; he is sixth in line for the throne, and the king will certainly marry again and continue to seek an heir. But I am intrigued by the idea of a king who knows the Ancient Writings. He would be a new sort. I wonder if that is the purpose He Who Knows Men's Thinking has in bringing us monks to the castle for these past years. Perhaps we are to influence the nobles toward He Who Knows Men's Thinking and the Ancient Writings.

To do so, we will need more interaction with them than we currently have. I believe I shall talk with Cormac about this.

Twentieth day, twelfth month, in the twenty-eighth year of King Saran's reign

WE have made a beginning. I spoke with Cormac about my thoughts regarding the need to influence the nobles. He agreed, and we both have been seeking new opportunities for conversation. Today I met Lord Allard, a young mid-level nobleman who would like to talk more with us in the future. He said he has become increasingly concerned with the state of Asael, and he thinks there should be greater collaboration between the nobles and the monks.

It is a better start than I had hoped. Lord Allard has the ear of the king, young though he is. Perhaps we will see results from this.

Tenth day, first month, in the twenty-ninth year of King Saran's reign

I sat today in Brother Cormac's office with him and Lord Allard for tea. As we talked, the conversation turned to the prospect of King Saran's marriage.

"I am quite certain he will marry again," Cormac said. "Though he will have to choose from among the lower nobles. All the higher-ranked nobles are either his close relatives or have only sons."

I thought I saw Lord Allard stir in his seat and turned to him, but he waved my attention away. I turned back to Brother Cormac. "What will happen if the King does not have a son?" I asked.

Brother Cormac looked at me for a long moment before responding, as if he were weighing a decision. "That is the question that will be on every tongue in Asael soon," he said.

"But not yet? He has outlived two wives already."

"Watch and wait, Brother Ezra," Cormac said. "His new queen will be young, healthy, and strong. Only if she does not produce him an heir will the questions begin to rise."

Lord Allard stirred again. He set his teacup down on the old sailing trunk Brother Cormac has as an end table in the room. "There is, of course, the indirect line," he said.

"Most nobles would consider it near treason to suggest such a thing," said Brother Cormac.

"We nobles may need to update our thinking," said Lord Allard. "We have lived for a thousand years under the rule of the direct line of kings, but everything breaks down in time. We rank ourselves based upon our relations to the king, but then we break our ranks for those who stand out in battle. Look at the Adamaris boys, for instance."

I nodded, thinking of the young men who had attended the king's dinners regularly over the past five years. Though their birth was relatively low, they had distinguished themselves in battle and, as a result, regularly rubbed shoulders with the highest of the nobility.

"I have often seen them but have not yet met them," said Cormac.

"They are remarkable young men," said Lord Allard. "Young Lord Adamaris is the youngest captain in the king's army, but even he is overshadowed by his younger brother's skill."

"What's so impressive about him?"

"Master Arnau was only eighteen when he fought his first battle for the king," said Allard. "He's an incredibly gifted sportsman, and I've never seen his like in the saddle.

When he and his brother practice war-play, young Master Arnau beats Master Richard every time, though he's four years younger. I wouldn't be surprised if he's made captain by the end of the year."

"He seems intelligent, too," I said. "He is always watching and observing when they attend the king's dining room. I feel he's calculating every move."

"Aye," said Allard. "Have you noted how he struck up a friendship with Lord Hakan early on? Master Arnau knows the rolls of royals better than anyone. He knows there is only one daughter among the children of Saran's siblings."

"Young Lady Abra Hakan?" I was surprised. The girl I had seen the day of the queen's funeral could not have been ten years old.

"Master Arnau is willing to bide his time," said Lord Allard. "The best chance of advancement in rank besides prowess in war is advantageous marriage. If he can accomplish both, he will certainly set himself up as a leader in Asael."

Brother Cormac cleared his throat. "You have thought this through," he said to Lord Allard.

Allard nodded. "I am a noble," he said. "Nobles must always concern themselves with rank and position. Careful attention is our *only* hope of ever holding any power."

He stood, then, and finished his tea in a great gulp before excusing himself. Brother Cormac and I sat quietly sipping our tea for a few more moments.

"It is interesting," said Brother Cormac, breaking the silence. "We monks are the same."

"Not quite," I said, remembering my considerations on the topic from years ago.

"No?"

"Careful attention to rank and position is not our only hope of holding power."

"What else is there?" he asked.

"Magic," I said. "Giftedness as a Practitioner offers power to those who otherwise might never gain it."

Brother Cormac continued to look toward me, but I could see his mind was elsewhere. He was considering my words, and he obviously saw some meaning in them I had not intended, for a smile spread slowly across his face. He set down his cup and saucer beside him and stood.

"I have letters to write," he said and moved to his desk.

I knew I was dismissed. I drank the last of my tea and stood. I walked to the door and went out into the hall. I am still not sure what it was that came to Brother Cormac with my words. Perhaps he will tell me in time.

Fifteenth day, sixth month, in the twenty-ninth year of King Saran's reign

I look back sometimes and wonder that I was so slow-witted. There are things that come about which I should have seen coming, but I always seem to find myself surprised.

King Saran announced today his engagement to Lady Elan Allard—Lord Allard's young sister. That day we sat together in Cormac's office drinking tea: I am certain that is when Allard thought of the match. The way he stopped when Cormac mentioned the king would need to marry a lesser noble, his talk of marriage being one of the ways to advance in rank. Allard himself is too old to wait for Lady Abra to grow up. There will be eyebrows raised if that is Arnau Adamaris' intention—such age differences are not typical except for King Saran's marriages.

Lady Elan is half the age of King Saran, but I do not believe she had any choice in the matter—and what lady would say no to a king? The wedding is to be next month, and I think Lord Allard expects a nephew to solidify his position within the year.

Sixth day, fifth month, in the thirtieth year of King Saran's reign

I sat in Brother Cormac's office today, drinking tea as we normally do. Lord Allard had dropped in. That was not unusual. No. None of it was unusual. But I think the results of this afternoon's conversation will ripple out like waves from a stone thrown into a pond. I cannot foresee what they will be.

Lord Allard is concerned. The whispers have begun. His sister has been married to the king nearly a year, and there is still no heir. Of course, most of the whispers are about the king, not Queen Elan, but still, he worries for her. And, I think, perhaps he worries more for his own position.

"The king has stopped asking me for drinks after dinner," he said today. "I have not spoken to him in weeks."

"You have fallen out of favor?" asked Cormac.

"So it seems." Allard took a drink of his tea.

"Your careful attention to rank and position seems to have gotten you nowhere."

Allard huffed. "I suppose I should give up any dreams I had of a measure of power."

Cormac studied him for a moment. "What if you did not have to?"

Lord Allard raised his head and looked at Cormac. "What do you mean?"

Brother Cormac looked down into his tea, and, staring into it, he spoke again. "You and I have long been proponents of a new system, one in which noble and monk treat each other as allies rather than enemies."

"Aye," said Allard.

"Brother Ezra reminded me of something some time ago. It was the day you spoke to us of the noble's hope for power being rooted in position and rank. When I said to him that we monks had the same system, he countered that we use one element for determining power that you nobles do not have."

"What is that?" Lord Allard looked back and forth between us. I had nearly forgotten that conversation, but it all flooded back to me as Brother Cormac spoke, and I suddenly realized why he had smiled that day.

"Magic," I said. "The youngest novice may gain power quickly if he is gifted in magic."

Cormac looked directly at Allard. "Do you see hope for gaining power in your current situation?"

"No," Lord Allard answered.

"Do you still believe that some cooperation between noble and monk is necessary for the survival of Asael?"

"Aye," said Lord Allard.

Cormac looked at me, but his words were still addressed to Lord Allard. "We have with us in this room one of the most gifted Practitioners of the age, and the system in which he finds himself will not allow him to advance to his fullest potential."

Lord Allard looked at me. "Are you really so gifted?"

I stammered something.

"He is," said Cormac. "Ezra, your modesty is fine, but do not be false. You know you are gifted. You have chafed under the strictures of the order. You have seen lesser men advanced above you in rank. I was here when you came in as a child. The head priest had never seen a child so gifted. There was discussion about whether you might be the promised Rose."

I felt my face flushing. I tried to protest, "No—"

"Do not speak, Brother Ezra," Cormac commanded. "I have watched you with interest for many years, and I have seen what you cannot see. The Ancient Writings' promise of the Rose is a false line of hope to throw to downtrodden peasants. It is not for us—we who know what it is to sit near the king's table and see the scheming and corruption in Asael."

Lord Allard nodded along with Brother Cormac as he continued to speak. "You are gifted beyond your years, Brother Ezra," Cormac said. "Would you not like to be recognized for the work you have done for so long? Would you not like to be known for the gifts you have, rather than squashed away behind closed doors, bowing and praying through the offices of the brotherhood?"

Lord Allard picked up the train of thoughts. "Asael is a broken land," he said. "The king has no heir and is not likely to ever have one. Who better to heal it than us in alliance—noble and monk together—seeking the best for this kingdom?"

"The monks and priests ruled Asael for a long time," said Brother Cormac. "They lost their power to the hands of the kings. Now that grip is tenuous, and it is up to us to restore it. United we can do so—noble and monk together, as Lord Allard said—united we can restore Asael to its former glory."

I was overwhelmed. Something I could not understand stirred within me as they spoke. I stood. "I must think on these things," I said, and I left the room.

I heard Lord Allard behind me as the door swung shut. "Should we go after him?"

"No," said Cormac. "Let him consider what we've said."

I still feel my pulse pounding in my head. Their words excited me, thrilled me even. I look at the state of Asael, and it is hopeless. The line of kings is nearly at an end—it would have to be a miracle of He Who Knows Men's Thinking for Saran to father a son after all these years. There have been dark times throughout Asael's history; I've read of them in the Written Histories. But I don't know that there have ever been any so hopeless as these days.

The stories of the Rose may be no more than legend. The Ancient Writings say that the Rose will be the one who practices Rosefire, though never trained. But no one has practiced Rosefire in hundreds—no, thousands of years. There is no rescue coming for Asael—we are it. We, the monks, are the only hope Asael has. There was an age of the Priests. There has been an age of the Kings. Perhaps it is the dawn of a new age.

Tenth day, twelfth month, in the thirtieth year of King Saran's reign

CORMAC is dead. Dead by a Kingsman's arrow.

Lord Allard imprisoned.

I am stripped of my rank.

The events of these last days have undone me. I—I cannot. I thought—but no, I was—Why am I still here? There is blood on my hands! Why have I survived this?

Seventeenth day, twelfth month, in the thirtieth year of King Saran's reign

I may find I owe my life to Aldan. He has stood for me when I faced punishment, as Lord Allard's sister stood for him. And I let him. Perhaps that is the worst of all. I let him stand when I know what I am.

My hair has been cropped short once more. I am stripped of rank, never to rise again.

And Aldan has offered me a cell in the monastery. I have a home for the rest of my life.

But no one knows I planted the seed of the idea in Cormac's mind. No one knows I considered my position, and chose to join them knowing they sought power for themselves. No one knows I sought it myself.

No one knows but—but He Who Knows Men's Thinking.

I realized just now as I wrote those words that I have not spoken to He Who Knows Men's Thinking in a very long time. I cannot even recall when I stopped. Oh, I have attended to the offices of the order, but I do not know that I have spoken to the Creator on my own in months, perhaps even years.

You know my thoughts. You know my will. You know what I have done. Can I be forgiven? Is it possible?

Eighteenth day, twelfth month, in the thirtieth year of King Saran's reign

I awake in the night with the images in my mind. I shall never be rid of the horrors.

Oh, Creator, erase my mind. Make me like a child again.
Wipe clear my memories!

I have seen the great beauty that is magic flowing from the fingers of a Healer. There are not many of us, and most of us are limited. I have been able to heal injury, but not illness. I knew a monk once who could do the opposite. I have watched flesh and bone knit together under my hands as I sought the power the Creator gave me.

It is an ugly thing when the flesh knits together over a man's nostrils and mouth, suffocating him. I would say it is the most horrible way to die had I not seen worse.

Take it away! It is burned on the inside of my eyelids, so
when I close them for sleep, it is all I see.

Allard has been judged. He will remain in prison for the rest of his life, in solitary confinement in the dungeons of the castle. His scheme to marry his sister to the king may not have panned out for him in terms of position among the leaders of Asael, but it served him well in this. She pled for leniency, and King Saran granted her wish.

I almost envy him his solitary confinement. Aldan visits me daily. He never asks questions. And I give him no answers.

I have no answers, Creator. I no longer have any answers. I am capable of such atrocity. I am a bringer of death.

It flowed from my fingers, the heat that killed him. I felt the power deep in my mind, and I drew it forward. I whispered, "*Sana,*" and felt the strands of heat stretch from my fingers and my palm. They wrapped about him where he sat on horseback. I smelled the singed horsehair and the smoke off his clothes. And still the power flowed. I wanted to show I was worthy of advancement, worthy of the rank that had been denied me for so long. I wanted to show I was gifted.

Your gift was beautiful. I mangled it. You gave me power. I abused it. Turn back time! Stop my actions before they began!

I still smell the singed hair. I still see the blistering flesh. I see his sword grow red with heat in his hand. I hear the crackle of the first flame. He died by my hand, my hand alone, and no one will ever know.

No one but You.

I saw the gruesome corpse before me, and it was as if a switch turned in my mind. I knew this was not the way. The Creator's gift is not this repulsive twisted power.

Will You take me back? Can I ever make it up to You?

You know my thoughts; You know my will. You know I swear this in truth; there is no falsehood in me. I shall never again wield the gift You have given me. I will serve my years as a Helper, but I will never seek the practice of magic again.

I cannot be trusted with the gift. I have used it for evil.

Sixth day, first month, in the thirty-first year of King Saran's reign

YOUNG Lord Arnau Adamaris was granted his reward today. Lord Allard saw it coming, seeing with the clear eyes of another noble. Adamaris has found the rank and position he desired. I wonder if he thinks it worth the cost. I wonder if he grieved when he came upon the smoldering remains of his brother Richard. I wonder if even in his grief, he still thought of the ways this death would serve his own benefit.

Young Lord Arnau Adamaris, younger son, is now the sole heir to his father's holdings in the north. In addition, King Saran has granted him a large estate from the king's own lands, right on the sea, not half a day's journey from the Capital, abutting the land of his brother Gennady's family. Young Adamaris has arranged his marriage prospect to Hakan's daughter, as Allard predicted he would. He will wait until she is of age, of course. It will give him time to build a house on his new estate, Marinel. His marriage will increase his land holdings even more. Lord Hakan's son recently died of an illness and his daughter is now his sole heir.

Is this Your repayment for my actions? That I watch this man—who schemed for power no less than I—gain more than he ever imagined? Or is that my own sense of justice?

I have been calling out to You for weeks now. Will You not answer? Why do You no longer speak comfort to me?

Fifteenth day, second month, in the thirty-first year of King Saran's reign

I heard He Who Knows Men's Thinking today. I rose from my prayers at peace for the first time in months.

I cannot adequately explain what it is like to hear Him. It is as if the most perfect note of music plays, and for a moment, you are the music, and you step from time and you live in the music. And in that moment, you believe the music could heal the world.

I finally stopped crying out. I believe that was all He was waiting for. He knew my thoughts, yet I felt the need for so many, many weeks to speak them aloud to Him.

I rose from my prayers today with a renewed purpose: I shall seek the Rose. I shall work to the glory of He Who Knows Men's Thinking. I shall follow the Creator only, all the days of my life.

Twentieth day, tenth month, in the fortieth year of King Saran's reign

A boy was born at the palace today. After more than ten years of marriage, Queen Elan provided Saran with an heir, Prince Loran. He evidently looks strikingly like his father, even in these first hours of life. I have no doubt. It is a miracle of the Creator, yes, but the line of kings is restored.

Creator, bless this boy. May he be a man of courage, of honor, of kindness, of grace. May he seek You and Your ways. May he find friends among the peasants and the monks so that he will see the kingdom as a whole and not the nobles alone. May he be the instrument You use to restore the land to Yourself.

Fourteenth day, seventh month, in the forty-fifth year of King Saran's reign

I heard news of Lord Adamaris and his young wife the other day. They have welcomed a son at Marinel. They named him Richard.

Lord Adamaris is now one of the most powerful noblemen in the kingdom, and he has a son to carry on his line. I have heard that he hates magic, that he came upon the smoldering, disfigured corpse of his brother and understood his death was at the hands of a monk; that he has sworn never to allow magic in his home.

Yet Lady Abra Adamaris, when she was a girl, studied the Ancient Writings. Her mother, Lady Hakan, saw to it that she was educated about the ways of the monks. I wonder if Lady Abra will teach her son to know He Who Knows Men's Thinking. I wonder if she will be allowed to do so.

The Ancient Writings teach us that death is not an

end; it is merely another step, and life goes on beyond the grave. If that is so, I hope Richard Adamaris is able to see his namesake. I hope the boy grows to make him proud.

Nineteenth day, ninth month, in the sixty-fifth year of King Saran's reign

I visited Lord Allard. He is allowed visitors now. I suppose Saran has forgiven him enough, or forgotten him enough, to lessen the strictures of his solitary confinement.

I had heard his mind is going. He lived alone with his demons for over thirty years. Perhaps it is no surprise.

He was lucid today, though. He remembered me and greeted me by name when I entered the small room where he sat on a bench beside a wooden table.

I sat down across from him. I knew why I had come, but I could not bring myself to start the conversation.

"You ran away that day," he said.

"Aye. When I saw what I had done, I could not take it."

"Have you been running since?"

"I stopped many years ago," I said. "But I have been working since."

"Working for what?" he asked.

"The reform of the order. We loved magic too much in the old days."

Lord Allard smiled slightly. "We loved power too much in the old days."

"Aye." I nodded as I spoke. "You heard of the death of Prince Loran?" I asked.

Lord Allard nodded. "It is a sad thing."

"He was beloved," I said.

"What will become of Asael?" Lord Allard asked. "Saran is too old to marry for a fourth time."

"I've heard rumors of a Council," I said. "Established by Adamaris."

He let out his breath in a laugh. "Of course he will be in power. Arnau Adamaris always finds the sunny side of trouble."

"He lost his brother," I said. I tried not to sound defensive. Disquieted as Lord Adamaris had always made me, I have come to the conclusion that his putting down of our rebellion was a great act. He Who Knows Men's Thinking used him to scatter us to the wind, striking a blow to the order that allowed for the reforms we have enacted in the past thirty years.

"I lost my whole life," said Allard. His gaze grew unfocused then, and he began to scratch at the tabletop, digging with a fingernail I could see had been bloodied with wear before. I thought I heard him mutter, "The dark." I could not get another straight word from him. I shall try to visit him again after the funeral.

Twenty-fifth day, tenth month, in the sixty-fifth year of King Saran's reign

MY visit to Allard has been delayed long enough. I can make no sense of the things I have seen. I went today, hoping he would be lucid once more. I had to tell him.

"You are here to tell me more of Adamaris' council?" he said. "I want none of it."

"I believe the Creator may have a plan other than the Council."

"And what is that?" asked Lord Allard.

"I have seen the Rose," I said.

He sat straight and looked at me keenly. His eyes were clear. "Where?"

"I sat at the funeral and lifted my thoughts to He Who Knows Men's Thinking," I said. "And he directed my eyes across to where the nobles sat."

"The Rose is not a noble!"

"I think we may have misinterpreted that passage all these years," I said. "The text simply says the Rose will be without honor. There are plenty of unrecognized nobles."

Lord Allard rolled his eyes. "Aye, but what of the Rose? Where did you look?"

"Lord Adamaris' box."

He shoved back from the table, turning over the bench with his energy. "Do not mention him again to me," he said. His eyes flashed.

"At his son and daughter and the servant girl who was with them."

"They must be children!"

"The young man is older than Adamaris was when he first came to court." I paused. "He is named for his uncle."

"And you believe one of them is the Rose?"

"I do. Clearly as a bell, I heard the Creator direct me to look. He has told me I would live to see the Rose, and when I saw them, I knew this was the time.

"Which one?"

"I don't know," I said. "I saw them again outside the cathedral after the funeral. They stood close together, stricken with grief. And I knew, like I have known nothing else in my life, that He Who Knows Men's Thinking had sent the Rose."

Lord Allard leaned down and picked up the wooden bench, setting it again by the table. He sat down upon it, wearily. "The Rose from the household of Arnau Adamaris?"

"It seems impossible," I said. "His hatred of magic is legendary in Asael. He has had no part in the religious reforms of recent years."

Allard sighed. "My mind is not always clear," he said.

"I know."

"But when it has been, I've studied the Writings."

"Aye?"

"We were wrong. All those years ago."

I nodded.

"The Writings say the Rose will save the line of kings," said Lord Allard.

"Through Rosefire."

"Aye," he said. "It's an act of magic that cannot be used for selfish gain. It cannot be used to get power. If it is, the practitioner's life will be demanded in return."

I chuckled. "So our plans for monk and noble ruling together, our desire to use magic to gain power..."

"If we had read the texts, we would have seen we were wrong."

"I had stopped listening to He Who Knows Men's Thinking," I said. "I listened instead to Cormac and to my own heart—I wanted recognition, and you were willing to offer it to me."

"The Ancient Writings tell us the Rose is the hope of Asael," said Lord Allard. "I believe that now, as I never did before."

"Aye," I said.

"So you must find the Rose."

I left him then, and came back here to this cell Aldan gave me all those years ago. I remember how his daily visits used to chafe, how I wished for Lord Allard's forced solitude. But he is a broken man now, and I am not. I have the Creator to thank for that. For His forgiveness of the horrors of my past. And Aldan, for his faithful love and care.

Word came through this evening that Lady Karan Adamaris has run away rather than marry Lord Gennady and has taken with her Lord Richard and a servant girl, Sephanya. No one knows where they have gone, and their father has been searching for days already.

I know I have seen the Rose. And I know I will again. He Who Knows Men's Thinking will show me the path.

It is time for me to put away this journal and spend my days on my knees. I will open the lid of the old sea chest in my cell that was once Brother Cormac's, and I will place this book inside. And perhaps someday someone will tell the rest of my story.

PART THREE

A faithful account of the genesis and activities of the Followers,
here written by Karan Adamaris

CHAPTER 17

WE'D brought the simplest gowns I owned, and not one of them was appropriate for the environment in which we found ourselves. I was no good at sewing, so Anya had given me the task of ripping out the stitches that joined the skirt to the bodice of one of the gowns. The plan was to use the skirt's fabric to make a new dress for me. I tried to do as little damage as possible with my clumsy fingers, but a part of my mind wondered whether it was of any use. As far as either of us knew, Anya couldn't sew either. She'd mended buttons and small tears in seams in the weeks that I'd known her, but she'd never even attempted to make new clothing.

I sat near the fire, using the light it gave off to see my work. Every few minutes, a gust of air would whirl in from the entrance and disrupt the smoke's dance upward to the cracks in the cave's ceiling, which served as vents, turning it into my face and setting me choking and coughing. Anya was on the far side of the flames, cutting up root vegetables for our evening meal: a stew to be cooked over the fire. Richard was out. He'd left early that morning to go deep into a nearby forest, searching for dry wood.

We heard noise coming from the entrance, a narrow cleft that wound from the outdoors between two walls of rock to the wide cave where we sat. Anya and I both looked toward the black crevice, frozen in place. In the week we'd been there, I'd still not become accustomed to that moment: the brief seconds between the first noise and the person's entrance into the cave. For the space of about half a minute, I had no idea if friend or foe had arrived and always feared the worst, imagining my father's figure emerging from the darkness.

Richard stepped into the light, his arms full of wood. I raised my eyes upward in relief but quickly closed them: the rough stone above our heads was a fearsome reminder that we were not safe—in my mind, it collapsed upon us a dozen times a day. All Richard's assurances that these caves had stood for hundreds of years did no good. I tried to shut out the knowledge that the fissured stone above our heads was supporting tons of earth: the moors and forests of my childhood.

I dropped my work and scrambled to my feet to help Richard. If I was active, my mind wandered less. I reached for the wood in his arms and found that it was damp.

"We'll have to spread it out along the wall and allow it to dry in the heat—there's no dry wood anywhere," he said.

"It's been raining for two days," said Anya. "Perhaps it's no wonder."

"We should have stockpiled more before the rain began," I said.

Anya chuckled. "I'll add that to our list of things we've learned about living in the wilderness."

"I've got more outside," Richard said. "Come help me with it?"

I followed him through the dark, narrow fracture between the stone that had become our front hall. We stepped out into the cool, misty grey day. I took a deep breath and looked about.

"You should be sure to step outside each morning," Richard said, watching me.

I drank in the sight of the sea, the rhythmic beating of the waves against the sand, the overcast sky. I lifted my face to the drops of rain that were coming down steadily from above and for a moment imagined that the stone roof of our cave was like this firmament above me now—which fell to earth in painless, nourishing precipitation, rather than the jagged shards of my imagination.

"There's so much stone," I said.

Richard smiled. "Aye. We are living in caves, after all."

I gave him a baleful look and began picking up wood.

"You should be sure to come outside every day, though," Richard said. "You are having a harder time with our accommodations than Anya and I."

I nodded. The first morning, I had opened my eyes in the flickering firelight and seen the rock above our heads for the first time. I had panicked and screamed. It took both Richard and Anya twenty minutes to calm me. Richard kept looking to Anya and asking if she could do anything. She had shaken her head at him and held me tightly, my head buried under her collarbone as she whispered words of comfort to me.

Later she had told us that a spell had come to mind which would have calmed me, but she had been certain that I needed to overcome the fear on my own. Richard was angry at her for not using magic to help me, but I understood—I didn't want to forget that fear or the panic it had brought. I needed it. I needed to know that this way was a sacrifice, too. That I was not simply shirking my part and making Anya and Richard suffer with me.

Because I was the reason they were here. I felt the guilt of that every time I saw Richard pulling a splinter out of his hands or struggling with a fire, every time I watched Anya cutting up vegetables or skinning game. They were here because I was not marrying Gennady.

"It's getting better," I said. "I learned to rip out stitches today."

"Who would have thought our greatest struggle would be finding you appropriate clothing?" Richard said. "You were always so picky about your dresses."

I threw a pebble in his direction. "I don't think I would call it our greatest struggle," I said. "Don't forget that you haven't been able to bring down anything larger than a rabbit with your bow."

"I consider it a sign of great skill that I have been able to get quick rabbits and not simply slow, ponderous deer."

I laughed. "Richard Adamaris: always able to present the facts in the most positive light."

It was nice to laugh again. The days following my eighteenth celebration had not lent themselves to much laughter. We all tried frantically to plan our departure in secret while still going on as if nothing were amiss with my father.

The afternoon after the celebration, Father had called me into his study. He praised my conduct from the night before and then picked up a letter lying on the desk before him.

"I received this from Gennady this afternoon," he said.

My chest tightened. I felt the fear creeping up on me again. I handed it over to He Who Knows Men's Thinking and took a deep breath. "Oh?"

"It is a formal proposal for your hand in marriage."

My breath quickened. "Do you approve of it?" I asked, my voice not quite steady.

He looked down at the handwritten text on the sheet and read aloud, "The Lady Karan's quick mind seems to be matched by a quick wit. She is lovely to the eye, and her connections—you, my Lord, and your late wife's royal blood—are beyond reproach. The line of Gennady can only be enhanced by such an addition." He stopped reading and looked up at me. "He laughed last night during your first dance. What did you say to him?"

"He asked about my faults, and I told him I can't sew."

My father chuckled. "You'll never have to sew again, my dear, with a marriage like this. If he can offer this much as a bride price, his father must have left their affairs in better order than I'd hoped." He looked back at the letter. "He's not put off by the size of the dowry, but now that he's actually offered, I may add something to it. I've let your tutor go. You won't have time for studies in the next two weeks."

I gulped. "Two weeks?"

He looked up at me. "Yes. Gennady suggests a wedding date in two weeks, and I agree. There's no reason to delay. Not when we're all in agreement."

I desperately fought to keep calm. Our plan was to leave in a week; nothing need change. "I will have much to do then, in the next few days."

"Yes." My father was already distracted, pulling out a blank piece of paper and uncorking his inkwell to write back to Gennady. He glanced at me, about to dismiss me. I must have betrayed some of my emotions in my expression. "There's nothing to fear, Karan. Married life is full of minor adjustments. You're quite capable of adapting." He paused as a thought struck him, "Perhaps I should have asked the Makrams to stay a bit longer. Lady Makram could have guided you through some of your questions."

I thanked He Who Knows Men's Thinking that the Makrams had departed early that morning. Having Edmund around any more than he had been in the past two weeks could lead to someone suspecting a connection between him and the rest of us.

"Oh, surely she could come a few days early for the wedding," I said.

"That's perfect," said Father. "I'll write and ask today."

The following days had been a flurry of activity. I had been so concerned about my father discovering our secret plans that I did not laugh much during that week. I wasn't certain how a bride should behave anyway. My father knew that I was not in love with Gennady, so there was no need to pretend that, but I had no idea how I should act—I knew I probably shouldn't be laughing.

I leaned down to pick up a last piece of wood. I hadn't had time to think about living in the wilderness, either. I could not have imagined how much work it would be. Preparing a meal took the efforts of all three of us. I was daily grateful for Anya, who seemed to know intuitively which root vegetables we found in the forest were edible, and Richard, whose hunting skills brought us meat—even if I did tease him about the size.

I was, again, the one without a skill that was useful in our new environment. So I carried wood and ripped out stitches and cut up vegetables, all the while hoping to happen upon that one thing I could do well.

I followed Richard into the cave, through the dark fissure and into the welcoming brightness of our fireplace. We spread the wood out along the wall and then joined Anya by the fire to dry off from our time outside. I picked up the dress and began ripping stitches again. Richard found the small, straight branches he had been stripping for new arrow shafts. Anya was finishing the last of the vegetables, dumping them into the stew pot. Then she sat back with a pad of paper to try to sketch out a pattern for my new dress.

We all worked quietly for a time. Richard and Anya had returned to their cool distance after we settled into the cave. Without the need to rescue me, they had no motivation to return to the easy comfort of the early days. Richard's refusal to tell Anya he thought she was the Rose still rankled her, and something else I couldn't quite identify continued to hold Richard aloof. Neither one was willing to broach the topic.

I paused in my ripping and watched them for a few moments before I finally couldn't take it anymore. "What's next?" I asked.

They both started and looked up at me.

"Next?" said Richard.

"In our plan," I said. "We've been here nearly a week now. Tomorrow is my wedding day. We've obviously burned that bridge, that plan—and don't misunderstand me, I am glad we did—but other than learning we should stockpile dry wood before the next rain, I don't really see what our future here is."

Anya smiled, "Next on my list is getting you into more reasonable clothes."

Richard shook his head. "No, you're right, Karan. We do need a plan."

"If we're going to gather followers of the Rose, then we need to be meeting people. I haven't seen a soul in days besides you two," I said, trying to tread lightly around the topic of the Rose.

Richard's eyes flashed at me, and then he looked over to Anya. He opened his mouth but closed it again before speaking.

I closed my eyes for a moment and tried a different question. "When we do gather followers of the Rose, what then?"

"We overthrow the Council, of course," said Richard.

"And replace their rule with what?" asked Anya.

"The Rose will rule."

"Where in the Writings does it say the Rose is to be ruler?" asked Anya.

Richard looked at her, his head cocked slightly. "The Rose is the hope of Asael," he said.

"It's a long leap from 'hope' to king," said Anya.

"How else is the Rose supposed to save the kingdom?" asked Richard.

"By saving the line of kings," said Anya.

"The line of kings died with Loran."

"Don't try to use that argument! You said yourself that the indirect line still stands."

"Yes, but Briyanne? Gennady? Is that the kind of rule you want? A wet fish or an iron fist? If that was the plan, then we should have left Karan to marry Gennady. Then at least when the Rose saved the line of Kings there would be someone with a heart near the throne."

"I couldn't!" Anya said, looking over at me. "I couldn't let you sacrifice yourself like that! Not when I might find another way later."

Richard pounced. "*You* might find another way? What do you mean?"

"I—I," Anya stammered. She knew where Richard was going, and she was not yet ready to join him there. "I meant *we* might find another solution! Something that will save the line of kings without sacrificing one girl's happiness—"

"Shh!" I interrupted them, putting up a hand.

"What is it?" asked Richard.

"Shh!" I said, more forcefully. I thought I had heard a noise at the cave entrance. "Get your sword!" I said to Richard.

He scrambled to his feet and picked up his sword.

I heard the noise again; we all did. We turned toward the dark crack in the wall, tensed.

In a single moment, all the fears of the previous weeks came rushing back upon me. I was certain my father had found us and was going to drag me back and force me to marry Gennady. Tears came to my eyes as all the things I'd ever imagined about life as the wife of a nobleman of my father's choosing came rushing back upon me.

I felt Anya come up beside me. She took my hand, and we stood behind Richard. "He Who Knows Men's Thinking knows your fear," she whispered.

I gripped her hand, and we faced the crack in the wall together.

CHAPTER 18

THE form that emerged from the darkness was that of Thayer. Richard lowered his sword, and we all relaxed.

"Thayer!" Anya cried. Lanica and Tay followed him into the cave, coming blinking into the light of the fire. Anya rushed forward to hug them.

"You've all come?" Richard asked.

"Aye," said Lanica. "Young Lord Makram told us of your plan, and we wish to be with you."

My heart jumped. "Edmund is at Marinel?" I asked.

"Aye," said Thayer. "He said to tell you all is going well."

Richard was the first to realize we were all still standing about. "Come in; sit," he said. He looked at Thayer. "Did you bring a horse? I can show you where we stable ours."

"Aye. And we have belongings in the saddlebags," Thayer said.

"Lanica and I can bring those in," said Anya. "Tay, will you help Lady Karan tend the stew?"

"Aye," the boy said, looking at me seriously.

"Come over here, Tay," I said, taking his hand and drawing him nearer to the fire. "It's warmer this way." The boy shivered and allowed me to lead him closer to the flames.

"How long have you been here?" he asked, looking around.

"Over a week," I said, following his eyes. "We haven't made it particularly cozy yet, have we?"

The boy applied his expert eye to the furnishings: piles of blankets in one corner, piles of food stores in the other, stone walls all around. "I think you need tapestries," he said matter-of-factly.

I laughed. "Well, it's a good thing your mother has come then, isn't it? Though I doubt you had the space to carry a loom on horseback."

"No, we didn't," the boy said. "But Lord Makram talked about bringing one soon."

Again, my heart jumped—Edmund coming soon? I knew everything must have been going well for that to be planned. I looked at the stew in the pot and stirred it, impatiently waiting for Thayer, Richard, Lanica, and Anya to return.

By the time they did, Tay and I had found bowls and spoons enough for all of us to eat. Lanica had brought more food for the stockpile, and we added fresh bread and cheese to the meal, making a celebration out of it.

We sat and talked, and Thayer and Lanica told us what had happened at Marinel since we'd left. Evidently, our father had hired men from the village to search for us and had spent the better part of two days on horseback himself, looking far and wide. The search parties hadn't come down the cliff face near our caves; Edmund had been right that few people knew of these caves.

After two or three days of searching, during which he had continued preparations for the wedding, hoping he could sweep our disappearance under the rug and go on once we were back as if nothing had happened, he had to make a decision. Lord Makram and Edmund had come down, at my father's request—further evidence of how much he trusted Makram. Edmund had been right about the strength of that bond, too. They were the only noble family at that point to know the truth of our disappearance.

It was Makram who convinced my father that it was time to stop the charade. If he was preemptive in his announcement, Makram reasoned, he could minimize the damage—painting us as ungrateful rebels and himself as a loyal noble whose commitment to the Council could not be questioned.

So that was his course. He wrote a letter to Gennady. I can only imagine what he might have said about us in it. With no hope of forging that connection, still, he had to walk a fine line—if Gennady were ever to trust him again, my father must show that we had duped him without making himself look foolish.

"They've laid most of the blame on Miss Anya," Lanica said. "Pointed to Lady Karan's strong character in getting her way with this new servant against her father's wishes. Then pointed to Miss Anya's wiles in convincing a young, still inexperienced girl to disobey her father who knew what was best for her."

Richard snorted. "And me?"

"You've been taken in by a seductress," said Thayer.

I looked at Anya, pained to hear these words were being said about her. She shook her head at me. "It is not true," she said. "It doesn't matter."

Edmund had managed to bring up the matter of him serving as secretary quite casually; they had been talking over dinner one night when my father had mentioned how angry he was at Richard for leaving him with so much work to do.

"Young Lord Makram was able to suggest that he might assist with the work to be done. I think both his father and yours took it as initiative on his part," said Thayer.

Lord Makram had returned home, leaving Edmund behind to work as my father's personal secretary. The next evening, he found time to get to the village and meet Thayer and Lanica—we had told him about them—and tell them everything.

"And your decision to come here," asked Richard. "How did that come about?"

"It was that night when Young Lord Makram was visiting with us. He told us how you came to believe the Ancient Writings," Lanica said.

"Lanica was raised among the faithful," said Thayer. "I thought the Writings were just stories until I met her. It was her father that led me to believe—he showed me the ways He Who Knows Men's Thinking is active in our world today."

"We have raised Tay in the ways of the faithful," said Lanica. "That day you healed him, Miss Anya, we didn't want to say anything for we didn't know how you'd take it—"

"But the night that Young Lord Makram came and told us your story—" Thayer gestured to all of us, "We knew we had to come join you because..." He trailed off.

"Because you think I am the Rose," said Anya.

There was a beat of silence. Richard's eyes widened and settled on her face. She looked directly back at him.

"Oh come, Richard!" she said. "You've been dancing around saying it for weeks now."

"I didn't want to force you—"

"And instead, you've insinuated and hinted."

"I'm sorry!" he protested. "I thought it would be better if you realized it by—"

"Well, I didn't! Karan let it slip, and it has been weighing on me for weeks—this expectation you have of me."

Richard turned on me. "You—"

Anya interrupted him. "No! You do not get to blame her in this! Did you ever think that maybe I would want to talk through such an idea, rather than having it there, in the back of my mind, feeling that it might be true, but not being able to say anything about it to the person I care most about because he has some foolish set idea that being the Rose means ruling the kingdom!"

Lanica, Thayer, and Tay were silent. I watched as the anger crackled between my brother and my friend. I had noted her statement that she cared for him. I wondered what Richard would say to it.

"Do you think you are the Rose, Anya?" Richard asked, quiet in the face of her anger. I could see him struggling to remain calm. Vestiges of the pain I had seen before when he spoke of Anya were in his eyes.

"I don't know," she said.

"What do you feel?" he asked. Already, he knew her well enough to know that her heart led her.

Tears sprung to her eyes. "I feel that you may be right, and I don't know what to do with such responsibility. I'm terrified!" The tears spilled over, and she put her face in her hands, quietly sobbing.

I looked back to Richard; the pain was all over his face as he watched her cry. He raised his eyes to mine and indicated with his head that I should go to her. I sighed and moved closer to her. Putting my arms around her shoulders, I let her weep.

After a few moments of quiet, the only sound Anya's sobs, Lanica gently broached conversation again. "Miss Anya?" She waited for Anya to stop crying and look up at her. "Miss Anya, the Writings never say exactly how the Rose saves Asael, but they are clear about one thing: the Rose helps the people. Perhaps that is the place to start."

"Remember the day you were there in our home in the village," Thayer said, "and the people came asking for help? We tried to turn them away, but you would not let us. I saw how it was not what you expected your afternoon to be, but when the people came, you were willing to help."

"You said, 'How can I let them go on like this, knowing I have the ability to help?'" said Lanica. "That's at the heart of the Rose's service to the people—being willing to serve. Perhaps that is all you need to focus on now."

Anya nodded and swallowed another sob. "I can do that much." She looked over to Richard. "Rose or not, you have been right about this—if I can help, I must. I will promise to help the people of Asael, to the best of my ability."

Richard nodded.

"Will that suffice, my Lord?" she said.

He started as if she had slapped him. Color suffused his cheeks, and his eyes glinted. Without a word, he stood and walked out of the cave.

Anya closed her eyes. "That was cruel," she said. "Will you go to him, Karan? Tell him I am sorry."

I scrambled to my feet, picked up my cloak and threw it over my shoulders, and followed my brother outdoors. The mist had cleared, but the sky was still overcast. I found Richard sitting on a small boulder, throwing pebbles at the waves.

"She says she's sorry," I said, coming up beside him.

"You told her? When I asked you not to?"

"It was an accident. I was telling her how Edmund was worried about me, and I said we should be worried about her; she's the Rose."

"And now she's angry at me for being the one to keep it from her."

"No, she's angry at you for acting like you have the right to determine the course of her actions."

He threw another pebble at a wave.

"You don't, you know," I continued. "You cannot force her to rule over Asael."

"I know, but if she would listen, she would see that the Writings clearly indicate the Rose will lead Asael."

"There's nothing clear about it, Richard. The Rose is the hope of Asael—that's all we know. And if she is the Rose—"

"If? Now you are doubting me as well?"

"No! I believe she is the Rose, but there's only one proof in the Ancient Writings: Rosefire. I can't see any situation where she's going to practice Rosefire, so we're all going to need to take it on a little faith."

"I am certain she is the Rose."

"I know you are, Richard. But she is also your friend. And she needs you."

"She needs you. You are a better support than I could ever be."

"She needs *you*. Didn't you hear—"

He scrambled up from his seat on the boulder and clapped his hand over my mouth. "Do not say it. Do not repeat it."

I pushed his hand away. "Why not? She cares—"

He stopped me again, his eyes blazing with anger. "I cannot distract her from her purpose. She is the Rose, the hope of Asael."

Suddenly it became clear. I understood his behavior over the recent weeks. He had been deliberately distancing himself. My heart ached for him, for her.

"Richard, we don't know that she's the Rose," I began.

"Do not speak those words to me!" he shouted. "Don't you think I tell myself the same thing in every moment of weakness? No. She is the Rose. I cannot stand in the way of her purpose and her destiny."

"Oh, Richard," I said. Tears welled up in my eyes for the pain he was causing himself. I reached out and pulled him into an embrace. He leaned his head down into my neck and wept.

When his tears had finally ceased, he sat back on the boulder and lifted his face to the cold ocean breeze. "This you must promise me will never slip out."

"I promise," I said.

"It is so much more important than telling her I thought she was the Rose."

"I know," I said, sitting beside him. I thought of the dream of the cabins in the mountains and the strength it had taken for me to wrench myself away from that path. I knew the danger of hope. "I will not tell her."

We sat in silence in the chilly wind for some time. I slipped my hand into my brother's, and we sat together, letting go of our dreams.

Perhaps half an hour had passed before Richard roused himself with a shiver. "We should go in," he said.

We rose and walked toward the cave entrance. As we reached it, an idea popped into my mind.

"Oh!" I exclaimed. "Thayer could make my dresses!"

Richard laughed, and I joined him, and we made our way into our new home.

CHAPTER 19

In the days that followed, we settled into a routine in the cave. Richard built frames of branches that we could set up with blankets over them to make sleeping areas separate from cooking and living space.

Lanica helped us organize the foodstuffs and fire into an orderly kitchen. Thayer built a small, makeshift oven from stones. Tay followed us around and asked questions incessantly. To get him out of the way, I began telling him stories from the Written Histories. Familiar as they were with the Ancient Writings, Thayer and Lanica had never seen a copy of the Written Histories.

"It is the nobleman's history," Thayer explained. "You don't hear much about peasants in them, I'd wager."

"Not much," I said, noticing it for the first time. "Is there a book of the peasant's history?"

"No book, milady," Lanica said. "We tell our stories. Like you have been to Tay, around the fire of an evening."

"The Spoken Histories," I mused.

"Maybe that's why we call the book the Written Histories," Anya said. "To differentiate the two."

I had not realized, before those first weeks in the cave, how much of Asael was built around separating the classes. The nobles had constructed for themselves an entire society that stood upon, yet was wholly insulated from, the peasant class.

The songs Thayer and Lanica sang around the fire after dinner were completely foreign to me. The stories they told of their history fit like a glove into the events of the Written Histories but were never mentioned in the text.

Richard and Anya had returned to their cordial distance. The tension was gone, but I could see neither one was happy with the state of their friendship.

Thayer had, bless him, taken over the project of sewing my new dresses. I tried to help, but we quickly learned that the change in environment had done nothing for my sewing skills, so Anya helped while I told Tay stories nearby so they could listen.

One day I told of the uprising known as Allard's Rebellion. It had taken place only about thirty years earlier and was in one of the addendums to the Written Histories. A nobleman sought to gain favor with the king, and offered his sister as a bride after King Saran's second wife died. But she did not have a son soon after their marriage, and seeing that King Saran had no heir, Lord Allard had sided with the monks to seize power using their magic. He had teamed with a monk named Brother Cormac. Allard had been convinced that he could control the monks and use their magic for his own benefit. Cormac and the monks who followed him saw Allard as a tool to get into the upper echelons of society, gaining power. The nobles faithful to the king saw Allard as rejecting noble rule by siding with the monks.

A hard-fought battle was waged in which no party came out unscathed. Cormac was killed, and the monks who survived quietly returned to their places and did their best to distance themselves from the Rebellion. Allard was imprisoned as an enemy of the crown.

"And a young nobleman named Arnau Adamaris made his fortune," Thayer said. "We have our own version of this story."

Richard sat straight and looked at Thayer. "Arnau Adamaris? Our father?"

"Aye," said Thayer. "Did you not know? Lord Adamaris led the forces which put down Allard's Rebellion."

"I had no idea," said Richard.

"He was a low-ranking nobleman, but his efforts in the battle won him the recognition of King Saran. His land holdings were more than doubled as a reward—the king used to own most of the land that is now Marinel," Thayer said.

"And the king offered him any bride he wanted. And he chose the king's niece," said Lanica.

"Mother," I said.

Richard looked at me. "How have we never heard this story?"

"I doubt Lord Adamaris likes to flaunt that his rank and position are fairly recent acquisitions," said Anya. "That would not do well for his standing on the Council."

"And it was a horrible battle," said Lanica. "I cannot imagine he wants to remember it often."

"What was so horrible?" I asked.

"The monks fought with magic," said Thayer. "Magic turned to evil; magic used for violence. It was one of the reasons the monks fell apart so quickly. A good number of them had no idea they would be dealing out magic to destroy other human beings, and when it came down to it, they couldn't stomach it."

"Aye," said Anya. "I don't think I would be able to handle that myself."

"Many of Lord Adamaris' men were killed by magic. His own brother Richard was killed."

Richard and I looked at each other, eyes wide. That we had lived our whole lives without knowing this part of our own history shocked me. But suddenly pieces began to make sense: Father's hatred of magic, his dislike of most other noble families, his deep love of Richard over me, even his desire to see me marry Gennady was now, in this new light, the strivings of a man to be accepted among those he knew were not his peers.

WE had all been together about two weeks when I went one day with Thayer and Richard to a village about an hour away in order to replenish our supplies. From the caves, we rode about a quarter of a mile up the shoreline before we came to the narrow, switch-back trail up the cliff face. Our horses were sure-footed, but from time to time as we slowly made our way up, I would glance down to the waves thrumming against the beach below, imagining the fall. The top of the path was almost indistinguishable from the rest of the cliff edge—the very thing that made it a per-fect hiding place. I took note of the landmarks by the path entrance, in case I would have to find it myself. I breathed easier when we turned to cross the moors. We rode along, our horses' saddle bags empty, dreaming of fresh cheese and eggs.

The village was one where we were unknown. Our hiding place was within an hour's ride of four different villages, and we had decided to visit them in a rotation so that we would not grow too familiar at any of them. As we rode in to the main street, I looked around. The only village I had ever been to was Thayer and Lanica's, and this one seemed quite similar. We stopped first at the tailor's, where Thayer picked up bolts of cloth and spools of thread. Then we moved on to the bakery. My mouth watered over the cakes and cookies, but our purpose was to purchase coarse flour and yeast. Lanica had been able to get the little stone oven working well enough for baking.

Our final stop was the grocer's, where I wandered about as Thayer haggled the price of eggs. There was a little girl, maybe five years old, sitting on top of a barrel of grain.

She caught my eye as I was walking and waved at me. I waved back and moved closer to her.

"Hello," I said.

"Hello. Do you see my doll?"

I looked at the knitted doll in her arms. "Aye. She's lovely. What's her name?"

"Sephanya," she said.

"Why, that's my friend's name!" I said, startled.

"Really?"

"Yes."

"Is she here?"

"No, I'm sorry. She's at our home."

"I got Sephanya for my birthday," the little girl said. "How did you meet your friend?"

I smiled slightly. For a moment, I wavered on how to answer that question, then a single clear thought went through my mind: If people are to follow the Rose, I thought, they need to hear her story.

"She arrived on my doorstep on a cold, rainy night," I began. "The servants knew that my father was a hard man and didn't give to charity, so they tried to shut her out in the cold."

The little girl watched me as I spoke, attending to every word.

"My brother and I heard the commotion and went to see what was happening. I heard her asking for help, and her voice was the prettiest voice I had ever heard. Then my father came to the door and took it away from the maid. As he began to push it shut on the girl's face, a new courage

I'd never experienced came over me, and I called out for him to stop."

The girl's eyes widened. "Did he?"

"Yes!" I said. "He stopped, and he turned to me. And my father, who always gets his own way, let me take in a waif from our doorstep on a cold autumn night. I reached down to help her to her feet, and my life has not been the same since."

I had not realized as I told the girl the story that a woman was standing nearby. She moved then, and I looked up into her face. Her eyes were bright, and her cheeks had spots of red on them. "*Thus I will come, like the unknown waif, and ye who welcome me will be blessed,*" she quoted.

I nodded slowly, not sure what I should do next. "Do—" I stammered.

The woman moved a step closer and put her arm around the little girl. I realized that they must be the wife and daughter of the grocer. "The Rose is really come?" the woman asked. "In this time of need, the Rose is really come?"

I didn't know how Anya would respond to a stranger coming to ask for the Rose. I didn't know if she would be angry with me for raising someone's expectations. I wasn't even sure she was ready to say that she was the Rose. But I had to follow my own convictions.

"She is. And she is the hope of Asael. Would you like to meet her?"

The woman nodded, her wide eyes echoed in the face of her daughter beside her.

"She is at our home. It is about an hour's ride."

"I will speak to my husband," the woman said. She turned and moved toward the grocer, who was still working deals with Thayer and Richard.

I grasped the little girl's hand and helped her jump down so we could join them. As we arrived, the woman was speaking low in her husband's ear.

I turned quickly to Thayer and Richard and said, under my breath, "I told the child the story of Anya's arrival, and the woman knows the story of the waif."

They both looked at me in surprise for a moment. Then Richard smiled. "Perhaps it is time to begin telling the story of the Rose."

The grocer heard him as his wife had finished speaking. "This girl, then, who arrived on your doorstep, she is the Rose?"

Richard nodded. "I am as certain as I have ever been about anything."

"She is a Practitioner," Thayer said. "One of the most powerful I have ever seen."

The grocer and his wife looked us over. We were a strange lot, Thayer with his simple tailor's clothes, Richard with his nobleman's hunting garb, and me, with a peasant's dress made out of finer material than the tailor in this village had in his stores.

"We've left our homes to follow her," I said. "We don't yet know what path we will be taking, but we are with her for the journey."

The woman's expression changed. I saw in it the expectation of the faces on the tapestry in my room. She looked at her husband.

"We must meet her," she said.

He nodded slowly. "The Lord of this estate is not a member of the Council, but he has already begun implementing new regulations and taxes upon us without the permission of the king. I fear it will only get worse if the Council takes power. They will allow him to run this estate as he sees fit, as long as they receive their cut of the taxes. Asael is in need of hope. If ever there was a time for the Rose to come, it is now."

"Will you come with us?" Richard asked. "We are living on the coast. It's only about an hour's ride. You could join us for our evening meal."

The grocer and his wife looked at each other, still deciding. The little girl reached up and tugged on her father's sleeve. "Papa," she said. "I want to meet Sephanya."

The man reached down and picked up his daughter. "We will come. I can close the store for the rest of the day."

And so it was that we left the village with three new friends, the newest followers of the Rose. And with that, our ranks began to grow, as the story was told by one to another, to yet another. Those who had believed for so many years that He Who Knew Men's Thinking would send the Rose at the time of Asael's greatest need found their hope fulfilled in the girl who had no past, and whose future was unknown.

CHAPTER 20

IN the following weeks, our numbers grew. Some, like Thayer and Lanica, left their homes and joined us in the caves. Others went on with their industries, still living in their communities. They visited us regularly and kept us supplied with food. It was mostly through their efforts that the story spread. They would tell their friends, tell their villages, and one village would report to another. Like flame spreading through a knot of branches, word moved from person to person that the Rose had come. The kindling was dry and ready for burning. With each new person who arrived at the caves, we heard more stories of the nobles oppressing the peasants on their lands, demanding taxes and unreasonable work hours.

Richard and I continued to travel regularly, sometimes with Anya, sometimes by ourselves. We told those we met the story of Anya's arrival, the story of how she healed Tay, and the stories we were daily seeing in the caves as followers came looking for the Rose.

Anya had accepted her role—still with concerns, but when people arrived needing help, she would stand and find out how she could serve. People came with illnesses, injuries, deformities, disorders of the mind, and we saw them healed.

Richard and I had returned from a long trip to a village far from the coast. We had been away for nearly a week. The journey itself took the better part of two days, and our time in the village had been extended when more and more people kept coming to hear the stories we had to tell. My voice was hoarse from so much speaking.

The wind had whipped us as we came across the moors, and we followed the path carefully down the cliff as we watched the breakers crash against the stony beach below. At the caves, Richard took the bags and went in to the living area while I took the horses to the stable to make them comfortable.

I removed their saddles and began brushing the road from my own horse. I curried her mane, thinking through the journey we'd returned from. It had been long, but we'd heard that there were people in that village interested in the story we had to tell. I saw in my mind's eye the faces of the men and women we'd spoken to. It was as if we were bringing water to thirsty people. They'd heard rumors of the girl without a past, with the hands of a Practitioner.

A group from the village was planning to follow us in the coming days; we directed them to the grocer and his family in the nearest village. They would put up in the local inn, and the store owner would guide them to the caves to meet Anya. It was a measure of caution we took, only leading the way to the caves, never telling it.

As people had joined us in the caves, we'd spread out. There were groups living behind six or seven fissures now. The stable where I stood was one of two, and both were nearly full.

Anya traveled with us from time to time, but more often than not, she stayed at the caves. Pilgrims had begun to flock to the nearby village, and the grocer's wife and daughter regularly brought those who were seeking healing, who came only because of the stories they'd heard. The lame, the sick, those in pain came seeking relief, but receiving so much more. As Anya spoke to them, her words pointed them to look away from her to the One whom she served.

When I told the stories in the villages, I tried to do the same—to point people to this girl I believed was the Rose. I told the stories of the Writings that pointed to her coming and the stories of the recent months since she'd arrived on our doorstep that pointed to the Writings. I told my story, of the way He Who Knows Men's Thinking had patiently allowed me to search, and how I had become convinced that this girl who had no past was the fulfillment of all His words.

And people were listening. As I had, many saw the way these stories filled the holes in the patterns of our lives, and they chose to follow. We did not know the final destination. We were pilgrims on the way.

"I think her mane is smooth now," a voice behind me said.

I jumped and blinked at the glossy mane under my brush.

"Karan?" the voice said.

My heart was in my throat. My pulse beat quickly. I heard it pounding in my ears. I set down my curry brush and turned to face the voice.

It had been weeks since those final moments we'd had in the garden. I'd wondered how he had been doing since I'd seen him last. When I'd heard of the responsibilities my father had given him, I wondered if they would change him. More than anything, I'd wondered if he had thought of me. I could not expect letters; I had no idea if or when I would see him. But I had thought of him daily, wondering if he was doing the same.

Edmund stood before me in the stable. He seemed no different than that night in the garden. He smiled.

"Can I help?" he asked. He picked up a brush from the shelf we had built along the side of the cave.

I blinked, trying to find the right words to say. "O-of course," I stuttered. "Killion still needs to be curried." I indicated Richard's horse in the stall next to mine.

Edmund walked over and began brushing the gelding. I picked up my brush and began currying my mare's flanks. I couldn't think of the right thing to say. I wasn't used to finding myself tongue-tied. I wracked my mind, looking for a topic. I peeked over the back of my horse, across the space between us to see Edmund's head bent over his work. He looked up and smiled at me. I ducked my head quickly, smiling myself. A question popped into my mind. I looked back up; Edmund was still smiling at me.

"How long have you been here?"

"Two days," he said.

"How long can you stay?"

"I leave in the morning. I need to get on to the journey toward my home before I can think of no story to cover the delay."

"How will you explain it?"

"My horse threw a shoe in the stretch between the estates of Lord Llewellyn and Lord Canella. None of the villages at the edges of their estates have farriers. It's half a day's walk to the closest one, and then there's the time to shoe the horse."

"Two extra days, though?"

"I may be stretching it slightly," he said.

"Is that safe?"

"No one suspects me at all."

"Yet!" I protested. "You must be careful. You can't call any undue attention to yourself."

"Would you rather I'd left before you returned?"

"I—" He'd caught me. I smiled sheepishly. "No."

I watched the smile spread across his face. "You're not disappointed to see me?"

"No!"

"I wasn't certain," he said. "You seemed a bit stand-offish when I arrived a few moments ago."

"Not at all!" I was stammering again, trying to find the right words. "I was surprised—" I broke off, seeing his expression expand into a wide grin. He was teasing me. I raised an eyebrow at him and moved to the other side of my horse, my back to him.

Half an hour later, we made our way back to the main cave. In the light of the fire as we entered, I saw Thayer showing Richard the loom he'd set up in our absence. Lanica had already begun weaving tapestries.

Lanica saw us come in and came to hug me in greeting. "Edmund brought my loom," she said. "We shall be warm this winter."

I looked around the cave, lit by the flickering fire. Anya and Tay were bent together over a game of some kind. A stew was bubbling over the fire for dinner. Richard and Thayer worked in the corner. The frames covered in blankets that set off the sleeping areas from the living areas would be covered with tapestries soon after they finished. I glanced up at Edmund beside me.

"I'm glad you came," I said. "Welcome to our home."

He looked down at me and smiled. "Thank you," he said.

THE fire had burned down to its coals. Lanica had long since taken Tay to their sleeping area and had not returned. We had talked for another hour before Thayer's yawns forced him to join them.

Richard, Anya, Edmund, and I had continued to talk in low voices around the fire until sleepiness began to overtake Richard first, then Anya. I didn't feel weary, despite the long day of travel.

Anya was trying to hide her yawns, and Richard had grown so quiet I wasn't sure if he was even fully awake.

"Go to bed," I said to Richard. "You're exhausted."

He shook his head hard, trying to clear it. "Edmund, I can't stay awake another moment. I'm sorry to miss these hours with you."

"Go to sleep, Richard," Edmund replied. "I'll see you in the morning before I leave." He looked over and caught Anya in a yawn. "You, too. We'll see each other in the morning."

She nodded. They both rose and said goodnight, Richard going back to the corner of the cave where he'd slept and Anya making her way to the pile of blankets we shared.

Edmund rose and added more wood to the fire. I watched as he stoked the coals back into flames. He set down the tools and came to sit beside me.

"Are you tired?" he asked.

"No," I said. "I should be, but I am not."

He glanced around the cave, taking it all in again. "I'm glad I was able to bring the loom," he said. "You will all be warmer this winter."

I looked around as well. Without thinking, I looked up-ward. Quickly, I closed my eyes, shuddering. In my mind, the roof began to break apart.

"What is it?" Edmund asked.

I was breathing quickly, trying desperately to keep calm. A few days out of the caves had done wonders for me, but I could ruin it all by dwelling on the thought of the tons of earth above my head.

"I—I have t-trouble with the caves."

Edmund glanced up and took in the ceiling. He looked back over at me. "Karan, you're pale as a ghost!"

"I'll be all right," I said, trying to take deep breaths. "I—"

Edmund stood and pulled me to my feet. He picked up my cloak and put it around me. "Outside," he said. "Now."

He held my hand and pulled me behind him toward the narrow entrance. As the walls closed in, my breathing became more ragged. "Hold on, Karan," he said. "Breathe deeply. We're almost out."

I directed my mind to focus on the feel of his hand around mine. It was real—flesh and blood and bone. Warm. The stone on either side was cold as I was pulled past it. *It hasn't fallen yet*, I thought, repeating Richard's words to me from the early days. *He Who Knows Men's Thinking knows your fear*, Anya's voice said in my mind. The warmth of Edmund's hand. The cool of the breeze on my face. The pounding pulse in my ears gave way to another throbbing—the surf against the beach. We were out, and Edmund's arms were around me. I continued to take shuddering breaths, my head buried in his shoulder.

He stroked the back of my hair, his other arm still tightly around me. "We're outside, Karan. There's nothing above us now but the sky. I'm here. You're all right." He went on speaking quietly as my breathing slowed. My racing heart rate subsided, and I steadied my breath to match the pounding of the breakers. The salt of the sea was in the wind. I breathed it in, and breathed in Edmund's scent, and finally began to relax.

I raised my head and looked up into his face. It was a dark night, the moon covered by clouds. The wind whipped at us from the sea, tugging at my cloak, pulling wisps of my hair out of its braid. It buffeted his head, tousling his hair across his forehead. I freed a hand and reached up to move the hair away from his eyes. Dark as it was, I could see them clearly—almost colorless in the darkness, but deep and caring, their expression tender. His hand moved from the back of my head around to my chin. He lifted it, leaned down, and kissed me.

WE sat on a boulder, looking out over the sea. Edmund had taken my cloak and wrapped it around us both to protect us from the wind. My head was comfortably settled on his shoulder as his arm wrapped around me.

"Do the attacks happen often?" he asked.

"Not too often," I said. "More when I've been away for a while."

"I wish we could find another way."

"Edmund, this is the other way!" I said. "This is my part. I hated to think that Richard and Anya would be suffering for my sake. At least I have some penance to pay."

"I don't think He Who Knows Men's Thinking is out to make you suffer," said Edmund.

"No, but this whole journey has forced everyone to sacrifice something. All because I didn't want to marry Gennady. I should have to sacrifice something, too."

"From what I've seen," Edmund said, "Most people seem to feel that the sacrifices were worth it. Anya is settling in here well. Yesterday, when the store owner's wife brought pilgrims to see her—I remember what you told me about the day in Thayer and Lanica's home. She was remarkable."

"She's the Rose," I said. "I think even she is beginning to believe it."

"And Richard seems to be doing well. At least he's happy not to be doing the Council's business."

"I think he is." I paused. Only I knew why Richard volunteered to be the one who traveled so much. Edmund was right. Richard was glad he did not have to do the Council's business. He thrived beyond the fist of our father. But Richard was not happy. As long as he remained convinced that he would be in the way of Anya's purpose as the Rose if he grew any closer to her, he would not be happy.

"Thayer and Lanica gave up everything to come here," Edmund continued. "And they are thriving."

"Yes," I said.

"This is right, Karan. This is what is supposed to happen. Your friends have not set aside their lives and livelihoods only for you. They've done it because they believe in the cause you're fighting for."

"But everyone except me has had to set something aside. I have only gained in this equation. And I'm still useless to the cause. All I do is cut up vegetables for stew and tell stories to Tay. So let my penance be the attacks."

"You tell stories to more than Tay," Edmund said.

"Well, yes," I said. "Lanica and Thayer and Richard and Anya listen in while they work, but all I'm doing is helping to keep Tay occupied."

"After I arrived the other day, we needed to take the wagon I'd used to haul the loom over to the nearby village—where the pilgrims come. Thayer rode with me to show me the way."

He paused. The rhythmic surf continued to throb quietly. The wind had died down, and a mist was settling in as the night cooled. Edmund pulled the cloak closer about us and rubbed my arm to warm me. I waited, not sure what the point of his story was.

"We had dinner with the grocer's family," he went on. "His daughter told me how you met."

"Her doll was named Sephanya," I said. "So I told her about Anya."

"After we returned to the caves, Thayer took me to meet some of the others who live here. One after another, they told me how they came to give up everything and come to join the Rose. Again and again, I heard the same tale: 'Lady Karan told us about the Rose.'"

"Aye," I said. "I've been telling how Anya arrived and how I came to believe. And so many of them have never read the Written Histories, so I tell them stories from there. And Thayer and Lanica have been teaching me the stories of the peasants, too. I've started telling those stories, as well."

We sat in silence for a few moments. I still wasn't sure what Edmund's point was. I told stories. Thayer made me clothing; Lanica cooked and now, with the loom, would weave us tapestries and cloth to keep us warm all winter; Anya healed the pilgrims who came seeking the Rose...and I told stories.

Edmund chuckled. "You don't see it; do you, Karan, love?"

"See what?"

"How would they hear if no one told them the stories?"

"What do you mean?"

"These pilgrims who come, they hear the stories from someone who heard the stories from someone who heard the stories from you. The store keeper's wife would never have put Anya together with the waif in the Writings if she hadn't heard you telling the story of Anya's arrival to her daughter. You tell the stories. That's your part. How can they believe if they've never heard?"

"But it's nothing!" I protested. "They would have the Ancient Writings and the Written Histories anyway."

"Why do they have those?" Edmund asked. "Because someone thought it important to tell the stories. To write them down. Would you have believed if you didn't have the stories?"

I had never thought of the Writings in that way. They were so old that, while I believed that what they said really happened, I never had thought of them being recorded. Someone thought the events important enough to record. Even the peasants' tales. Someone thought them important enough to tell to their children, who told them to their children. Would I have believed if I didn't have the stories?

"No," I said.

"That is your part, Karan." Edmund smiled at me. "You tell the stories."

I opened my mouth to speak again, not quite sure how to respond. I thought of how easy telling stories was for me. How natural it seemed. I wanted to protest that it couldn't be so simple. My task couldn't be so—so *right*. Before I could speak, though, we heard, above the thrumming of the surf, the sound of footsteps on the rocky beach. The noise grew louder, the tramping of feet against stones.

I looked up at Edmund, my eyes wide. He put a finger to his lips and stood, pulling me up from the boulder to face the sound. The mist had thickened around us, and we couldn't see up the beach in the darkness. But from the sound of it, there were many, many feet, shoe against stone, shoe against stone, over and over, closer and closer, drowning the beating of the waves.

Edmund grasped my hand, and we stood together by the boulder, facing the dark mist, as the first figure came into view.

CHAPTER 21

FROM his bearing, I could see it was an old man. He was dressed in a monk's habit with the hood pulled up over his head. One by one, other figures came into view through the mist, all monks. The old man in front stopped and looked at us, his face in shadow. Behind him, the other monks came to a halt as well. Before anyone spoke, I heard footsteps behind us.

"Karan?" Anya's lovely voice floated through the darkness. "Edmund? Where are you?"

"We're here," I said, and the steps came closer.

"I can barely see anything out here," Richard's voice said. I heard a falter in the footsteps. "Watch your step there."

"By the boulders," Edmund said.

"I woke up, and you weren't in the cave, Karan," Anya called through the darkness. "I got worried and woke Richard."

The footsteps grew closer, and finally Richard and Anya emerged from the mist. They stopped short at the sight of the monks spread out before us.

"What woke you?" asked the monk in front. His voice held the grit of years.

Anya shrugged. "Nothing particular," she said. "I was suddenly wide awake."

Richard stepped forward. "Who are you? How did you find us?"

"We are seeking the Rose," said the old monk.

There was a pause. We waited for the monk to answer Richard's questions.

"We are seeking the Rose," he said again.

Another pause. I glanced at Anya, who had come up beside me. She took a deep breath. She stepped forward to join Richard. "I am she."

The monk nodded his head. "I know."

"Who are you?" Anya asked.

"My name is Ezra," said the monk. He put up his hands and pushed his hood back from his head. As he did so, I saw his hair was cropped close, showing that he held the rank of Helper. Far above, the clouds broke, and the moon shone through, reflecting off every drop of mist. Everything brightened slightly, and we could see the old man's face. I gasped as I saw Richard and Anya's eyes widen. It was the monk from Prince Loran's funeral.

We stood staring at him for a few moments. Edmund gathered himself first. "How did you find us here without a guide?"

Brother Ezra continued to look at Anya. "Were you deeply asleep?"

"Aye," she said. "I rarely wake at night."

"And you woke just a few moments ago."

"Aye."

I didn't understand. The old monk nodded to his brothers. "The time is right."

They nodded in return, and all reached up to push back their hoods. There were monks of all ages and ranks, Helpers, Masters, Priests, boys, young men, old men like Brother Ezra. They stood behind Brother Ezra, disappearing into the mist and darkness beyond what I could see. There had to have been over a hundred of them.

AN hour later, we sat by the fire in our cave, across from Brother Ezra and a priest named Aldan. We'd woken Thayer and Lanica and settled the monks into the largest of the caves. They said they needed no fires or blankets, so we left them as they lay down, one by one, on the hard stone floors. Brother Ezra and Father Aldan had returned with us to our cave, still mysteriously silent as to how they had found our hideaway.

I sat beside Anya, my shoulder touching hers. Richard stoked the fire and sat on her other side. Thayer and Lanica were to one side, and Edmund was behind us, pacing back and forth.

"You have not told us how you found us," Richard said.

"Seven nights ago, I rose from my prayers with a certain path in my mind," Brother Ezra said, his voice low. "I gathered my brothers, and we came to find the Rose."

Edmund laughed. "Just like that, a hundred monks and priests followed an elderly Helper?"

"No," said Father Aldan. "We have been preparing for weeks for this journey."

"Since I saw you at Loran's funeral," said Brother Ezra.

"We saw you there," Anya said. "We saw you watching us."

"Aye," Brother Ezra said. "I know."

"Why?" I asked. "Why were you watching?"

"I was certain my search was over."

"Your search?" asked Richard.

"For the Rose. I have been seeking the Rose my whole life." Father Aldan gave him a sideways glance. Brother Ezra ignored it and went on. "I knew when I saw you, with a certainty deeper than any I have ever had, that I had found the Rose."

"Why didn't you approach us then?"

There was a pause. Father Aldan spoke, "It was not time."

"The time was not right. I saw three young people and knew I had found the Rose," Brother Ezra said. "But I did not know which was a Practitioner."

"How did you know tonight?" I asked.

"We have been hearing rumors of a girl gifted in magic beyond her training," Father Aldan said.

"The stories are everywhere," said Brother Ezra. "People tell them to the monks. Rumors of a girl with no past."

"So you knew it wasn't Karan," Richard said. "You know she's the daughter of Lord Adamaris."

"Aye," said the monk. "But we did not know where you had gone."

The priest nodded. "Until Brother Ezra saw the path."

Brother Ezra looked directly at Anya. "What woke you tonight?"

Anya's brow furrowed. She gave her half-shrug. "I told you. Nothing particular."

"But you woke, wide awake when only a little while before you were tired from a long day."

"I—" Anya paused. She nodded. "Yes."

"He Who Knows Men's Thinking woke you," Brother Ezra said. "Just as he gave me a path to find you."

"It is time," Father Aldan said.

"Time for what?" Richard asked.

The old monk's eyes moved from Anya to Richard. "Time for the Rose to save Asael."

EDMUND departed in the grey pre-dawn. We stood around his horse as we said goodbye. He shook Richard's hand. "I'll stop on my return and make a report. I'm sure there will be talk among the nobles at the disappearance of the monks."

Anya hugged him, and he kissed her on the cheek. "Now I've seen it with my own eyes," he said to her. "I believe you are the Rose. Don't fear it."

He shook hands with Thayer and thanked Lanica for her excellent meals. He tickled Tay, making the boy laugh and run behind his mother.

Then he turned to me. With the arrival of the monks the night before, we'd never had a chance to talk further. I looked up at him, uncertain of what to say. He gripped my shoulders and kissed my forehead. "Keep telling stories, Lady Karan," he said.

He mounted his horse. "I shall see you all in a week," he said.

I stood, watching him ride away, feeling alone. I heard Lanica call for Tay and walk back toward the caves.

Richard turned to Thayer. "The monks will be awake soon," he said. "We should begin thinking through some plans." Thayer agreed, and they turned and made their way after Lanica.

I heard Anya shift behind me. She stepped forward and put her arm through mine. Together we watched the dark horse and rider disappear into the morning mist.

"Last night, it was 'Karan, love,'" I said.

Anya squeezed my arm tightly. "It is 'Karan, love,' even if he doesn't always say it," she said.

"How do you know?" I asked.

"You should have seen how impatient he was the past two days, waiting for you to return. You should have seen his face the night of the ball as he watched you dance with suitor after suitor of your father's choosing."

I took a deep breath and looked over at her. "I suppose there is something more important than me and Edmund, isn't there?"

Anya smiled. "Do you mean the hundred monks who arrived last night to inform me that it's now time to overthrow the rulers of Asael?"

"That's not quite how they put it," I said. "They merely implied that the hope of the kingdom lies squarely on your shoulders."

"Oh, yes," Anya nodded. "That is so much more comforting."

I laughed. "Don't look to me for comfort," I said. "You're the one that was born to this role. I only volunteered."

Anya smiled ruefully. "I wish I could remember being born to this role. Then maybe I'd know how to do it."

"No, you wouldn't," I said. "I still haven't figured out how to be a noble, and I've been doing it my whole life."

Anya sighed and looked out at the sea. "I wish I knew where I came from," she whispered. "I wish I knew who I was."

I had never heard her express anything resembling concern that she had no past. "You are Sephanya," I said. "You arrived at my doorstep the night the heir to the throne died. I used to think that was a coincidence. But now—" I broke off. Assurance filled me, and I spoke what I knew to be true: "You're the Rose, the hope of Asael."

"How do you know?" she asked.

"How do you know?" I replied. "Last night, you didn't even hesitate when Brother Ezra said the monks were seeking the Rose."

She nodded. "I knew it the moment I woke in the cave. I felt a single, flaming branch of my power sticking out from the circle in my mind and I knew the Rose was needed. I thought you were in trouble or something, that's why I came looking for you, but what my magic was telling me was that the Rose was needed, and I had to respond."

"The monks say it is time," I said.

"But what does that mean?" asked Anya. "I do not believe the Rose is to be a political leader, but in the current state of things, I don't see another way to save Asael. We must work through the political system."

"Well, at least you have Richard by your side. I said to Edmund once that he could lead nations if he put his mind to it. And he's put his mind toward making sure you do."

Anya was silent. I looked from the waves over to her. She seemed lost in thought.

"Anya?"

"Hmm?"

"Did you hear what I said? Richard will help you. He can navigate the politics of kingdom saving."

"Aye," she said, still distracted. "I heard what you said."

I couldn't determine what it was that had caught her attention so. She seemed to be turning an idea over and over, examining it from all angles. "Anya?" I asked. "Is everything all right?"

She smiled, still looking out at the sea. "Aye, everything is all right."

THE next few days were full of activity and planning. For much of each day, we sat together over maps, the rhythmic thrumming of Lanica's loom setting the undertone for murmured conversations. Brother Ezra and Aldan the Priest continued to speak for the monks, and we came to know them better.

I learned little of their lives before the funeral of Loran, but from what I gleaned, I learned that they had known each other since they were boys. For some reason, Brother Ezra had halted in his rise through the ranks of the monks, and Father Aldan had continued to become a priest. Though he was higher in rank, he still looked to Brother Ezra for guidance, wisdom, and insight.

As we worked together each day, the plan took shape. When the moment was right, we had a system for calling together all the followers of the Rose. The monks and some of us who had been in the caves for a while had routes to take which would move us from village to village, spreading the word to gather. There was some disagreement as to what would happen when we reached the Capital. Richard was all for storming the Council offices with a small army. Anya would have none of that plan. Brother Ezra was opaque on the subject. Father Aldan advised caution.

"If we're not to overthrow the Council, then what are we doing?" Richard asked. "You said it was time for the Rose to save Asael."

"The time, aye," Brother Ezra said. "But we do not yet know the way."

"It's the only way to deal with the corruption. Cut it out from the top."

"And the king?" Brother Ezra asked.

Richard paused. "The king barely holds power. It is all in the hands of the Council now."

Anya stood from the maps. "We cannot start a war." She walked over to the stew bubbling above the fire and began to stir it.

I sighed. I didn't see how to reconcile them. I saw Richard's point; if we didn't rid the kingdom of the Council, there was no hope for Asael. But I didn't want war, either. I didn't want to see my friends in danger.

I stood as well and moved over to watch Lanica. She had been weaving almost non-stop since Edmund had brought the loom. There were tapestries hanging on each frame and against the walls of the cave. It was easier for me to pretend there was no earth above me when I couldn't see the walls. I had thanked her for that. Plain though they were, the tapestries felt like a bit of home.

That evening she had stopped working on the loom and had moved to a frame Thayer had set up for her. From the top of it hung hundreds of strings, warm golden yellows and whites. She had weighted them by tying each to a bar that hung nearly at her feet. She held a shuttle in her hand

and with it pulled strings from colored spools set in a rack on one side of the frame and threading them through the yellow strings to hooks on the far side.

"What are you doing?" I asked.

"We do not weave the picture tapestries with the loom," she said. "They are too complex."

"You're making a picture tapestry?"

"Aye," she said. "A small one. My head was aching from leaning over the loom for so many hours. I needed to stand."

"What will it be?" I asked.

"Only the weaver knows that," said Brother Ezra, coming up beside me. "We must stand back and watch the picture unfold."

He indicated a pile of logs, and I stepped back to join him sitting on them. As we watched Lanica work, he began to tell me about watching a weaver as a young boy. He had seen the man pick up a shuttle from the rack and called out to him that he'd taken the wrong color. The man paused and looked over his shoulder at Ezra.

"'Do you know the picture I am weaving?' he asked me," Brother Ezra said. "I told him I did not. 'How then do you know I chose the wrong color?' he asked. I righteously informed him that he had selected blue on the previous pass, and this time, he had chosen green. 'I have finished the sky,' the man said, and he turned back to his work. Only then did I look at what had already been completed in the picture and see that it was a landscape scene, with trees not yet planted in the ground growing against a sky of blue."

Lanica and I laughed quietly, and I continued to watch her work for a few more moments. Still watching her, I asked Brother Ezra, "How can you know it is time for the Rose to arise and not know how to go about it? Why doesn't He Who Knows Men's Thinking give more clear guidance?"

Brother Ezra chuckled. "When you have been guided by He Who Knows Men's Thinking, has He ever given you all the information?"

"When I've been guided? I haven't!"

"How did you know to come here?" asked Brother Ezra.

"We came up with the plan ourselves," I said.

"And why did you follow the plan?" he asked.

"Because it was right," I said.

"How did you know?"

"I—I just—I just did. Deep inside, I knew."

"I have rarely seen one so young as you so attuned to He Who Knows Men's Thinking. The Rose told me you fear the caves, yet you have learned to give over that fear."

"Not perfectly," I said.

"But how did you learn that?"

"I did it one night before we left home. My father was going to make me marry Lord Gennady. I was terrified. And one night, I lay in bed, and I thought, *If He Who Knows Men's Thinking is here, I can give Him my fears.* And so I did. One by one, I handed them over to Him."

"And you were no longer afraid?"

"I was no longer holding my fears," I said.

He nodded. "I have rarely seen it in one so young," he said again.

"But that is not the same thing!" I said. "I can give over my fears, yes, I can name them. But patience has never been a strong point for me. How can you sit back and wait for guidance?"

Brother Ezra sat back and watched Lanica for another moment before speaking. "Each of us has a role to play in the story unfolding before us. Sometimes that role is simply to stand aside and let the tale unfold. He Who Knows Men's Thinking sees every thread of the tapestry being woven, how they each fit together into a glorious pattern. We usually only see a single strand and think it is in the wrong place. Without a view of the whole tapestry, we cannot know. We must trust He Who Knows Men's Thinking. After all, the story is His to tell."

Suddenly there was a commotion behind us. I heard a voice outside call out, and Richard jumped up from where he sat talking with Aldan and Thayer to run out the entrance. A moment later, he came back in with Edmund, covered in mud from riding hard. It had only been three days since Edmund had left. He was not supposed to return for a week.

"What is it?" asked Anya.

"I am on my way back to Marinel urgently," Edmund said. "King Saran is deathly ill."

CHAPTER 22

THERE was silence in the cave.

"I cannot stay long," Edmund said. He pulled a folded paper from his pocket. I saw my father's purple wax on the broken seal. He handed the paper to Richard.

Richard opened it and began to read aloud:

Edmund,

Word has come that King Saran is on his deathbed. The Council will gather to make Briyanne abdicate. Make haste and join me before I leave for the Capital. We must be there, ready to move when the king dies. Tell your father to gather his fighting men and join us in the Capital within the week. We shall need all those loyal to our cause. I heard word this week that monks have gone missing from the Capital. I did not think much of it until this news came through. We may find the establishment of the Council more difficult than we thought.

Come quickly.

Arnau Adamaris, Lord of Marinel

"Stop for half an hour," Richard said. "Eat a bite, and we will tell you what we've planned."

I picked up a bowl and ladled stew into it. Anya handed me a spoon, and I gave the bowl to Edmund. He smiled at me quickly as he thanked me for it.

Richard, Edmund, Thayer, Anya, Brother Ezra, and Father Aldan gathered around the maps. Lanica went back to the loom and began working on the heavy cloth she'd started after she finished the tapestries for the cave. I stood for a moment by the fire. I knew the plan; I did not need to be in the circle. I looked down and saw Tay standing beside me.

"Tell me a story, Lady Karan?" he asked.

I smiled, settled down next to the fire, and invited him into my lap. To the rhythmic thrumming of the loom on one side, so like the sound of the surf far under my window at Marinel, and the quiet murmur of voices around the maps on the other, I began to tell him the story of the last King of Asael, whose reign had seen some of the darkest days of the Age of Kings, and who, weak though he was, loved his kingdom. When Saran's son died, the great hope for his kingdom and his will to live died with him, and Saran quietly moved toward his grave, never knowing that the Rose had come never knowing a greater age had already begun.

THE group around the maps stood and shook hands. Lanica rose from the loom and wrapped bread and cheese in an oilcloth for Edmund to take with him. Anya stood before him and put her hand on his head. He bowed it, and she spoke a blessing.

"Go in peace," she said when she was done. "Go safely."

"We shall keep in contact," Richard said. "Remember—"

"Use the code from when we were boys," Edmund said, nodding. "I know, Richard. You've only told me ten times."

"You remember it?"

"I remember it."

The priest shook hands with him, and Brother Ezra gripped his shoulder. Lanica handed him the food, and he thanked her for it.

He waved to Tay, still sitting in my lap. "Goodbye, Tay! I shall see you again soon!" Then his eyes moved up, and he caught mine. We looked at each other across the cave for a moment, and then he turned and went out the entrance.

I sat quietly for a few seconds, my arms around Tay. The little boy leaned his head back against my chest, settling it comfortably under my collarbone. "Master Edmund didn't say goodbye to you, Lady Karan," he said.

"No," I replied. My throat grew tight. My father expected trouble. He was calling on the fighting men. We could be that trouble. And there was no knowing where Edmund might be if fighting broke out. "Excuse me, Tay," I said. I set him on the floor beside me and jumped to my feet. I ran to the entrance, through the narrow gap, and out into the open air.

It had started to snow since I'd been out last, and the wind whipped white flakes against my face, their sharp edges scratching at my skin. I shivered and tried to see through snowflakes piling on my lashes.

"Edmund!" I cried out.

"Karan?" I heard him off to my left. I stumbled toward his voice. I practically ran into him, where he stood beside his horse. He'd put the food into his saddlebags and looked as if he were about to mount. "Karan, you don't have a coat! It's freezing out here."

"I couldn't let you go without saying goodbye," I said, raising my voice to compete with the wind.

"Karan, love—"

I cut him off. "I love you. Whatever happens, know that. I've loved you ever since we played on the moors together in the old days, and you and Richard would tease me about liking Prince Loran. When Father wanted me to marry Gennady, my heart was breaking because I only ever wanted you. And the only reason I ever agreed to go along with it was for the good of the kingdom. Serving the Rose is more important than my happiness."

He stopped my words with a kiss. "I know, love," he said. "And when I teased you about Prince Loran, I always brought up the reasons it wouldn't work, remember? I didn't ever want you to really like him. I always hoped someday you'd love me like I loved you."

I felt tears pricking at the corners of my eyelids, fighting off the snowflakes with their heat. "Go in peace," I said. "Go in safety. Go with my whole heart."

"And you keep mine," he replied. He took my face in both his hands and kissed away the tears from my cheeks. He stepped back and mounted into his saddle. He smiled down through the whipping snow at me. "Tell the stories, Karan, love."

OUR plan was to target key villages in the kingdom, the trade villages of each estate. If the stories of the Rose had spread as much as the monks thought, our task in each place should be simple. We were to gather those who wanted to follow the Rose and tell them to make their way to the Capital. Even with their fighting men, the nobles would be no match for the thousands upon thousands of peasants in the land. If it came to a fight, there were plans for that as well. Richard and Thayer would serve as generals. They'd trained a group of men from the caves to be their lieutenants.

Richard and Thayer left first, planning to go far to the north and west before circling back around. There were one or two lesser nobles Richard wished to visit on their journey, particularly his friend Bellamy Mumina. Richard hoped he and his sister Cecily would join the cause. He was fairly certain that Lord Mumina would believe once he heard the story.

In pairs, the monks went out, walking west, north, south, every direction to take the message over all of the kingdom. Some of the peasants who had joined us in the caves went, too. Others returned to their home villages to take the word there. Still more remained in the caves and prepared to go to the Capital in time to meet us all there. Father Aldan asked Anya if she would travel with him to a few monasteries where he had connections. They departed a few days after Thayer and Richard.

Lanica, Tay, and I remained a bit longer in the caves with Brother Ezra and the peasants who stayed. Every day I sat with Ezra, listening to him tell the stories of his life and of the histories of the monks. Pilgrims continued to come, seeking the Rose. We told them she was away in service of He Who Knows Men's Thinking, and we told them the stories of everything that had happened. Some remained with us; others returned to their homes with promises to meet us in the Capital.

We'd received one message from Edmund before Richard left. He'd written that our Father was moving everything to the Capital and leaving Marinel practically empty. He'd dismissed the staff and left the house in the care of the old cook, Garima. It was perfect. Richard and Thayer, Anya and Aldan, and Brother Ezra, Lanica, Tay, and I planned to gather there before going to the Capital. We could regroup and make further plans based upon the information we'd gained in the intervening weeks.

Lanica, Tay, Brother Ezra, and I decided to make our way to Marinel a few days early to get the house ready for the others to arrive. We left the responsibilities at the caves to some who remained and packed our things onto horses for the journey. Winter had fully settled in, and the snow had fallen deep on the moors. We left early in the morning, knowing the going would be slow. It took us nearly the full day to get to Marinel.

I knocked at the kitchen door when we arrived. I knew the cook well and knew she would not betray us to my father. She opened the door cautiously, a lamp in her hand.

Her eyes widened at the sight of me. "Lady Karan! Is it you?"

"Aye, Garima," I said. "It is."

"And who do you have with you?" she said. "Where's Master Richard and Miss Anya?"

"They'll be coming in a few days," I said. "They're each traveling. I have Lanica the weaver and her son here with me. And a monk from the Capital named Brother Ezra."

"A monk? Coming here to Marinel? What would your father say to that?"

"I don't doubt he would say many terrible things," I said. "But since he doesn't have to know, why should we bother wondering?" I looked Garima straight in the eye.

She looked back at me for a moment. Then she nodded. "Aye, why should we?" She stepped back to let us in the door.

"I'll settle the horses," Brother Ezra said and turned back to take them to the stables.

Lanica and I moved into the kitchen, with Tay at our heels. He looked out from behind his mother's skirts at Garima.

"Is this the boy what was nearly dead?" Garima asked.

Lanica put her hand down and hugged Tay against her leg. "Aye," she said.

Garima looked at me. "'Tis really true Miss Anya healed him?"

I nodded. "She did."

"They been saying in the village since you left that the story your father told us was a lie. They been saying that Miss Anya is a Practitioner."

"She is," I said. "And more."

Garima nodded. "I heared that, too. Don't know as I believe it yet," she said. "But I'll bide my time before I decide."

"That's fair enough." I smiled at her. "Is there food in the larder? We've been journeying all day."

"Aye," Garima said. "More than enough for all of you."

"We'll have more guests in a few days," I said.

"It will be good to have folks to cook for. Now, get yourselves upstairs and wash the journey off of you. Though he shut up the house, everything is kept in readiness. The fires are stoked in the boiler rooms, so you can get hot water on your hall. I'll send the monk up to the room next to Master Richard's when he gets back in."

I smiled. Garima took everything in stride, not a feather ruffled.

"Now go!" she commanded. "You look as though you've been living in dirt like nothing I've ever seen before."

I laughed. "We've been living in caves," I said.

"Well, then, it's no wonder. Go get yourself clean and looking like a lady," she said. "No dawdling."

I dragged a bathtub from the boiler room to the wet room in my chambers and ran back and forth with pitchers, filling it with water. I sank into the hot bath, letting the water pull at every knot in my muscles. It had been months since I'd had a real bath, and I couldn't think of anything I missed more from my life as a noble. I didn't even care that I'd had to prepare it myself; just being able to soak in it was heavenly.

When I was clean and relaxed, I dressed in a fresh gown—one of the ones Thayer had made; I was not ready to reclaim the buttoned dresses in my wardrobe. I stood for a moment in front of the mirror, letting my feet sink into the plush carpeting. I remembered Anya's reaction to the rooms the first night she arrived, and I looked around them with new eyes, taking in the luxurious furnishings. I looked back at the girl in the mirror. She looked the same as she had that night. It had only been a few months. She had thinned out a little, perhaps, and the last time she cut her hair, she had shortened it significantly. But outwardly, there was very little different about her. Nothing to show that a different woman lived within, one who was fighting for a cause, one who had friends from every rank of society, one who could recite whole passages of the Ancient Writings, one who loved a good man and knew she was loved in return. Perhaps there was something of that story written about her eyes, but the story of a soul is hard to see from the outward appearance.

I gathered my hair into a braid and went out to the hall. I knocked on Lanica's door, and Tay opened it, his skin pink and rubbed clean.

"Lady Karan!" he said. "Have you sat on the bed? It's so soft!"

I laughed. "Aye, Tay," I said. "I have."

Lanica joined us by the door. "Is it time to go down?"

"If you're ready," I said. "I'm sure Garima has prepared a feast in the past half hour. Please don't be overwhelmed. She has probably put out the full settings of silver."

Lanica smiled. "We shall live as the nobles, then," she said.

We went down to the front hall and met with Brother Ezra there. He told us Garima had set up dinner in the dining room. I led the way and opened the door to be dazzled by the glittering silver on the table.

Garima stood by the sideboard. "I'm sorry not to be able to serve you like in the old days," she said. "But I thought perhaps you would be able to serve yourselves from the buffet."

I laughed. "Oh, dear Garima. Of course, we can. You needn't have gone to all this trouble."

"No trouble at all, Lady Karan. It's my part, you see, serving you food since you was a girl. And if what you say about Miss Anya is so, then it's a good thing I do, feeding you all. If you don't mind, I'll get one or two of the maids back from the village, quiet-like, to help out for the next few days."

"Aye," I said. "Do so. Carefully—my father cannot know we're here—but do so. I hate to see you put yourself out for us."

"No trouble at all," she said again.

"And tell us how we can help," I said.

Garima looked shocked. "I shouldn't like that," she said. "Milady or milady's friends working next to me in the kitchen. No, Lady Karan, you keep to your ways up here, and I'll keep to mine below."

I glanced over at Lanica, trying very hard not to laugh. Her eyes sparkled back at me. I looked to Brother Ezra, and there was a twinkle in his eye, too. Garima bowed herself from the dining room, and we turned to the buffet to fill our plates.

"I believe I heard Master Richard talking one day about a new society for Asael," Lanica said as she scooped potatoes from the warmer to her plate. "I seem to remember him saying there would be a day when there was no class distinction in the kingdom."

Brother Ezra helped himself to the meat. "There may be a few who have problems with that idea," he said.

I laughed. "And not only among the nobles."

We ate our dinner in comfortable conversation, and then each made our way up to our rooms. I entered mine again and walked toward the window. I could hear the pounding of the surf, far below, the sound of all my years in the room. I turned back and looked around it once more. On the desk, I noticed a book I'd never seen before. I walked over for a closer look. It was a beautiful volume, bound in leather. I fingered the etchings on the cover and realized that it was a miniature of the image on the tapestry on my wall.

Curious, I opened to the first page. There was an inscription, written in a familiar hand, *Tell the stories, Karan, love. –E*

I smiled, tracing the words with my fingertip. I turned another page and saw that it was blank, lines on paper. I paged through. The whole book was empty.

I closed the cover again and stood for a moment fingering the etching. I looked up at the tapestry on the wall. Again and again in the previous months, I'd seen those expressions of expectation on the faces of all who came seeking the Rose. I heard Edmund's voice in my memory, *Someone thought it important to tell the stories. To write them down.*

I sat at the desk, uncorked the inkwell, and picked up the pen. I opened the book to the first page, dipped my pen in ink, and began to write: *A faithful account of the genesis and activities of the Followers, here written by Karan Adamaris.*

CHAPTER 23

TWO days later, Anya and Father Aldan arrived. The largest monastery in the kingdom was the one in the Capital, where Brother Ezra and Father Aldan had lived with the monks they brought to find us. However, across the middle of the kingdom, there were other, smaller monasteries. They had gone to them, one by one, and Father Aldan had introduced Anya as the Rose. The monks had believed, and they planned to meet us in the Capital.

I had grown comfortable with Brother Ezra and Lanica in the days since I'd seen Anya, but I missed our friendship. I was delighted to have her back. The time had been good to her. She seemed steady and calm. We settled into my room with cups of tea in our hands the evening she arrived.

"The pilgrims and the peasants were one thing," Anya said. "So many of them believed because I could heal them. I tried so hard to direct them to He Who Knows Men's Thinking, but so many of them were more focused on me. I don't want to be the focus."

I smiled, remembering the first time Lanica tried to bow before Anya. "Aye, I know."

"But the monks already know the Writings. They know that I am only a part of a bigger plan, a bigger story."

"I have been surprised at how sound the thinking of the monks is," I said, reflecting on my conversations with Brother Ezra over the previous weeks. "How is it that for so many years, they have known the Ancient Writings and understood them, but it has had no impact on the nobles?"

"Father Aldan said this understanding of the Writings is fairly new among the monks. There was a long time when there was very little focus on the Ancient Writings in their studies. After their fall from power, there was a movement among the monks to focus study on magic rather than on history. Only in the past thirty years or so have they focused on the Ancient Writings again."

"What made them change focus?" I asked.

"He didn't say. A crisis of some kind among the monks. Did you notice that there were not many old men in the group that came to the caves? Brother Ezra and Father Aldan, and maybe one or two more, but most of the others were younger. I saw that in the monasteries, too. The bulk of their numbers are younger men who have joined in more recent years."

"Did you hear word from any of the other travelers?" I asked.

"The monks sent messages to Father Aldan regularly. They found village after village smarting under the caprice of the nobles. The response to our message seems to be good. Any word from others here?"

"Not from the travelers." I smiled. "Edmund left me a book."

"A book?"

"Blank, to write down everything that's happened."

Anya looked over her teacup at me. "He's right, of course. Someone should."

"He says that's my part."

She nodded. "Aye. I wonder that I didn't see it." She took another sip of tea. "Do you know where he is now?"

"Brother Ezra has gotten messages from the monks in the Capital. The members of the Council have all gathered. They've been meeting in the palace for days now. Lord Makram has arrived with his fighting men, and others are coming daily. My father is there, and Edmund with him."

"So, we wait for Richard to return, and then..." Anya trailed off.

"We go to the Capital," I said.

"Aye." Anya stared into the fire. "We must."

RICHARD and Thayer arrived the following evening with Lord Mumina and his sister Cecily.

"I knew they would believe when I told them every-thing," Richard said to me in the hall after we had shown them to rooms. "I remembered all the conversations I had with Bellamy in school and the conversations we would have with Cecily when I visited their home. They were ready, they didn't even know what for, but they were ready."

"We've not tried to tell many nobles about the Rose," I said. "I wonder if there are others who might be interested."

"Among the older generation, no, I don't think so," said Richard. He indicated the closed door of Bellamy Mumina's room with a tilt of his head. "His parents died last year, both of fever. Old Lord Mumina would never have listened."

"We ran away," I said.

"We were fortunate to have a Father who paid very little attention to us," said Richard. "Lady Mumina watched her children like a hawk."

I nodded. "Perhaps among the young people, though. Perhaps this will not be split so evenly between the classes."

Richard put his arm around my shoulders, and we made our way to the main hall. "See you downstairs for dinner soon?" he asked.

"Aye," I said. "I must go check in with Garima to be sure she has everything she needs."

I turned and made my way to the back stairs down to the kitchen. Garima was now cooking for ten guests and the extra maids. She would be horrified if she knew I was concerned that she could do it at such short notice. I wasn't really, but I knew that Cecily Mumina had been raised in a nobleman's house, and I didn't want our lacking hospitality to be her first impression of the followers of the Rose.

I made my way upstairs twenty minutes later, shooed out of the kitchen by an indignant Garima. Chuckling, I tripped up the steps and walked to the front hall. The door to the sitting room was open, and I approached it, making little noise in my leather house shoes. I paused at the entrance, taking in the scene before me. On the far side of the room, Richard and Cecily sat in a window seat, looking out into the darkness, talking quietly together. Cecily leaned forward to the window, cupping her hands around her face to peer into the darkness, then looked back over her shoulder to Richard and made some comment about what she saw.

He laughed aloud. A real laugh. A laugh like I hadn't heard from him in months. Cecily sat back and laughed with him, smiling up at him, her golden curls dancing about her face as her body shook with mirth. I felt someone come up beside me, and Richard looked up.

"Bellamy! Karan! Come in! Cecily has been telling me her theory on how snowflakes are made." He laughed again and stood, taking Cecily's hand and drawing her up with him.

Lord Mumina was behind me, and we stepped into the room together. I smiled at Richard; there was no false note in his joy in the moment. He was happy. As I walked forward, out of the corner of my eye, I saw something move. I turned in time to see a figure, dressed in black with long dark hair, disappear from the other door into the sitting room. Anya had watched the scene, too.

At that moment, Brother Ezra arrived at the door where Bellamy and I had entered. Richard greeted him and began the introductions to the Muminas. No one else had seen Anya.

"I must check on one more thing in the dining room," I said, hurriedly excusing myself from the group. I went out the far door and stood in the hallway for a moment. All the doors were closed, and the narrow hall was empty. I walked forward and opened the door to the breakfast room.

Stepping inside, I shut it behind me. Anya stood by the window on the far side.

"Anya?" I asked.

She didn't turn from the window. "I've never seen him laugh quite like that," she said. "Even with you."

"He hasn't laughed like that in months," I said.

"Because of me."

"No! Because of everything."

"Tell me that if I had not come, all the rest of this would have happened anyway," she said.

I didn't speak. I wanted to assure her that she was wrong, to tell her that all of this was bigger than her. I wanted to give her the words of comfort I could take—that I was a piece in the story He Who Knows Men's Thinking was telling. But I couldn't say that. The Rose was the story being told.

"I am glad he is happy," she said, finally turning away from the window to face me. Her face was pale and set. "We will all face much harder things before this is done. Let him be happy now." I watched a wave of agony sweep over her, and I remembered Richard's tears that day on the beach. I alone knew that Richard loved Anya. Never before or since have I wanted to break a promise. I knew it would bring them happiness.

"Anya, he—" I broke off. My promise to Richard stopped me. I couldn't fail him again. I desperately wanted to comfort her, but I had nothing I could give.

"We should join the others for dinner," she said.

"Aye."

She stepped past me and opened the door. "Come, Karan," she said. "They're waiting for us."

I stepped forward and caught the door as she let go. I stepped out, pulled it shut behind me. I watched her walk away and took a deep breath. For the first time, I understood why she had worked so hard to find another way for me so I wouldn't have to marry Gennady. I looked at the set of her shoulders and saw the same determination I'd had to do my part. But I could not offer her another way. I could not give her hope for a bright future. She was the Rose, and I was her servant.

WE sat together over the meal, a strange band to break bread together. We were gathered for a single purpose: a peasant girl with no past, an elderly Helper, an old Priest, two sets of noblemen's children, and a family of peasant clothiers. In this room was the hope of a kingdom.

Richard gathered everyone's attention. "We go to the

Capital tomorrow," he said. "We have each heard bits of news coming from there, and in our journeys have gathered information. The king is dying. I am surprised he has held on this long. The Council is already behaving as though they are in control of the kingdom. As we traveled, we all heard story after story of the nobles seizing power over those beneath them. We have told the peasants to go to the Capital. We will meet them there tomorrow. When the king dies, the Council will make its move. We must be prepared for whatever they do. It is time to decide, once and for all, which course of action we will take."

Brother Ezra nodded. "There has been no word of Briyanne's decision."

"If he has abdicated," Aldan said, "would it have been made public yet?"

"I'll send a message off to Edmund tonight," said Richard. "He may be able to tell us more by the time we reach the city tomorrow."

"Have him send his response to the monastery," said Father Aldan. "We will go there when we arrive."

"If Briyanne does not abdicate, what will happen to him?" asked Thayer.

"He will be imprisoned," said Anya.

"Or killed," I said. "I wouldn't put it past Gennady to do away with him."

"Either way, the Council is in control," said Richard.

"Why have they not made it known?" asked Lanica.

"The nobles know," said Bellamy. "We weren't given all the details, but we were notified that since the king was dying without direct heir, a Council has been formed to determine the course of action for the governance of Asael."

"And they don't care about the peasants," said Anya.

"That is the Council's greatest weakness," Brother Ezra said. "They have underestimated the peasants. They believe that the nobles can control their tenants."

"Why haven't there been more demonstrations or riots?" asked Cecily. "If I were a peasant and the king had died, and I had no knowing what my life would look like once everything was settled, I think I would be shouting about it somewhere."

"Lords of estates hold absolute power over their tenants," said Lanica. "My father worked his whole life as a successful businessman and died without a penny to his name." She looked at me and Richard. "Even my loom belongs to your father."

"When Loran died there was great sorrow," Thayer said. "We had hoped he would have more influence over the Lords of the estates. He knew what our lives were really like."

"But what could we do?" said Lanica. "With Loran gone there is now no one in power who looks to the needs of the peasants. If we were to protest against the Lord of Marinel, he could and would take away everything."

"So everyone resumed their normal lives," said Thayer. "For a thousand years, things have been this way. For generations. We are used to groaning under oppression, great and small. Why would the peasants rise up for no reason?"

"Until they heard of the Rose," said Richard.

"Aye," Lanica smiled at Anya. "And you should hear the way they talk in the village here. When she stands, they will stand with her."

Anya shifted in her seat. "I do not want violence," she said.

"We're prepared either way," said Richard. "But until we know how the Council will respond, we cannot rule it out."

"I don't want to see my friends struck down at the hand of my father," I said.

"Is that a concern?" asked Bellamy. "Surely, with the monks on our side, we would win easily."

Anya turned to look at him. "What makes you say that?"

"They can fight with magic," said Cecily. "Like they did with Lord Allard."

"No!" Brother Ezra stood so suddenly all the dishes on the table rattled. "There will be no magic used in battle."

Richard looked from Bellamy and Cecily to Brother Ezra. "They may have a point," he said. "It's an untapped resource we hadn't thought of using."

"No," Brother Ezra's voice was steely and quiet. "Not in battle."

"But—" Richard began.

Brother Ezra cut him off with a shout. "No!"

There was silence around the table. Brother Ezra's anger boiled just under the surface. He stood, alone, and the rest of us stared at him in confusion.

"It is time, Ezra," Father Aldan said.

"No," said Brother Ezra. "No."

"They have to know why."

"I do not want to."

"Then I will," said Father Aldan. Brother Ezra closed his eyes, his expression pained. "He has seen magic used in battle," Father Aldan explained.

Brother Ezra broke in. "I have seen what is good and beautiful taken up in anger and twisted into blackness and horror. I have seen spells of heating used to burn the flesh off men. I have seen spells that heal broken skin used to cover the nostrils and mouths of young men, leaving them to suffocate in their own flesh. I have seen what happens when magic is used as a weapon. I will not be a part of it."

Anya had been sitting next to Brother Ezra. She stood and put a hand on his arm. "Brother," she said. "When did you see these things?"

Brother Ezra looked down at her hand on his arm. He looked into her eyes. "I saw them when I fought in battle against King Saran. I saw them when I joined Lord Allard's Rebellion." He turned and looked across the table to Richard, and then to me. "I saw them when your father's brother was killed by magic from my own hand."

CHAPTER 24

QUIET reigned. Anya's hand did not move from his arm. "You said you spent your whole life seeking the Rose," she said, her voice low.

Tears formed at his eyes and began to make their way down through the wrinkles of his craggy face. "Aye," he said. "And but for then, it is true."

"You joined Allard?"

"I planted the idea of rebellion in his mind."

Father Aldan spoke, "Brother, it was not entirely your doing. Cormac—"

"Cormac never had me fooled," Brother Ezra interrupted. "I knew he coveted power for himself. I knew why he sought me out." He put his hand over Anya's on his arm and looked down at her. "I lost faith," he said. He sank into his chair and put his elbows on the table. He coughed, the sound rattling deep in his chest.

Anya sat again. We all waited in silence.

"He Who Knows Men's Thinking had not spoken in so

long," Brother Ezra said. He looked over at me. "I told you I had not seen your sensitivity in one so young. I have not, except once: I was a prodigy among the practicing monks. My skill with magic led some to ask if I might be the Rose. But I knew it was not so. I knew it with certainty every time I rose from my prayers. He Who Knows Men's Thinking was a real, living presence in my times of meditation... until I began to listen to Cormac. His voice drowned out the quiet whispers of He Who Knows Men's Thinking until I could no longer hear the Creator at all. And so I began to believe Cormac's words that magic was the only power worth having and that, since I was gifted in it, I had the right to wield it over my fellow men." He looked over to Father Aldan. "I knew I was stronger than him," he said. There was another moment of silence. "Allard was Cormac's pawn. Cormac was mine."

Father Aldan breathed heavily. "You never said."

"No," said Brother Ezra. "And you offered me asylum when it was all over. Oh, my crisis was real! I saw the ugliness that we had twisted magic to be—I saw it flow from my own fingers—and I could not go on. I ran from the fight. Without me by his side, Cormac fell, and Adamaris captured Allard and put down the rebellion." Brother Ezra looked to Richard and me. "It was the best thing your father has ever done," he said.

"And your search for the Rose?" asked Anya.

"Aldan protected me after the Rebellion. He argued for me in the face of those who would have destroyed me. I was stripped of my rank and any opportunity to progress through the ranks of monks for the rest of my life. And I vowed never to use magic again. I spent months in solitude, trying to remove the images of that battle from my mind." He was quiet for a moment. "I could not. I begged He Who Knows Men's Thinking to wash my mind of them. And I heard no answer. Finally, I stopped crying out. And when I was quiet, at long last, that was when I heard Him again. When I rose from my meditations, I was certain that I would live to see the Rose."

"Ezra has been the driving force behind the reforms among the monks for the past twenty-five years," Father Aldan said.

"Futility," said Brother Ezra, spitting out the word. "Laying down deed after deed. I know they can have no effect." The tears continued to make their way down his face.

We sat again in silence. I knew that no words from me or from Richard could do any good. I knew that Thayer and Lanica would not speak, that Father Aldan, Bellamy, and Cecily had nothing to say. We were all waiting for the one person who could speak to this moment. She was the hope of Asael and the hope of every soul who had lost its way. Only the Rose's words would have any merit in this moment.

"No," Anya said, her voice still low and quiet. "Deeds can have no effect."

Brother Ezra sobbed.

"The Creator does not consider deeds," said Anya.

Brother Ezra turned to look at her. He waited for her to speak again.

"*The Creator knows the man's thoughts and the man's will— better than the man himself,*" Anya quoted from the Ancient Writings. "The Creator does not consider deeds. He knows the thoughts and the wills of men."

Brother Ezra raised his hand and wiped the back of it under his chin, where the tears had gathered and were dripping down.

"Do you believe the Rose is the hope of Asael?" asked Anya.

"Aye," said Brother Ezra. "And I have lived to see her."

"Then your past actions cannot count against you any more than they can count for you," said Anya. "You are a follower of the Rose. You seek the way of the Creator."

Anya stood and turned to address us all. Her voice rang out as it had that first night we met, rising in the silence now as it had above the hubbub of voices then, beautiful and clear. "Tomorrow we go to the Capital. We shall not use magic to fight. '*Skill in practice is only a sign*'; it is not a tool to be wielded for power. The Ancient Writings teach that our war is not against our fellow men but against death itself. The Council strives for power as they strive for strength and life. They fear the end of these things; they fear the end of their own lives. We go to the Capital tomorrow. There is only one hope of Asael. It is not the Council. That is the course of action we will take, Richard. We will introduce the Council to the Rose."

I sat alone later that night in the front sitting room. I had Edmund's book with me and was recording all I could remember of what had taken place in the previous months. The door to the hall opened, and I looked up as Brother Ezra entered. I was curled up on a sofa, and he sat down on the far end.

"I breathe easy tonight, as I have not for thirty years," he said.

I watched his profile in the lamplight. I could not imagine living with a secret like his. Lord Allard's Rebellion had been the darkest moment of King Saran's reign. And sitting on the sofa with me was the man who was responsible.

"I wanted to apologize to you," Brother Ezra said. "Your uncle died at my hand."

"I didn't know him," I said.

"Your father grew hard after his brother's death," said Brother Ezra. "I've come from speaking with your brother. He told me how harsh a man Lord Adamaris has become."

"Aye," I said. "He is."

"Richard tells me you often bore the brunt of your father's anger."

I considered this for a moment. My mind reached back over my life, looking for a time when I had not feared my father. Until the night Sephanya arrived, I could not think of a single one. "Aye," I said.

"I cannot say what might have happened had Lord Richard Adamaris not died by my hand in that battle," said Brother Ezra. "But I know something of what happened because he did. And I know you have hurt because of it. I wish there were better words to explain the sorrow this places in my soul. I breathe easy tonight, but your pain has been a part of every labored breath for the past thirty years—even before I knew you." He began to rise from his seat.

"Wait," I said. He stopped and looked over at me. "Sit, please."

Brother Ezra sat again. He turned slightly, so he was facing me.

"You said once that He Who Knows Men's Thinking is weaving a tapestry, and we only see the mess of strings."

"Aye."

"We think He may have picked up the wrong one, when really if we could see the picture being woven, we would know to trust the artist."

"Aye."

"My father is a cruel man," I said. "And Richard is right: I bore much of that cruelty as we grew up." I swallowed. "I feared him."

I paused again. Brother Ezra waited.

"When I was a child, I would lie in my bed at night and think over all the encounters I had had with my father during the day. Each one terrified me and kept me from sleep. One by one, I would run them over in my mind. As I did so, it was as if someone took them away, and, when I was done, I always slept peacefully."

One side of Brother Ezra's mouth rose, forming a half-smile.

"You remember how surprised you were at my sensitivity to He Who Knows Men's Thinking when we met?" I asked. "How listening for His guidance came so naturally to me?"

He nodded, the other side of his mouth rising. "Aye," he said.

"That night that I gave over my fears to He Who Knows Men's Thinking, I was doing nothing new," I said. "I had only discovered the One who had been there all the time."

"And a string in the tapestry makes a picture," said Brother Ezra.

I smiled at him. We sat quietly for another moment.

"What are you writing?" he asked.

I looked down at the book in my lap. "More tapestry strings," I said. "Edmund Makram gave me this book to record what has happened."

"You tell the story of the Rose well," Brother Ezra said. "I heard you many times in the caves, when the pilgrims came."

"When I finish recording this, I shall have to record your stories," I said to him. "They should not be lost."

"I have written since I was a boy," Ezra said. "The volumes are in the monastery in the Capital. I shall show them to you when we are there."

"I would like that," I said.

He rose, wished me a good night, and left. I heard his cough echo in the front hall as he made his way up the front stair. I went up to my rooms an hour later, my eyes drooping with weariness. Anya was already asleep in the cot, and I quietly blew out the burning lamp and slipped into bed.

Tired as I was, I found myself lying there listening to the distant beating of the waves and thinking of what the next days would hold. We were to go to the Capital and enter the Council's chambers. And we were going to tell them that the Rose had come to save Asael.

I smiled a little, rueful in the dark. They would laugh us out of the chambers.

Yet, as I turned over the idea in my mind, I found myself again certain it was *right*. The Rose had spoken, and I was to serve her purpose. I heard Anya breathe and shift in her sleep. My friend, the Rose of Asael. There was something new about her since her return from visiting the monasteries, a set purpose that I had not seen before—as if she now knew the direction she was meant to take. She would tell us what we needed to know when we needed to know it. We were, after all, servants of the Rose.

WE woke early and packed up our things. I did not know if I would ever see Marinel again. If we failed, my father would never invite me back into his home. I gave my thanks to Garima and her helpers as we prepared to leave.

"I spoke with the weaver last night," Garima said to me.

"Did you?" I said. "I know Lanica was grateful for your hospitality."

"Aye, she said that," said Garima. "And she said you are

all going to the Capital to face the Council."

"We are," I said.

"You believe this whole thing that much?"

"Aye," I said. "The only hope for Asael is to turn back to He Who Knows Men's Thinking."

"Miss Anya was down here yesterday, too," said Garima.

"Oh, yes?"

"I asked her if I should have one of the girls injure themselves so she could heal it and show us her skill with magic."

I tried to stifle the giggle that arose. "Really? And what did she say?"

"She said these meals I've made in the past few days were sign enough," Garima said. "Nobles and peasants and monks and priests all eating together in one room."

"*Those who would not share bread will break it together before me*," I quoted.

"Aye," said Garima. "I never thought I'd feed the Rose talked about in the Writings. I always thought the Rose would be too high and mighty to eat the likes of my cooking."

A lump rose in my throat, and I felt a hotness around my eyes. She believed. I reached out and hugged her. "Oh, Garima!"

She waited out my hug and then stepped back. "Now look at you, milady, getting flour all over yourself. You best be on your way now and come back safe."

I ran up the stairs and out the door where the others had gathered with the horses saddled. Lanica was driving a wagon with the bulk of our provisions and luggage. Tay and Cecily rode with her, and the rest of us were to go on horseback. The day was chilly, but the roads were much clearer than they had been a few days earlier.

I was the last out the door. At the sight of me, Richard called for everyone to mount. He and Lord Mumina took the lead, and Brother Ezra and Father Aldan followed. Thayer rode close to the wagon, leaving Anya and me to bring up the rear.

She held my horse's head while I mounted and then handed me her reins to hold while she did the same. When she was in the saddle, I handed them back to her.

"So we're off to the Capital to face the Council," I said.

"Aye."

I grinned at her. "Do you think they'll crown you immediately when you arrive, or will they take some convincing to make you queen?"

She arranged her skirt and looked up at me. "Oh, I will not be queen," she said.

"Well, you'll be the Rose, of course," I corrected myself.

"The Rose is not a ruler," said Anya.

I stared at her for a moment. "Then who will lead Asael?" I asked.

"Richard," she said, turning her horse toward the road.

"What?"

Anya gently tapped her heels against the mare's sides, setting her off after the wagon. She looked back over her shoulder at me and laughed at what must have been the utterly shocked expression on my face. "Come on, Karan," she called back. "You said yourself he could lead nations if he put his mind to it."

CHAPTER 25

WE entered the city by raft late that night. We'd been greeted in a narrow stretch of farmland to the west of the Capital by a group of Helpers, most of them younger than me. They'd bowed their heads quietly when they saw Anya and taken the horses' reins at Father Aldan's order. They would ride the horses in through the gates the next evening as if coming in from working out in the fields owned by the monastery.

We, more recognizable than a group of young monks, needed to approach the city under the cover of darkness, avoiding guards at the gates. There were rafts that the monks used to transport equipment and produce between the monastery and their fields. This night they transported us.

I sat on the bottom of the raft, pulling my shawl about me and shivering in the cold wind that blew down the river from the mountains into the city. Father Aldan and Brother Ezra helped the young monks pole the rafts toward the stone bridge ahead. Once we went under it, we were within the city limits. I glanced at Cecily on the far side of the raft. She caught my eye and waved with a quick smile. I smiled back, unable to free a hand for a wave. I liked her. I couldn't help myself. She was joyful and energetic. I had been surprised at how quickly she and her brother had believed, how eager they had been to throw in their lot with us. Lord Mumina's land holdings were small and far from the Capital, diminishing their value even further. Even so, I thought, the prospect of losing everything—your way of life, your rank and status in society, your home—was daunting. I asked myself if I would have been open to the Rose had she not arrived on my doorstep, had I not been an unhappy, fearful daughter of an angry father. I did not know. The raft swayed as we moved across the smooth water, under the bridge, and into the Capital.

We reached the monastery without incident. There was a culvert into which we followed a diverted stream off the main river. We followed the stream in the dark for a few minutes. Once through the culvert, we were in what seemed to be an underground cave. The walls and ceiling were covered with murals depicting moments of the history of Asael. I glanced over them as the raft came to a stop at a small dock. Richard stood and reached down to help me to my feet.

"We're under the monastery," said Brother Ezra. "This is the entrance to the storage areas and kitchens."

A young Helper assisted us off the raft onto the dock, and Brother Ezra led the way up narrow, dark stairs. We passed through the kitchens and went on. When we came to a dark door, Brother Ezra pushed it open. He ushered us through, and we found ourselves in the front hall of the building.

A middle-aged monk stood there and smiled at us in greeting. "Brother Ezra, Father Aldan," he said. "It is good to see you again."

"Thank you, Brother Derenik," said Father Aldan. "It is good to be back home."

The younger monk looked us all over. "Which is Young Lord Adamaris?"

Richard stepped forward, "I am."

"A message arrived for you less than an hour ago." Brother Derenik held out a paper.

Richard took it from him and opened it. "It's from Edmund," he said. I moved closer and looked over his shoulder. My skill with the code the two of them had always used for writing messages to each other was limited. I recognized a word here and there, but I couldn't decipher the text on the page.

Richard looked up from the page, his face ashen. "King Saran died tonight."

There was a moment of silence in the hall. "It begins," said Father Aldan.

"The Council will declare themselves in the morning," said Brother Ezra. "We must forestall them."

"How?" asked Cecily.

"The Rose must go out among the people—let them see she is here."

"Can we avoid bloodshed?" asked Anya.

"I do not know," said Brother Ezra. "But for now, we should catch an hour's rest."

We were shown to small monks' cells in a narrow hallway off the front hall. Brother Ezra opened a door and beckoned Cecily, Anya, and me. "We have extra cells, but no extra cushions," he said, indicating the room. I looked in. On one end, the floor was nearly covered with two large cushions, about three feet wide and six feet long. "I thought you would like to be a little more comfortable all together than to each have your own room."

Anya, Cecily, and I looked at each other. Cecily grinned. "Aye," she said to Brother Ezra. "I would appreciate the cushions. Shall we, friends?"

I looked to Anya; she shrugged a little and smiled. "Aye," she said.

I gripped her hand as she stood beside me and looked back at Cecily. "I would appreciate the cushions, too," I said. "I've grown soft this last week back at Marinel."

Richard and Mumina were put into a cell across from ours, and Thayer, Lanica, and Tay were next door. Brother Ezra had told us he would wake us in an hour, so once everyone was settled, we three girls made our way to the cushions and dropped onto them without much conversation. As I was drifting off to sleep, I heard Cecily, beside me, whisper, "I'm glad we're all together. These stones would be terrifying if I were all alone." I smiled a little, thinking how strange it was I trusted these man-made stone walls over the caves that had stood for centuries. Then I reached over and hooked my arm through Cecily's, gave it a squeeze, and fell sound asleep.

I woke to a gentle knock at the door of the monk's cell. I heard Brother Ezra cough, and then his voice came through the door.

"We will eat together in half an hour," he said. "In the kitchens."

Anya was waking beside me, and I turned and shook Cecily on my other side.

"That was *not* enough sleep," Cecily said.

I laughed a little. "Welcome to life as a follower of the Rose," I said. "She's a taskmaster."

Anya elbowed me. "I seem to remember it being Richard and Brother Ezra who decided we needed to arrive in the night," she said. "This comes as a result of throwing in our lot with the nobles and the monks."

Cecily's laugh echoed off the walls as we rose from the cushions to get ready for the day.

It was good to laugh. I was reminded of the early days when it was just Anya and Richard and me. In the recent weeks, with the reality of our purpose becoming more clear, we'd lost some of the moments of laughter. The seriousness of our purpose weighed on us. Now King Saran was dead, and the Council was prepared to take over the governance of Asael. We knew what the nobles would do with unrestricted power over the peasants on their lands. We'd seen glimpses of it in the past months as the injured and sick came to the caves seeking the Rose.

I glanced over at Anya. She wore the same simple black dress she'd put on the night she arrived at Marinel. She was pulling her hair back into its single long braid. With the early grey light of morning filtering in through the window and washing over her, I was struck by how young she looked. This girl was the hope of Asael. Somehow, through her, all would be made right.

I remembered her off-hand revelation from the day before: Richard would be king. Anya would not rule. As surprised as I'd been to hear her make that statement, I'd seen that she had been considering it for quite some time. There was a certain set about her shoulders that had indicated she'd decided, and there would be no arguing the matter. I wondered how she planned to tell Richard that she intended him to be king. I knew she wouldn't back down.

Anya, Cecily, and I made our way down to the kitchens once we'd dressed. Richard, Mumina, and Brother Ezra were already there. We served ourselves porridge from a crock on the stovetop and sat with them on long wooden benches along either side of a table worn smooth by the years. We ate silently, quickly. Thayer and Lanica joined us, as did Father Aldan. Tay slept on. He would stay in the monastery under the care of the young Helpers. Our destination was no place for a child. We were going to the Council's chambers.

Finishing our meal in silence, we rose and handed our dishes to a Helper who took them to the scullery. Brother Ezra took a deep breath, triggering a short fit of coughs. When they quieted, he breathed again and looked at Anya.

"Are you ready?" he asked.

"Aye," she said. She looked to Richard, then to me. "To the Council's chambers?"

Richard nodded. "Aye," he said. "We shall introduce them to the Rose."

"Lead us," Anya said to him.

Richard led the way up the stairs to the main hall. A Helper opened the doors, and we stepped out into the pearly morning light. The skies were overcast, but at that early hour, the sun would not have been far above the horizon anyway. Our troop—two noblemen, two monks, two simply-dressed noble ladies, a peasant couple, and a girl without a past—made our way through the silent courtyard to the street gate. It was dark wood, heavy planks tied together by wrought iron joints. Bellamy and Richard lifted the wooden bar that held it shut. Thayer and Father Aldan pulled back one side of the gate, and Brother Ezra led the way through it out into the streets of the Capital.

The streets were busy. Much more full than I expected them to be at that early hour. We made our way down from the monastery toward the river. It took longer on foot than it had floating down the underground stream the night before. Looking through gaps in the buildings, I could see the government buildings, the palace, and the cathedral on the far side of the city. My father's city house was within a few blocks of them—that was the area of the Capital I knew. We would cross the river by going over the bridge of boats in the center of the city and make our way up the hills to the Council Chamber in the government buildings.

"Why is the Monastery so far from the cathedral?" Cecily asked.

"The monks have always wished for solitude," said Father Aldan. "A small number stay in the living quarters near the cathedral, but most of us live on this side of the city, nearer to our fields, further from the hubbub of the king's palace."

"I've not spent much time on this side of the river," I said.

"No," said Brother Ezra. "Not many nobles do. The river has served as a dividing line for centuries."

I looked around at the buildings about us. The architecture was much simpler than the buildings on my father's street. Though they were in good repair, the stones were worn and old, and there were few ornate carvings.

Bellamy Mumina caught my eye. "We've lived separate in so many ways," he said.

"Aye." I nodded. The people of the Capital were not under a single nobleman's rule but were directly under the power of the king. I wondered what they had thought for so many years when they went through the streets of their own city and saw such a difference from one side of the river to the other.

The crowds multiplied as we got closer to the river. More and more, I felt eyes on us. We were beginning to be recognized. Some who did followed us as we made our way toward the bridge of boats.

"Anya," said Richard quietly. "I see people in the crowd from the caves and from the villages we visited."

Anya nodded to him. "Aye. They came, as we asked them to."

The streets narrowed, and the crowd compressed around us. Cecily grabbed Anya's hand on one side, and I took hold of the other. Richard and Bellamy went before us, pushing through and making sure we were close behind them. Thayer and Father Aldan flanked Cecily and me, and Brother Ezra and Lanica brought up the rear. We kept close, by necessity and by desire. I had no wish to be lost in that crowd in a part of the Capital I didn't know.

We reached the river at last, and the crowd grew even larger. From the buildings that faced the river to the low wall before the docks was a roiling mass of people. It stretched in either direction as far as I could see.

"Anya." I was struck breathless by the sheer quantity of people. "They came. They're Followers." I glanced over at her. Tears shone in her eyes.

Richard and Bellamy began to push toward the bridge of boats. The Capital was not a very large city; the river, going through its center, was only about two miles long. There were only two bridges across it: the stone one we had come under the night before and this bridge of boats lashed together by ropes that crossed at the center of the city. Liveried officers of the king stood at the end we approached, but not the other—another sign of the forced separation between the nobles' side and the peasants' side. Along the riverfront were hundreds of small docks with tiny craft moored to them. Most people used these for fishing in the short stretch of rich feeding ground downriver from the city before the river stretched out into an unnavigable delta or to traverse the water from one side of the city to the other. Some winters, it grew cold enough for the river to freeze, and then the people simply walked the quarter-mile to the other side, but so far that year, there was only a little ice at the river's edges.

As we approached, I saw Richard loosen his sword in its scabbard. We did not know what we would face with the guards.

We reached the low wall that separated the riverfront from the street beside it. As we were about to pass through the gap by the bridge of boats, we heard a shout from the crowd.

"Miss Anya!"

We turned toward the voice, but we could not tell who'd called out. Another shout rang out from the other direction: "Miss Anya! We wish to help!"

Another voice, then another, and another joined the first brave shouts. I couldn't make out the words any longer, except to hear Anya's name and the word "Rose" again and again.

Richard stepped to Anya. "They are calling for the Rose," he said. "You must speak to them."

Anya took a deep breath. She closed her eyes for a moment. Opening them, she nodded. "Get their attention for me," she said to Richard.

Richard climbed up the low wall and stood tall. His torso was above the heads of the crowd. Everyone could see him.

He raised his hands for silence, and the shouting faded away. Richard cleared his throat and called out in a loud voice, "I am Richard Adamaris, Follower of the Rose."

The crowd erupted into cheers. Richard raised a hand again, and they grew quiet once more. "I have seen some of you before. Many of you have met the Rose and know first-hand that He Who Knows Men's Thinking has gifted her with magic well beyond her training."

Cheers rang out again. The hand raised. The crowd quieted. Anya and I exchanged a glance. Richard could rule nations if he put his mind to it.

"The Rose arrived on the doorstep of my father's estate like the waif in the story from the Ancient Writings. Over and over again, I have watched as she has fulfilled what was written. I have, like many of you, seen her power first-hand. But some of you have come here today simply because you heard the stories—the stories that have run through the villages of Asael like a fire through kindling. You have come to see if they are true." Richard paused for a moment and looked down into Anya's face. He smiled and turned back to the crowd. "To you, today, I wish to introduce Sephanya, the Rose of Asael!"

As Richard reached his hand down to help Anya climb up onto the wall beside him, the people burst into their loudest cheers yet. Anya stepped up beside Richard and smiled at him. He moved to step down, but she put a hand on his arm, keeping him beside her. She turned to the crowd. I wondered if she might announce right there her idea that Richard was to be the next king. I waited, my breath coming quickly, to hear what she would say.

The crowd grew quiet, and she spoke. I vividly remembered the first time I heard her voice, rising above the noise of the storm and the servants in the front hall at Marinel. The lovely tones of it rang out as clearly as that night. "Today is a sad day for Asael," she said to the crowd. "In the middle of the night, we heard the news that King Saran died." There were gasps. The Council's heralds had not yet taken to the streets in the early morning. I doubted whether they knew the Capital was so full of people. Anya glanced down at us and at Richard standing beside her. "My friends are coming with me to the Council's Chambers. We understand that they plan to announce today their new plan to govern the kingdom by Council rule. I go to speak to the Council because I fear they do not have in their hearts the best interest of the people of Asael. I go to speak for you."

The crowd burst out into cheers. Then, as Anya seemed ready to step down from the wall and proceed toward the bridge of boats, we heard the cheers change into shouts and yells. I couldn't make out what they were saying, but Anya must have understood them before me. She froze, and her eyes flashed with the anger she rarely showed.

She turned back to the crowd, and they began to quiet. I then heard what people were yelling.

"We'll fight with you!" I heard someone yell.

"My sword for the Rose!" another voice called out.

Anya looked to Richard, and he raised his hand for silence. The shouts faded away.

"War—violence—is our last resort!" Anya said, her face flushed. "I go to the Council Chambers to speak for you. I will not represent warmongers! Follow me if you will, but leave your swords behind you!"

She jumped down from the wall and strode toward the bridge of boats. The crowd parted before her. Richard watched her for a moment. Then he unbuckled his scabbard from around his waist and lifted it above his head as he turned to the crowd.

"I will follow the Rose, and I leave my sword behind me." He set down the scabbard on the wall, jumped down, and followed Anya, all of us falling in behind him and the crowd following after us. The liveried guards watched in silence as first Anya passed, then our troop. When the first members of the crowd approached the bridge, I glanced back. I watched as the guards unbuckled their swords, set them down, and joined the people following the Rose, eager expressions on their faces.

CHAPTER 26

AS we made our way into the part of the city I knew, I saw that the crowd following us had formed itself into a unit. There were probably several hundred of those who had been at the river who continued on with us, and they seemed to be an organized battalion. A force to be reckoned with, even without swords.

The streets in this half of the city were nowhere near as full as those on the other side of the river. From time to time, we saw servants hurrying by on early morning errands. I was certain the nobles who owned the homes on either side of the streets were still sound asleep. We were a few streets from the government buildings when we heard the steady thrum of feet marching in rhythm on the cobblestone streets. We turned a corner and saw what was making the noise.

A large troop of soldiers, uniformed and armed, approached from the far end of the street. I saw Gennady riding a horse at their head. He reined his horse at the sight of us and raised a hand to stop the soldiers behind him. He waited our approach.

Anya did not falter. She continued to stride forward with the same purpose she'd shown at the bridge of boats. Richard walked by her side, and the rest of us followed. As they drew near Gennady, Richard and Anya slowed. I saw Anya look to Richard and nod slightly. As he had at the dock wall, he understood her intentions. He raised his hand, and we fell in behind him, the crowd at our back standing silent.

"Gennady," Richard said.

"Young Lord Adamaris," said Gennady. "I am not certain whether your father will be glad to see you alive or disappointed he must now live with the regret of having a traitor son."

Richard was silent.

Gennady looked over Richard and Anya at me. I quaked under his gaze but handed my fears to He Who Knows Men's Thinking.

"Karan," Gennady said, nodding. "It is a shame you chose this path rather than the one I offered you. I expect your life will be much less comfortable than it would have been as the wife of a Council leader."

"Lord Gennady," I said, nodding back. "If I wished a life of comfort, I would not have left my father's home."

"More's the pity you did," he said. He surveyed us again. "Monks and peasants, Richard? This is who you choose to surround yourself with?"

"I surround myself with the Followers of the Rose," replied Richard. "May I present Sephanya, the Rose of Asael?"

Gennady's glance flicked over Anya, and he addressed himself to Richard again. "This waif? Oh, Richard, you have been sadly misled. Did she promise you favors if you would be her protector? She may know the tricks of the trade, but I promise you can find better-endowed women on any street corner."

I gasped. Anya's head jerked back as if she'd been slapped. I watched Richard shift forward, ready to run and drag down Gennady from his horse. Anya recovered herself to reach out and grasp his arm, restraining him.

"Milady Karan," Gennady addressed me again. He looked me up and down. "You may have ruined your matrimonial chances for good, but if you've learned a thing or two from this friend of yours, we could still talk terms. I've a delightful little cottage on my property where I could put you up in exchange for a visit now and then."

I cried out, and Richard broke free of Anya's hand. "You filthy brute!" he yelled, rushing forward, reaching for his sword—but it lay still in his scabbard back at the river. He hesitated.

"Richard!" Anya called out to him as he stuttered in his rush toward Gennady's horse. He stopped and looked back at her. His eyes still blazed with anger. "Richard," Anya said, her voice steady, "we have a purpose here today."

Richard took a deep breath. He looked at me. I could see Lord Mumina tensed to fight beside me. I could hear Cecily breathing heavily. I could feel the red anger in my cheeks. I wanted Richard to rush the horse and pummel Gennady's filthy mouth until he had no remaining teeth. I could sense the crowd behind me, strung tighter than a bowstring; I heard their shuffling feet and angry murmurs. But Anya was the Rose. We were her servants.

I closed my eyes for a moment and took a deep breath, letting the tension leave my muscles. I opened my eyes and found Richard's again. I slowly shook my head once.

I watched the fire crackle in his eyes as he fought against his own anger. He looked from me to Anya.

"It's the last option," Anya said to him.

"Aye," said Richard, his voice tight. He turned back to Gennady. "The Rose would like to address the Council," he said.

Gennady chuckled with false good nature. "A common whore in the Council Chambers?" he said. "That will be the day!"

The crowd behind us broke. We were shoved to the side of the street as men and women rushed forward at Gennady.

"No!" cried Anya.

But it was no use; the fight had begun. Followers of the Rose, weaponless, charged the armed soldiers and, wave after wave, were cut down.

From where we stood on the sidewalk, I looked up at Gennady on his horse in the middle of the fray. He laughed as he watched the carnage unfold.

"We must do something!" Mumina said. "Miss Anya, your magic!"

Anya had tears streaming down her face. She looked at Brother Ezra, a pleading expression in her eyes.

"It is worse than this," he said.

Mumina pleaded with her. "Miss Anya!"

Anya sobbed and shook her head.

Cecily wrapped her arm around Anya's shoulders. "No magic in battle, Bellamy! Father Aldan! Richard! Brother Ezra! Thayer! All of you, get them to retreat! Back across the bridge of boats." She shook Anya gently and grabbed me with her free hand. "We sound the retreat now; we will fight another day."

The men scattered. Lanica said something about the wounded and followed after them, calling directions to people in the crowd as she went.

"You're all right?" Cecily said to me. "He was only trying to force a fight."

"Aye," I said.

"Anya," Cecily turned her so they faced each other. She was shorter by nearly a head than Anya, but she gripped her shoulders with a steely strength. "You must call for the retreat as well."

Anya lifted her head and looked over to where the worst of the fighting was happening. "I told them to come unarmed," she said.

"And you were right to!" said Cecily. "But we must now address the reality. Call for retreat."

Anya nodded. She took a deep breath, stood straight, and made her way into the crowd, calling out for people to retreat.

"Let us assist Lanica in getting helpers for the wounded," Cecily said to me. She turned and moved into the crowd. Before I stepped off the sidewalk, I looked over again at Gennady. He was watching from his perch above the heads of the crowd and saw the turning of the Followers back toward the river. I saw him see the advantage and choose to press it.

"Soldiers!" he yelled. "They flee! Give chase!"

And as the street began to clear, I watched a line of Followers who had wrested swords from the dead and living hands of soldiers in the skirmish stand together and hold back the charging troops, fighting to the death to give us time to retreat.

I joined those assisting the wounded, and we hurried back through the streets to the bridge of boats. Those who had crossed before us had cleared the crowd back away from the dock wall. Bellamy Mumina, Brother Ezra, and Father Aldan were directing people away from the bridge area as they came across. I saw Richard and Anya standing by the riverbank and joined them as soon as I'd helped the wounded man I was supporting to the triage area that Lanica and Cecily were setting up.

We watched as a few more stragglers came hurrying across the boats. I had been near the back of the retreat. After the last of the Followers came Gennady on horseback, leading the chase.

"We must stop him," I said.

"Anya," said Richard. "Burn the boats."

"But—" I could see her about to protest about using magic in battle.

"Quick, now, before Gennady and his men reach them. You won't hurt anyone," said Richard.

Anya glanced back across the bridge of boats and realized the truth of his words. There was a gap just big enough between the last of the Followers and Gennady's horse. The line of men who had held back the soldiers had sacrificed their lives for that gap.

Anya concentrated, gathering her strength, pulling out the single line of burning flame from her mind. She reached out her hand and whispered, "*Igniculus.*"

One by one, starting on the far side of the river, the boats that made up the bridge began to burn, the ropes that held them together breaking apart. They separated, destroying one of the only two bridges in the city.

"Mumina!" Richard turned and called. Bellamy came running to us. "Take archers and defend the stone bridge," Richard said. "Do not provoke a fight, but be prepared to hold the position. We shall organize reinforcements later."

Bellamy Mumina jogged away, calling for anyone who could handle a bow to join him.

Gennady had pulled up his horse on the far side of the river. It was difficult to see him through the flames rising from the burning boats between us, but I thought I saw a look of surprise on his face. One moment the bridge of boats had stood, floating as it had for as long as anyone could remember, and the next, it was gone, the boats floating in the river each aflame. This was magic beyond—it seemed—his expectation.

A few hours later, we had moved most of the wounded up to the monastery, where Lanica was coordinating their care with some of the monks. We had no way of knowing how many had been lost in that morning's battle. There were seventy-five with wounds that needed continued care and more who were able to go after the monks dressed their wounds. Richard had gathered more archers and gone to the stone bridge to consult with Bellamy about setting up a defense rotation there.

The morning's events had happened so early that the normal traffic of boats back and forth across the river had not begun. A few small vessels were moored on the far side of the river, but most who used boats for crossing were the shopkeepers and delivery men. Being peasants, they all docked their boats on the monastery's side of the river. When the flaming debris in the water dissipated, we would need to be prepared for a few small parties in boats, but other than that and the stone bridge, the river itself became our protector. It broadened into impassable marshes less than a mile from the Capital as it flowed east to the sea a few miles away, and upstream it widened into treacherous rapids as it came down out of the mountains. In the city, it was not deep—the boats were all flat-bottomed—but the rocks on the riverbed were treacherous and sharp. The kings of old had built the Capital there for that very reason. All traffic moving north or south through Asael was forced to go through the city and pay the tariffs associated with such travel.

By midday, Richard had returned from the stone bridge, and we had gathered with Anya, Brother Ezra, Thayer, Cecily, and Father Aldan at the riverbank where the bridge of boats used to begin. The weather was turning cold, and I wrapped my cloak tightly around me to ward off the breeze that came up from the water behind me.

"Lanica is tending the wounded," Thayer said. "She said she will stay at the monastery."

"Aye," said Anya.

"Mumina is training the stone bridge defensemen," said Richard. "He will join us when he can."

Anya nodded. We waited for her to speak. She looked at Richard. "Thank you," she said.

"For what?" he asked.

"For leaving your sword behind this morning." She swallowed back a sob. "Those deaths are on my shoulders," she said. "You did what I asked."

Richard nodded. "I am sorry," he said.

"For what?"

"For losing my temper with Gennady," said Richard. "My anger fed the crowd's."

"You were defending our honor," I said. "And you checked yourself."

"Not soon enough," he said.

Brother Ezra broke in. "This morning went regrettably wrong. We grieve those we lost. But we cannot live in our regrets. That debris in the water will not burn much longer, and we must look forward."

"Yes," said Cecily. "What did we learn this morning that can help us?"

I smiled at her. "We learned that you keep your head in a crisis, Lady Cecily."

"Aye," said Anya. "You may have saved all of our lives."

Richard reached down and gripped Cecily's hand. "Thank you."

She blushed a little. "Enough of that!" she said. "What else did we learn?"

"Gennady was surprised when Anya burned the boats," I said. "It was hard to see him, but I don't think he expected real magic from you, Anya. He seemed taken aback by how quickly it all happened."

"Good," said Brother Ezra. "He will have a healthy fear of her from here on out."

"Maybe it will stop him from spewing such filthy—" Richard began.

"Richard," Anya cut him off, warning in her tone. "We are looking forward now."

Father Aldan nodded. "The people are able to fight," he said. "Even without swords, there were some who got the upper hand of the soldiers. They can be trained, Miss Anya, if it comes to battle."

Anya shook her head. "I wish I could still say I hope it will not. But I fear we may have no choice. Richard, can you and Mumina and Thayer train others as you are the defensemen?"

"Aye," Richard said.

Thayer nodded. "We prepared for this at the caves," he said.

"You are our generals," Anya said. "There are two rules that must be primary, though: We use no magic to fight, and violence is our final option."

Richard and Thayer nodded. "Aye."

"This is all good," I said, "but what is our next step? If the Council will not even speak to Anya, then how do we proceed?"

We stood in a near-circle at the river's edge. I was facing away from the river, and Cecily was almost directly across from me, next to Richard. Her eyes widened at something in the distance behind me; then she glanced up at Richard's face before looking back behind me.

"Richard," she said, gripping his arm. "Is that your father?"

I turned. We all did, moving to face the expanse of water and our enemy's territory across it. The debris that had once been the bridge of boats was burning itself out and was beginning to be pulled downstream by the current, which was very slow through the city. We could see clearly across the water now, and Gennady had returned, still mounted. Flanking him on either side were Lord Briyanne and my father.

I took a deep breath. It had been months since I had seen my father. So much had happened in the intervening time that it might as well have been a lifetime. As I tried to decipher the emotions I was experiencing, I saw him put a hand out to his side as if he were waiting for something to be placed in it.

From behind him, a young man moved his horse forward. My heart leapt. I watched as Edmund placed a large cone-shaped device in my father's hand.

CHAPTER 27

FATHER raised the conical device to his mouth.

"Where is the peasant styling herself the Rose of Asael?" His voice came across the water to us clearly, magnified by the cone.

Anya glanced around our circle and stepped forward onto one of the docks. Her distinctive voice rang out as she called back.

"I am the Rose," she said.

"Turn yourself in, tell your ring leaders to stand down, and the Council will look with mercy on the peasants you have misled. We will allow them to return to their homes."

"The lives to which you would return them serve a system constructed to fail," said Anya.

"We are at the prelude of a great age for Asael," my father said.

"The Council's work will come to nothing," said Anya. "You are serving yourselves alone."

"And you serve an antiquated system of ritual."

"What will you do for King Saran's funeral?" asked Anya.

I thought at first that her statement was a non-sequitur. But then my father, whose responses had been immediate up to that point, hesitated. I saw a grin flash across Edmund's face before he quickly replaced it with the stoic expression he'd carried since he'd come into view.

Father gathered himself together. "The king will receive a funeral worthy of his position."

Suddenly I understood. If belief in He Who Knows Men's Thinking was an antiquated ritual, then calling upon a Priest to perform the funeral rites for the king undermined the Council's purpose. Anya had struck a blow.

Gennady moved his horse closer to my father's and said something that we could not hear. Father turned to him and seemed to speak sharply. Gennady moved back, seemingly chastened.

Father raised the cone to his mouth again. "Richard Adamaris!" he called out.

Richard went forward and stood beside Anya. He raised his voice to shout across the water. "Aye, Father."

"So you still recognize I hold that role?"

"You are still my father, Sir. You are not my leader."

"No!" Our father's voice was sharp. "You choose the way of the traitor."

I saw Richard's back straighten and his fists clench. He glanced at Anya, and she shook her head slightly.

"Anger will get us nowhere," she said.

"I cannot defend our choices in a shouting match across the river!" said Richard. "Shall we establish terms for a meeting of our two sides?"

Before Father answered, we heard a commotion in the crowd behind us. A runner, one of the young Helpers who had been tasked to the stone bridge with Bellamy Mumina, burst through the mass of people to the water's edge.

"Soldiers!" He panted, trying to gain breath to share his message. "At the bridge! Our defensemen are under attack."

Richard shot a furious look across the water. "A waste of time!" he said.

"A parley is never a waste," said Anya.

"This was no parley," Richard said. "It was a distraction." He looked about at us. "Thayer, you are in charge here. I doubt they will attempt a crossing with one of their boats during daylight hours, but keep men at arms near the front as defense. Father Aldan, Cecily, assist him."

They nodded. Brother Ezra took a deep breath and coughed to clear his throat.

"We are going to the bridge?" he asked.

"I need you and Karan to command the Helpers." Richard had agreed to abide by Anya and Ezra's dictum. He would not command the use of magic in battle, but he wanted those gifted in it nearby. "You have Healers?"

Ezra looked back to the crowd. Near the front were a group of monks who had not returned to the monastery with the wounded. "Aye," he said. "Some are still here."

"Bring them." Richard turned to Anya. "You would rather heal, I know, but I need you with me at the front. They must see you."

Anya nodded. *They* meant both the soldiers and our own people.

I glanced across the water. Our father had given up his attempt to parley and seemed to be coordinating his men as Richard was. I had no doubt that they would send reinforcements just as we did.

"We must hurry," said Richard. He called out to a group of men standing near, "Divide yourselves between defense here and those who will come with the Rose to the stone bridge."

Already that morning, Richard had organized the Followers willing to fight into some semblance of order. At his call, his lieutenants gave instruction to their men, dividing into two groups.

Thayer called on men near the front of the crowd to force a path for us. The runner led the way, and we followed—the Rose, her general, a monk, and a girl, leading a troop of men and women and monks running through the streets near the river, making our way to the stone bridge.

Brother Ezra stumbled a little by my side. I gripped his arm to support him and called out to Richard and Anya to go on. They continued to hurry forward, the fighters behind them, and I dropped back with Brother Ezra and the Healers.

By the time we reached the bridge, Brother Ezra was coughing—a deep, wracking cough. "Brother?" I asked.

"Should I get a Helper?" I looked around. A battle was being waged at the bridge, and the Helpers were clearing space for a makeshift clinic near the rear.

"No!" Brother Ezra got the word out between coughs. "I will not have a Healer!"

We stayed back from the worst of the fighting; I helped Ezra to the stoop of a house where he sat on the steps and recovered himself. His cough worried me. It had been growing worse and worse since our time in the caves. Being outdoors all day in the chill air could be doing him no good. But he wouldn't allow me to do anything, instead waving me away and telling me to oversee the organization of the Helpers.

Already there were wounded who needed tending. I appointed two Helpers to be in charge of triage and another to lead a team that would go forward to bring people back from the battle. The rest of the Healers had their hands full working on the wounded. I shouted directions and assisted where I was able.

I do not know how long it had been before Brother Ezra joined me. I looked up from the man's chest where I staunched a bleeding wound with my bare hands, to see him beside me. His skin held a grey tint, but he seemed to be breathing easier. He lifted my hands from the wound for a moment and shook his head.

"Miss Anya could heal this, but none of the Helpers," he said.

I looked down at the man lying unconscious before me. Tears pricked at my eyes. I looked up into Ezra's face again.

"Can you?"

His eyes widened at me. "I have not used magic since the day I killed your uncle," he said.

"I know," I replied. "But this is why He Who Knows Man's Thinking gave us magic—to restore, not destroy."

"Aye," he said quietly.

I closed my eyes for a moment. I could feel the beat of the man's heart under my fingers. I knew it had slowed since I put my hands to his wound. I knew there was not much time before it stopped altogether. I concentrated on the rhythm of the beating heart. It was the same rhythm of the waves against the shore, the rhythm of the loom at work. I feared its stopping.

My eyes still closed, I lifted my fear up to He Who Knows Men's Thinking. The sounds of the battle faded from me. I felt the fear taken from my soul and a new assurance set in its place. I faltered for a moment as I considered this new thing. I turned it over in my mind. It was grievous, but not tragic. I was saddened, but not destroyed by it.

I opened my eyes. Brother Ezra knelt directly across from me, on the man's other side.

"You are dying," I said.

He nodded. "He Who Knows Men's Thinking saw fit to show you this?"

"Aye," I said. "And one thing more."

"What is that?"

"It is time to use your magic again. His heart beats with a rhythm I've long known. His life is a thread in the tapestry. I do not know what part of the picture it will make, but I know it cannot be cut off. He Who Knows Men's Thinking would have you use your gifts again."

I watched as tears filled Brother Ezra's eyes. He swallowed hard. He looked deeply into my eyes as if trying to read my soul. The assurance remained. This was *right*.

Clashes of swords and the thump of released bowstrings went on in the distance. The sharp smell of iron filled my nostrils from the blood that covered my hands. Brother Ezra leaned forward on his knees. The sounds and the smells around us faded away as we both focused on the life between us.

Brother Ezra put one hand on the man's forehead and another over mine. He was quiet, and I imagined him finding the magic deep in his mind like Anya described it. "*Sana*," he whispered.

I smelled a faint hint of roses as I felt the flesh beneath my hands knit itself together. As I felt the wound closing, my fingertips sensed the throbbing of his heart growing stronger. His breath changed from shallow gasps to full breaths.

I looked up again to Brother Ezra's face. He had paled even more. Using magic took much of his strength.

"He will live," I said.

"Aye," said Brother Ezra.

I wiped my blood-covered hands on my skirt. I reached out to grip Brother Ezra's. "I will miss you," I said.

He nodded.

I looked around. The sounds of the battle in the distance

returned to me. The shouts of the Helpers flowed back in. The man before us was breathing easily, still unconscious but quiet. He would recover.

"I smelled roses," I said.

Brother Ezra nodded. "That is the scent of magic used to restore," he said. "Have you never been so close?"

I shook my head. "No."

Brother Ezra struggled to his feet and put out a hand to assist me up. "There are others," he said. "Let me use my strength for He Who Knows Men's Thinking while there is still time."

We went from person to person, assessing the needs. Those who would not otherwise survive, Brother Ezra healed, each time growing a bit more pale, each time leaning more heavily on my arm as we walked to the next wounded man.

I learned later that Anya and Richard had joined Lord Mumina at the bridge with their troop of Followers. Mumina's defenders had held position until reinforcements arrived, though outnumbered five to one.

Anya and Richard's arrival had been greeted with cheers from the Followers and a renewed vigor in the fighting. Gennady and Briyanne arrived soon after them, reinforcements with them as well, and the battle continued.

The Followers held the bridge, and the bulk of the fighting took place in the narrow street on the far side of the river. Anya remained on the bridge itself, next to Bellamy Mumina, whose skill with a bow and arrow made him invaluable in such a position. He picked off Lord Briyanne's horse, forcing the old nobleman to fight on his feet rather than raining down blows of his sword on the heads of the Followers from his perch on horseback. Anya served as an extra set of eyes for Bellamy, directing him to shoot toward areas of the battle where he would be less likely to accidentally hit our Followers.

Richard led the infantry forward on foot. He told me that he was trying to make his way to Briyanne and Gennady, but never got so far. Helpers joined the fight, and there was a brief lull in the attack when they did so. But, seeing no magic being used, the soldiers pressed forward again.

They'd fought for nearly an hour when more reinforcements arrived on our side. Thayer had reorganized his troops and was able to send more to the battle at the bridge. Our father and Edmund had disappeared from the waterfront. Thayer said they rode in the direction of the Council Chambers.

All of this went on without my knowing. I stood or knelt by the side of men and women again and again with Brother Ezra. I supported him as he wound between the bodies laid out in the streets to find the next person, and the next person, and the next person who needed help.

I forced him to pause from time to time, when he seemed so weak he would not be able to get to another wounded Follower. I got water for him, and food, and did my best to slow what I'd set in motion—I watched him sap his strength before my eyes, and I knew that his death, which had been coming, was now imminent because of this day's actions.

As darkness fell, the nobles called for their soldiers to retreat. Richard and Mumina set up defenses, and Anya worked with the Helpers to get assistance for all the wounded to be returned to the monastery or other shelter. Brother Ezra moved toward the bridge, and we crossed it, and among the fallen, we found men on both sides of the battle whose hearts still beat. By each one, whether they wore the livery of the Council's soldiers or the plain clothes of peasants, Brother Ezra knelt and found his power and whispered words of healing over them. While men and women Followers carried away the dead, a monk knelt to restore those whose hearts still beat.

It was full dark when Richard and Anya came to find us. "The fighting will begin again in the morning," I heard Richard say as they approached. "And they will send out men late tonight to take away their dead. We should go."

"The riverfront?" Anya asked.

"Thayer has it defended. I expect there to be a skirmish or two there overnight. They will find it safe to use their boats in the darkness. But their boats are small. They cannot carry many soldiers."

Brother Ezra knelt by the side of a young woman. Richard and Anya reached us. I held a hand up to them, and they stopped.

Ezra leaned over her. She had a gash from a glancing blow of a sword across her shoulder. It had missed her head and neck by inches, but she had been knocked unconscious and bled heavily. Her breaths were shallow, and her pulse was weak.

"*Sana*," he whispered, his voice cracking with wear.

Anya gasped at the word. The wound on the woman's shoulder healed itself, and she lay quietly, her breathing eased.

"Brother?" Richard began.

"I'll explain everything, Richard," I said. "But not here. He needs assistance back to the monastery. Anya, help me. Richard, please carry the girl."

Anya and I helped Brother Ezra to his feet. He put his arms around our shoulders and stumbled along between us as we began to move, bearing most of his weight. Richard knelt down and picked up the young woman and followed behind us as we made our way back over the bridge and began the walk back to the monastery.

CHAPTER 28

BROTHER Ezra would not allow Anya to heal him.

"It is my time," he said. He lay on the cushion in his cell. Father Aldan had offered him special accommodations in the infirmary, but he had waved them away, choosing instead the bed that had been his for thirty years. Richard had helped us get him onto his mat before going to check that all the defenses were in order. Anya and I sat on the floor by Ezra.

"But Brother," Anya protested. "You still have years you could serve Asael."

"My service is coming to an end," Brother Ezra said.

"I don't believe that," said Anya.

"You are the Rose, child; you must believe it. The Rose must see this world for what it is. You cannot shove the darkness to the side and pretend it doesn't exist." He began coughing, and I helped him to sit up, hoping it would bring him some relief.

When the coughs subsided, Brother Ezra looked at Anya again. "We will speak again before the end, my dear. I have days, not hours."

A tear slid down Anya's cheek. "I have grown fond of you in these weeks since you arrived on that stony beach."

Brother Ezra reached out his hand to her. She gripped it, squeezed, and then turned to leave. I eased the old monk back to his cushion and pulled a small blanket up over him.

"Thank you, my child," he said, settling in.

"It is nothing," I said.

"For this, yes, but for today more." He closed his eyes for a moment. I thought he had fallen asleep, but then he spoke again. "I did not know the Creator had that task for me before the end."

"But you knew the end was coming?"

"Aye. Each of us is destined to die once," he said. A cough stopped him. I felt as though he had more to say, but I did not press the topic. When he recovered his breath, he opened his eyes to look at me again. "I told you I would show you my writings," he said.

"Aye, you did."

"They are in the chest in the corner."

I turned in the direction he gestured. An old sea chest stood in the corner, its locks broken but its walls sound.

"They are yours," said Brother Ezra. "Young Lord Makram was right. You are the keeper of our story, we Followers of the Rose." He settled down into the cushion and pulled the blanket up about his chin. "They are yours," he repeated. He closed his eyes, and I saw his expression ease into sleep.

Quietly, so as not to disturb him, I rose and went to the sea chest. I stood above it, thinking that it must have its very own story—how the broken chest of a sailor made its way to a monk's cell. But within, I knew, was the history of the old man who slept near me. And, where his history intertwined with my own, there were stories that served as the foundation of my own experiences.

I reached out and ran my fingers over the surface of the chest. The metal straps that wrapped the wood were cool to my touch, the wood worn smooth. I touched the broken latch, gained a grip, and raised the lid.

I sat all night in Brother Ezra's cell, listening to his quiet, ragged breathing, reading his journals. There must have been a hundred books in the chest like the one Edmund had given me. The oldest ones were filled with a child's scrawl and told, in simple words, the story of a young peasant boy gifted in magic whose parents were considering sending to train with the monks.

He recounted the nights he would lie awake in the loft, with his brothers and sisters sleeping about him, straining to hear what his parents said in the kitchen below.

"I'll miss him around the farm," his father said.

"But if the Practitioner thinks he's gifted, he should be given a chance," his mother replied.

"He's only a simple country boy," said the father.

"According to the Writings, the hope of Asael is without honor."

"He's not the Rose!"

"You don't know! We don't know," his mother replied.

They debated for weeks about whether he should be sent to train as a Helper. They wondered if they could spare his labor on the farm. They questioned the village Practitioner's assessment of the child's skill with magic. They weighed the benefits of the freedom of childhood on a farm with the honor of being a Practitioner.

All these things the boy had recorded; I'm certain he did not understand much of it. He was seven years old when he entered into training, and he didn't return to his home village in the south of Asael until his father's funeral twenty years later.

The intervening years were filled with training. I scanned through the journals, wanting to get an overview of the man's life before I got caught up in the details. Again and again, I saw evidence of how attuned he was to the voice of the Creator. He Who Knows Men's Thinking appeared often in Brother Ezra's writings in the early years. It became clear to him and to those around him that he was not the Rose, but also that he had special skill with magic. I had seen the skill that very day and saw that his power was evident early on in his life.

As he grew in influence and rose in rank among the monks, I read fewer and fewer of Brother Ezra's prayers in the journals. His days were busy, and the entries I read recounted the activities of them and the people he'd met. He rubbed shoulders with the high priests and with the king's aides. His journals were filled with names that I'd read in the Written Histories.

Skimming through the pages of the journals, I saw faithlessness come, bit by bit, unnoticed by the writer himself. His world filled with opportunities for influence and power, and little by little, they pushed aside the sensitivity of the gifted boy. By the time I first saw Brother Cormac's name written, the child noticed by the village Practitioner was a man of authority among the monks and the nobles.

The aftermath of Allard's rebellion was there in black and white. An insider's perspective on the great betrayal of our age. Reading it, I began to see clearly how it laid the foundation for the Asael I knew. When that last alliance between noble and Practitioner combusted and disintegrated, both sides were damaged beyond repair.

I wondered how I would have viewed the Practitioners had my father ever told us the story of his brother's death. I wondered if, when the monks arrived that night on the beach, I would have feared them. Had our father recounted the story of Allard's rebellion, Richard and I might have distrusted magic in the same way he did.

The new alliance might never have occurred.

I dozed off before morning, sitting on the stone floor with my back against the wall and a journal in my hand.

I came to as Brother Ezra woke. He tried to sit up, and I scrambled to my knees to assist him. Even with my help, he didn't have the strength to raise himself. He fell back onto the cushion with a sigh.

"I shall spend my remaining time on my back, then," he said.

I smiled a little. "Brother, we can get extra cushions and prop you up."

"Aye, that would be a good thing." He looked at me. "You spent your night in here, Lady Karan?"

"I was reading," I said, gesturing to the pile of journals on the floor.

"The stories of my faithlessness."

I nodded. He did not deny it; I could not protest it. "But also the stories of your faithfulness," I said. "Both are there." I glanced at the books, then back to Brother Ezra. "Yesterday, when I—I learned you were dying, you already knew."

"Aye."

"How?"

"None of us knows the day we are destined to die," said the old monk. "But I once begged the Creator to let me live to see the establishment of the Rose. He stopped my begging and commanded me not to speak of the matter again. We near that day. And I know I shall not see it."

A Helper knocked at the door and interrupted us. He carried a tray with a bowl of thin porridge on it. I smelled it as he came in, and my stomach grumbled.

Brother Ezra heard it, and smiling, said, "Lady Karan, go find yourself some breakfast and get some rest. I will have them call you if there is any change in my strength."

I asked the young Helper to be sure to get cushions for him and left the cell, making my way down to the kitchens.

Cecily and Richard were already there, deep in conversation. I quietly served my porridge and joined them at the table, listening as they talked.

"We must hold our positions," Richard said. "If we give an inch, the enemy will take a mile."

Cecily shifted. "But I still don't like calling them the 'enemy,' Richard," she said. "If my father were alive, he would be on the other side of the river. They are men of Asael over there."

"Aye," Richard nodded, impatient. "I understand, but if we are to fight for the establishment of the Rose, we must draw the lines somewhere."

"This is where Anya is struggling with you, though, Richard," said Cecily. "What you said there—'fight for the establishment of the Rose.' You say 'fight,' she says no violence. You say 'establish the Rose,' she says the Rose is to be the hope of Asael."

"It's the same—"

"No, it's not," Cecily cut him off. "I was reading the Ancient Writings last night. I couldn't see anywhere that indicated the Rose was to be a political leader."

"Yes, but—"

I jumped into the conversation. "Cecily has a point, Richard," I said. "We need to keep our focus on what the Ancient Writings say."

"And trust the Rose," said Cecily. She laid a hand on Richard's arm and squeezed it encouragingly. "That's why you're here, isn't it? It's what you said when you came to find Bellamy and me. You said, 'She's the Rose. I am a Follower.'"

Richard looked down at her hand on his arm and sat quietly for a moment.

"I am her Follower," he said. I could not read his tone. There was a note of regret in it, and looking at his face as he raised it, a moment of pain, too.

"We are all her Followers," said Cecily. "Followers of the One promised in the Ancient Writings. We shall be led by her and by them."

"Aye," Richard nodded.

We turned back to our bowls, and a moment later Bellamy and Anya entered the kitchen. Lanica remained in the infirmary, and Thayer had already returned to the waterfront after he'd been spelled overnight.

We sat around the table in the kitchen, eating quietly together.

"How is Brother Ezra?" Cecily asked after a few moments.

I was silent for a moment. "I don't know quite how to answer that," I said. "He is dying. But—but I have never seen someone face death with no fear."

"His death will be our loss," said Richard. "He has great wisdom."

"He is leaving much of it with us," I said. "I read many of his journals last night."

"But we will not be able to ask him our questions anymore," said Anya.

"No," I said. "If you have questions, you may wish to speak with him today. He seems to enjoy talking with us, though he tires quickly."

Richard rose from his seat. "I must get down to the bridge."

"Have they attacked again this morning?"

"Not yet," he said. "And there were no forays last night. They seem to be regrouping. I think our defense took them by surprise. They did not expect us to be as strong as we are."

Bellamy and Cecily stood as well. "We will come with you," Cecily said.

Richard nodded. He looked to Anya.

"I would like to speak with Brother Ezra before I come down this morning. As long as all is quiet."

"It is for now," Richard said. "I'll send a runner for you if you're needed."

Anya thanked him, and he left, Bellamy and Cecily with him.

"I know you need rest, Karan," Anya said to me, "but please come with me to speak with Ezra."

"Of course," I said. "But why?"

"I wish for his insight," she said. "I have questions for him."

I was curious what questions she would ask. When she had said nothing of her plan to make Richard king the day before, I had wondered if she'd given up the idea. But I saw the same determined expression on her face I'd caught that day we left Marinel, and I wondered if that might be one of her questions.

"Come," Anya said. "Let us go speak with him."

I stood back at the door as Anya knelt by Brother Ezra's side. She laid out for him her conviction that Richard was to be king.

Brother Ezra nodded as he listened. She asked him about his interpretation of certain passages of the Ancient Writings, and he explained how he had understood them.

"The Rose is not to be a ruler." Anya repeated her common refrain.

"But the Rose will save the line of kings." Brother Ezra mused. "Yes, I can see your point."

They continued their debate over a few other passages, examining them in light of each other, looking for a whole among the pieces. As they did so, my mind wandered back to the passage which had caught me the first night I read the Ancient Writings in the library:

And you shall know the Rose by this sign. This One will practice Rosefire, though never trained. All the signs which come before will be confirmed in this one act. And the act will save the line of kings.

The act of Rosefire would save the line of kings. I thought of the scent of roses I'd smelled when Brother Ezra healed the wounded man the day before. Rosefire was a mysterious thing to me. As far as anyone knew, it had not been practiced in centuries. I'd read the passages in the Ancient Writings that spoke of it. I knew its dangers. If Anya's motives for using it were not completely pure, her life would be required of her in return for the life she brought back.

Neither Ezra nor Anya mentioned Rosefire in their discussion that morning. I leaned against the wall, so tired that my mind struggled to stay engaged in what they were saying. I thought to open my mouth and ask about Rosefire, but my sleepy mind couldn't seem to form whole words. I would mention it to Anya later, I thought. After a little while, Ezra's strength began to fail him, too.

"I must rest again," he said, and he looked over Anya's shoulder to me. "And you, Lady Karan, you did not really sleep last night. Go lay down your head."

I smiled at him, stepped forward, and knelt down to kiss his cheek. "I shall."

Anya and I left together. Weariness was washing over me, and I didn't think to ask her about Rosefire as I'd intended.

I was so tired I swayed on my feet. Anya directed me to our shared cell. She helped me get to the cushion and pulled a blanket over me.

As I faded into sleep, I heard her say something about going to the waterfront.

I woke in the dim light of the waning day. We were in the short days of winter, so I knew it was not too late, but I had slept the daylight away.

I rose and went into the hall. The stone walls, off which every sound of shuffling foot echoed, were silent. I made my way to Brother Ezra's cell and peeked in. He was sleeping peacefully, a Helper by his side.

I went on to the infirmary. I had not been to visit yet but had been told that Lanica and the Healers had organized a system of wards for the wounded. I knew the most critically injured were all together in one large room, with many Helpers available to assist the Healers as they worked. There were none with Brother Ezra's or Anya's skill with magic here. The Healers were gifted in discovering what treatment the wounded needed and mixing herbs to assist in healing.

Lanica greeted me quietly. She seemed as tired as I had been that morning. Father Aldan was with her, having arrived to relieve her. They showed me the smaller rooms, where those whose injuries were not as severe were being kept, five or ten under the care of a single Healer.

Then they showed me the large ward. I gasped as we entered. One wall of the room was made of glass—some of the clearest I had ever seen. It was better quality than the glass in the windows of my father's house at Marinel. On the other side of the glass was a garden, a courtyard entirely enclosed from the elements by glass and filled with rose bushes in bloom.

A door to the garden opened off of the ward, and Father

Aldan led me through it. The scent of roses struck me as he opened the door. The garden, warmed by stoves and the daily sun, was a breath of spring or summer in the midst of winter.

"They bloom year-round," he said. "Different bushes in bloom in different months."

I reached out to finger a deep red country rose. In the fading light, it seemed almost black. I leaned in and breathed in its scent.

I wondered why the monks would grow roses year-round. My still-awakening mind was about to form a question when there was a commotion in the infirmary. A runner was directed through to us in the garden.

He came in, breathing heavily. "Lady Karan, Young Lord Adamaris thought you should know that boats have been launched from the far bank of the river."

I was alert immediately. "You left as they launched?" I asked.

"Aye, milady."

"Take me there immediately," I said. "Perhaps I can be of some help."

"Master Richard thought you would want to be there," he said.

I thanked Father Aldan for showing me the roses and kissed Lanica as I passed her. I grabbed my cloak from my cell as we ran past and followed the young Helper out into the deepening darkness, running toward the waterfront.

CHAPTER 29

COLD. My most distinct memory of that night is of the cold. The temperature had dropped well below freezing over the course of the day. It seeped into every building and forced those fighting to wear extra layers and cloaks. Along the edges of the river, the ice had thickened, more ice had formed away from the banks, and the water resembled slush across the open expanse.

But the boats came anyway, one after another, each landing at a different spot along the waterfront, with ten or twenty men aboard. They rushed out at the Followers, like stinging insects, never letting up. As soon as men jumped to shore or dock, the boat captain would maneuver away faster than we could react, back across the water for another load. The Followers were left with the landed soldiers, fighting for their lives.

It was a brilliant strategy, one we should have seen coming. We knew they had few boats, but we had not considered they could use them each multiple times.

We had no cannon. A single cannon and our problems would have been solved, but beyond our archers, we had no way of doing damage at a distance. And in the darkness, our archers were useless against the boat captains.

So we fought. Richard, Bellamy, and Thayer had spread out along the waterfront, each with their lieutenants and the Followers under their command. Anya was with Thayer, closest to the bridge. The soldiers seemed to be ignoring that route so far, focusing their energies on the boat attack. When I arrived, I joined Richard's company. The Helpers were already in action at the back of the fighting, finding open houses where they could care for the wounded out of the cold. I assisted them, wishing Father had allowed Richard to teach me fighting with a sword. My nerves were wound tight, and I wanted to be in the action.

Instead, through the long night, I labored again near the fighting but not in it. Every time I heard my brother's voice rise above the din to shout a command, I thanked the Creator that he still lived. I knew Cecily worked as I did behind her brother's company. I thought she must feel the same as I: glad to be near her brother but terrified for him with every clash of weapons she heard.

Somewhere near the middle of the night, I heard Anya's voice in the front hall of the house where I worked. I went down to meet her.

"I must speak with Richard," she said. "It seems to be quiet out there right now." She shivered; her cloak was pinned tightly around her.

"Come to the stove," I said. Even working indoors, I had been chilly all night. I couldn't imagine how cold she was, having stood with Thayer for the past few hours.

I sent a Helper to find Richard down at the waterfront and took Anya into a quiet backroom outfitted with a stove. I settled her into a rocker with a cup of tea.

We did not wait long for Richard. He came into the room looking tired and worn. His hand was loose about his sword hilt. The blade was bloody and dinged, and he set its tip to rest on the stone floor as if it was too heavy for him to carry.

Anya stood and moved toward him as he entered. "I have been thinking of Brother Ezra all day," she said. "We must pull back."

I was confused. The statements did not seem to connect.

Richard blinked at her for a moment. "We're holding our own," he said.

"I see that," said Anya. "That is not what I mean."

"Why would we pull back now? The frazil ice is growing thicker. It is only going to get colder tonight. By morning they will not be able to use their boats."

"Brother Ezra healed the soldiers," said Anya. "Not just the Followers." She paused, looking at us both to see if we understood her. "Asael will not be won by war. The Council thinks it can use soldiers like cogs in a machine, sending them battalion after battalion to their deaths. Those soldiers are Asael as much as the Followers are."

Richard was quiet. Her words had struck him.

"We cannot rise on the oppression of the weak," Anya said. "If we do not stop fighting, we will be no better than they."

Richard moved across the room to the rocking chair Anya had vacated and sat down in it. He stood his sword tip-down before him, his hands on the cross guard, and rested his forehead against the pommel.

"*Death is not an end, but an enemy, and in the war I shall overcome.*" He said it quietly as if he'd been living with the words all day.

"Aye," said Anya. "And we are dealing out the very thing we should be fighting against."

"Then how do we defeat them?" he asked, his voice low.

"We hold fast to what we know," said Anya.

"And what is that?"

My sluggish thoughts seemed to finally catch up with the conversation, register and catalog the things they'd said. "We know the Rose is the hope of Asael, Richard."

He lifted his head. "And I am her Follower," he said.

Anya frowned. "I do not wish you to be under my rule any more than you wish me to be under yours, Richard."

"No," said Richard. "But Anya, you are the Rose. If I believe the Ancient Writings, I must be your servant—there is no other option for me."

Anya swallowed hard. I watched a moment of pain cross her features. "No," she said. "I suppose not."

"What you are saying," said Richard, "even though it seems strange and foolish, could be exactly how the Creator intends to save Asael."

"I do not have all the answers, Richard," Anya said. "From the night I arrived at your doorstep, I have followed this path without knowing what comes next. I know it is my path. I can feel when I have strayed from it. But I know this: He Who Knows Men's Thinking is able to turn a retreat into a victory."

Richard was quiet for a few more moments. He looked back and forth between us. "Victory or defeat." He chuckled slightly, shrugging his shoulders in imitation of Anya's familiar gesture. "I seem to remember that we once before found another way."

He stood. There was a sudden energy about him as if his limbs had been recharged. He smiled at Anya—a friendly, open smile—and opened the door for her to lead us out. "We had best go tell our generals," he said.

We made our way toward the front of the house. As we reached the front door, we heard a commotion in the street outside.

Richard pulled open the front door and stepped out, sword in hand. "What is this?" he demanded.

Two Followers had a man between them, his hands bound in rope, a grain sack over his head.

"This man says he's one of us, but Michael there says he saw him jump off the boats with the soldiers."

"I'd swear it was this man," the one called Michael said. "Saw him hop right from a boat to the docks." He pulled at the grain sack, roughly tugging it from the man's head.

"Edmund!" I cried. I pushed past Richard and ran to

him. A gag stopped him from speaking. I fumbled at the knot on the gag, trying to remove it.

"He was telling the truth," Richard said to the two men. "Thank you for your diligence to your duty, but he is one of us."

I finally got the knot undone and pulled the gag down from Edmund's face. He spit out the cloth they'd stuffed inside his mouth and smiled at me. "My thanks, Lady Karan," he said. "Could you get the knot on my hands, too?"

I threw my arms around his neck and gave him a kiss on the cheek, then set to work on the knots in the ropes holding his hands together. I had them in a moment, and Edmund shook the ropes off his wrists and rubbed his hands.

He stepped forward and shook hands with Richard. He smiled to Anya, who still stood in the doorway.

"What brings you to us?" asked Richard.

"It was time to break with them," Edmund said. "I can be of no more use to you there, and I have important information for you. Richard," Edmund's voice grew serious. "The Council is planning an all-out attack in the morning. The Followers must pull back."

WE found ourselves back at the monastery a few hours later. Richard, Thayer, and Bellamy had sent their troops back to their beds as the night continued to grow colder. The ice in the river was solidifying into a sheet, and the boats had stopped running.

We had even left the stone bridge unguarded, though it was the last defense we removed. The Followers sheltered in the city, and we and the monks gathered to the monastery. We had brought some of the wounded to the infirmary and some of the Helpers remained in the temporary care facilities we'd set up in houses that night.

When everyone was settled within, Father Aldan had the gates and doors closed and barred. He gathered us all to the kitchen and asked a Helper to prepare tea and sandwiches. I looked around the table where we sat together. We had been surrounded by death and battle for two days and nights, and yet the group gathered here was only short one face from the group that left from Marinel.

"How is Brother Ezra?" I asked Lanica, who had joined us from the infirmary.

"There was no change the last I checked," she said. "He was resting quietly. Shall I send a Helper to find out more?"

"Please."

She stepped out of the kitchen for a moment and then came back in and sat again next to Thayer. We were quiet, sipping our tea.

Anya and Richard sat at the head and foot of the table. She held her teacup in her hands and nodded to him.

"We have pulled back," Richard began, "because we cannot be like them and still serve our purpose. It is our purpose to save Asael, but we cannot deal out death and oppression upon her people in order to do so. We must find another way."

"We came to the Capital to speak to the Council leaders," Anya said.

"They are coming to you," said Edmund. We all waited for him to continue. "As soon as morning comes, they plan to rush the bridge. If the river is solid by then, they'll come on foot over it, too. Many noblemen have arrived in the past day from the south and brought their fighting men to join the soldiers. They are throwing everything they have into the attack. I watched as they drew up the plans, and I knew I had to come tell you. I could not allow you to be overrun."

"Well, they will now find no defense," said Richard.

"No. And they will make their way directly here. They know the monastery is your stronghold."

"So we will let them in," said Anya. "The Council leaders. We will welcome your father and Lord Gennady and Lord Briyanne—"

Edmund cut her off. "Briyanne is dead."

"Dead?" Mumina asked, surprised. "When?"

"In the fighting at the bridge yesterday. He was mortally wounded in the fighting after his horse was taken out from under him. He died early this morning."

Bellamy blanched. I remembered seeing his arrow strike down Briyanne's horse.

"Briyanne is dead," said Anya quietly.

"Lord Adamaris and Lord Gennady remain the ringleaders."

I saw Anya's eyes flick toward Richard at the mention of Gennady's name. I suddenly realized Richard was second in line for the throne. The line of succession was one step shorter.

"Then we shall speak with them tomorrow," said Anya.

The Helper Lanica had sent to check on Brother Ezra entered the kitchen. "I think he's growing weaker, ma'am," he said. "His breathing is much shallower than it was before."

I stood from the table. "I must go to him," I said.

"We should tell him our plan," Richard said. He and Anya rose as well.

I looked to Edmund. I didn't want to let him out of my sight. "Will you come?" I asked.

"If you wish," he said.

"Aye." I put out my hand, and he took it, standing and coming with us.

We walked down the hallway together, the four of us, and I thought of the last time it had been just us four and how much had changed since then. We had dreamed of a movement among the people; we had promised to work to raise up Followers of the Rose. I thought of the massive crowds that first morning in the Capital and of the battles of the past two days—it had been but a few months, and we had turned the world upside down.

WE entered Brother Ezra's room, and I knelt on the chill stones by his head. Edmund stood behind me, close enough that I could feel his warmth. Anya settled herself at the cushion's edge and picked up the old monk's hand in hers. Richard stood by his feet.

Brother Ezra opened his eyes. His breathing was labored and shallow, but he could still speak. He looked at Anya.

"I have lived my whole life in hope of seeing the Rose, Miss Anya," he said. "I am above all blessed that He Who Knows Men's Thinking granted me this."

"We have stopped the fighting, Brother," Richard said. "The soldiers are men of Asael; they are not our enemies."

"No," said Ezra. "The enemy is darkness and fear. When I came to this cell after the Rebellion, I was consumed by darkness. But every day, Aldan would visit. His loyalty and love brought me through those dark days. Push back the darkness with love, and you need not fear."

"What are we to do without you, Brother?" asked Richard.

"Oh, my son, you will follow the Creator in the way you should go."

My tears came too thickly to allow me to speak. I reached out and touched his weathered cheek. He turned his gaze to me.

"Tell the story, Lady Karan. Tell the story of a boy who became a monk who became a traitor. Then tell the story of the Creator who loved him and pursued him and forgave him and gave him purpose once again in an ancient prophecy of the hope of Asael. Tell the story of the Rose."

I nodded.

"You will see the image on the tapestry one day, Karan. He Who Knows Men's Thinking told me so."

I swallowed, trying to clear the tightness from my throat.

Brother Ezra looked up at Edmund behind me. "Young Lord Makram, you lived in the den of the lion, and you were not maimed. The Creator has a purpose for you."

The old monk sighed. I could see he was taxing his strength. He closed his eyes again, and we remained quiet for a few more moments. Then Brother Ezra put his free hand atop Anya's.

"I am weary. I am to die." He opened his eyes. "The Rose could restore life, but that gift is not for me."

The color drained from Anya's face. "Rosefire?" she said. "Brother, no—"

He interrupted her. "You will, child. I have already seen that you brim over with love. The act of Rosefire is the deepest love. You will practice Rosefire, and it will show the world you are the Rose." He looked into her eyes for a long moment, then turned his gaze to Richard, who stood at the foot of the bed. Neither one spoke, but I was certain Richard was somehow listening to the last words of wisdom from the monk.

"And now," Brother Ezra said quietly. "Sit by me a while as I rest. I am ready for sleep."

Richard moved to sit on the edge of the mat behind Anya and laid a hand atop the covers over the old monk's knee. I rested my hand on top of his head and leaned back into Edmund's chest when he knelt down behind me. We sat together into the night as first Ezra's breathing slowed in sleep, and then, in the quiet, it stopped altogether.

CHAPTER 30

I stood alone in the chapel as dawn's light illuminated the stained glass window behind the altar. The colored glass painted an image on the stone floor before me, vague and undefined, a ring of green and red and gold around a colorful center.

I stared down at the ring as it brightened. If I lifted my head to look directly in front of me, I would see clearly the image leaded into a pattern in the window. But instead, I studied the image on the floor, feeling that I knew it, feeling that it represented something far greater than a mix of colors creeping across stones.

"I have been thinking about a passage in the Ancient Writings." I would know Anya's voice anywhere. I had not heard her come into the chapel. She came forward and stood beside me. "It is one of the parts that always catches me with its beauty and leaves me thinking I may never understand its meaning."

I continued to study the colors on the floor as she began to quote:

"The shadows pass, they pass, they pass
Yet there is a stillness outside of time.
And for a moment, in the sound of a note,
In the path of a tear, in the laugh of a child,
In the fire of a rose, in the dapples of light,
A glimpse.
And afterward the shadows pass, they pass.
Eternity loses meaning. Roses fade.
But the glimpse remains, displacing fear."

"I have never seen someone face death without fear," I said.

"No," said Anya.

"It has always been the terrible unknown, perhaps beautiful, perhaps harsh—but an end."

"Aye."

I considered the words she had quoted. "I think I saw the glimpse," I said.

She nodded. "It is not an end."

"No," I said. I continued to watch the light painted on the floor. "But I still do not see it clearly."

Anya put her arm through mine. "We cannot see it clearly with these eyes."

I raised my head and looked at the stained glass. It was a similar motif to the picture on the tapestry hanging on the wall of my quarters at Marinel: a circle of branches with gold and red around an image of people, expectant expressions on their faces.

Anya squeezed my arm. "There is food in the kitchen," she said.

We turned and made our way back through the center of the chapel toward the door. There were no rows of seats in this chapel as there were in the cathedral; here, the monks stood or knelt for worship.

The door opened to the front hall where we'd been greeted the night we arrived by the young monk bearing Edmund's letter. Ice crystals had formed on the metal fittings of the front door, and hoarfrost crept across the flagstones. The cold had not abated with the dawn.

In the kitchen, Richard and Cecily sat together at the table, and Edmund and Bellamy were serving themselves porridge from the pot on the stove. I saw Anya glance toward Richard before we moved to serve ourselves. He looked up and caught her eye, smiling, before returning to his conversation with Cecily. I could not read their expressions.

Something had changed between Anya and Richard. I could not quite place my finger on it, but I thought back to our conversation in the warming room the night before. Where so often in the past they had fought one another, now they seemed to have found a rhythm for pulling together. There was an easiness about their interactions that had only shown itself in fits and starts before. I wondered if, perhaps, they would find a bright future after all.

Anya and I joined the others at the table, and a few minutes later were joined in kind by Thayer, Lanica, Tay, and Father Aldan. It all seemed so normal, sitting around the table with this small band, quiet conversations going on here and there.

Edmund's hand over mine raised me from my thoughts. He gave a comforting squeeze. "It's almost enough to make you think we haven't lost a great man," he said.

"Or that the hope of the Kingdom wasn't in the balance," I replied.

"It feels strange—this not-action."

"It is rebellion, in our own sort of way," I said.

"How so?" asked Edmund.

"We are rebelling against the need to control the outcome. We do not know exactly what He Who Knows Men's Thinking has planned, so if we are to fight His battle, then we must wait for Him to move us."

Edmund chuckled. "All along, I've wondered if we really understand how mad this all is," he said. "We've gone against everything common sense would dictate, and yet here we still are, sitting around a table, noble and peasant, priest and child, ready for whatever is to come next."

I smiled. "I suppose it does sound strange."

"I don't doubt for a moment that what we are doing is right," said Edmund. "But I've spent the past few months surrounded by those who strive for power by grasping at it rather than by letting it go. Gennady alone—" He broke off, seeing my expression. He gripped my hand again. "If for no other reason, I am glad we are on this path."

"I think Richard would have killed him in the street the other day had Anya not stopped him."

"For Richard's sake, I am glad she did," said Edmund. "But he is a cruel man and cares for others only in relation to how they support his own ends."

"And my father?" I asked. I thought back to what I'd read in Brother Ezra's journals. My father's motivations were not so clear to me as Gennady's.

"Your father is more complicated," Edmund confirmed. "He seeks power, yes, but where Gennady would use any means to gain it, your father is principled. He truly believes the Council is the best hope of Asael."

"If I did not believe in the Rose, I might as well," I said. "The Council is certainly a better option than Gennady alone. There is, at least, the hope that someone would speak for the peasants."

"I think your father is driven by fear," said Edmund.

I nodded. "He fears death. And I think he fears magic."

"Aye," said Edmund. "He fears magic. Gennady was lofting ideas one day and said we should force the Priests and monks in the cathedral to fight for us. Your father snapped. I've never seen him resort to physical violence before. But he practically threw the table at Gennady. He yelled something about never using their wicked witchery and stormed from the room."

"His brother was killed by magic," I said. "In battle. At Brother Ezra's hand."

Edmund's eyebrows raised.

"It is why we used no magic in battle," I said. "Brother Ezra fought with Lord Allard and saw what magic used for war looked like."

I watched as Edmund's eyes grew wide. It was as if I'd solved a puzzle for him. "That's who it was," he breathed.

"Who?"

"That night, after your father had calmed down, he took Gennady and me to the castle dungeons and forced Gennady to talk to a prisoner. I only saw him for a few moments, but he was not right in the head. Neither of them ever explained, but Gennady never suggested using magic again."

I remembered skimming past an entry in one of Brother Ezra's recent journals that mentioned Allard. I had thought it a reference to the past when the name caught my eye and hadn't read on, thinking I would do so later. I wondered now if Ezra had visited Allard in prison.

"You saw Lord Allard?" I asked.

"I saw the shell that was once Lord Allard," said Edmund. "He raved like a lunatic the night we went. The guard said that some nights he didn't rave but simply moaned over and over, 'the dark, the dark.' No one pushed back the darkness for him."

I shut my eyes. I'd gathered enough of the horror from reading Brother Ezra's journals. I could not imagine having to live in a prison cell with the memories from that battle for the rest of my life.

We heard a commotion in the hall, and a Helper hurried into the kitchen. "There are soldiers at the gate," he said.

Father Aldan turned to Anya. "What shall I have them do, Miss Anya?"

Anya looked to Richard. "We will tell them we wish a summit. Here, on our terms."

Richard looked around the table. There were nine of us, not including Tay. "If we invite them to bring the same number, we will be eighteen in the room," said Richard. "Where can we meet in such numbers?"

"The chapel?" Anya turned to Aldan. "Will that be acceptable?"

"Aye," said Father Aldan.

We rose, leaving our breakfast half eaten and Tay with the Helper, and went to the hall.

"Richard, Karan," Anya addressed us. "I believe you must bring them in."

Richard looked at me with a grin on his face. "Well, I've never been voted least likely to be struck down by enemy weaponry before, sister. How about you?"

I laughed. For a moment, the tension left me. Perhaps this would work.

Anya turned to lead the others to the chapel. Edmund took a step to follow, then turned back, grasped my arm, and pulled me to him, kissing me.

"Oi!" said Richard. "We're in the middle of a diplomatic mission here, Edmund!"

I blushed as Edmund stepped back.

"Sorry, Richard," he said, shrugging. "I just realized I hadn't kissed her yet since I came back and didn't want to send her out there unfortified."

Richard scoffed. "Get yourself to the chapel, you young rogue, before I call the law on you." His tone turned serious. "No weapons, friends," he said. "Let us show good faith. Leave them outside the chapel door, so they can see them as they come in."

A Helper had gotten my cloak from my cell and Richard's overcoat. We pulled them over our shoulders as the Helper unlocked the door and opened it to the frigid air. Richard took my hand, and we walked down the steps together into the front courtyard.

As we crossed the open space, I glanced up at my brother. "What are you thinking?" I asked.

"Wondering if we should tell Father about you and Edmund at the beginning or end of the day's proceedings," he said, his tone light again.

I hit him in the arm. "Really," I said.

"I am wondering what it will take for Arnau Adamaris to come to believe Sephanya is the Rose, the hope of Asael."

"Aye." We were both quiet. I listened to our shoes crunch against the cobblestone courtyard.

We reached the front gate. There was a small door in one side of it with a shuttered window that could be opened to speak through. Richard put his hand to the shutter knob and looked at me. "Here's hope for a miracle," he said.

He pulled open the shutter and looked out. "Where are your leaders?" he called to the soldiers.

I heard movement, then my father's voice. "We are here."

"I am going to open this door and Karan, and I will come out," said Richard. "I trust that we will not be shot on sight."

"You shall not be," said our father.

Richard unlatched the door and opened it. I stepped through, and he followed behind me. We stood together, our backs to the monastery gate. I looked around. Soldiers trained arrows at us, but no one moved.

Richard rubbed his arms. "Brrr, it's cold out here," he said, conversationally. "Did the water freeze hard enough for you to cross it as you'd hoped, or did you have to come by the bridge?"

Father blinked. Then his eyes narrowed as he realized the implications of Richard's words. "So the boy Edmund is a traitor as well," he said.

"Now, Father," replied Richard. "I wouldn't talk like that. It's quite likely he'll be your son-in-law someday."

I felt my eyes widen and my pulse quicken. I had not expected Richard to take this approach. He was relaxed and jovial. He sounded like the brother who teased me about flirting with the stable boys. It was the polar opposite of his encounter with Gennady in the street two days earlier.

"Have you come out here to tease, Richard?" Father's tone was weary; he, too, was familiar with this banter.

Richard shrugged. "I'm only saying," he continued, "based on the kiss I saw him give her in the front hall a few moments ago, I would be expecting a formal request for her hand to be coming any day now." There was a chuckle from back among the soldiers. Richard turned slightly, and his tone became razor sharp. "I am sorry, Lord Gennady. I suppose this means your engagement is truly off now." He paused ever so slightly before spitting out the next sentence. "Or any other plans you might have had."

"Richard!" Father shouted. "Why are you here?"

"The Rose requests a formal summit with the leaders of the Council," said Richard. "And as it is bone-chillingly cold out here, we invite you to enter the monastery for our talk."

Father's eyes narrowed again. "We will be outnumbered."

"Inside these walls, there are wounded, Healers, holy men, and a small band of the Rose's most trusted Followers. You will be entering the front door of the monastery and immediately progressing to the chapel off the entryway, where the Rose and her Followers await, unarmed. It is a holy place, not a place of battle. As we would wish all things to be fair, the Rose has offered that you may have men accompany you equal to the number who await you in the chapel."

There was a pause as Father considered the terms. He turned to Gennady and nodded, then back to us. "How many men?"

"Nine in total," said Richard. "You may come armed to the door of the chapel, where we will all leave our weapons." He pulled back his overcoat and rested his hand on his sword's hilt.

Father commanded Gennady to select soldiers to attend them and strode forward. Gennady followed, seven soldiers behind him, and Richard gestured for me to lead the way. I stepped through the door, Richard right behind me. He took my hand, put it through his arm, and led me across the courtyard as if we were walking into a ball. Every move he made was perfectly choreographed. I had danced with him often enough to follow his lead. I raised my head and put my shoulders back, carrying myself as a noblewoman should.

The monastery door was opened for us, and we proceeded into the front hall. Richard divested himself of his overcoat and handed it to the Helper who had opened the door, then assisted me in removing my cloak, passing it off as well. His easy frankness had been covered over by the pristine façade of nobility.

Father and Gennady led the soldiers inside but did not remove their coats. Richard raised an eyebrow as if he was slightly offended by the action. He made no comment but put out his hand to me again. I laid mine atop it, as I would if I were being led to the dance floor. At the chapel door, Richard stopped.

He dropped my hand and unbuckled the belt of his scabbard. He laid his sword down next to the pile of weapons already there.

I gestured nonchalantly toward an empty space of stone on the other side of the door. "You may lay your weapons there," I said.

Richard stood again and put out his hand for me. We waited patiently, while the soldiers removed swords and knives and set them down on the floor. Father and Gennady unbuckled their scabbards and set them on top of the pile.

"All ready?" Richard asked, still oozing nobility.

Father's expression was nonplussed. "Aye," he said, sighing. He knew Richard as well as I did and could see when he was putting on an act.

"Well, then," said Richard. "Gentlemen, I invite you to join me at the summit of the Rose."

He turned to the chapel doors, plain wooden ones with hinges that would swing out toward us, stepped forward, put his hands to the handles, and pulled them wide with a flourish.

Then he took my hand again and led us inside.

CHAPTER 31

THE Rose and her Followers were staged across the front of the chapel before the altar. Anya stood in the center of the room, with spaces on either side of her for Richard and me. Then, back a step, Edmund and Bellamy on one side and Father Aldan with an empty space beside him on the other. Another step back, flanking them, were Cecily and Thayer and Lanica.

Richard led me to my place at Anya's left and took his position on her right. We turned and watched Father and Gennady and the soldiers awkwardly sort themselves into positions. Father and Gennady stood together at the front, Father on my side, Gennady closer to Richard. Then the soldiers fanned out behind them.

"My Lords," Richard said, still formal but genuine, "May I present Sephanya, the Rose of Asael."

"Lord Adamaris, Lord Gennady," Anya said. She inclined her head toward them—not enough to be called a bow, but rather an indication of recognition.

I saw my father open his mouth as if to reply, but he seemed to realize that he didn't know what to call Anya. Any title would seem like an admission of recognition that she held any authority. He shut his mouth again and instead bowed ever so slightly at the waist. Gennady followed suit. If we were to go by appearances, the Followers of the Rose were looking better in this stand-off.

My father surveyed our tableau. He paused on Edmund.

"You were not lost in battle last night, then?" he said. His tone was clipped.

"I can make no defense for our actions in sending a spy into your ranks," said Anya. "Though surely had you had the opportunity to do the same, you would have, so perhaps it is justified."

My father's eyes flicked to her while she spoke and then went back to Edmund. The muscles of his face set themselves into hard lines as he stared. He continued his scan of the arrangement, moving past me and Anya and Richard before his eyes lingered on the empty space between Richard and Aldan. I watched them grow cold.

"Where is your monk friend?" he said. "Brother Ezra, if I'm not mistaken."

"He is dead," said Anya.

This surprised him.

"He died after healing the wounded at the bridge two nights ago," I said. "Soldiers and Followers alike."

"It was his actions that prompted this summit," said Richard.

Gennady broke in. "Why did you have no defenses in the city this morning?"

"Your soldiers are men of Asael," said Richard. "Our purpose, as Followers of the Rose, is the restoration of Asael, not the destruction of her citizens."

Gennady scoffed, then looked about as if he wondered why no one else was jeering. "You're a fool!" he said. He turned to our Father. "They won't fight back? Why are we even here? We should walk out the door and gather our forces to breach the gates."

I saw Richard lean in. All easiness was gone from his manner. "We will defend—"

Anya interrupted him. "Richard." He looked at her, and she shook her head slightly.

Gennady laughed aloud. "She really has lured you into her trap, hasn't she?"

Richard was perfectly still. His tone was icy. "What do you mean?"

"You truly think this peasant seeks anything but her own progress in the ranks of society? She would let you die to climb the ladder."

Anya raised her hand. "Lord Gennady," she said. "Whether you believe my intentions or not has no effect on them. I have called this summit so that more men of Asael do not die needlessly." She directed her attention back to my father. "Lord Adamaris, surely you have seen enough of battle."

Father cleared his throat. "When it is forged fairly, the wounds heal."

Anya nodded. "We have not used magic against you."

"That was Brother Ezra's doing as well," I said. "He would not have it."

My father turned his eyes to me. I trembled, feeling his fury pour over me. I took a deep breath and held his stare. There was anger there, yes, but hidden beneath it, I thought I saw pain—and the kind of fear that I had held all those years before I found the Ancient Writings. He feared the magic we could wield. I realized then that he would not attack, though we promised no defenses. He had seen the battle I'd read of in Brother Ezra's journals. In a way, he, too, had been trapped in a prison cell with those memories ever since, setting a cage around his life to ward off magic. I thought of all the things I had experienced since I broke from the rules my father had laid for us.

"I will not mourn that monk's death," Father said, spitting forth the words again. He turned back to Anya. "What is your purpose in calling a summit? Do you wish to negotiate a truce of some kind?"

"I wish to speak with you about the future of Asael," said Anya.

"Ah, yes," Gennady broke in, his tone lofty. "The bright future of Asael planned by the peasants and their madam."

"Shut your foul mouth." Father spat the words like he would at an animal. He did not raise his voice. It was low and burning. "And do not open it again until I give you leave." He turned fully toward Gennady, staring him into silence. It was the worst of his anger, far worse than when he yelled or slammed doors. It was the kind of outburst

Richard used to try to fend off when they were directed at me—the kind that sent me trembling to the horse stables when I saw just a glimpse of them. The kind that always made me wonder how he managed to keep from doing physical violence, such was the wrath that boiled within him. Then he focused back on Anya.

Gennady paled. He'd not had my father's wrath directed at him before that. I could see him seethe under the enforced silence. He stood straight, his eyes flicking toward Father every few moments.

"We are without a king," Father said to Anya. "The line of kings is broken, and there must be some rule."

"Aye," said Anya. "There must be rule, but it must be under the guidance of the Ancient Writings."

"The monks lost their authority in this land a thousand years ago," said Father. "You are grasping at what is lost, girl. The people will not follow the priests."

"They won't," said Richard. "Unless the priests follow the One who the Writings speak of."

"You truly believe this peasant girl who arrived on our doorstep is the great hope of Asael, Richard?" Father said.

"I do," said Richard. "And she would rule more fairly than any of your Council members." He threw a pointed glance in Gennady's direction. "You've surrounded yourself with the vile and the weak who only want power for themselves. They will stand on the heads of anyone to achieve it."

"Power is only achieved through stepping up," Father said. "There will always be those trodden underfoot."

Gennady looked from Richard to Father and back again. I watched as his face registered first surprise, then distaste. Disappointed and angry as my father was with Richard, he treated him as an equal as they stood across from one another in this summit. Where he had spoken to Gennady like a dog, he spoke to Richard like a peer.

Father turned back to Anya. "So instead of the Council, you would establish the monks in a hierarchy of rule under your leadership? You would take Asael back a thousand years and set yourself up as Queen in all but name?"

"No," said Anya.

"No?"

"The Rose is not a ruler."

"Oh, I see," said Father. "Do go on."

Anya swallowed. Edmund shuffled his feet as he stood at ease behind me. Even Richard began to relax.

"We will restore the line of Kings," said Anya.

Father's eyes widened. I saw him shift them in Gennady's direction, a bit of question in them. "And just who do you have in mind to rule?" he asked.

"Richard will be king," said Anya.

Richard's head snapped to stare at her in shock. I heard Cecily breathe out sharply with a surprised laugh. I saw, in my periphery, Edmund and Bellamy and Thayer come to attention. I watched, as if in slow motion, my father's mouth drop open slightly as he looked from the girl before him to his son.

And, as all these things happened together, in the blink of an eye, Lord Gennady made his move.

He must have had the dagger hidden in his boot. I wondered later if he'd had thoughts of assassinating Anya, but she was not his target in that moment. As Richard's focus moved to Anya, Gennady lunged across the flagstones and gave one thrust—quick, sharp, and perfectly aligned to slip the blade between the ribs and into the heart.

I screamed. Gennady twisted the blade and jerked it out. Richard swayed and fell as I stepped to him, sinking down to the floor with him. I covered the wound with my hands, trying to staunch the blood. I was flanked in an instant by Lanica and Cecily, both jumping into action to use the skills they'd learned in the infirmaries.

Gennady's knife had done its damage. Richard never spoke. He gasped a few breaths. His eyes never left our faces. And I felt the steady pulse of his heart falter, skip, and disappear from beneath my hands.

I raised my eyes to Anya's face. Her eyes were wide, round. She breathed in quick, shallow breaths.

It had happened in the space of a moment. Gennady still stood over us; the dagger was still shuddering where he'd dropped it to the floor. Edmund and Bellamy and Thayer were still moving to defensive positions. Father Aldan was moving forward to stand over us like a protective bird as we tended to Richard.

And Anya still stood across from my father. She turned her face back to him. He had been frozen, watching it all unfold in horror. Something in her expression released him. He let out a scream like a wild cat and turned on Gennady with fists and feet and teeth. He attacked with all the violence I had never seen him display. The fury he so carefully controlled and channeled into wrathful gazes burst forth and rained down on the murderer of his son.

Edmund, Bellamy, Thayer, and most of the soldiers jumped forward at once to stop him, but he fought them off as he continued to beat Gennady. It took five men to pull him back, grasping arms and legs and holding him about the waist. Edmund stood before him, gripping his face in both of his hands, trying to calm him enough to communicate with him through the blood rage.

"My Lord!" Edmund shouted, right in his face. "Lord Adamaris! Killing him will accomplish nothing, my Lord!"

I watched it all with tears running down my face, my dead brother's head in my lap. Cecily Mumina had her arm around my shoulders and was weeping with me. Anya stood, silent and still, straight and tall and unmoving: quivering like a reed but indomitable.

My father's screams echoed off the stones of the chapel, assaulting my ears in time with the cries of my own heart. When his anger was spent, his breathing slowed into ragged, sobbing breaths. He looked down to where Gennady lay, senseless on the flagstones. He looked over Edmund's shoulder to where I sat, into my eyes, then down into the staring dead eyes of my brother. Then he looked at the quiet girl standing silent and still before him.

"If you are the Rose," he said. "You can bring him back."

Edmund stepped back, surprised. Cecily gasped. Everyone looked to Anya.

"Aye," she said.

"Anya," I said. I wanted to warn her, remind her of the danger.

She turned her eyes to me. In them, I saw my own agony reflected. My heart constricted. I alone knew of Richard's love for her. I suspected she loved him, too. I thought of the passage in the Writings that said they would burn, knowing the pain of the Rose. I was terrified. I alone knew the true danger of this act. She held my gaze for a moment.

Before I could speak, she took a deep breath. She closed her eyes, breathing in and out. When they opened again, her expression had cleared. She had made a decision. In place of the agony, I saw the profound concentration I had seen many times, whenever she was reaching deep within for the knot of branches or flames she tapped for her power.

"Bring me roses," she said. Her voice was steady and calm.

There was a moment of silence. No one moved. Then Father Aldan stepped forward.

"Bellamy, Thayer, Cecily, please assist me."

He moved across the flagstone floor toward the chapel door. Father shook off the men holding him, including Thayer and Bellamy. Cecily rose from where she knelt beside me and went to them. Bellamy put his arm around her shoulder, and they followed the others out the door.

"Bring him near the altar," said Anya.

Edmund paused to see my father was settled. Then, together, they came for Richard's body. Edmund crouched beside me. He reached up and drew my head into his chest in an embrace. He kissed my hair and then let go, leaning in to grip Richard's shoulders. Father took his feet, and they carried him toward the altar, laying him before it.

I stared at the blood-covered stones before me. Lanica rose, moved to Gennady, and began a cursory examination. I watched her. I wondered if he would die if we left him there unattended. I weighed the prospect in my mind.

"Will he live?" Anya asked.

Lanica had her hands on Gennady's head. "Aye," she said. "We will move him to the infirmary later."

The prospect was taken away from me. I do not know if I would have left him to die. I was not tested.

I rose from my knees and walked toward the altar. Anya was concentrating deeply. I skirted her and went to Edmund. He put his arm around my shoulders and hugged me to him, intertwining the fingers of his other hand with one of mine, disregarding the blood on it. We stood by Richard's head; directly across from us was my father. He did not move his eyes from Richard's face. The face held a slightly surprised expression as if Richard still hadn't recovered from the shock of Anya's announcement that he was to rule when he'd been stabbed, and his face had frozen that way.

A moment later, Cecily, Bellamy, Thayer, and Father Aldan returned with their arms full of rose branches. I saw stains of blood on their hands where their skin had been pierced by the thorns in their hurry to gather them.

Deep, dark, red blooms covered the boughs, framed by green leaves.

"Pile them here," Anya gestured to the space around Richard's body. They came forward and placed the rose branches before us, surrounding him. They stood, and we formed a half-circle around the body. The soldiers stayed back, but the rest of us were there.

Anya knelt and pulled the branches over him; they caught together, forming knots and tangles. The thorns cut her hands, but she didn't even flinch.

I watched as she reached her hand into the midst of the knots of branches and concentrated on reaching her power in her mind. She was still for a few moments, and I saw her lips moving in a prayer to He Who Knows Men's Thinking.

The roses burned sweet. Something of their scent lingered even in the fire. I watched as the flames licked the branches, mingling with the leaves, their bright colors dancing with the rose blooms. I almost could not see the difference between the leaves and the flames in the brightness. I'd seen the image before, wrought in cheap silver, on the pendant Anya wore around her neck.

The roses burned and burned, but they did not blacken or grow brittle. Anya continued to kneel, her hand deep in the midst of the flames. She did not seem to be in pain. She breathed deeply, her energy entirely focused on the task before her.

Suddenly, the flames brightened and disappeared. With them, the rose branches, leaving nothing but a fine dust of ash behind.

CHAPTER 32

ALL was still. The colored light had moved across the
floor since early that morning, and it now lit the folds of
Richard's clothing, the ridges of his facial features. Father
Aldan, standing beside me, shifted a little. As he moved, a
small shower of ash rained off the sleeve of his habit.

Anya still knelt by Richard. She had not moved since
the flame and the branches disappeared. She opened her
eyes and took a deep breath. Then she laid her hand on
Richard's chest.

I watched, and as I did so, the passage Anya had quoted
the night before—those last words of the Writings—came
unbidden to my mind: *The man who remembers his Creator need
not fear death. Even death is not an end. Not an end, but an enemy,
and in the war I shall overcome.*

It was a moment before I realized that Anya's arm was
moving gently up and down. My eyes snapped to Richard's
face. I saw him blink, and the surprised expression melted
from his features.

"Richard!" I cried. I fell to my knees by his head and pulled him toward me. He slowly raised his hand, reaching up to grip my arm.

He blinked a few times, took a deep breath, and moved to raise himself to a sitting position. I pushed his shoulders, helping him to rise.

"How am I—?" he broke off, looking at me. "I was not here," he said.

"Gennady killed you," I said. I gulped back tears. "Anya brought you back."

I watched his face as my words filtered into his understanding.

"You mean she healed—" he began.

I cut him off. "No. She brought you back."

I'd not seen the pain in his eyes in many weeks. He still loved her. Whatever had changed between them had not erased it. *Torment comes through love*, I thought.

"*Rosefire is the deepest act of love*," Brother Ezra had said. His words had confused me at the time, but watching Anya and Richard, I thought—perhaps—I understood. She loved him; of that, I was certain. But this act would not cost her life as it did the Practitioner in the Ancient Writings; of that, I was certain as well. The deepest love is that which denies itself.

Then Richard closed his eyes. His jaw clenched. And a tear ran down his cheek. He opened his eyes again and turned to Anya. "Rosefire," he said.

And for a moment, his pain was reflected in her face. "Aye," she said. She put her hand to his cheek; it was more tender than a kiss. "Asael needs you." Then she closed her eyes, dropped her hand, turned her face away, and rose to her feet.

Bellamy and Edmund leaned down to assist Richard and me to our feet. Cecily stepped forward tentatively, and Richard smiled down at her. Her cheeks were still wet from her tears; she'd wiped them away with her hands and left a smear of blood from the pricks of the roses. Richard reached out and cleaned it away with his sleeve. Then he wrapped her in an embrace.

Letting go, Richard shook hands with Father Aldan and Thayer and kissed Lanica on the cheek before turning to face our father.

They stood, eye to eye, their faces unreadable. Richard looked over to where Gennady still lay, unmoving and broken.

Father glanced that direction as well. "I nearly killed him," he said.

Richard turned back to face him. "For a traitor?" he asked.

Father breathed in and out, studying Richard for a moment. "For my son."

"I am a Follower of the Rose," said Richard.

Father nodded. "Aye," he said. He looked over Richard's shoulder toward Anya. "The Ancient Writings give a proof: '*This One will practice Rosefire, though never trained*.'"

"We have fought against each other for a long time," said Richard.

"But we can make an end of that," Father said.

"The end of that is the beginning of something new," said Richard.

"Aye," Father nodded. "But I'm not afraid anymore."

He lifted his eyes and caught my gaze. My throat tightened, and tears sprang to my eyes. It was a moment that was gone in an instant and yet will last forever. The man before me was transfigured. His steely eyes had grown gentle, and there was no fear, no pain, no fury in them. He had been reborn.

I sometimes wonder what my children will think when I tell them the Second Age of the Kings was established in the kitchen of a monastery, where monks of all ranks and nobles, peasants and royalty sat around an old wooden table, worn smooth with age, together breaking coarse loaves of bread and cutting slices of cheese.

They may laugh at me and wonder why I would retell such a detail, for I hope they will live in a world where such a combination of people from different walks of life is no oddity to them. But history is a pattern of remembered moments, and those moments are eternally present in my memory. They are surrounded by the footfalls of what might have been—if a noble lord had trained his children in his fear of magic, if a girl had not brought a waif in from the rain, if a monk had sought power for himself, if a small band of Followers had not stopped fighting to seek the path of He Who Knows

Men's Thinking. But I shall tell them the stories of what really happened, because the moments of the future are contained in the moments of the past, and what might have been and what has been both point to the present in which we live—unable to see the whole picture for the mess of threads before our faces.

We sat in the kitchen, and between our bites of bread and cheese, Richard turned to Anya and asked how long she'd intended that he should be king.

"Since the caves," she said. "When the monks came."

"And you didn't think I should know this piece of information?" he asked.

"It wasn't time," she said.

"I can't be king, Anya," Richard protested. "I don't know how to be king."

Anya smiled at him. "You do," she said.

"I do?"

"You hold fast to the Ancient Writings. You listen to He Who Knows Men's Thinking. You follow His ways."

"And if I get my own motives mixed up with them? If I find myself seeking power for my own sake?"

Anya looked hard at each one around the table, one by one, Father Aldan, Bellamy, Edmund, me, Thayer, Lanica, my father, Cecily, and finally, back at Richard. "You surround yourself with those who will hold fast with you. You ask them to be your conscience, your right hand, your guides, your friends. You rely on them more than you rely on yourself, and together you all rely on He Who Knows Men's Thinking."

Richard looked around at all of us. He smiled, the expression in his eyes still a little unsure. "I could not ask for better counselors," he said.

"You are the next in line for the throne, Richard," I said. "Not counting Gennady."

Gennady lay in the infirmary. Lanica had tended to his wounds, and Anya had healed the worst of them.

"Gennady will be brought up on charges," said Edmund. "According to the Charters of the Kings, he cannot serve in government if he is found guilty."

"What charges?" Richard said. "I am alive. Does murder count when the victim is brought back from the dead?"

Edmund chuckled, shaking his head. "Only you would ask that, Richard. No, he will be brought on charges of treason—he undermined a summit in a time of war. No matter which side came out of the summit holding power, he betrayed a peace negotiation by bringing in a weapon. It's a treasonable offense, according to the Charters."

"Who judges such a case?" asked Thayer.

"The king appoints the judges," said Edmund.

Richard looked at Anya. "I think the Followers of the Rose should judge this case."

Anya glanced around the table. "Are we not all too closely connected?" she asked.

"Not these Followers," Richard said. "All of them. The people of Asael. Let them choose their king."

Anya smiled. "Aye," she said. "For a king should hear his people's voices."

IT took weeks to take the news of everything that had happened to all the corners of Asael. We all became messengers of the Rose again, this time taking the story of the conflict between the Council and the Followers in the Capital and the question of Gennady's treason before every peasant and noble in the land.

The winter had lost its hold by the time we gathered again in the Capital for Richard's coronation. Spring was still a long way off, but you could once again smell the earth and feel warmth from the sun when it shone in the sky. It was hard to realize that it had all started only months before, on a stormy autumn night when the heir to the throne died, and a girl without a past arrived on my doorstep.

In the weeks since that day in the monastery, Richard had gathered a group of Followers and nobles to examine the Ancient Writings, the Written Histories, and the Charters of the Kings. He wanted to write new Charters for the Second Age of the Kings, built upon the principles from all the Writings of Asael's history, centered on the truth that He Who Knows Men's Thinking is active among us today and laying a groundwork for new relationships between nobles and peasants and monks. I joined in when I was not traveling, but most of my time in those weeks was spent out in the villages with my father and Cecily, where we each told our story of the path we took to follow the Rose.

I grew to know my father in those weeks as I had never known him when I was a child. Anya's act of Rosefire had done more than raise Richard. It was the battering ram breaking down my father's fear. And as he fought daily to overcome his long-seated fear of magic, I fought to overcome my fear of him. Neither was a simple task. Both of us had lived our lives cut off from good by blind fear. So every day we asked He Who Knows Men's Thinking to open our eyes to see what we had been unable to look at before, and we walked through those days together, treading where we had never gone, able to do so because we knew Death had been subsumed in love—and that there was no fear anymore.

Richard's coronation was the greatest celebration I had ever seen in Asael. The cathedral, which I'd only ever seen stripped of adornment for a funeral, was decked in gold and red. The risers on each side, where the nobles and monks had once sat, had been removed. Everyone—noble, monk, and peasant—stood together on the floor of the nave, a rope creating an aisle through the crowd. Richard approached the throne set below the altar wearing the robe that the kings of the First Age had worn, a heavy fabric woven of silk. But when he arrived at the front, he removed the robe from his shoulders and laid it carefully before the altar.

He stepped back, and Cecily and I went forward to put around his shoulders a new robe, tailored for him by Thayer from a piece of fabric Lanica had woven in the caves. It was a rough, coarse material made of wool. Wearing that, he addressed the people who filled the cathedral, peasant and noble alike.

"I am here today because He Who Knows Men's Thinking saw fit to defeat Death. I knew a man, a monk, who faced his physical death with courage. He lived his life steeped in the truth that death was not an end, that he was more than his physical form. He lies buried in the yard outside these doors, next to the Kings of the First Age.

"I had not yet learned to live that truth when death came to me. It was a fearsome thing; my little faith did not yet comprehend its powerlessness. He Who Knows Men's Thinking chose to rescue me from the pyre of death by fire—to show Himself the overcomer and to show the One He sent us, true."

Richard looked to Anya. She stepped forward beside him and addressed the crowd.

"The Creator is the cause and the end of all our movement, the One we seek, even when we do not know that we seek," she said. "He knows our thoughts, and He knows our wills, and He reaches to meet us when we lose sight of Him.

"The new Charters for the Second Age point our eyes to He Who Knows Men's Thinking. But we know from our own history how easily we lose sight. May we ever keep the Writings before our eyes. May we ever tell the stories of these days."

"May we ever remember the Rose," said Richard. "May we speak of her to our children, and our children's children, and may we remember why she came to us—to point us back to our Creator." He turned to Anya and bowed low. Everyone in the cathedral followed suit.

There was a moment's silence as Anya took in all of us bowing before her. "Rise," she said. Richard stood again, and Anya smiled at him. "It is time to crown your King," she said to the crowd.

She led Richard to the throne and took a copy of the Ancient Writings from the stand beside him. She held it out to him, and he placed his hand upon it.

"Do you, Richard Adamaris, seek to serve and uphold He Who Knows Men's Thinking above all?"

"I do," said Richard.

"Do you seek to love and serve the people of Asael above yourself?"

There was a moment of silence—a beat. Not a hesitation, but I could see Richard trying to regain control of his emotions.

A tear rolled down his cheek. "I do."

"Do you seek to walk in the role of king as long as you are able and to teach those who will follow you in the leadership of Asael the truths of the Ancient Writings?"

"I do."

Anya set the text back on the stand and took a simple golden circlet from a cushion Bellamy held. With both hands, she placed it around Richard's head. She stepped back, and Father Aldan and the High Priest of the cathedral stepped forward together. Father Aldan poured a small stream of oil over Richard's hair. As it ran down over his face and around his ears, dripping onto the rough robe over his shoulders, the High Priest spoke a blessing from the Writings over him.

When they finished, Richard stood. The crowd could hardly contain its composure through the standard bows and curtsies required before the king. They burst into cheers, clapping, and shouts of joy.

The entire day was a celebration. The streets were filled with people from all over Asael. I saw men and women from villages I had visited during our time in the caves and nobles and peasants my father and I had met in our travels. After the celebrations in the streets, we returned to the castle, where a feast was laid out before us like none I had ever seen, followed by a ball far more grand than my eighteenth celebration.

Through it all, I was with the people I loved most in the world: Richard and Edmund and Anya and my father. The very fact I could put my father in that list brought me joy. Edmund was the first on my dance card, and Richard and Bellamy and Thayer and Aldan and my father each had a spot as well. I laughed and danced, and joked with Cecily and Lanica, and smiled across the crowded ballroom at Anya, who was constantly surrounded.

Late in the night, as I finished a waltz with Richard, I caught Anya's eye, and she tilted her head toward the door before walking out. I excused myself and made my way out as well, eventually finding her in the castle gardens. The day had been quite warm, but as darkness had fallen, the cold air had settled down again. I could see my breath in the light from the lanterns hung from trees throughout the garden.

She stood, quietly, looking back at the castle, aglow with light. I joined her, turning to look where she looked.

"This is *right*," I said.

"Aye."

"We are all here together, and all is well."

"I'm leaving," she said.

It took a moment for her words to register. When they did, I knew the extent of their meaning without even asking, but I still tried to pretend I'd misunderstood her.

"Leaving?" I said. "Oh, yes, go rest. It has been a long day—"

She cut me off. "Karan," she said. "You know that's not what I mean."

I blinked, holding back the tears that tried to come when I thought of the prospect. "You can't," I said. "We've only just begun."

She shrugged her shoulders—that familiar, beloved gesture of hers. "I must go." She paused. I waited for her to continue. "Do you remember when I first felt my power? I wondered if it was more a tangled vine or a burning twist of flame. Now it is a pulsing light inside my mind, never-ending, compelling me to go."

I reached down and took her hand, gripping it tightly.

"I do not know where, exactly," she said. "But I feel as if I shall know the place. It will be home, just as I have felt at home here by your side all this time."

I watched the castle for a moment. "But Richard—"

"Richard is king. A king who follows He Who Knows Men's Thinking. He is the king Asael needs."

I could hold my promise to Richard no longer. I turned to Anya, pleading. "But Richard loves you. He told me he loved you like his own soul and—" I faltered for a moment, looking into her eyes in the flickering lantern light. "And you love him."

"I do. Like we are two parts of a whole."

"So stay!" I pleaded. "We could find—"

She cut me off. "You—better than anyone—know I cannot."

I sighed. I wanted to weep. "My heart breaks for you both, though."

A small, sad smile crossed Anya's lips before she spoke. "But we both gave up that hope some time ago. Asael needs Richard far more than he needs me or I need him. *We* have He Who Knows Men's Thinking. *They* need a guide. One who will resist the desire for power or magic, who will only seek the Creator and point others to Him."

"But one day, when Richard is gone, who will be Asael's guide?"

"I think he will find his bride. He will love her as she loves him and raise sons and daughters who will seek He Who Knows Men's Thinking and follow the Rose," she paused a moment. "But even if he never does, your own children will succeed him, raised to lead a kingdom to seek the Rose."

"But—"

She reached out and put her finger to my lips. "No more protests, Karan. You do not mean them."

I sighed. She leaned forward, kissed me on the cheek, and we embraced. When we let go, she turned and walked away through the castle gates. I watched as her figure faded away into the darkness. The girl without a past became the girl with an unknown future, whose present had intersected with mine for a brief moment and forever altered my eternity.

EPILOGUE

A faithful account of the genesis and activities of the Followers,
here written by Karan Adamaris

I sit here at my desk in my room at Marinel, writing these last words in Edmund's book. I have reached the final page and the end of this tale—but the end is where we start from.

I keep pausing to listen to the sound of the waves surging against the shore down the cliff outside my window. I have traveled the length and breadth of Asael, and everywhere the rhythm is the same—in the thump of a loom or the beat of a heart. It is the rhythm of the magic of this world, the steady beating that says a Hand conducts the symphony, keeping the instruments in time.

I look at the faces on the tapestry on my wall, and I know them for the first time—I see Thayer and Lanica, Richard and Cecily, Bellamy and Father Aldan, Edmund, my father, myself. We all follow the path marked out for us by the knots of roses, ever expectant, ever hopeful.

Lanica is weaving a new tapestry for the castle in the Capital at Richard's request. He asked that it tell the story of the Followers of the Rose, but looking at this one against the wall of my chambers, I realize that our story has already been told—every thread woven in the right place, even if we do not see the picture they make when we are walking among them.

I hear Edmund below. He has arrived to take me back to the Capital for our wedding. Nearly everyone else is there already; Thayer has my dress finished—he made it without a single button—and Tay has been stuffing himself with the test cakes from the kitchen for weeks now. But I wanted a few days back here at Marinel before all of it, to come back to where it all began and finish writing it down in this book.

I catch glimpses, now and again, of the eternity I now know is out there, of which this tale is only a part. I never can quite see it clearly, but from time to time, it is there—in the beauty of a tapestry, in the love from Edmund's eyes, in Lanica's hands as she works the loom, in the set of Richard's head when he kneels to pray. I cannot hold the glimpses, and I only half understand them. But in those moments, I know what love is, and I have no fear.

I write this account to tell the Story of the Rose. I am Karan Adamaris, Follower, sister of the King, companion of the Rose. Let Him, who knows men's thinking, judge the truth of my words.

AFTERWORD

I began the first draft of *Rosefire* in 2008 and then set it aside—picking it up again from time to time over the next few years until it actually started to be something.

Then came 2012, a year full of loss and grief. The wheels nearly came off. I jotted one scene in a journal during church one day in January: the scene of Anya's departure from the final chapter—far ahead of where I currently was in the story. I hadn't known until that moment how the story would end.

I'll never forget the night my friend Saritha came over for dinner that summer. I don't remember details of what we talked about, but when she left at the end of the evening, I pulled out a notebook and began working again. Saritha told me later that she began painting for the first time in months that night. It was a grace to both of us.

Late that summer, my roommate Christine returned from travel and asked if I'd begin reading *Rosefire* to her, and that kept pushing me forward to finish. The day I got to the final chapter, I had to go digging back through note-books to find that scene I'd written. In the process, I realized I'd not written anything—at *all*—for more than six months. This story only exists because of these two friends, and I will be forever grateful to them both.

In addition to these two friends, *Rosefire* would not exist if it weren't for two lines of poetry.

Ash on an old man's sleeve

Is all the ash burnt roses leave.

I have spent much of the past twenty years of my life in T.S. Eliot's *Four Quartets*. They are poems that reward the repeat reader, poems that are rich in depth, meaning, language. Poems that confound. Poems that soothe. Poems that challenge. Poems that enlighten.

The image in two lines above (from "Little Gidding" II.54-55) can be found in *Rosefire's* final chapter, but other ideas, themes, and images from *Four Quartets* are embedded throughout the text. There are portions of the Ancient Writings that echo Eliot's language; there are ideas that confront our characters which are drawn from segments of the poems. Themes of time and eternity in *Rosefire* find their essence in *Four Quartets*, as do themes of love and fear, of knowing the moment only after the moment is passed.

I could point spot for spot the moments in *Rosefire* that are inspired by *Four Quartets*, but I might only interest myself—and I would find as I went through that more and more moments kept presenting themselves. When one lives with a text, it bleeds over into one's thinking in ways one cannot even put a finger on.

That's true, of course, for the Christian Scriptures, too. If you know them, you will see echoes of them in this text. They are my Ancient Writings. They are the words I turn to for truth, comfort, direction, guidance, hope. He Who Knows Men's Thinking is patterned after the God I know, who walks with me daily, to whom I turn over my fears, and who has overcome the fear of death.

I've no end of inspirations for *Rosefire* beyond the two mentioned above. If Anya's philosophy of government sounds familiar, it may be that you've heard it in Josh Garrels' song "Resistance." If there are moments that remind you of Robin McKinley's *The Blue Sword*, that could be because I was reading it while I wrote a whole section of *Rosefire* when I had no power during Hurricane Sandy. And I am certain I would not have been able to write a single skirmish if it weren't for Howard Shore's *Lord of the Rings* soundtrack.

Art begets art, and *Rosefire* is no exception—begotten of the words and works of men and women who have sought to paint, to write, to compose, to bring to an audience words and images of hope, of truth, of insight, of power. It is my prayer that *Rosefire* may one day be the work that begets another work of art. May you be that artist.

Karan, Anya, Richard, and Brother Ezra first introduced themselves to me over a decade ago. Their journey to being introduced to the rest of the world has been long and circuitous. But as I re-read their story here in 2021, I can't help but think that perhaps we need to hear it now, more even than we did when I finished the first draft of this manuscript eight years ago. We have always lived in a world fraught with struggles for power, and we have seen the ugliness and horror of those struggles on our screens more and more every day.

The Followers of the Rose had to learn that authority without love leads toward destruction and sows fear. May we learn the same thing today.

Carolyn Clare Givens
January 2021

ACKNOWLEDGEMENTS

NO art is birthed in a vacuum. *Rosefire* is the labor of many hands, and I need to say some thanks:

To my parents, Elizabeth and David Givens, for your encouragement, typo-finding, and support in so many ways.

To my sisters, Jessie and Loren, for being listening ears and sounding boards and for reminding me to always share what's going on in my life with you, good or bad. To your families, too—I love you all.

To my Bandersnatch Books team, Rachel Donahue and Annie Beth Donahue, for tackling this adventure with me, for being friends and colleagues, and for complementing me so well. Not a bad start for three women who decided they wanted to launch a publishing company in the middle of a pandemic. I appreciate that you're as crazy as I am.

To Kelly Collins, for your incredible line art, which showed the world what was in my head when I thought of the flames and roses intertwined.

To Jason McFarland, for your amazing cover design and your ongoing encouragement over our years of friendship.

To friends who have shared so much wisdom about the process of making a book and running a Kickstarter, running a publishing company, and ALL the things: Charlie Hurd, Tim Briggs, S.D. Smith, Josiah Smith, Andrew Mackay, Glenn McCarty, Paul Hinton, and anyone else who has allowed me to pick your brain for wisdom over the years.

To my brainstorming partners, especially Seth Antes who spent most of an eight-hour drive from Maine to Pennsylvania mentally mapping out the landscape of Asael with me.

To my early readers, who include some of those named above and others like Anne Smith, Melissa Lewis, and Samantha Wipf, for your feedback, insights, recommended name-changes, and more typo-finding (clearly, I can't type, that's what we're learning here).

To our Kickstarter Launch Team, who volunteered to spend a month talking about a book they'd never read for nothing more than a rough advance copy and my thanks. You knocked it out of the park, friends, and I'm so grateful.

To our Kickstarter Backers, the 314 individuals and families who decided *Rosefire* and Bandersnatch Books were a project worth supporting. We've said it many times, but we'll say it again: we are so grateful. Thank you for bringing *Rosefire* to life.

ABOUT

Carolyn Clare Givens

Carrie is a displaced Northerner exploring the foreign ways of the South. She works in church communications and the arts in North Carolina and does freelance editing and writing. Carrie lives in Charlotte with her two literary cats, Lord Peter Wimsey and Harriet Vane. She has previously bumped around the world, both as a missionary kid and adult. She's the author of *The King's Messenger* and *Rosefire*.

ABOUT
Bandersnatch Books

Bandersnatch Books is a publisher of treasures found off the beaten path, books that might otherwise be overlooked in the vast world of publishing. We don't look down on small ventures, but focus instead on making excellent books accessible. You'll often hear us quote Zechariah 4:10, "Do not despise these small beginnings, for the Lord rejoices to see the work begin" (NLT).

Bandersnatch Books

bandersnatchbooks.com